**Praise for
Mollie Gregory's
previous novels . . .**

Triplets

"Glitzy, fast-paced . . . crackles with tension, lots of glamour."

—*Booklist*

Birthstone

"A perfect diamond . . . ~~~~~~~~~ ry, fascinating characters, a~~~~~~~~~~~~~~~~~~~~~~~~~ ing author

"A no~~~~~~~~~~~~~~~~~~~~~~erful men and women, ~~~~~~~~~~~~~~~ce, and most of all, primitive~~~~~~~~~~~gh places."

~~~~en Dean, bestselling author of
~~~ashington Wives and Capitol Secrets

"Dazzling . . . glitters from the first page to the last."
—**Rex Reed**

"Finely etched characters, intricate plotting, and raw human emotion illuminate this rich novel of a Hollywood family caught in a web of secrets."
—**Carolyn See, author of
Golden Days**

PRIVILEGED LIES

Mollie Gregory

JOVE BOOKS, NEW YORK

If you purchased this book without a cover, you should be aware that this book is stolen property. It was reported as "unsold and destroyed" to the publisher, and neither the author nor the publisher has received any payment for this "stripped book."

PRIVILEGED LIES

A Jove Book / published by arrangement with
the author

PRINTING HISTORY
Jove edition / December 1993

All rights reserved.
Copyright © 1993 by Mollie Gregory.
This book may not be reproduced in whole
or in part, by mimeograph or any other means,
without permission. For information address:
The Berkley Publishing Group, 200 Madison Avenue,
New York, New York 10016.

ISBN: 0-515-11266-6

A JOVE BOOK®
Jove Books are published by The Berkley Publishing Group,
200 Madison Avenue, New York, New York 10016.
JOVE and the "J" design are trademarks
belonging to Jove Publications, Inc.

PRINTED IN THE UNITED STATES OF AMERICA

10 9 8 7 6 5 4 3 2 1

ACKNOWLEDGMENTS

I am indebted to friends and acquaintances for their good advice. In Washington, D.C., Barbara Bode heads the list for her generous introductions and her enthusiasm. Others shared insights about the executive branch, congressional campaigning, and filming in and around Washington: Ellen Malcolm, Judy Corley, Edward Coyle, Vincent Clews, Brad Fitch, J. P. Philips, Pat Wait, Ernest T. Sanchez, Susan Jenkins, Judge Stanley Frosh, and Ruth Prokop for her steadfast assistance.

In Los Angeles, friends offered advice and read the manuscript at various stages: Krista Michaels, Phylis Geller, Judith Bustany, Katherine Rembold. Special thanks to: Jerry Virnig, who shared his rich fund of filmmaking lore; Gordon Smith, who did the same; and to Charles C. Neighbors for his editorial assistance and for his faith in this book. To Leslie Gelbman, my splendid editor at Berkley, my gratitude. She is a delight to work with.

PROLOGUE

THE DAY FELT abnormal, the air looked orange. Sweating, impatient, Faye Ferray was standing in the noonday sun outside the old Gower Studios, waiting for her friend to pick her up.

"Hot for March, isn't it, *querida*?" Della Izquerra said as she jerked to a stop. "I'm glad you could make it on short notice."

Della had chosen El Portero, a grimy garden dive off Melrose, instead of their usual lunch spot. Despite the heat, Della refused to sit inside, so they settled at a tattered umbrella table on the patio, where the roots of an old sycamore bulged the already uneven bricks.

Faye flung herself at life, counting on her wits to cushion any rough landings. She began immediately. "What's wrong? You said something was—"

Della held up her hand like a traffic cop. "Please," she said, "be calm. Let's have some iced tea first." She smiled. "Now, how's your work going? You producing anything *good* this year?"

"C'mon, Del," Faye said, "forget the chitchat. Just tell me what's bothering you. Did something happen in Washington?"

"Oh, it's all so loco." Della picked up a menu.

Della was dressed in a sleeveless yellow sundress. At thirty-five, she was a flamboyant woman with a mane of black hair and expressive large black eyes. Energy flowed from her.

"I ran into your ex the other day." Della put down the menu without reading it.

Faye shrugged, then raised both hands shoulder high in surrender. "Gabe?" she said. "The sexual beast with the warm grin? The one who slept with all my friends?"

A hint of the old Della appeared. "Tch, tch. Really, *querida*, you must get past all that. Besides, he only slept with *one* of your friends."

"That we know of."

The waitress arrived and took their orders.

Faye placed her elbows on the table, twined her fingers together, and made a bridge for her chin. Although Della looked the same, she seemed tense and watchful. "I was thinking about all of us in law school—you, Nadine, Tot, me. Only twelve years ago, but it seems like fifty—so far away."

"Life is really very short." Della slipped on a pair of dark glasses. Behind them, Faye could see Della's gaze touring the patio.

"What are we all doing with our lives?" Faye asked her. "Do you ever think about that?"

"We're doing the best we can," Della said, as the waitress delivered their iced teas.

"You know what I dread?" Faye said. "Not having a child, not doing any work good enough to be remembered even next year, and not being loved again the way I was." She wrinkled her nose. "How about you?"

"De ser deshonorada," she said. "Being dishonored."

Faye was shocked. "That would never happen to you, Della."

Carefully, gently, Della stared at her oldest friend. How much should she tell her? Should she involve her at all? "You were always the fixer of our group," Della said. Her eyes tracked the freckles floating over Faye's slightly arched nose down to the few stuck pleasantly to her upper lip. Faye, tall, had wavy red-brown hair. Today, she was dressed in nineties L.A.—checked Geoffrey Beene skirt, flowered silk blouse, heeled sandals. There was a fancy diver's watch on her wrist. Pure Faye.

Finally, Della said, "Something's come up in my work." Her private law practice handled the work of nonprofit public interest organizations. "Recently, I've been rustling up private grants or federal financing for drug rehab programs, arts programs, battered women."

That was the public Della Izquerra. Faye was better acquainted with the private, more radical Della, buttressed by passion and belief. Although Della had grown up in comfortable surroundings, she'd chosen to apply her legal training to the service of her compassion.

"What's come up, Della?"

Della glanced away. "We don't know who we are until we're threatened."

"Who threatened you?" Faye was alarmed. "Del, please tell me what's going on."

"Richard," Della said, a little too quickly. "The custody war over the twins."

"Forget it, Del. We're not hiding out in this delightful cafe to talk about Richard." Della's life with her ex-husband—before and after divorce—had been a melodrama of vituperative exchanges and banging doors.

"In fact, Faye, I need a new lawyer. Any suggestions?" She ran a hand across the crown of her thick black hair.

"Jeez, Della, I don't practice law—I'm a film producer," she snapped, impatient and distressed.

"Oh, I don't mean you, *querida.* I want someone outside my circle to get a restraining order against Richard. I want him kept away from the twins."

Faye felt the sun baking her hair through the tatty umbrella. As she crunched down on an ice cube, the waitress delivered a pair of weary iceberg-lettuce salads. The moment she left, Della leaned toward Faye and whispered, "I might be disbarred."

"Disbarred?" Faye barely contained a shout, ending the word in a whisper that matched Della's. "You couldn't have done anything that serious."

"Has it occurred to you there are clever, ruthless people out there?"

"Sure. I work with a few." Faye hunched over the table. Della slash-wiped her mouth with a nervous hand. Her eyes scoured the patio again. Faye continued, "You've been hyper for months, Della, banging back and forth between here and Washington, and each time you seem more frantic. How can I help if you won't level with me?" Della opened her mouth, then closed it. "If I can't help you, then for God's sake talk to Nadine."

Della stuck a green onion into her mouth and bit down. "We may have suffered through law school together, but Nadine's a better friend to you than to me. She's high gringo back there in Washington."

Faye tried to lighten up. "Yes, I'm afraid Nadine really does think our government personifies a 'kinder, gentler' way of life."

"Nadine lacks courage," Della stated flatly.

"She does not!"

"Okay. I only meant I don't know how far she'd be willing to go."

"Then talk to Tot. Despite what she did to me, she's a damn good reporter."

Della gulped the rest of her tea and rattled the ice in the glass. "I don't trust her."

Della's scared, Faye thought, *that's what's so different about her.* "C'mon, let's talk it through, figure it out. Where's my old 'Della the Brave'?" But Della's grace was gone, her tawny skin had no light left in it. She hadn't touched her salad. Even in the heat, Faye felt chilled. "I can see you're afraid—"

"I'm not."

"The hell you're not."

Della quick-scanned the intense conversational groupings at the other tables, sheltered by the ragged striped umbrellas.

"Over the years," she began in a voice so low Faye had to lean forward, "I've helped pump millions of dollars from grants into urban neighborhood programs in this state. But I have this problem. Where exactly is the money going and who's actually spending it? All of a sudden there are an awful lot of new Latino faces connected to the biggest program I ever got funded—CDEE."

"What's that?"

"Centro Docente del Economía y Ecología Internacional— the Educational Center for International Economics and Ecology. It was a wonderful program—it's helped a lot of people."

" 'Was'?"

"I don't think it's the same program anymore. But I can't for certain tell you how."

"Well, what's wrong with a few new faces?"

Della sighed and stared at her plate. "All right, let's say I help get a grant funded for a drug rehab center and I have some people in mind to set up the program, people I know will perform well. Okay, we get the program funded. Then, let's say one of those great community workers disappears— that's happened once—or they have to go to Missouri, or wherever. Someone else pops up to handle this program, sitting there all funded, then that person starts to build a power base that isn't really connected to the program. Get it? And the feds—they don't care!" She lit a cigarette with shaky fingers, striking the match three times before it ignited.

"When did you start smoking again?"

"Yesterday." She peered at the end of her cigarette. "One of my good people has been killed."

"Killed," Faye repeated, frowning.

Della puffed on the cigarette. "Nothing splashy, not a drive-by, not drugs, just your ordinary unsolved L.A. Latina killing."

"Who?"

"A woman who worked for me. A small-time druggie painter who'd let me know if one of my funded drug centers was dealing or receiving. Naturally, I wrote her in under another job description," Della said. "But her task was to keep tabs on the programs for me."

Faye sat back. Being with Della was always a little destabilizing, but now Faye felt disconnected from an entire section of contemporary life. "Del, how can I help?"

Della raised a long arm to flag down the waitress and order a glass of wine. "Listen to me, I guess. Be my friend."

She is *scared,* Faye thought. Faye had seen frightened people before—fearing for their jobs, their marriages, their reputations. But Della's fright was palpable and more intense. A sense of powerlessness invaded Faye; she didn't know how to help. "You know I'll always be your friend, Del."

"CDEE really bothers me," Della said. "It's a major federally funded operation, see, and it's out of sync. I went down there and found a fleet of limos, office furniture right out of Rockefeller Center, and all the board members were in Rio de Janeiro taking some training seminar. They're not doing what they were set up to do. If they're not, they could be indicted for fraud. And if they are, what do you think will happen to my reputation? They'll tube it."

"Della, I know you, you're not merely concerned about your reputation. This isn't about that."

"No." She crushed out her cigarette. The waitress brought the wine and the check.

"So are you going to tell me what it's about?"

"I don't know. CDEE held board elections the other day. Royal Diaz is the new chair."

"Royal Diaz," Faye snorted. "Sounds like a comic strip."

"Faye, he's one of the El Salvadoran judges with alleged connections to the death squads there."

"Oh. Definitely not a comic strip."

Her features set, Della force-marched them back to her parked car. Her black hair rolled on her shoulders, her long strides ate the sunlit pavement. Faye struggled to keep up, pushing a damp lock of hair off her forehead, hefting her briefcase.

"Here, give me that," Della said, taking the case. "I know it weighs a ton, you damn techno-nut." Her voice was lighter; obviously, she felt better. "You got a cellular phone in here, right? Maybe a hand-held computer? Faye, you have to rebuild your *human* relationships."

Faye grinned, wide and winning, fluttering the freckles across her high cheekbones. "All right, so I'll quit sleeping with my computer and join a video dating service."

The car seat was a griddle. Della started the engine, made a lunatic U-turn, screeching down Melrose toward Faye's office. Faye gritted her teeth.

When Della slowed down, Faye said: "Get a lawyer, Del, someone who knows fraud, liability, collusion—all that good stuff."

"Yeah, I guess it's time."

"And call me every couple of days, more if you want. Really stay in touch."

"Okay."

Della pulled against the curb near the corner. Faye got out and leaned into the open window on the passenger side.

"Will you keep in touch? Please?"

"I promise." Della smiled, her eyes settling on Faye's face. "You're a good friend, you always have been."

Touched, connected, Faye reached out and clasped her friend's bare arm. "I count on you, Del."

Della tossed a wave, gunned the Buick's motor, and took off so suddenly Faye had to leap away.

"Damn!" Faye yelled. Della was accelerating straight into the traffic. "Della, you asshole, watch out!" The Buick dodged a slow-moving Chevy and came to a halt in the middle of the intersection, waiting to turn left. Faye bent down to retrieve her briefcase.

The roar of the explosion, loud and sudden, was a physical force, thrusting Faye against the signpost. She banged her head, dropped to her knees. Bits of glass peppered her.

An eerie silence followed. Shakily, Faye regained her feet. Isolated cries: a woman screamed, a man bellowed something. Faye realized she was facing west. She turned.

Della's car, still sitting at the intersection, was canted to one side. The air was filling with acrid smoke. People on both sides of the street were stealing out of their own cars, dazed. Faye stepped off the pavement toward Della's Buick.

Della was at the steering wheel, her head resting on it. Someone across the street was yelling, "Call an ambulance!" A man's voice near Faye was saying, "Don't touch her, don't touch her."

Trembling, Faye reached out and inventoried her friend. Della seemed intact but she was too low in the seat.

"Don't touch her," the man repeated, grabbing Faye's hand. "She'll sue!"

Faye wrenched away from him. "This is my best friend. Get away from me." She pressed her fingers against Della's throat and felt a faint pulse.

She whirled. "Get the paramedics!" she yelled, feeling a surge of energy and hope. The producer in her took over. "Get moving! Do it!"

Della stirred. "Don't move, Delly," Faye said. "You're going to be okay, just hang on." Faye's knees were turning to rubber. She didn't feel the tears rolling down her cheeks.

A crowd formed at the edges of the car like a chorus line, moving and swaying. She yelled at them to call for help. She reached down and stroked her friend's head with shaky, feathery fingers. "Delly, help is on the way, we'll stay here, wait for them. . . ."

How come Della was so low in the seat? Faye, suspended, elastic, bent to look under the car. She was staring under it, trying to figure it out. The car was only a couple of inches from the street. Now, Faye was air itself, rising, looking at Della in the seat, looking down at Della's legs. There was a big hole in the car where the pedals should have been, there was the street just below the hole. Della's legs were poking through the hole and Faye was floating again, hanging on to the outside of the car door to keep from soaring up and drifting away. She felt the blood in her arteries reversing, pouring out of her head and plunging into her belly.

Della had no legs. The blast had blown out the bottom of her car, amputating her friend's legs at the calf. Della was bleeding to death.

Faye was galvanized. She seized the door handle as she ripped off her skirt belt. Another man, his face chalky, swam into view. He was hanging on to the car, too. "Get the ambulance," Faye said through her teeth, "and give me your belt." Now she knew she was crying but inside she couldn't feel the pain of her tears. She yanked viciously at the door. It would not budge. "She's bleeding to death! Get them to hurry up. Just get them here!" The man leaned into the window of the car.

"A Mex," he sighed, turning away.

Faye grabbed his collar and jerked him back. "Give me your damned belt! Open that other door!"

"Faye . . ."

"Right here, Della." Della's head was lolling to one side, her eyes wide. "The ambulance is coming. Hang on. Fight. You're good at that, *you fight—*"

"Am I hurt?"

Faye leaned across the open window. "Yes. Bad. You gotta fight hard."

"Bomb?"

"I—I guess so. Who would do that?" Faye shrilled. When she hauled on the door again, the car rocked.

From the other side, the man said, "I can't get this open."

"Try harder!"

People around the car resembled dancers, receding and advancing, eyes hollow and wide open, their faces dripping with sweat. *What the fuck were they doing?*

Riding the thick warm air, a high tenor voice, like a chime, sailed across the stalled, congested intersection. Somewhere, someone was practicing. Faye hunted for the source of the sweet sound. It would save them.

Della was whispering. Faye leaned closer. "I don't understand . . ." Faye said.

"Sham . . . selections," Della said. She closed her eyes, then opened them again. "Tia . . ."

The wafting effortless tenor glided into "La Forza del Destino."

"What about 'tia'?" Faye asked.

Irritated, Della grimaced. "Bigger . . ." she muttered, "bigger than I said." Faye strained past the window frame, half in and half out of the car, trying to get her ear close to Della.

"Del, I'm going around the other side, climb in the window. We gotta stop this bleeding."

A hand seized Faye's shoulder. A paramedic.

"I couldn't get the door open. Her legs . . ."

The paramedic peered inside the car, immediately bent to look underneath it, then straightened, raked a hand through his blond hair and exhaled powerfully. "Mike!" Another paramedic was running toward them.

Faye tugged at the first medic. "Her legs . . ."

Paramedics were storming the car. Police were every-where, gesturing at the crowd. Bleating car horns drowned out the tenor. The first paramedic was racing around the car for the other door.

Faye stepped up to the window again. "Della, who put the bomb in the car?" she whispered.

"Don't let Richard get my twins," Della said. Her face was gray.

"I won't, Del."

"Sham . . . Bye . . ."

"No, no byes," Faye said staunchly. "You can't give up." Faye was sobbing and deep inside her body she felt the agony of the sobs.

"Faye . . . warn Nadine. . . . Stay clear. . . . "

The paramedics had pried open the passenger door and were in the car with Della the Brave. On the driver's side, Faye hung on to the window frame, her forehead touching its searing heat, staring at her own feet. She was standing in a pond of Della's blood.

ONE

FAYE SAW HER ex-husband, Gabriel Mittelman, the moment she got out of the car in front of the Catholic church in a wealthy suburb of Los Angeles. Gabe had a way of standing, his weight on one long leg, ready to move. Her life with him came back, a rush of nostalgia, injury, elation. She turned away, focused on a row of stucco homes across the street in the old Encino neighborhood. The press, armed with cameras and mikes, were lined up on the curb like goshawks, poised, waiting.

Faye felt Gabe take her arm and simply stand beside her. She accepted it.

"Della was 'sunshine in a shady place,' " he said, quoting Marlowe. "I'll always remember her."

She looked up, felt the comfort of being near him again, this tall, soft-spoken man with the reserved, almost courtly manner, and watchful eyes.

He glanced at her carefully. "How are you holding up, Faye?" he asked quietly. She tossed her head in a way that told him that she wasn't doing very well. "You just barely escaped yourself."

"Yes." She didn't want him to go on. She concentrated on the new streaks of gray in his dark hair. He still wore his mustache. "When did you get back in town?"

"Yesterday. First time in two years." He knew that Tot, the woman he'd left his marriage for, would probably be there, too. Funerals summarized, closed, and restarted the machinery of life. For Gabe, Della's murder and Faye's narrow escape had brought him out of what felt now like a state of suspension. He trusted what was coming, and he dreaded it.

"I didn't think Della was into drugs," Gabe said.

"She wasn't."

"Press thinks so. Cops found crack in her car."

She didn't respond. The press had persistently pumped the story of Della's explosive end, but the police appeared to have few leads, other than a possible drug connection.

Nadine Stern Ferray, Faye's brother's wife, and her best friend from law school, stepped out of a limousine. She was blond and slender, somewhat austere. Faye tried to wave but a cluster of relatives was surrounding her: Faye's mother, her brother, Rob, her younger sister, Annie.

Gabe offered his ex–brother-in-law his hand. Rob shook it briefly. He was a year older than Faye, a chunky man of medium height with brown hair. He hadn't spoken to Gabe in two years. Nadine took Gabe's hand instead of kissing his cheek or hugging him.

They all stood uncomfortably together until Annie reached out and hugged Gabe. "Are you back in town for good, Gabe?" Her voice rang with enthusiasm.

Annie had a horror of passing unperceived. Even in a dark suit, she managed to look dramatic and voluptuous. Her tinted contacts deepened her green eyes. The two sisters shared only the color of their reddish hair. In Ferray family lore Annie got the looks, Faye the brains.

Faye's mother took Gabe's hand. "Della was like another daughter to us," she said. Her powder and perfume curled in the air.

"I know, Coo," Gabe said. The nickname still suited her. Even in funeral attire, she looked blowzy, one of those redheads whose face thickened with age. But behind the pancake makeup, anyone could see traces of the beauty that shone in Annie.

A solemn group of about twenty Hispanic men and women in black were walking from the parking lot toward the church.

"Who're they?" Nadine asked.

"People from Della's good works," Faye said. And at least one of them, she thought, knew what kind of crossfire Della had been caught in.

Nadine watched Gabe covertly. His easygoing style masked an inner energy. It was, she decided, the combination—that placid exterior, the volcano beneath—that attracted women, especially Tot.

"I think I'll go on in," Gabe said. He moved toward the steps of the church as Tot Jencks came around the corner from the parking lot.

Petite and compact, Tot carried herself alertly, like a dancer. Her frizzy brown hair framed her round and strangely beguiling, almost innocent face. Seeing the Ferrays, she smiled wistfully, then moved back, keeping her distance.

"Funerals," Rob said, spotting Tot, "stick the past right back in the present. She should have stayed in Washington, D.C. It's bad enough I have to deal with her there."

"Rob, don't," Faye said. She hadn't seen her old friend for a year, but she could still feel the rot of jealousy and anger unfold inside her. Had that been simmering there all this time? She shivered. She found herself in her past, listening to Gabe end their marriage. She was holding a spiral shell she'd picked up on a beach during their honeymoon. Gabe, behind her, anguished, was saying, "I do love you, but it's hard to live with you, Faye. Tot and I have something different." She'd cried, "Tot? Not Tot!"

In the crowd, Faye pressed her palm to her mouth.

From the top of the steps of the church, Gabe watched Tot, respecting her, regretting her. He glanced at Faye and knew instantly that she was reliving the past. Her jaunty good looks were compressed; her black straw boater cast a deep shadow across her face. He'd come to help Faye if he could, but he doubted that was possible. He caught Rob staring coldly at him. Gabe went into the church.

Another limousine had rolled to a stop. Two agile men

leaped out and held the door open for a tall, broad-shouldered, genial-looking man in a gray pinstripe—Senator Mark Drummond. Rob Ferray, who worked as the senator's press secretary, went up to him.

Faye saw Tot smile at the man who'd once been their civil law professor; the senator didn't notice Tot. Then an expression she knew well crossed Tot's face: the reporter in her had taken charge. Faye looked back at Mark. His solemn face of mourning had changed: the press was swooping toward him. Ah, Faye thought, he loves this. Tot had seen it, too.

"Mark's schedule's a mess," Rob said to his wife. Nadine frowned. "We can't switch San Diego around." Rob turned to Faye. "We're on a swing around the state." It was the warm-up for the campaign heat that would soon sear them. "We'll have to leave right after the service, Nadine. I know I said I'd stay tonight, but it can't be done, sweetheart." His manner was upbeat—the square-shooter who saw only solutions, not problems.

Nadine nodded. "See you in D.C." Her eyes closed, long lashes brushing her cheek. "Faye, why don't we go up to your cabin tonight?"

"I had to sell it, Nadine."

"Oh," she replied with a bewildered smile. *Having* to sell a cabin was outside Nadine's experience. "Well, let's go up to Dad's. No one's there."

"Nadine, I need some time alone," Faye said. "How about letting me stay there tonight? You come up tomorrow and we'll talk about Della, about what we can do."

"Sure, Faye. But what can *we* do?"

"A detective questioned me," Faye said, "but since then I haven't heard anything. I think we should do something. We knew her better than anyone."

"How about Tot?" Nadine whispered. "I mean, the four of us . . . we were always together . . . ."

Faye stared at Tot. "I'm not over it. If you want her there, you ask her." They started up the steps. "Annie, we're going to go up to Nadine's cabin tomorrow, talk about Della."

"Really? You're asking *me*?" Annie was flattered.

Mark Drummond came up to them. "A very sad time," he said in the deep, warm voice he'd developed in the classroom. "I'm glad you're safe, Faye."

"How are you?" Faye asked him.

"Why, very well. . . ."

She looked into his big, handsome face. There was fear in his eyes. "Mark . . . ?" He was looking over her head toward the church door. Faye turned. A muscular, good-looking man with black hair and a black mustache was staring back at Mark Drummond. "Who is that, Mark?" But Senator Drummond had turned to Nadine, taking her hand.

"Annie," Faye said, "who's that man?"

"Where?"

"Up there, by the door."

He was gone.

The press stirred. Della's father, Izzy Izquerra, the aging TV comic, was shepherding his twin grandsons away from the insistent press, trying to make it to the steps. Rob broke away to help him.

Izzy was saying, "Della was my only daughter. But I have a son, and my grandsons—"

"Fellas," Rob said to the press, "you gotta excuse us."

Izzy stumbled against Faye. His grave face was damp with tears; he was poking blindly at a handkerchief in his pocket. He finally freed it and pressed it against his face like a mask. Then he took Coo's arm. "It's good her mother didn't live to see this day." He turned to Faye. "Della left something for you, Faye," he said, his Spanish accent thickening.

"What?"

Iz Izquerra shrugged. "A big box and a sweater."

The cool nighttime mountain air smelled of pine and sage. A decorator had worked hard to make the Sterns' spacious cabin seem rustic. Faye was dozing on the couch. A fire in the oversized stone fireplace made the room rosy and warm.

Again, the explosion echoed in her head, and woke her up. Once more she wondered why she had escaped so narrowly. Her life felt stunted: she was thirty-five, her bio-clock was running down; since the divorce, her career had deteriorated.

She pressed her fingertips to her forehead. There had been worthier times, happier times. She remembered receiving an award for a television film she'd made about battered women; she remembered waltzing with someone in a ballroom; she remembered standing in a hotel hallway with Gabe. He was holding a key, his hand shaking so hard he couldn't get it in the lock.

"I've never done this before," he'd said shyly.

"Bullshit," she'd laughed. He'd tilted his head and smiled at her, acknowledging that between them guile was not going to work. He'd won her right then.

Inside her hotel room, he'd walked around, stopping at the window, his back to her. She'd sat on the bed, smugly amazed at her intense attraction for this man she'd just met that day at a film festival. She stared at his back.

"Where are you from?" she finally asked.

He turned around. "Los Angeles."

"You couldn't have been there long or I would have met you."

"It's a big town."

"It's tiny."

He folded his arms and studied her. "What's your name again?" He was mocking her, or himself. A smile moved his mouth beneath his mustache. "I'm nervous," he'd said. He was very honest, fresh and strong.

Between them, an intersection, a sea. She blew across it, collided, kissed him hard. He gripped her around the waist with both hands, kissing her face, neck, ears, groaning and holding on to her so hard she felt she was going to pass right through him. She was trying to get his shirt off. She popped a button. He wrestled with his sleeves, not letting go of her. She was trying to get out of her skirt and he was trying to get out of his jeans. Naked, they fell together on the bed. She was opening her legs. "So much for pretense," she'd sighed, grabbing a lock of his hair, pulling him to her, kissing him, not wanting ever to stop.

A log rolled out of the fire. She got up from the couch, pushed it back in, poked it. All that was eleven years ago. Why was she thinking of that now? Because she'd felt so alive then, and didn't now.

She fell asleep, feeling the crowded forests around her stacked on the San Gabriel mountain range. Below, not many miles away, unseen but known, the Los Angeles lights throbbed on the plain.

A car crushing the gravel and pine needles outside woke her up. When she heard steps coming toward the cabin, she hiked herself out of the chair and went to the door.

"Gabe!"

"I hope this is okay."

"What's up? Is anything wrong?"

"No."

She stood back, running a hand over her hair. He stepped inside and closed the door.

"I was concerned about you." He smiled at her, ran a finger across the bottom of his mustache, a neutral gesture, not artificial, like a pause between words. His mouth turned up, a gentle, self-mocking smile, creasing the lines in his cheeks.

"How'd you know I was here?" Had Tot told him?

"I overheard Nadine speaking with her dad."

"What do you want?"

"The funeral was rough today. I thought you might want to talk."

"I'm not pining away up here."

"You seemed so sad at the church, so lonely."

"Don't push it, Gabe."

"Sorry. But I knew you'd be missing Della a lot. Friendship's important, most of all to you."

"I came up here to be alone."

"I felt lonely, too," he said.

She turned and went toward the kitchen; he followed her. "I used the last of the coffee," she said. She stared into the cupboard, then into the refrigerator. "Wine?" she said, smiling tentatively, studying him with her shrewd hazel eyes. He nodded. "You've been in Maine all this time?"

"Yeah." He grinned. She didn't.

"Been anywhere else exciting?"

Gabe was addicted to travel. He used film festivals as the excuse, though he needed none, to create eccentric itineraries involving trains and boats, and sometimes bikes.

"Morocco. And Ireland."

"Have you been working?"

"Life's more than making a picture."

"Ah, Gabe, you love the game. So do I."

"There's bigger game," Gabe said. As usual, Faye was darting around the kitchen, hunting for glasses, rinsing them, finding a bottle of wine, a corkscrew. He gazed at the freckles on the lift in her nose, at the part in her hair. He wondered if she still made those little snuffling sounds in her sleep.

"Anyway, tonight, I couldn't stay at the hotel. Where was Jerry today?"

"He's ill, Gabe."

"Nothing serious, I hope."

"Leukemia."

"What?" Gabe said, stunned.

"We just learned. He's doing all right."

"I'll go see him," Gabe said. "I thought he'd outlive us all."

Faye was hunting in a drawer. "Yes, we're here one day and not here the next," she said.

"Is he doing chemo?"

"Yes." She shut the drawer.

"Poor guy."

"Pop thrives on chemo. It hasn't made him sick at all." She began unwrapping the foil around the wine bottle. "Maybe his body's absorbed so many poisons that massive doses of chemo are—nourishing."

The words sounded cold, but she was close to both her parents. The words were like her and her father: don't look back, don't feel sorry for yourself, get it together, say what you mean.

"Do I hear a little denial?" he asked.

"Pop and I understand each other," she said. "You know that." She turned back to the wine bottle.

"Faye, when I heard about Della and how close you'd come to death, I felt—reprieved. As if I'd been standing at a crossroads for a long time and, suddenly, I could take a road. You know how fond I was of Della—if I could bring her back, I would. But you're alive and I felt so lucky because I had a chance now to tell you . . . talk to you again." He watched her work the corkscrew into the cork. "Love's so mysterious, whether it's going right or wrong. I turned our lives upside down. What I'd lost with you, I thought I'd regained with Tot. But I didn't."

She popped the cork. "Gabe, I don't want to hear this. I'm vulnerable right now, I don't want to get into something heavy, you know?"

"I wanted to talk about life."

"Yes, well, since we split, I've spent the time finding ways to live without you and with"—she searched for a word that wasn't completely accusatory—"injury. And now Della's dead, and I feel fragile, very fragile."

"I only came up here because I wanted you to know I care about you. You were almost killed and you might have died thinking I didn't care about you. I needed to tell you that."

"Okay," she whispered. She pushed the wine bottle back.

"Don't retreat."

"I don't want to talk. I was getting my life back, starting to get over you—"

"We won't get over each other, shayna, sweet Faye," he said gently, "if we don't deal with this." He felt her eyes pass across his face like a brush stroke. He shifted his weight, uncertain. What was it about some women who touched those inner spaces in a man, thrummed them, and long after separation, left a man listening too hard for the echo?

"It's too hard to see you," she said. She leaned against the drainboard, resting her forehead against the cupboard. A tear started down her cheek. "I felt such pride in you, in us, and then you and Tot—just blew it up."

"Faye, I'm not with Tot."

"Oh, I heard, and what difference does *that* make? Gabe, I can't handle this now."

"All right. I'm sorry. But I care about you and that's not going to change." He left the kitchen.

He stopped at the front door. "No," he said. He went back into the kitchen. She had turned and was leaning back against the drainboard. He ran his hand down her hair. "Faye . . . I can't leave like this."

"If you love me at all, don't, don't do this."

He grasped a firm hand around her arm, turned her to him and held her. "Oh, honey . . ." he sighed. She cried in spurts. She felt her loneliness like a sledgehammer. She put her arms around him, feeling his familiar curves, and the smell of him, the soft comfort of his lips against her temples, the resistance in him, and in herself. She felt hungry and dishonest. She pulled back, knowing what life was like without him, wanting him, not wanting him.

They moved into the living room, staying close, and sat down on the couch, hugging each other. He stretched out, made a hollow for her head on his shoulder, stayed that way. Her hand on his chest felt his heart beating and the breath moving in and out of him.

Against his better judgment, he wondered if they had a second chance. Did he want one? Did she? He tightened his arms around her, feeling the length of her, stroked her face, kissing her slowly.

The sea swell of emotion, of longing, caught them, lifted them. They were separate, then together, like sleeping then waking and being aware that the dream of making love was real. Her arms dropped away from him, letting go.

At two in the morning, he made pancakes. She held him about the waist as he measured and mixed and plopped creamy batter into the steaming pan. They stuffed themselves and grinned at each other, and thought there might be a second chance after all. She felt alive. She loved the feeling of her body returning to her. Nothing was forever, but these moments, whatever they meant, were hers: she wasn't merely a witness. She held on to his familiar body and felt the bone and muscle of him. Long after he'd left, she could smell the faint aroma of his skin and the feel of his mustache brushing her lips.

TWO

As HE EXPECTED, the call came at seven o'clock in the morning.

"Cowboy, this Izquerra business is appalling," the Chief said.

"Tragic," Cowboy said, "tragic."

"Didn't anyone see this shit coming? What's behind it?"

"Hard to say," Cowboy replied, choosing his words carefully. "She was giving CDEE a hard time."

"How could she have been doing that?".

"Mistakes were made," Cowboy replied. He had, in fact, known she'd been suspicious; he probably shouldn't have used an organization so close to her, but that had been convenient and corrupt. "Someone panicked and did something stupid."

"The whole thing was bungled! She had someone with her in the car. What do you think *she* overheard?"

Cowboy smiled. The Chief was being very circumspect. "Nothing, I'm sure."

"Check it out! Check it out! How about the, ah, accident investigation?" the Chief asked.

"It's being handled," Cowboy assured him. "It won't go anywhere." He glanced around his office, radiant with the Southern California winter sun.

"Make sure. Jesus Christ."

Cowboy didn't reply. He knew who had ordered the car blown, and why.

"Christ, we already had a big hole in Leo's operation," the Chief was saying. "Who can ride shotgun now?"

"I've been talking to Leo. He's seeing a replacement."

"Whoever it is, he's got to handle the receiving organizations a whole lot better."

"Leo's got just the man, a true believer," Cowboy said. These conversations with the Chief bored Cowboy because the Chief assumed he was in charge. In fact, Cowboy had been running things a long time.

The other man was grumbling. "Everyone's nervous. The elections are coming on." Over the telephone, Cowboy could hear the rustle of papers. "I don't like it, Cowboy, that CDEE outfit's out of hand, unreliable." Cowboy didn't say anything. "We don't want that jerk involved. Cut him out of the fold."

"He was a judge."

"I don't care. He's got a screw loose, and he can't control his people. The Friends don't want him involved."

"If you're talking about Diaz, he swears he had nothing to do with it," Cowboy said, alert.

"The Friends won't go for it!"

Cowboy sat back in his chair and pursed his lips. "Hum. Well. We've pumped a lot of money through them."

"No. I'm drawing the line in the sand right here."

"They have certain expectations," Cowboy said. "It wouldn't be wise to make changes now. Blowing up that car was a message aimed right at the Friends, Chief. Are you reading me?"

The Chief's voice became muffled. "We have to talk, just you and me. We'll see the others later after this dies down."

The line went dead. Cowboy hung up. He tapped a gold penknife against the edge of his desk. Someone's going to keep digging, he thought. Of course, the program *was* unraveling, not noticeably, but there it was. He dropped the knife into his pocket. Obstacles, setbacks, were part of the game's challenge. He would find the errant threads, knot them, go forward, win.

So, on this morning, Cowboy didn't feel as bad as some people. He felt the thrill of the chase.

Cowboy was sixty-five, but didn't look much over fifty. One of those men of average height and weight who faded into a crowd, he'd been born in a small town in California, the surprisingly late second child of a farm-equipment store manager and a math teacher. He remembered them fondly and often claimed to quote them to prove the wisdom of simple, hard-working Americans.

He was proud of being an American born and raised in the West. He was proud of a land that rewarded initiative. He loathed Easterners' scorn of the West. He was proud of what he'd done in his life. But because Cowboy's father and grandfather had died at age sixty-five, he felt he was standing at "the barn doors." Chances were good he wouldn't reach his seventies.

Perhaps more for that reason than any other, he'd permitted himself a daring and risky maneuver—riskier and more far-reaching than any movie he'd helped to fund, any government program he'd run, or any candidate he'd supported. If he could hold this colossal program on course, the same one Della may have discovered, then those Americans who counted would finally recognize the power of Californians.

But the program *was* unraveling. L'affaire Izquerra had proved what Cowboy already knew: the weak links always showed the wear first.

He bounced to his feet, toured his office with his hands behind his back, his short legs propelling him past the floor-high windows of the forty-ninth floor and his vivid high-rise view of downtown Los Angeles. The opposite wall was solid mirror reflecting the sky and cityscape of the window, shadowing Cowboy's perambulations.

Nothing was as much fun today as politics. And the new venture was a great challenge. He stopped and peered down at the plaza, El Pueblo, the old rowdy heart of the city; it seemed small and tidy from up here.

Back at his desk, Cowboy pulled out the daily National Security Council print out log. He appeared to be and claimed to be working in the private sector, but he actually functioned in a curious zone—part private enterprise, part government effort—a shadowland. Basically, Cowboy was carrying out a form of government policy far beyond the purview of elected officials. In that region anything was possible. He was no better than he ought to be—service to his country first, mankind second.

He sipped tea from a fussy, undersized Spode cup, glancing again at the printouts, then sat back and lifted his pale blue eyes to the Paul Klée painting across the room. A ray of light angling from the glass corner of his office struck it. When his eye locked on the dominant red figure in the painting, he knew he'd found a way to patch up the CDEE breach.

Cowboy checked his watch: quarter to eight. He tapped the rim of his cup with the overly long nail he cultivated on the little finger of his left hand and heard a satisfying "ping." For the next hour he tested the plan from various approaches, snaking his way through moves and counter-moves. He walked his office, back and forth in front of the mirror. Finally, he sat down, a brief smile stretching his thin lips. Worst-case scenario: a careful leak or two could throw blame for a smaller event on someone else, while the operation moved to safety, perhaps into some other agency's budget. He didn't want to move it; it was well set up where it was. All in good time. He shouldered an imaginary Sharps .50-50, squinted into the sights, squeezed the trigger.

"Boom," he said.

The business about Faye Ferray being with that Izquerra woman before she died worried him.

The soft buzzer sounded on his telephone. He lifted his hands in delight.

"Excuse me, sir," his assistant said through the speaker. "Mr. Jay Harper is on line one; Mr. Leo Townsend is on two."

Cowboy nodded pleasantly. "Louise, I'll take Leo first. You just set up an appointment with Mr. Harper—whenever it's convenient today." He ting'd his nail against the Spode cup. "And, Louise, I'll have another cup of that herb tea you're pushing this morning."

* * *

"We can't just go back to our lives as if nothing happened," Faye said.

"But what can we do?" Nadine asked.

"The police are handling it," Annie said.

"The police are *not* handling it," Faye said. "They don't know who did it, or why, and the drug thing is an easy out. They have hundreds of killings a year. We've got a responsibility here. This is about friendship; we can't just do nothing."

Everyone was still. "Faye's right," Nadine said, invigorated as always by Faye's energy.

In the late afternoon sun, the deck of the Sterns' cabin, enclosed by glass, provided a view of pine trees, boulders, and melting snow. Annie reclined on a chaise, her rounded haunch lit by the pale sunshine. Daintily, Nadine sat upright in a wicker armchair. Tot was slouched in a cane chair, one thin arm around the back of her neck. Lunch remains lay on a low table.

"Tot, is there any press scuttlebutt?" Nadine asked.

"Drug wars."

Faye sat on a bench, thinking what a bad idea it had been to ask Tot to come. She wished for a more generous heart, for greater tolerance. Even after last night with Gabe, it was hard to be in the same room with Tot. But the old corrosive jealousy *was* fading; in its wake came sadness. Tot had once been a close friend; Faye had missed her. Of course, a residue of anger persisted, too. How could Tot even sit here with Faye after what she'd done? Where Faye had once prized the steel in Tot, now it dismayed her.

She sat up. "We have to remember when we saw Della last and what she said."

"Well, there were all those weird organizations she worked with," Annie said.

"Social change," Faye replied in her wise older-sister tone.

"But wasn't she involved in drugs once?" Annie shot back, unchastened.

"Recreational, I'm sure," Tot interjected, swiveling her round, pretty face toward Annie. As a television reporter, she used her deceptively innocent and youthful looks to inspire trust during interviews.

"We're getting off the track," Faye said.

"Anyone could have blown her up," Tot said. "Lovers, ex-husbands, angry employees—"

"This is *Della* we're talking about!" Faye said, disgusted.

Everyone began talking at once. They'd always argued, the legacy of their first-year study group in law school where they'd talked fast to build their points before the inevitable interruptions from their classmates.

"It was a public execution," Faye said. "Who would do that?"

"We probably won't ever know," Nadine replied.

"I can't accept that," Faye said. "You weren't there, talking to her, while she bled to death."

"If someone asked me which of the people I know might be killed," Tot said, "Della's name would be on the short list."

"What?" Faye exclaimed.

Surprised, Tot backed off. "I only meant she took risks, lived on the edge of things."

"We were arrested together," Nadine recalled. "We went to jail together."

"For abortion rights," Faye said. "We didn't do time together."

"The last time I saw her, she hinted something was wrong with one of her programs," Nadine said. "She was very emotional about it." One hand moved to her temple, smoothed her hair. "I had a feeling she needed us. I didn't quite believe it, though. She said she was thinking of chucking it, going back to Berkeley and teaching."

"About three months ago," Tot said, "she asked me for some information about some Salvadoran group. We talked after that, but she never asked me again. I forgot about it. I didn't take it too seriously."

Nadine expected Faye to blow up, but she only said, "God, how far do women have to go before we take seriously what we do, what our friends do? Della needed us and we didn't come through."

"I take what I do seriously," Annie said.

"I wonder if any of us really do." Faye seemed drained.

"Okay, Faye," Tot said, surprising everyone. "I admit if some guy I'd known for years asked me to find something out, I would have."

Tot's admission sharpened Faye's sense of regret for her old friend and for the life she herself had once had with Gabe. "Let's analyze," Faye said. They examined their last meetings with Della.

Annie dove in with excitement until she admitted she'd only seen Della once that year. "At an afternoon benefit. We sat under a tree." Annie loved gossip and stories. She began playing her part and Della's, changing voices and gestures. "She talked about the power of television in elections: 'building hope where there was none,' was what she said, I think, and after that she said the nicest thing about my show *Take This Life,* that it had humanity, that I brought humanity to the role."

Faye smiled at her sister's unerring instinct for self-congratulation.

"My God, how could I forget this?" Nadine cried. "A month ago when I was out here, Della called me at three in the morning. She was a little tight." Nadine swept a hand to her cheek. "Didn't I even *care* about Della? I *did* care, we all did." She stared at Faye. "We *did* care."

"Nadine, what was it about?" Tot asked.

"The LAPD had had her in for questioning. They suspected her of being involved in the death of a man who worked for her."

"Ridiculous," Tot said. "Why?"

"I don't know. She'd been with him an hour before he died—it was all lunatic." Nadine was pacing back and forth in front of the french double doors in the waning light. "That was the last time I saw her. We had breakfast together that morning. She was talking about Richard, the twins, some of her clients—I don't know what she suspected her clients were doing. But she seemed really—changed."

"How?"

"Outraged, but controlled, too. I can't explain. Different."

"She was just plain scared by the time I saw her," Faye said. "She denied it, but she did talk about being disbarred."

"Disbarred?" Nadine and Tot chorused.

"She told me about this urban program she'd helped get funded, but she was so uneasy about it. She didn't know where the money was going or who was actually spending it."

"What program?" Nadine asked.

"CDEE. Some international study center for ecology and economics. She said she didn't think it was functioning as the program she'd funded, that the personnel had changed and so had the center. And that though *she* found the changes very disturbing, the feds, who'd provided the funding, didn't really care."

"Maybe Della was doing more than fundraising or advising for those groups," Tot said.

"Like what?"

"Well, misappropriating funds. Money laundering?"

"She would never do that," Faye proclaimed.

"She might," Tot said.

"Let's look at that," Nadine said.

"Oh, Nadine, you never understood her," Faye said.

"No, but I admired her."

"We all admired her," Tot said.

"Did you?" Faye said, looking directly at Tot. "Della never got scared when she had the answers. It was when she *didn't* have the answers that she came apart."

"I do believe *that* about her," Nadine said.

"She was a trained lawyer," Tot said, "and she had street smarts, for a spoiled Chicana who grew up in Encino."

"She kept saying at that breakfast," Nadine murmured, " 'Something's not right, it's not right.' " Nadine fell silent. Then she said, "Driving up here, I kept thinking how law school bonded us."

Annie closed her eyes against their law school memories.

"No, Mark's campaign did that," Tot said.

"A great high, that night of the big win," Faye said. "I felt powerful, as if democracy was real, not just words. Didn't you? Remember how bummed out everyone was in 1980? The hostages in Iran, gas wars, Carter losing his grip, and we're working our tails off on this uphill, underdog campaign for our old law prof—just ordinary Americans deciding to make a difference—and *doing it!*"

"That was sweet," Nadine said, thinking of the early days with Rob—a space and time she wanted to go back to where goals were palpable and possible, where bone-deep friendships couldn't be fractured.

"I was watching Mark yesterday," Tot said. "He's different."

"Of course he's different," Faye said. "He's a powerful senator, no longer a freshman." She remembered the man Mark Drummond had been staring at on the top step of the church.

"He's basking in media glory," Tot said, "and he's almost part of that group of politicians who're leading men. They're not trained in government, they're entertainers who look good on TV." Tot smiled, looking cute. "As Hollywood goes, so goes the nation's capital."

"That's really cynical, Tot," Nadine said.

"Faye, why did you go to law school?" Annie asked.

"I loved the work, even though I wasn't tops at it like Nadine and Tot. I felt the discipline would show me that even though I'd come from nowhere, I could have at it with the best."

"What do you mean 'nowhere'?" Annie said. "Mom and Dad were known all over the world."

"A song-and-dance team is a long way from law school."

"Then why didn't you practice?"

"Because I met Gabe and found out I was a better producer than a lawyer."

"So what good was it all for?" Annie said, gloating.

"It showed me that I could do it."

Annie rose, stretching her lips into her big smile. "I have to go. I have an early call."

Nadine hugged Annie. "How's your daughter?"

"She's fine and likes living with her dad, thank God. He's a good daddy."

"Are you in something I should watch for?"

"I'm in a mediocre TV pilot. But it looks like they've changed locations on us so we might end up in Virginia in ten days. I'll let you know. We can have lunch."

Outside in the sharp air, Annie listened to the sound of her feet crunching pine needles. She stopped beside her car and looked deep into the dark trees. Being with three trained lawyers was boring. But that wasn't what bothered her. She wanted to feel good about herself *as* Faye's sister and Rob's, but she didn't. Faye loved her like a sister, but she didn't respect her, and Annie could feel it like a burn.

She got into her car, turned on the ignition. The light beams poked through the trees. Annie wanted to smooth out her discontented feelings about Faye. She didn't know how to do that. She put the car in gear. "I guess it's really Faye's problem," she muttered, driving away.

Inside, Tot was making a telephone call in the bedroom. On the deck, Nadine lit a hurricane lamp. The stillness of the forest around the cabin enshrouded them. "I wish I were as close to Annie as I am to Rob," Faye said to Nadine.

"But Annie's got all that wonderful emotion—gushes of feeling," Nadine said almost plaintively.

"She appears to be emotional," Faye said quietly, "but it's all a little calculated."

"Is she smart?"

"Yes, but she hides it." Faye sat on the bench, stretching out her long legs. "We used to be close, at least I thought so. Now, we're involved in this weird competition."

"How many years younger is she?"

"Eight. She's so ambitious, so needy. . . ." An owl hooted. Faye stretched her arms above her head, held them there. "And then there's Tot." She considered telling Nadine about Gabe being with her at the cabin last night. She dropped her arms. "Everything's breaking up, changing, and you and Tot and I will never be like we were. That makes me feel lonely, not like myself at all."

"Maybe someday you and Tot can be friends again."

"Maybe."

"Good. That's good, Faye." Nadine sat down on the bench next to her. "You go out to Izzy's and get whatever Della left, I'll check out which groups she got major grants for— her big clients."

Faye's face crumpled. "I'll miss her so much." Nadine, the stoic, put an arm around her. "It comes in waves—I'm still leaning over that car window, trying to hear what she's saying, and—and I can't remember! I'm standing there in her blood—I can hear her voice—I can't remember the *words*!"

"You will." Nadine hugged her. Faye was the sister she had never had. Across the room, she saw Tot in the doorway, her short arms by her side, her tiny body balanced, alert, a witness at once detached and troubled. Nadine couldn't figure out how Tot contrived the balance.

"Tot, why don't you fix us all a drink?" Nadine asked her.

"I know just what to make."

Tot went into the main room and opened a cabinet in the corner where Nadine's father kept the liquor. Nadine wandered in after her. Faye dried her eyes, got up and stepped through the doorway.

"What's in that?" Nadine was asking.

Tot was pouring a jigger of dark rum into each highball glass. "Don't ask," Tot said. "Gabe was over a couple of nights ago, and he— Oh, I need limes." She turned. She hadn't expected to find Faye in the room. "It's—soothing," Tot sputtered.

Faye nodded, and went back on the deck. Night had rushed in. The crowd of trees outside had settled into the side of the mountain.

Was Gabe still sleeping with Tot, too? Just five minutes ago she'd felt she could move on, but now she felt mired in a fresh sense of dishonesty. It was, simply, awful. Would she ever trust Gabe again? Or Tot? Did she trust Nadine? Had Della been the person she'd always believed her to be? I should get away from here, she thought, get a whole new life, I can't patch up this old one. At the bottom of her discontent, she realized she didn't feel up to maintaining the standard she'd always set for herself, one she couldn't see, but knew was there. One that grounded her.

THREE

ANOTHER DETECTIVE HAD taken over the Della Izquerra case. Phelps. His NY Yankees baseball cap was cocked back on his thick dark brown hair. In his forties, Phelps was bulky but trim, with sharp features and anguished hazel-gray eyes the color of gravel. He was attached to the Detective Support Division that investigated bombings and gang-related felonies.

"Are you going to put me in the movies, Ms. Ferray?"

Irritated, she shook her head. *What a smart ass.* "I'm here to find out what's happening on Della's case. Where's the other detective?"

"Shot. In the hospital."

"I'm sorry."

He fished a tissue from the paper littering his desk and blew his sharply pointed nose. "Cold."

"Do they still call you guys narcs?"

"Not me. I don't make midnight raids."

He wore a jacket and sports shirt. The only detective Faye had ever met was a retired consultant to a reality-based police TV series. "What's happening with Della's investigation?"

"We believe there was an internal squabble over drugs," Detective Phelps said evenly.

"I was one of her closest friends and I can tell you Della never used drugs."

"Friends often don't know."

"But you're checking for other suspects?"

Phelps let one hand drop onto a stack of folders. "For openers, Ms. Ferray, you could help by remembering some more of what she said. The time between the call and the arrival of the paramedics was twelve minutes. A lot can be said in twelve minutes."

She glanced around his dreary Hollywood office. "I've told you what I could recall."

Phelps blew his nose. "We don't have much to go on."

"You have her character, her professional reputation! Is this investigation on hold somehow because I can't remember everything she said? That makes me feel really bad, like I'm responsible."

"We've checked the kind of explosives used—plastique— a bungled job. It should have blown the car apart, but it misfired. We are checking for professionals whose MO fits this crime, checking to see which of them was in town, which are still alive." He gave her a narrow look. "Motive and opportunity, y'see. If we find anyone like that, we'll haul him in for questioning. But this one feels like an amateur and he's probably long gone. We're checking our informants and her secretary, her associates, we're going through her files looking for her drug associations—"

"She didn't have any!" Faye yelled. "Why won't you believe me?"

"I believe evidence." He turned to toss away the tissue.

"Why would a drug dealer go to all the trouble of blowing her up? God, this is so grim."

Phelps sniffed glottally. "Yes, they could have just sprayed her with a nine-millimeter. . . ." He thought about that. "The reason was that they wanted it known."

"Yes, yes, and?"

"Yeah, on the surface she was a lawyer, but maybe she was more. A Latina, Hispanic, whatever—it's a rough life. They get killed."

"Now, wait a minute, *my* friends don't get killed. If

you think this isn't serious because her father came from Mexico—"

"Don't misunderstand, Ms. Ferray. This is frustrating for us, too, you know."

He looked away. "If you remember anything else she said, call me."

Faye rose. "I'm not satisfied. I want to see whoever your superior is."

He waved a hand vaguely. "He's out sick." Phelps was writing on a pad. "Feel free to call him."

Faye took the note. His sharp solemn face had stilled. "Ms. Ferray. We're not sure this was meant just for Ms. Izquerra, though chances are it was. You be careful, too. Just in case."

"Me? Who'd want to kill me? My last film flopped, but—"

"Keep your eyes open," he said without humor. He sneezed and swallowed.

Faye hit the street. The weather was cool, the gray skies typical of March. It was eleven o'clock in the morning. The detective frustrated her; she had no trouble communicating with a wide assortment of people, but she couldn't reach this Phelps. She didn't think he gave a damn about Della, a woman, a Latina—last in line for his time. Yet, in brief moments, the distress in his gravel eyes had startled her. He had a shit job, a killer job; his eyes showed its cost. Burnout.

Despite all appearances, the greater Los Angeles basin was, and still is, a desert. It's been dubbed "a gigantic improvisation" because, like a decorated sound stage, everything's been imported—the water and the trees, the flowers and the people. Even the weeds came from somewhere else.

Los Angeles began as El Pueblo, a violent assembly of saloons, bordellos, and gambling dens devoid of trees, sidewalks, laws. Captured from the Spaniards, who'd wrested it from the Mexicans, who'd stolen it from the Indians, it had few traditions to check its rush toward an uncertain destiny.

In 1876, the railroad hooked up Los Angeles to the rest of the country: El Pueblo grew. Twenty years later, oil was discovered and by 1907, when Teddy Roosevelt was in his second term as President, William Selig was shooting movies in Santa Monica. Another boom began. For the next thirteen years, by 1920, the first swarm of movie stars, among them Theda Bara and Charlie Chaplin, had conquered America's hearts. By 1924, the corporations that shaped the stars—United Artists, Universal, Warner Brothers—were flourishing. Even in laid-back Southern California, everything moves fast. The studios were sweatshops in company towns and from their looms for thirty-five years came visions of American life that simply would not fade.

No more company towns or little factories, Faye thought as she stared out the window of Herbert Yount's top-floor outer office in Los Angeles. Like other studios, this one was only an ornament in a corporate necklace of book publishers, record companies, magazines, cable TV systems, distribution networks, parking lots, shoes, insurance, plastics.

A few miles east, the downtown skyscrapers thrust into the smog. Below, on the lot, the studio writers' and producers' buildings were laced with scaffolding—a reconstruction program to put the old ship back the way it used to be. Faye wasn't looking at any of it: she was mourning Della and wrestling with her dislike for Detective Phelps.

She heard Herbert Yount in the hallway. "World War Two? Who remembers that? It's retro!" Faye grinned. For Herb, the world began around 1980. She tugged at one of her over-the-knee boots, straightening the short black skirt she wore over a rose-colored catsuit. Trying to relax, she rolled her shoulders inside her black suede jacket.

Herb Yount strode through the door, jabbering to his attendants. A cool, somewhat arid man, Herb Yount's deep connections in life were entirely business related, but he was capable and Faye liked him. At twenty-nine, he was the youngest studio production chief in Hollywood.

"Faye!" he said. "Does she look great, or what?" He was walking straight through the reception area. "How are you doing—holding up? Tragic about Della, tragic." He pushed open his door and stalked across the vast room. His entourage made sympathy sounds at Faye—Norma Goldstein, twenty-nine, a senior vice president of production, and Bob Simon, a younger, lesser vice president, her assistant.

"Love your boots," Norma whispered to Faye.

A Sheraton-style table was set for four in an alcove by the window. "Boy," Herb said, "this town is loco. Did you see Rafe's column in the trades? I tell you, talking to columnists is viral." Herb, head of the studio's production, had come from television; in the year he'd had the job, he'd been proving he could turn out hit features, too.

"Now, who's that friend of yours, Faye, the blonde I met at the funeral?"

"She's an attorney with the National Security Council in Washington."

"A woman that gorgeous shouldn't be hidden away in some bureaucratic cubbyhole."

"Nadine wanted to make a difference."

"No one can do anything with the government," Herb said loftily. "Still, we must keep trying." He was a steady supporter of liberal candidates and causes.

"Della and Nadine and I knew each other in high school out here. We met Tot in college, and then we all went on to law school together. There was some talk Annie would go to law school, too."

"*Annie*—in torts class?" Herb chuckled.

"We were going to form our own law firm—sex-discrimination cases," Faye said. "We might be suing your ass for equal pay today if it hadn't been for Mark Drummond."

"I wanted to talk to you about him," Herb said. Flocks of candidates from all over the country were flying in and out of Hollywood, drilling for money and star support. "Thank God he doesn't have any primary competition. Faye, I'm getting up a fund-raising committee for him, and I want you on it. I want a celebration for the senator who really listens—some blast to knock the socks off the opposition, raise a few mil."

"Very ambitious, Herb. After all, the Hollywood Women's Political Committee raised a million and a half with Barbra Streisand, and that—"

"Yeah, yeah, I know all about the HWPC," Herb said. "That was a few years ago. We can do better. If the senator gets a stiff race, it might cost fifteen or twenty mil to keep him in the Senate." He turned to Norma and Bob. "Faye worked on Mark's first campaign, didja know that?"

"Herb," Faye said, "my time's really tight, doing a lot with the HWPC—we're besieged by candidates, too."

Herb Yount smiled. "I know you'll find the time, Faye. We can always serve on another committee."

Looking serious, Bob nodded his head up and down.

A steward came in with the main course. "Do you think Sparks will be the senator's opposition?" Norma asked.

Faye hadn't thought about politics since Della had been killed. "Rob thinks so," she said. She searched for some insider gossip, aware that some of Herb's interest in her revolved around her family political contacts. "But Langer looks interesting—she's running a real grass-roots campaign." The steward left.

"She's a Republican," Herb muttered.

"I said she's interesting. I didn't say I was supporting her."

Herb poked at his food with his fork.

Faye felt light-headed, quite unlike her usual self. Her mood deepened as Herb and Norma discussed luminaries who'd serve with Faye on the Drummond committee. She thought about the sequence of her pitch—the story line, its crises and characters; the prospect made her feel tired. Did this movie bore her? Bottom line, all she wanted to do was to walk out of that room with a green light to start production. True, she needed the money, but more than that, she needed to get back to normal.

"What do you think, Faye?" Herb asked.

"I think we better hurry up and finish eating because I have a hell of a film. I want to start production tomorrow."

Herb chortled. "Always the cutup," he said. "Everyone's pal until she's crossed. I like people who fight for their pictures."

Faye smiled without feeling any pleasure.

"The line between TV and film is blurred, very blurred," Herb said, "but you've crossed over, Faye. I sure wish you and Gabe were back together. You made a good team."

Norma stopped eating her salad.

"I can still pitch," Faye said.

"You don't have to pitch," Herb said. "You're way past that. Just tell us the story."

That was bullshit: pitching *was* telling the story. Herb made a show of shoveling food in his mouth, which was disagreeable because he had a small mouth and his movements were precise—he was a man who could not clown.

He pushed back his chair. "I'm done," he said, "shoot."

Norma's large dark eyes were gazing at her. If she liked a script she'd go to the wall for it, if she didn't, she'd flush.

The performance mantle dropped over Faye. "*Lights Out* opens with a ten-alarm fire . . ." She stood and claimed the room. Herb smiled; Faye was good at this and she enjoyed it. He liked people to enjoy their pitches to him.

As she raced through the story outline, Faye began to sweat: she was hearing an echo. She was describing a film she'd already made—*Sally and the Drifter*. She stumbled. "I mean, after the fire, Paula—not Sally—feels she's being followed, but Raymond, her son . . ." At about the second turning point in the story, Faye realized *Lights Out* was like every movie she'd ever made for television. She knew the beginning, middle, and the end; she knew the exact moment to slug in a major confrontation between characters; she knew the twist at the end—some adaptation of the chase. *Is this what I want to do for the rest of my life,* she thought as she roared ahead describing the story. *Where are my values? I don't want to make* Lights Out, *I want to make* The Jungle Gym. She grimaced at her little audience. *How can I be in the middle of a pitch and not have known that it is* Gym *or nothing*? She hadn't thought about *Gym* for a year. *What is wrong with me?*

She labored to conclude the *Lights Out* story. "See, Paula learns with Ray just what life's really all about."

Herb nodded, as if he could personally appreciate what life was really all about. He opened his mouth.

"But that's not the one I want to make, Herb," Faye said.

Herb closed his mouth, and frowned thoughtfully. "It's passion that directs us," he said.

"Right, Herb." Faye felt disconnected from her body. "*The Jungle Gym* is a picture I just can't get out of my system."

"*Jungle* what?"

" 'Gym'—G-Y-M." *This is nuts*, she thought, *don't do this*. But she couldn't stop. "It's a story that can win awards."

"Box office?" Norma put in.

"Money, too."

"Jungle Gym?" Herb asked again.

"It's about justice and being brave." Norma blinked. Bob picked up a roll. "It's about a man and a woman who witness major life-threatening chicanery—and blow the whistle. It's about ideals and sticking to them and winning."

"Is this new?" Herb broke in.

Faye sailed on. "The lead's a stubborn laboratory administrator, a doctor named Celia. Think Streep, think Cher— cool, smart, feminine. She works for a government health agency, administering the research division. And she's a widow with a teenage child. Lives in Virginia. One day, in the lab, she finds evidence that a project's research has been compromised—fiddled with—but when she takes the papers to her boss the next day, they've been altered: this is not the set of experiments she'd read the day before. Her boss doesn't believe her, but Celia knows the drug has had some really bad side effects—causing convulsions. Celia claims the agency's research is covering up the side effects. Her job and her reputation are on the line but she decides to go over her boss's head—a dead end."

She was stirring concrete. Norma, who raised pedigreed boxers, resembled one, jowly and glum. Herb's smile was barely civil.

"Celia is threatened; there's a chase along the Chesapeake, an underwater scene in the bay when Celia and her kid manage to escape from her car. Weaving through her ordeal is the unique atmosphere of living and working in Washington, surrounded by our national symbols, which to her still mean something. There's romance, too, a first-term congressman from Virginia, who has a zany but repressed sense of humor. He's afraid of closeness, of making waves. And it's time he grew up—"

"Faye," Herb said, "I remember this, it's got an abortion scene in it, doesn't it?"

"Well—"

"Didn't we already pass on this?" He'd passed on it at the

network. Herb rose, put his hands in his pockets, and walked around the room. "Forget the jungle thing, Faye. *Lights Out* is dynamite. Norma, what do you think?"

Norma was smiling and nodding. "A great vehicle for Kathleen Turner."

"We could shoot it down at Long Beach," Bob said.

"Thanks, but how about *Gym?*" Faye asked.

Norma checked Herb with her eyes. "I can't get a take on it," she hedged. "Definitely nix on any abortion scene—"

"It's about principles, not abortion."

"Nix on them, too."

Herb was laughing. "Faye, quit kidding around. It's not for us."

The meeting was deteriorating. Faye tried to turn it around. "Herb, I'm not kidding, I haven't pitched it very well, but it's got a terrific love story, danger, great visuals, *and* it's a story that hasn't been—"

"—told," Herb finished for her. "Faye, I never thought I'd hear that old chestnut come out of your mouth!" He started folding his napkin. "Faye. This *Gym* picture isn't worthy of your talents. You have to set your sights higher—"

"Higher than justice?"

"You know what I mean. Justice is okay as a background story."

They were in a contest. Faye tried to pull out, but Herb wouldn't let her. Norma and Bob became spectators, swiveling their heads like tennis fans.

"You're respected," Herb went on, "but I'm warning you— that picture's a big mistake. You've got to build a career, now you don't have Gabe. You got to keep the product coming, audiences know what to expect from your movies. There aren't any men in this movie, and no action."

"Yeah," Norma weighed in, "sounds like the guy is an afterthought."

"Movies skewed to women make money," Faye said. "It's been proved again and again. Why won't you believe that?"

Herb was disgusted and his gestures were getting choppy. "They *don't* make money. This jungle thing, where's the foreign resale? How about video? The Japanese won't like that movie."

"A lot have!" she insisted.

"Flukes! Shit, Faye, you're one of the few women in the world who produces features, for crissakes; you want to risk what you have on some picture that won't make a dime?"

"If you don't want it, Herb, I'm disappointed, but I can take it somewhere else."

"You already took it around—am I wrong?"

"This year the timing is perfect. It's a nineties film."

"Faye," he said, approaching her, the cajoling dictator. "Don't you trust me? I know the markets. Don't shoot yourself in the foot here. I know what's best for you."

The awful part of it was that Faye liked Herb and she knew he was right.

"Make *Lights Out*," Herb said. "We all like *Lights Out*." The little audience grinned. "You're listening to me, aren't you? This is for *your* good."

Faye became aware of Norma's hound eyes. "Could I have a word alone with you, Herb?" Yount nodded.

"It's wonderful to see you again," Norma said on her way out. Bob said, "*Lights Out* is great."

Primly, Herb sat down in a side chair. Faye pulled over another. "Shoot," he said, looking at her freckles.

"Herb, I can't go on making the same old stuff."

"Now, you listen to me, Faye. It's your job. You're good at it. People love your stuff—"

"I'm dying inside, Herb. I have to stimulate myself." *This is dumb*, she thought. *He isn't interested in how much I care or don't care about my work.* "Repetition is not creative. I can't even remember why I got into this business."

He smiled. "We know you can be trusted, Faye. You know how to develop a project and keep it on track. You're just feeling burned out, Della and everything. Millions would like to be where you are. They're scaling the walls. Shape up."

"I'm sorry I pitched *Lights Out*," she said recklessly, "but I want to make *The Jungle Gym* with you. I'd take any director we agree on." She flashed him a smile to let him know it was a joke. He squinted hard at her as if she'd poked him. "There are actors out there who'd kill for the roles—"

A minute chime like a one-inch silver bell sounded twice. Instantly, Herb changed. The meeting was over. He rose. "Send the script, Faye, but I don't want to do any movie about a whistle-blowing scientist. What goes on in labs isn't sexy—it's confusing!" He stopped halfway to his desk. "Unless it's about making poison gas." He lifted his head, hearing old strains of story music.

"It's about saving lives, Herb, not destroying them. It's about honor. We need movies about ideals in this country—"

"Shooting in D.C.—we've seen the Lincoln Memorial a jillion times—" Solemnly, he shook his narrow head. "You be a good girl and think about it."

"Dammit, Herb, you're younger than I am! Don't give me that 'good girl' shit!"

"Faye, *Jungle Gym*'s a loser."

"If I'd been this fired up about it when Gabe and I were together, you'd have bought it—from Gabe!"

"I'm buying from *you*—so give me something that'll make a buck! Do I have to put someone in your office to look over your shoulder?"

"Like you assigned Ned Davis to patrol my production last year? He hasn't made a film in fifteen years! I had to explain the equipment to him. I don't need a babysitter!"

Herb Yount froze. "Get the fuck out of here, Faye, before we both say things we don't mean."

The door opened and she started through. "Remember, Faye, my door is never closed to you," he said, activating the electronic button beneath his desk. The door swung shut.

No green light.

Herb's voice—condescending, adamant, concerned—trailed Faye out of the building, out of the parking lot, and over to the building in the Gower Studios on Sunset where she rented office space.

She wasn't angry at Herb, she was angry at herself. She'd committed a kind of suicide in there. She was a professional, she knew what was expected, but she'd blindsided herself by pitching a story she hadn't prepared. And, why hadn't she realized how dumb *Lights Out* was until the middle of her pitch? A tide she hadn't seen coming was sweeping over her: she'd failed . . . she'd go on failing. She hadn't felt that way since her first law school exams. The old panic was crunching her bones.

FOUR

"HE LOVED IT, right?" Steve Crimean, Faye's ebullient assistant, grinned at her when she got back to the office. He was twenty-five and wore his long, sandy hair in a ponytail.

"Herb loved *Lights Out*. I don't want to make it. I pitched *The Jungle Gym*."

"Oh, no."

"What can I say, I think one way and the studio thinks another. I've lived here all my life and inside I still feel like an outsider. How many women are producing features, Steve?"

"Two or three. Three or four. Well, maybe five."

"And how many features are made each year?"

"Few hundred."

"I rest my case," she said.

"So, do *Lights Out*."

"Today, a movie's just a piece of organized information. In a few years, we're all going to be producing entertainment data for pay-per-view cable. As it is, we're making software."

"You're just depressed."

She walked through the connecting door and flung her briefcase on the couch.

Her office had a view of a courtyard: two olive trees, a patch of grass, and some croton shrubbery. Her dark blue desk was covered with books, scripts, loose papers, two rolls of 16mm film, and a stack of cassettes. Floor-to-ceiling shelves were bloated with dog-eared scripts. The entertainment center took up one wall: television, extra monitor, two VCRs, CD, and tape decks. A merry-patterned blue rug lay over polished peg wood floors.

Faye broke out a bottle of Evian and gazed at a Jack McLarty oil painting titled "Myself As a Royal Rosarian"—a man in a boater lofting a flowery, open umbrella, shaped like a giant nose. Usually, it made her smile. Not today.

Steve had regrouped. "On your schedule, you have a relationship-maintenance lunch tomorrow with Paul—"

"That's not relationship maintenance, Steve. He's a good friend."

"I found your keys." He held them out.

"Thanks." Since Della's death she'd lost her keys and her wallet, she'd mixed up her appointments, she'd forgotten entire conversations.

"Sign these." He put a file folder of letters on her desk. "And these came." He dropped some more papers on her desk.

"Where's Gail?" she asked.

"Having her mammogram."

"Oh. I feel rotten. I'm going to take a half-hour nap. Get everyone together for a staff meeting at five. We've got to talk about what I've just done."

Faye was an independent producer with a staff of five. Gail, her development chief, had found *Lights Out* and *The Jungle Gym*.

"I thought you had a faux date tonight," he said.

"Canceled. Everything's changed."

"Gabe called." He put down the phone messages.

Faye stared at the pink slips. She didn't want to hear his voice. "Excuse me, Steve. I need to be alone."

She dialed the number Gabe had left. "Gabe?"

"Faye, how are you?" His voice was cheerful and energetic. "Are you free for dinner?"

"No, sorry. Gabe, I—"

"How about Saturday? That better?"

"Gabe, let's just leave things as they are."

"How are they?" His voice dropped.

"Let's not do this again."

"What's happened?"

"I can't go back."

"How about going forward?"

"We're not heading in the same direction. I cannot do this again."

"Do what again? Feel?"

Is that it? she thought. "I don't want to be involved with you again."

They hung up. She thought of Gabe in Tot's arms, a picture she'd seen many many times. She thought of all the women attracted to Gabe, drawn by his unusual looks, his dignity, his director's talent with actors, his inner strength. *They* hadn't lived with his silences, his remoteness, his itch for getaway. But she'd been glad for him; he liked the attention, he deserved it, she'd learned how to handle it and she'd always felt they were a team—until Tot.

She picked up the papers Steve had left, pulled off her boots, and lay down on the couch. The photos fell out of the envelope. She leaned down to get them: Della's face was staring at her from a press room in the Beverly Wilshire Hotel. It was shot at an AIDS benefit only four weeks ago.

Faye threw her head back. She remembered Della laughing, ripe and full, dropping back in her chair in a tangle of long legs and arms. Della had been the only person who'd laughed during their first law exams. Tests were frail measurements of knowledge, considering how much hung on the grades. Nadine and Tot had been excellent exam-takers; Faye and Della not so good. Exams reminded Faye of pitching a story: both were shorthand about what you knew, but underneath lay a lot more untouched by test or pitch. "What kind of lawyers are we turning out?" Della had often demanded.

"Yeah, Del," Faye said out loud from her couch, "what kind of movies are we turning out?" Movies that sound great in the pitch. Movies any fifth-grader could understand.

The sparrows chirped outside, but Faye was hearing Della's whispers at the wheel of her car. The scene was vivid, as persistent as her own heartbeat. Had the bomb exploded a few seconds earlier, she wouldn't be seeing the palm trunks swaying in the breeze like rubber poles; she wouldn't have been with Gabe at the cabin, or retreating from him now; she wouldn't have the sinking feeling that her own life was unraveling.

She wanted to prove to herself there was a reason for her survival—that it counted. That's why she'd pitched *The Jungle Gym*—because the story reminded her of Della.

Faye was breathing water again. She marveled at this new skill, swimming underwater in a warm, gray sea. She couldn't see the bottom or the shore. She had the sense Della was near her. As she swam on, the water grew darker.

An immense white shape loomed up ahead, alive and enormously threatening. She froze, terrified, as it swept toward her, moving fast.

"Faye!" Steve shouted. He was shaking her. She heard herself crying out.

She was on the sofa in her office. Her heart was pounding fast.

"Bad dream," she panted.

"Humongous."

She sat up. She didn't like the look on Steve's face. "Guess I better get some real sleep," she said. "Change our staff meeting to tomorrow morning at ten."

"Okay," he said. He was reluctant to leave. "Maybe you should see a doctor or someone."

"Yes, okay. I'm fine."

After Steve left, Faye checked her watch; she'd been asleep fifteen minutes. The first days after the accident, Faye had dreamed either of the explosion, or of standing beside Della's car, trying to hear what she said. Faye believed in dreams, the flip side of everyday existence, but no less revelatory. She tried to replay this latest reverie, but could remember only the eerie sensation of breathing underwater. Symbolically, that was telling her something she didn't want to remember. Something about Della's death.

*   *   *

Gabe Mittelman was having dinner at a handsome Thai restaurant on Sunset Boulevard with the man who was like a father to him.

"You've been gone too long," Samuel Pike said, obviously pleased to see Gabe.

"Jeez, Sam, I tried to get you up to Maine for a few days."

"No, no, I didn't want to interfere."

"Sam, you could never do that."

"Well! Now that you're back, we'll have to get into our monthly dinners—right?"

Across the aisle from their table was a mirrored wall. Gabe glanced at their reflection: Sam was trim, handsome, about sixty, maybe. Gabe wasn't sure. He combed his hair straight back from his forehead, a style that accentuated the short jut of his nose and the hard bright mischief in his eyes.

"You haven't talked about the foundation," Gabe said. From a modest background, his mentor was a respected California man, former ambassador to Brazil, former executive with a multinational, behind-the-scenes facilitator of media financing, friend and adviser to the CEOs of motion-picture conglomerates, to Cabinet members, even to Presidents. Both liberals and conservatives courted the influence of the politically unaffiliated Samuel Pike. Currently, he was head of the Stansbury Fund, a foundation whose philanthropy spanned the globe. "Who's up, who's down, who's in, who's out?" Gabe asked. "Who's getting the money?"

When Sam smiled, his eyebrows jumped toward his hairline. "We've finally created a revolving fund for experimental film development."

"Great!"

A delicate eater, Samuel Pike plucked one of the last appetizers off the plate. Gabe had started on his pho beef soup. "You haven't spoken about Faye," Sam said.

"Saw her at the funeral with all the Ferrays."

Sam glanced around the jammed room with the curiosity of a tourist. "How's Faye holding up?"

"She didn't look so good."

"It must have been a terrible experience for her," Sam said. "I heard she was with Della before she died."

Gabe always made Sam think of himself at a younger age, had the times been different. Who knows? Sam might have been a director or a producer. But he didn't regret who and what he was, nor did that change the fondness he felt toward Gabe.

"Close calls like hers can change people," Pike went on. "She'll need to talk about it, she'll need support."

"Not from me."

"You might make the offer."

"I already did," Gabe said.

Sam Pike's dark eyebrows hopped up. "Ah?"

"No dice." Gabe grimaced at his soup.

Sam considered that. "You know what always struck me about Faye?"

"That she had more energy than a steam engine rolling downhill."

"That she's tolerant of other people and has great confidence that mistakes can be ironed out. Nice qualities." Gabe was a well-liked director, but for all the years Sam had known him, Gabe had a way of getting into trouble. "Sometimes major gaffes can be repaired."

Gabe checked Sam's expression and found acceptance there. "I know you'd like to see things back the way they were, and a few days ago I might have said there was a chance, but I was kidding myself. There isn't. She said so herself." Gabe's well-shaped hand made a chopping motion above the table.

"Ah. Les girls," Sam said with appetite. "Well, wooing works, or so I'm told."

Gabe laughed. " 'I'm told.' Don't kid me—you're a ladies' man and I know it."

"Now, now, Gabe. I'm a married man and I'm faithful."

"Your wife lives in Laguna Beach and thinks a trip to L.A. is a form of penance."

"True, but my original point was about wooing."

"I'm not a high woo king like Herb."

"High woo?"

"Ardent schmoozing."

"No, you're not that." Sam Pike beamed affectionately at Gabriel, his surrogate son. "But Faye needs emotional support. Are you still—in touch with Tot?"

"No, Sam. That's over. I saw her at the funeral and one evening for dinner. That's all."

"Well, Nadine—she's close to Faye. I saw a lot of this in the war, Gabe." World War II was the only real war to Sam Pike. "She won't get over an experience like that with Della right away. Maybe never." Pike nudged his plate without moving it. Instantly, the waiter whipped it away.

"Well, she won't take consolation from me," Gabe murmured. He glanced at Sam's reflection in the mirror. Sam appeared to be deep in thought.

"Faye hasn't done a film in quite a while," Sam was saying as the waiter placed a bowl of soup in front of him. "She might really be looking. Maybe she needs money?"

"She wouldn't take a cent from me. We split the house down the middle. She would have cut the sofa in half to make her point."

"Strong-willed," Sam mumbled. "Best kind. She'll need to get something mounted, not only for the money, for her career. How are *you* doing for money? You haven't worked in—what?—a year?"

"About that." Gabe frowned. "Sam, I had a lot of time to think back there in Maine."

"You sound as if you went back there whipped. You weren't whipped—"

"No, I just needed time out, and—" Gabe held up a hand. "Just let me get this out. One of the things I realized, Sam, was that I'd never expressed how grateful I am to you."

"Now, Gabriel, no need—"

"Yes, Sam, there is," Gabe said, his face shifting, allowing his deeper feelings to show. "You saved me . . . I can remember distrusting you, looking for your hidden motives, wanting to use you—"

"Ah, you were only a little lost kid, Gabe."

"Why'd you do it, Sam?" Gabe's dark eyes fixed on Sam Pike's face.

Sam leaned back in his chair, seeing the twelve-year-old boy caught in the cone of light of his flashlight, his arms loaded with food from Sam's refrigerator. "It was the way you were standing," he said briskly. "You were caught stealing and you weren't going to give an inch. You didn't cower and you didn't attack. You didn't drop the food, either." Sam chuckled softly and began to fold his napkin neatly. "I didn't catch you with my TV set on your back. When a kid's stealing food, there's something really wrong—not with the kid—with his circumstances."

"How old were you back then?" Gabe asked.

"In 1963? In my thirties. I was in the Bureau of Educational and Cultural Affairs for the United States Information Agency, stationed in Washington, D.C., but I did a lot of work for them in L.A. and that's why I was out here that month. You scared the hell out of me."

"*You* were scared? *I* thought you were a cop!"

Sam Pike, not that many years out of Army discipline, had ordered the boy to put the food back. "Now you tell me what's going on here." But Gabe wouldn't say anything.

"I'll hand you over to the cops," Pike had threatened. Gabe remained silent, stubborn.

"What's your name?"

"Gabe Mittelman."

"Hmm. Don't know many Jewish boys who break into other people's houses."

No response from Gabe.

"Parents?"

Gabe shrugged.

"Okay. I'll let you keep the food and you can go, but you have to come back here and atone." He'd paused to let that sink in. "You have to clean up my yard every other day for as long as I'm here."

Sam had let him go. "I didn't think I'd ever see you again, but by God, you came back the next day." Soon, Pike had learned Gabe was always in trouble, even at his Yeshiva.

Sam Pike looked at his reflection in the mirror as if he'd made a discovery. "Enough of memories, right?" He saw the waiter approaching with some skewered beef with onions. "Ah, bo dun," Sam said.

* * *

Outside, after their meal, the day was gloomy and raw.

"You keep in touch," Pike said. "And get busy! Don't lie around fallow. Not good for you."

Gabriel grinned and wrapped the shorter man in a hug. "Right, Sam, I will. You take care of yourself." He watched Sam Pike strut away with his characteristic buoyant bounce, one arm raised in a wave.

FIVE

THE NEXT MORNING, Faye locked her keys in her car again. It took an hour to set them free. Then she crowded onto the freeway and tried to make up the time to Izzy's house, far out in the San Fernando Valley past Encino.

"Sorry to be late, Izzy."

"Sure, sure, I understand, *querida*."

Izzy Izquerra held out his short, thick hand. His curly gray hair was mussed and unkempt; bushy eyebrows sprouted over his black eyes. He was a comic who had no fun left in him and she'd often wondered how much being America's funny man from Mexico had cost him.

From the outside, his house appeared ordinary, but inside, spacious rooms were crowded with the modern art Izzy adored.

"Herb Yount tells me you're going to do a wonderful movie with them," he said. "Something called *Lights Out*."

"I'm not doing that, Iz. I'm working on a picture about a research doctor with a federal agency who finds out they've been fudging the research on this drug . . ." Izzy's attention flagged. "The drug has terrible side effects, which they've been covering up—"

"Heya, come look at this Louise Nevelson I just got." He

53

steered her to a corner of the living room where the wooden sculpture was hung near a James Goldsmith paper collage. "I'm starting production myself, did Herb mention it?"

"Yes, he did," Faye lied.

"Haven't been in front of a camera in seventeen years. Are they using the same ones?"

"Smaller now." The last time she'd seen Izzy on a screen was during his hit TV show when she was in junior high.

Della's twins burst into the room. They were ten and traveled as a set. "Oh, great," Faye cried, delighted. They slipped away from her outstretched hand like bright fish in a stream. "They look so much like Della," she murmured to Iz.

Take care of my twins. Della had said that! The words in Faye's head drowned out the noise the boys were making. Faye felt herself welded to the window frame of Della's car, struggling to hear her feeble voice. *Take care of my twins.*

The boys were staring at her.

"David, Doug, how have you been?" Faye said, rattled. She sat down.

"Long time no see," David said. Doug shoved something the size of a videotape at her. "Can you play this?"

It was a hand-held Nintendo game called Game Boy.

"I don't know—want to see me sweat?"

"Yes," they said greedily.

"Okay, you're on. After I talk to Iz."

They went off. Iz opened the hall closet and pulled a carton out of it.

"What's in it?"

"Law school stuff. And this—" From a shelf, he took a folded blue sweater in a plastic covering. "The last time Della was here she said she wanted me to put this in the box for you."

"When was that?"

"About a week—before."

"Do you think she knew?" Faye asked softly.

"She knew she was in trouble and she didn't go to anyone," he said angrily. "Terrible, like we were strangers."

"Maybe she wanted to be sure the twins were safe," Faye offered.

"It was stupid!" he yelled, changing into the Izzy she

knew best—fiery, explosive. "She could have come to me! To her brother! She was—stubborn. Didn't she care how *we'd* feel?"

"Of course she cared!"

"I'm grieving, Faye, you know it, but Della always held things back—"

"It's terrible to lose a child," she said lamely.

"No, I'm okay, I have my son. He's a lawyer, too."

"The miracle of American democracy. Everyone's a lawyer!" She shut her eyes and sat down in a chair in the hall. "I'm sorry, Iz. I just—since Della died, I—"

He put a hand on her shoulder. "I understand. No need to explain."

She wrapped her arms around his pudgy waist and began to cry.

The air seemed thick. She was driving east on the Ventura Freeway when she remembered the twins and her promise to play the video game. She picked up the car phone. "Steve, send a hot new video game out to Della's twins and put a card on it saying I'll be back to play it soon. And make two more sets of keys for me."

She phoned the number Detective Phelps had given her. "I said I'd call when I remembered something. Della said, 'Take care of my twins. Don't let Richard get them.' "

Phelps was coughing. "We checked her ex out. We don't think he's involved."

"Richard wanted the twins!"

"Not enough to blow her up. That's a really expensive way to get them back."

She pulled into the fast lane. She had three appointments stacked up that day to talk about *The Jungle Gym* and she had to be at Le Dôme on Sunset in fifteen minutes; it would take at least thirty to get there. She drove fast, telephoning the restaurant as she went. She yelled at the windshield: "I'm going to spend my whole life pitching this turkey no one wants."

At Highland, she careened off the loaded freeway and plunged into the local traffic.

* * *

Halfway through lunch she mentioned the turkey. "Sure, Faye, glad to look at it," her friend said. He was now a vice president of production for Columbia. "But weren't you hawking a story like this about a year ago?"

"All stories sound alike now. This one's the same, but different."

"Aren't they all?" he drawled. She knew he had to be aware she was hitting up everyone in town.

"It's a woman-in-jeopardy story. She's with a federal agency and she discovers a drug they've okayed as safe is dangerous."

"Kind of idealistic whistle-blower?" he said.

"I'm adding Uzis for the D.C. scenes."

He smiled tentatively. "What's the budget?"

"Twenty-four."

"Mmmm. Who's the male lead?"

"A congressman. Muscle-bound, high profile," she lied, adapting the story.

"Bruce Willis type?" he asked, hopeful.

"Nah, I'm kidding. He's a retarded Woody Allen–Jimmy Stewart. It's a Karen Silkwood story."

He shook his head. "Didn't do much business, Faye, and the foreign rights were the pits."

Everything around her was fossilizing. She jammed her fork into the radicchio salad. All films were difficult to mount, excruciating to produce, hell to distribute. *The Jungle Gym* was going to be like working in the mines.

A light rain began to fall as she pulled away from the restaurant. But the air felt warmer. The weather was all screwed up and the day felt dirty.

She telephoned her lawyer, Karen Steiner. Her melodious voice had helped build careers.

"I've changed my mind about *Lights Out*," Faye said, dodging a pickup and turning right.

"Didn't Herb like it?"

"He did. I don't. Karen, remember *The Jungle Gym*?"

"Is that the one with that half-assed, loony-tunes congressman? You better make *Lights Out*."

"I'm right about this, Karen. I've fought before—for an actor, a cut, a location, more money—"

"You're not right about this one, Faye."

She signed off, promising to call her later. The rain was streaming down the windshield. There was a hard rain a few months ago when she and Della had driven to the offices of a group Della had helped to fund. For a nonprofit outfit, the physical setting had seemed fairly grand to Faye. The furniture was ritzy-office, a conference room was being paneled in oak; even the phone and fax systems were extremely sophisticated. Della had been upset. When she'd questioned a vice president, he'd snapped back that the federal money was now corporate. "You can't touch it!" he'd sneered.

Faye pulled onto a side street and checked her diver's watch. Using her car phone and her hand-held computer, she switched appointments around, then headed east on Olympic Boulevard.

The old neighborhood near Ninth and Western had once been rather grand. Now the people on the street were Korean and Hispanic, the signs read *Papusas* and *Carniceria*, or they were in Korean. Downtown were the graffiti tunnels; here the graffiti was on every wall; here the hip-hop groups and cultures clashed for real.

Faye pulled into the parking lot. Next to a radio station stood a three-story thirties building with rounded corners and arched windows. A large banner hung from the roof: CDEE.

CDEE. Was this the outfit Della had spoken of at lunch? Faye sat in her car, staring at the sign, wondering what excuse she could use to get inside.

The curved reception desk dwarfed a young woman.

"Hi, my name's Faye Ferray." She gave the receptionist a card. "I'm looking for some locations."

"Oh, a producer?" the woman said, pleased.

"An acquaintance of mine once suggested your building— it's pure thirties, isn't it?" Faye had gone on plenty of location searches, but it had been some time since she'd done the opening leg work herself.

The receptionist shunted Faye up the ladder to Ricardo Mendez, a vice president. He was a dapper and outgoing man in his thirties.

"A TV production company used the exterior of our building last year," he said, as his secretary, a pretty brunette, offered Faye a cup of coffee.

"I'm even more impressed with the inside," she raved. "What kind of programs does CDEE handle?"

"Mainly ecology—the links between the Central American rain forest with Northern America—atmosphere, weather, animals—everything is interconnected." His whole face smiled. She liked him. "It is a very important program. And recently, we've received more funding for another center in Central America."

"Then the production fee would be put to good use," she said, referring to the money that would be paid to shoot on their property. "Perhaps you could show me around?"

They made the tour. "It's a wonderful building," she purred, passing one busy office after another. "The remodeling you've done must have cost a fortune."

"Sure, but we're saving the building. It was going to be torn down."

As they moved along, Faye searched her memory for architectural questions about pilasters, masonry, tile work.

They were back at the main entrance. Faye was babbling about using the front reception area and Mendez's office for the shoot. Señor Mendez waved at a man turning away from the reception desk. "I'd like to introduce Señor Royal Diaz, one of the founders of CDEE."

The man in front of her was the one Faye had seen at Della's funeral, the man Drummond had been staring at on the church steps.

Diaz shook her hand as Mendez went on: "Ms. Ferray is a film producer looking for locations."

"Ahhh," Diaz replied. He was good-looking, powerfully built, with a warm, expansive manner.

"Señor Diaz is a naturalized American citizen from El Salvador, and is a candidate for Congress," Mendez said.

"We are testing our electoral muscle," Diaz said, releasing her hand. "With the redistricting, we have a good chance."

"Royal is an unusual name," she said.

"It was given to me as a young man. They called me El Rey, so here in America it is Royal. Haven't we met before?"

"I don't think so," Faye said.

"But I am sure," he insisted. In his eyes, in his tone, Faye felt he was saying "I know where and with whom we have met." "Maybe at Della Izquerra's funeral? Perhaps you were a friend?"

"I did know her," Faye said.

His black eyes flared with interest. "I, too, was there. Such a wonderful woman, I was so fond of her. A great loss."

"Yes. Thank you so much for all your help. I'll be in touch." When she shook hands with Diaz, his palm felt hard and damp.

She drove away quickly, longing to rest, to be with someone who was on her side, someone who understood her.

In 1951, Faye's parents had bought the little house in the San Fernando Valley for eighteen thousand dollars; they'd added a pool, a deck, a second story, and some landscaping. It was on the ridge between Beverly Hills and Encino in a grove of oak trees, and was now worth three quarters of a million dollars.

From the back veranda, as Faye's mother called it, a bumpy carpet of low buildings—the Valley—stretched all the way to the Santa Susana and San Gabriel Mountains; from the front picture windows they could see Los Angeles, Bel Air, and on clear days, Catalina Island. Today, clouds streaked the sky, turning red at the distant sea.

From the street, Faye heard a Puccini opera glorifying the atmosphere outside the house. Inside, the music, at full volume, would be saturating the comfortable, messy, lived-in rooms. She started up the outside steps.

The Ferrays were a happy family despite the fissures created by strong personalities and by the inconstancy of show business. As the family had settled into its final shape, Faye and Rob drew closer to Jerry, while Annie, being the baby, had formed a tight bond with Coo. Theirs had been a warm family to grow up in and Rob was a jovial and generous older brother.

On the steps, Faye passed the spot where Annie had fallen as a toddler, rolling like a stuffed toy down the stairs.

Annie had always seemed underfoot—the little cuckoo, Rob had called her. Now she tinted her hair bright red and, like Coo, she'd become a voluptuous woman. Marmalade, that's what Annie had always reminded her of, Faye thought, passing the small tree Annie had snatched at on her way down the steps. Laughing, Rob had grabbed her before she hit bottom. Faye skipped up the last few steps two at a time.

Her father was on the deck, holding a copy of *Spy* magazine, and talking with Judge Ballard Stern, an old family friend.

Jerry Ferray peered at her over the rims of his glasses. "You look like an extra out of *The Cat People* in that getup. Those are real fuck-you boots, aren't they? What's new in the media business that's not in the papers?"

She kissed his forehead and smelled decay and illness. "Nothing I'd tell a vicious gossip like you."

"You think those hummingbirds out here care what NBC is buying?" He waved at a new glass feeder hanging from the eave. "I had four birds nosing up to that thing this morning like fighter planes being refueled in midair."

At sixty-seven, Jerry Ferray resembled a bird himself, bony, short, and efficient.

"Judge, it's nice to see you again," she said, pulling up a canvas chair.

"Why so formal, Faye? We're like family, aren't we?"

Ballard "Buck" Stern was Nadine's father. He'd been an entertainment contracts lawyer, whose clients had included Della's father and Faye's song-and-dance parents. Later, his political interests had made him into a backroom political rainmaker. He'd been appointed to fill a term in the Superior Court, and now he was on the U.S. Court of Appeals.

In his buff-colored slacks and striped polo shirt, with a sweater looped over his shoulders, Buck Stern looked as if he'd be at home with a tennis racquet in his hand. His white hair gleamed against the reddening sky. "I can't stay much longer," he said, his merry eyes lighting first on Faye, then on her father. "But Jerry and I have had a fine old jaunt down memory lane."

"My favorite route," Jerry said, "talkin' the business, talkin' politics."

"How do you feel about Senator Drummond, Buck?" Faye asked.

"I've always been a big admirer of Mark's," he replied, flashing his warm smile.

"I thought Sparks would be your man," she said.

"Well, let's see who wins the primary. Anyway, it's all moot—I can't take sides anymore."

"Yes, how do you like being a federal judge?"

"Well, it's more sedate, Faye." He folded his hands across his silver Western belt buckle and winked at her. Judge Stern's complexion was reddish, wrinkled, but his features were handsome. Fondly, she recalled the old days at his house in the Palisades, the good days.

"I hear all you girls had a powwow up at my cabin."

"We had to talk about Della," she said. "So far, we're not happy with the investigation. I met with that Detective Phelps, the one in charge of Della's case."

"We've always had a hard time keeping Faye out of jail," Jerry grumbled happily.

"I may be crazy, Buck—"

"Take *that* with a grain of salt," Jerry put in.

"But this drug stuff about Della—it's not right."

Judge Stern crossed one leg over the other. "Even our best friends change with time, Faye."

"Of course they do, but would you mind calling some big chief down there for us and find out what's really being done?"

"Of course, Faye. But remember, they're the professionals. And they're probably right."

"Della wouldn't do drugs."

Judge Stern rose. "None of us ever know what our friends are really like."

"That may be, Buck, but Della was one of my friends who'd hung on to her ideals."

"Yes, she was a remarkable woman," he said, "but, you know, everyone thinks there's a vast gulf between ideals and venality. Actually, the gap can be pretty narrow."

"Judge!" Faye said, shocked.

He was already shaking hands with Jerry. "Great seeing you, Jer. You bring Coo to that banquet, hear?"

Judge Stern strode off the deck, an ad for a healthy diet and right living.

Before his illness, Jerry Ferray's face had seemed gnarled and puffy, his prominent nose blunted. Traces of alcohol abuse still remained in the color of his skin, and in the deep furrows in his face. But as his illness advanced, his nose had grown more beaklike, his hazel eyes sharper from pain and impatience. He still dyed his hair brown, which made the white at his temples look blond.

"Everyone's making the pilgrimage," he said, "now that the news is out."

"How's Mom?"

"Good. Out saving the desert turtle."

She saw a bottle of champagne sticking out of an ice chest underneath the table. "Pop!"

"Bah! That's for display only!"

"You and Buck were sitting here having a nip!"

"No, we weren't." Two hummingbirds zeroed in on the feeder. "I have mixed feelings about Bucky some days. He can be pompous, doesn't really understand the law, but he's mighty entertaining . . ." Jerry Ferray's thoughts turned inward.

"Pop, did you ever start talking about something and find out in the middle you were really talking about something you'd already done and never wanted to do again?"

"Nope."

"I actually pitched a film to Herb Yount and I was halfway through before I realized I didn't want to make that picture. I ought to be put away."

"I said that to your mom years ago." Jerry patted Faye's arm. "Della was a good friend and she's left a big hole in your life."

"Pop, I have to do something about her, but I don't know what, except to keep harassing that detective."

"Keep after Buck. He knows everyone."

"Oh, Pop, I'm not close to them anymore. It was really a strain seeing him here."

"Sic Nadine on them."

"Nadine hates her parents, Pop."

"Still?"

"Yes. Well, maybe hate's too strong. She—distrusts them, I guess. Longs for their attention . . ."

Jerry watched his daughter brush a curl of red-brown hair off her cheek. Her eyes were hazel-green in the fading light. He loved the odd scatter of freckles on her pale skin. She was the only person who never asked him how he felt. And he loved her for that, too, because he always felt rotten and he hated to lie.

"Herb Yount's put me on his Drummond committee."

"I'm not voting for Drummond. Twelve years is all they get from me. Corrupted by then, and he probably doesn't even know it."

"Oh, Pop, for God's sake, Mark's not corrupted. He's a senior senator. You kick senators out after twelve years, they don't get on the powerful committees."

"I don't care, I'm not voting for him. Just remember that motion pictures and politics are *both* performance arts and he's only playing senator now. I tell you, all the fun's gone out of the political game. It's not like in the sixties when Buck and me and some of the guys . . . that was the best time. The *fifties* were hell, real bottom-feeders." He slapped the arm of his chair. "But the *sixties*—! Remember when Kennedy came out here and stayed with Bing Crosby instead of Sinatra? Bing was a die-hard Republican! What a hot time! Jesus, was Sinatra pissed. But later, in sixty-four, we really took a pasting with George Murphy."

"The Senate race," she put in. She'd heard it before.

"We figured we had it made with Pierre Salinger. Who'd elect an old right-wing hoofer like George Murphy when they could have Kennedy's press secretary? Were we ever wrong! He beat the pants off Salinger." He peeked at the champagne. "Don't let Buck kid you, he plays both sides of the fence. He was for Carter in seventy-six, but he bankrolled Reagan in eighty. But he's one of this country's great gentlemen and you can always count on him for good advice."

"He lets his wife run him."

"Helena doesn't run him, that's an act, take it from me." He shifted uncomfortably around in his chair. "Faye, your problem is that your life's all work. Get it in balance. I'll bet you haven't heard an opera in a year. Very cleansing. Why don't you pick someone out and get married and have a child?"

"Have a kid or go to an opera. Is that your advice?"

"For openers. How's your waddyacallit—biological time clock?"

"Pop, there aren't any available men in this town and all the good ones are gay."

"I'm sitting here on my last legs with three children and only one grandchild—Annie's. Robbie's the only one of you three who isn't divorced. What's the matter with you all?"

"I want to make that film."

"What film?"

"*The Jungle Gym*. Herb hates it." She put a finger to her cheek. "But the story reminds me of Della. I think I can say good-bye to her if I make it."

"Then make it, take *any* work—commercial shit—just get busy again."

"I won't make any old thing, Pop."

"All right, make the film you want to make. You're not a nobody."

"It was a lot easier with Gabe."

"Forget Gabe. Make your own life, kid, it's all we've got. Have a drink." He reached beneath the table and poured champagne into two tiny paper cups.

"If you drink that, I'm leaving."

"Forget it, babe, I'm only holding." He handed her a cup.

"You know, when the news of our divorce broke publicly," Faye said, "people came out of the walls to tell me when they'd seen Gabe and Tot together at Morton's or out at the beach."

"Yes, it was a shock," Jerry said. "You and Gabe were more than husband and wife, you were a great team."

"It's a lot harder without a male partner."

"Whoever said it would be easy? Get up off your knees." Jerry swatted the air, irritated at his body and at his daughter. At one time he would have sung a two-octave scale, up and back. Now, he didn't have the energy or the voice.

"I love him and I hate him." She felt the pain and the magic, and a terrible longing for Gabe's company. She woke up each morning wanting him and cursing him. She did not like herself for that obsession.

"Everything's love-hate. I love sitting here doing nothing and I hate the reason for it. If I'd sat here more often when I was healthy I might not be ill today. Damned fucking leukemia—Faye, you don't let yourself be really close to anyone, not the way you did. Not emotionally."

She thought of telling him about seeing Gabe, about her hope, about her withdrawal. *What's wrong with me?* she thought. *What kind of woman am I? Am I worthwhile? Will anyone love me again?*

"Why did Tot and Gabe split?" Jerry asked.

"I don't know. Maybe the fire died. Nothing's forever," she said.

"Thanks."

"Don't mention it."

Annie flopped back against the bank of down pillows and drew the satin comforter toward her lush bare hips. She raised her dimpled arms and, with a low giggle, looped them around Sam Pike, preventing him from getting out of bed. She slouched closer to him and they lay together feeling the sweat on their bodies merge.

"Champs!" she said, disengaging. She threw off the comforter and uncurled from the bed. She was magnificent, all curves and cushioning. There wasn't a hair on her except for the rolling waves of reddish locks on her head, and a razored curly triangle between her peach-colored thighs. He knew his admiration fed her. Her insolent haunches disappeared through the doorway.

Sam was attracted to talented people and he had a weakness for truly sensual women. He was also tantalized by Annie's guile, deeply hidden beneath layers of pagan, feral impulses.

When her insouciant body returned, it bore a tray with champagne and glasses. Annie carried it propped under her generous round bosom, which rested on its surface, the bottle propped between, another offering.

"You are frisky," he said.

Her eyes twinkled at him. If Sam hadn't been important or rich, she would still have liked him, but she wouldn't have seen as much of him.

With a grin, she lowered the tray away from her breasts and set it on the bed. Sam poured, stowing the bottle and bucket on the floor.

Annie's bed was crowded with pillows and coverlets and ruffles. Every chair in her room was ruffled and overstuffed; a large oval mirror with a lacy, gilded trim hung over a dressing table covered by a platoon of ornamented perfume flagons.

"Sammy," she said, sipping the wine, "what do you think Della did to get herself killed like that?"

"Oh, I expect it's as the newspapers say, drugs."

"Faye's sure it wasn't."

"Well, Della was her best friend."

"Faye's obsessed."

"What you can do for her is listen, Annie. You're probably her only real confidante." Annie pitched forward, laughing. Sam seemed shocked. "Why, who else would she talk to about something so awful?"

"She used to talk to Gabe. She talks to Nadine, but she's so far away."

"You see? She really only has you."

"Believe me, we don't have that kind of sibling relationship."

Sam wanted Annie again, the ache was like an itch he couldn't reach. But she had something else on her mind and he could feel it forming. "Are you pleased about your TV show?" he asked, running a finger across her nipple.

"No, it's a stupid part. And you know it. Can't you help me get something better, Sammy? You know everyone." She turned to him, rolling on her glorious Rubens hip and sliding her soft hand along his chest.

"Mel's a good director," he said, feeling the itch consuming his body. "You're doing the pilot to work with him again."

"But it's television."

"Oh, TV, film, what's the difference anymore? Be patient, do the work. Something better will turn up."

When his hand slipped toward the floor next to the bed, she thought he was reaching for more champagne. Instead, he held up two pink silk cords.

"New ones," she said.

He took her champagne glass and set it aside, then bound one cord around her wrist and fastened it to a bedpost. He secured the other.

Sam was attracted to what Annie called "edge games," which flirted with dangerous designs. They did not excite her. She knew they came from corruption or boredom, though she didn't think those were true of Samuel Pike. She hid her thoughts, winked at him, and said, "Sammy, you are soooo naughty."

He grabbed each side of her bounteous waist and buried his face in her satin skin.

"Aren't you ever going to get rid of that trash?"

Across the narrow street, Faye's neighbor stood on the curb, aiming an accusing finger at some scrap lumber and a lump of cement the workmen had left a month ago.

"I'm sorry, Boyd, but it's not in anyone's way."

"It's an eyesore!" The man had a crude, critical face; his scrawny legs were a disappointing conclusion to his expensive Bermuda shorts.

"I ran out of money—I'll get it cleared as soon as I can!" She stumped up to her front door, and he stumped back to his.

Faye's house had been her parents' first home before Rob was born. A small 1931 bachelor pad built by a silent movie star who'd died in 1940 under mysterious circumstances, it perched on a rise off Franklin Avenue above Hollywood Boulevard. The place was cheap in 1945, when Jerry and Coo had moved in, because the star's ghost was said to appear in the windows, and moan in the garage. When Faye and Gabe separated and their house was sold, she'd asked her mother if she could "hide out" in the haunted house. Her mother had been against it: the foundations were going; the wiring had to be redone. After Faye started the renovations, she'd been forced to take temporary recesses. The last one had been permanent.

Built of concrete and smooth plaster with copper trim, the little house was an unconventional structure. The foundation had been strengthened; the nest of little rooms that had divided the main floor had been made into a single large area—dining, living, and a lounge-study with a wall of paned glass. She wanted to replace the molded stucco fireplace, a disgrace, according to her designer friends; she wanted to reconstitute the rooms' modernistic detailing; she wanted to construct a rock garden off the bedroom, one flight below the main floor.

She kicked the door shut behind her and flipped on the hall light switch: the damned house felt unlived-in. The open, unfinished walls in the hall and living room had been peeled back to the studs. She was idiotic to blow off *Lights Out*—she needed the money. Putting down Della's box, she turned on more lights, picked up the mail, noting that her bank statement had arrived, and went through the archway into the living room and on into the kitchen. This, too, was unfinished, the old counter tiles chipped, the cabinets dreary. She popped open a soda as she went back to the hall and down the stairs to the bedroom, a large room with a chaise, bookcases, two dressers, and a wall of mirrors—the last thing she'd added before calling off the decorators.

On top of the bedspread, one side of her bed was entirely covered with newspapers, trade magazines, books, and scripts, the bed of a woman who had no lover. Faye sat down on it. Since her divorce, she wasn't sure if she'd been seriously propositioned; she couldn't remember even looking closely at a man except a kindly TV actor. Dimly, she recalled some writer putting his arms around her in a pitch session in her office. But maybe she exaggerated.

She went back upstairs for the box left by the railing that overlooked the stairwell down to the bedroom. Carefully, she carried it down, dropping it in her bedroom. She sat on the bed and stared at it.

A phone was ringing. Faye fumbled for it on the nightstand.

"Hello," she mumbled.

"Faye, it's Della."

"Della?"

"I was waiting for you but you didn't show up," Della said. The connection was fading in and out.

"What?" Faye's other hand was reaching out for a lamp. The air felt heavy and moist.

"I've got a lot to tell you," Della was saying.

"Did I miss lunch?" Faye felt she was swimming but she couldn't feel the water.

Della's voice faded in and out between the static. " . . . I left it for you in the box . . ."

Faye could see the far shore, misty and gray. "What about the box?"

"Faye, Nadine's in trouble. She doesn't know how to ask for help, she didn't grow up loved like us . . ." Della's voice was trailing off.

"Delly, don't go!"

"Take care of Nadine!" The line went dead.

Faye was sinking below the surface of the lake. She'd been here before and she knew she could breathe the dream water again. She was enjoying it when she realized Della had died in her car weeks ago.

The shock stiffened her body. She started pumping upward. A white shape as big as a house climbed out of the shadows right in front of her.

"Oh, my God, oh, my God," she moaned, terrified, trying to swim away from it. But the water, like gel, held her fast. Enormous and silent, the white shape seemed to have no beginning or end, yet it was an entity, a presence. And it was malevolent.

"Help me," she was screaming as she woke up.

Fully dressed, she lay on her bed, her face wet with sweat. She stumbled into the bathroom and splashed cold water over her face. The shape in the water went with her, filling the room behind her. She was terrified of it. Next to her bath, a small room held a treadmill, weights, and an old TV set. She turned the set on: Janet Gaynor was kissing Fredric March. Faye flung herself into a major workout, showered, and went back into the bedroom.

To the box. She opened it. Signed copies of the law review, Della's papers from law school, photocopies of cases with notes in the margins, old photos. An exhumation. She found a photo of herself, Tot, Della, and Nadine, twelve years younger, standing in front of the law school in Berkeley. Tears welled up. By the time she reached the bottom of the box, she felt drained.

She put everything back. The sweater was last, Della's lucky cardigan she'd always worn for exams. Faye unfolded it, held it up, then crumpled it against her chest. "Oh, Della," she sobbed softly.

She was refolding it when she felt something hard in one pocket. A three-inch computer disk.

SIX

NADINE STERN FERRAY, Faye's sister-in-law, made one last call before leaving for lunch.

"I got the disk, Faye, and I'll look at it tonight, but it'll be late—Rob and I have to go to a reception. What else did Della have in that box?"

"Law school stuff. Izzy said the police checked that, but I don't think they've seen the disk—it was in her lucky sweater."

"Give it to them. Did you make a copy?" Nadine asked.

"Yes. It's just a list of names and places—I don't know what it means. I'm sure it's important. CDEE is in there."

"Well, we'll see." She heard Faye sigh loudly. "I'll take a real careful look. I will check it out."

"How about her clients?"

"I haven't checked them yet. I will."

"This is important, Nadine. We can't just let this go."

Now Nadine sighed. "I'll check everything out. I have to run to lunch—at the White House Mess, no less!"

"You're taking Annie to the hottest lunch spot in town?"

"Yes. And Tot."

"*Tot?* Rob won't like that."

"Faye, his bitterness toward Tot has gone on too long. It's

not worthy of him. He's got to work with her—she's part of the press gang out here."

"Okay, I understand. At least Annie will dress up the table, right?"

"Right." Annie's television series had been canceled two years before, but it was in rerun, and it had made her face and name well-known. "Actually, I can't remember when Rob and I last met for lunch. Anyway, I'm going to speak to Tot after. I'm sure she's not sleeping with Gabe."

"It doesn't matter," Faye said.

"It *does* matter."

"Okay, it matters," Faye admitted, "but, you know, in another way, it doesn't. I can't get back with Gabe again."

"Does he want to?"

"I think so. Sort of. When he was here for the funeral, I was a mess. I'm still a mess," she laughed. "I'm having the worst dreams. I come out of them and feel I'm temporarily blinded, trying to find my way back to real life. . . ."

Nadine had no use for imagery; she was a realist. "It's the shock, Faye. You're still in shock."

Just like Los Angeles, Washington, D.C., had evolved despite its location. All attempts to make it commercial, and therefore successful in the eyes of many, had failed.

Unlike L.A., the nation's capital had sprouted not from a desert, but from a festering swamp—a tidal zone—that fluctuated seasonally between fierce winter winds bearing sleet and ice, and suffocating summer heats. An old canal, an extension of Tiber Creek, snaked through the city. An open sewer, tides regularly overwhelmed it, spilling out and seeping back, servant to a force no Congress could control. Some thought it the source of "bilious fevers," but most informed people in the early days knew these statements to be shabby alarmism. Siding with the extremists, however, an enterprising Washington city council believed the canal a menace to public health so they urged Congress to drain it. In its wisdom, Congress, much like today, ignored the request.

Nadine Ferray was walking toward the White House and thinking about Tiber Creek. It still gushed under Constitution Avenue, slabbed over like a recurring family sin, rushing unseen through generations. Like the fate of Tiber Creek, there was, she thought, something hidden and covered over in Della's cruel death.

If she hadn't become a lawyer, Nadine would have taught history. She liked to look up arcane tracts and to study musty maps; she liked to read accounts of real events. She skirted the President's Park at the south of the White House. Its trees had been donated by or were associated with former Presidents: an American elm for John Quincy Adams, a magnolia for Andrew Jackson, a giant sequoia for Richard Nixon. She passed the Old Executive Office Building, an ornate Victorian confection known in Washingtonspeak as the OEOB, where she worked across the street from the White House.

The West Wing is a staff wing, home of the Oval Office and the Cabinet Room. Below, a two-story basement houses the Situation Room and some of the National Security offices. Nadine entered the West Wing basement, where an officer checked her ID against his list and waved her into a reception area. She'd arranged the lunch in the Mess through her boss, Leo Townsend, deputy to the President's adviser for the National Security Council.

Nadine let herself absorb the atmosphere of the center of all power in the known universe. She tried to look blasé, but she'd only been in a few meetings at the White House, and to a couple of receptions. She sat down, smoothed the skirt to her gray-and-white-checked suit. She was nervous about the lunch.

When her White House escort arrived, they went down a hallway to the elevators. Since her first year of law school, Nadine had wanted to be a lawyer for a government agency. Though top appointments were political, she'd had the law school grades and the connections—through Mark Drummond's 1980 upset Senate victory and through her father, Judge Stern.

When she started out as an attorney for Drummond, she was one of his most conservative staff members, though registered as an independent. Her father had introduced her to Leo Townsend from the State Department and to an attorney, Adrian Anderson III. When they moved over to the National

Security Council, she went with them. Rob had not wanted her to take it: he called the NSC the President's high-tech spy outfit. She called it the President's foreign advisory group.

Annie and Rob were already seated at a table in the wood-paneled Mess, which was crowded with senior White House staff. Rob smiled at her, but his eyes continued to canvass the room.

"What's the President really like?" Annie was asking as Nadine sat down.

"A family man with conservative beliefs," Nadine replied. "I love that," Annie gushed. "The White House alive with the sound of children."

Annie had on theatrical-strength makeup. She was dressed in an apricot outfit whose main feature was a thigh-high skirt. A black belt compressed her soft flesh, a long black chiffon scarf floated around her neck. Even old executive branch cynics eyed her closely.

They ordered from the steward.

Annie was impatient, rattling her bracelets. "Come on, Nadine, tell me what the President's *really* like."

"He's only been President six months," Rob said. "He's still called the Veep, but he's the don of our California types inside the government."

"We do stick together," Nadine said. But Rob, so merry a moment before, glanced at his wife crossly. "That's true," Nadine protested to his frown. Once she and Rob would have played the handoff together, each trying to top the other.

"Annie," Rob said, "he's merely filling out Masterson's term."

Annie drew herself up, pushing her prominent chest forward. "Well, I *know* he *was* Vice President, Rob, but do you *like* him?"

"He has all the intellectual fortitude of a Granny Smith apple," Rob said cheerfully. "He'll be reelected by a landslide."

"Don't listen to him, Annie," Nadine said. Rob was a Democrat and their two-party family had once been a strength. Now, it was showing the strain.

Much had been left unsaid. Like Hollywood, Washington was a city of rumors. The stories circulating around the Veep detailed his inattention, his lack of experience, his sudden stubborn opinions about how soon the old Soviet hard-liners would climb out of their foxholes and begin World War Three.

The food arrived. "So how's Drummy?" Annie asked.

"Don't call him Drummy," Rob said. "He is a powerful senator."

Rob wasn't handsome, but his face and manner transmitted a California wholesomeness. Men and women alike felt warmed by his good humor and ready laugh. As Senator Drummond's press secretary, Rob, together with his staff, created and tended the senator's public face. Rob controlled all the senator's media reactions, interviews, statements, speeches; he wrote or commissioned Drummond's op-ed essays for California newspapers.

"LaSalle's retiring from our nineteenth-century version of the Supreme Court," Rob said. "Now the President'll put a new man on and maybe he can push it into the eighteenth century."

"Rob always forgets the eighteenth century invented democracy as we know it," Nadine said. "What are your plans, Annie?"

"We're still shooting this TV movie in Virginia. It's about a mother who gives up her illegitimate child for adoption, then changes her mind."

"What's wrong with that?" Rob asked.

"We've only seen it a dozen times."

"We all compromise," Rob said. His eyes shifted quickly to Nadine, then away.

"Well, I don't," Annie said airily, flashing her big smile. "I need a serious role. That's how careers are made, Robbie. Faye could mount something for me, but she's revived *The Jungle Gym*."

"I'm sure she has her reasons," Rob said loyally. "If I remember that picture, Annie, it's a wonderful story with a great woman's role."

"Rob," Annie said soothingly, "remember Lili Zanuck and *Driving Miss Daisy*? For years she struggled to get that Academy Award-winning film made. *Years*."

Rob backed off. Annie's moods ranged from giddy sunshine to sullen pouts to screaming fits. It'd take an act of Congress for Faye to mount any project for Annie. She had a typical younger-sister complex, jealous and respectful of Faye, who fatefully had the power to give Annie what she needed most: roles. Rob did not want to be drawn into the middle of their battle. He ate faster. Beneath the table, he pressed a button on his watch that would make it chime in ten minutes.

"I have a confession," Nadine said quietly. "I invited Tot to have coffee with us."

"How exciting," Annie said, looking at Rob.

"Isn't it enough I have to put up with her around town?" he said.

"We can't keep avoiding her," Nadine said. "Faye agrees."

"I don't," he said, his good humor gone.

Tot showed up toward the end of lunch. "We had a tip the Veep was going to make a statement about D.C.," she said, sitting down. "Erroneous. But all was not lost. I had a talk with a White House gardener."

"Ohhh," said Rob, sarcastic, "a really big scoop."

"I thought you did national stories," Annie said, "with the network."

"Anything the President says is national."

"Are you covering the President?" Annie asked, awed.

"No, Annie, I just go where I'm assigned." Tot's expression was grave. "The Veep's known for his charitable concerns," she said. "He makes sure big trucks of food go out to the hungry on Thanksgiving and Christmas, and today we can add another concern." Tot paused as a steward brought her a cup of coffee.

"What?" Annie asked, going along.

"Birds."

Rob, his mouth full of lettuce, coughed. Nadine smiled, touching a beautifully manicured finger to her lips.

"Well, what's so funny about that?" Annie said.

Tot straightened up. "Right, Annie. We're talkin' important business of state here." She lowered her voice. "They'll never let me do a piece on it, but the gardener said the Veep has asked them to build more birdhouses because some thrush has taken up residence in Lyndon B. Johnson's Darlington oak. It's right outside the Oval Office." She lowered her voice even more. "The Veep's a bird freak." She chirped. "Veep-veep."

Annie and Nadine giggled, and Rob tried hard not to laugh out loud in a room of White House staffers.

"Nadine, will you check Leo on it for me?"

"Certainly not," she replied. "I'm not asking my boss about the thrush in the President's oak tree." She patted a wave of her blond hair. "I mean, friendship goes only so far."

Rob's watch alarm went off. He excused himself, casting a flat look of reproof at Nadine. "I guess I didn't charm him back to my side," Tot said after he left.

Nadine, Tot, and Annie were walking back to the old EOB. The day was cloudy, but pleasant.

"So, Tot, are you and Gabe going to get back together?" Annie asked.

"No."

"Why not?"

"Things change," Tot said. "You've been damned decent, Annie, not making me feel like some bitchy homewrecker."

"Faye always survives."

Nadine eyed them. Annie was smirking and Tot sounded callous.

"How did you and Gabe get together?" Annie asked.

"It was an accident, one of those moments when you see an old friend with new eyes."

"So who are you seeing now?" Annie asked Tot.

"A shooter—a cameraman. Who's that soap-opera guy the magazines say you're dating, Annie?"

"We're not dating," Annie shot back. "We're screwing our brains out."

Annie waved at a dark blue Lincoln, which pulled to a stop at the curb. "My car and driver," she announced. She kissed each of them on the cheek. "Bye-bye."

Tot fitted a blue beret over her curly brown hair, which made her look cute and even younger. "I knew Annie would ask about Gabe."

Nadine narrowed her eyes. "You sounded cold, as if breaking up Faye's marriage wasn't accidental."

"What can I say to Faye? 'I'm sorry?' I *am* sorry. It took Gabe and me like a firestorm."

"But Faye was one of your best friends."

"I feel awful about that."

"At the cabin, it sounded as if you and Gabe were still sleeping together, at least seeing each other—"

"Not so! I saw him for dinner one night!"

Nadine searched Tot's face. "Why?"

"We talked about Della," Tot hedged. Nadine was staring at her. "I think he called to make sure I understood it was over between us."

They were standing awkwardly in front of the Old Executive Office Building. Tot readjusted her beret. She had no relatives and no hobbies. Both her parents had died a few years ago. Nadine felt she was one of those women who might end up having no personal life because she was so busy covering other people's lives. "You want to walk a little?"

They started around the block, Pennsylvania Avenue to Seventeenth, and back again. "Rob's uncomfortable with me," Tot said. "What happened between Gabe and me— well, until something like that happens to you, you just don't know how—compelling it is. I felt like I was drowning in the most blissful way—it was ecstasy, it was sorrow. *I could not help myself,*" she said, separating each word. "You think I didn't consider Faye? I thought of her every hour. So did Gabe. I never meant to harm her."

"But you did, and I don't think you've faced it."

They walked in silence, the petite, solid woman with frizzy brown hair and the slim, blond fashion plate with the smart dark eyes. "Are you still trying to get pregnant?" Tot asked.

Nadine smiled. "Yes. I had more tests two months ago. I try to think positively."

"I'm trying to be assigned to the California campaigns, but there're a lot of senior people ahead of me." She tugged at her beret.

"Oh, shoot," Nadine said. "I forgot to check out that stuff about Della. I told Faye I would."

"Just remember, when you start investigating you better be ready to find out things you might not want to know,"

Tot said. Her short curvy mouth smiled innocently.

"Not about Della." Self-consciously, Nadine put a hand to her temple to lift the skin and erase the first new lines of her jaw. She was beginning to understand life without total beauty. She was losing her shield. "I'm thinking of getting a face lift," Nadine said.

"How silly."

"You can never be too beautiful," Nadine stated. "You know how many beautiful and powerful women there are in this town? I feel—Rob—sometimes I just don't feel good enough."

"Something's wrong between you and Rob."

"Oh, no," Nadine said, walking on. "We're fine. Well, it's hard right now. We really want a child. And the work's nonstop. Mark's very demanding—and Rob's hours are long. Sometimes, I wish we were all back in law school—"

"Back in that sewer?" Tot cried. "We couldn't wait to get out of there, don't you remember? If it hadn't been for you and Faye, I would have quit my first year. And Della. We made a pact never to give the school a dime of our money after we graduated!" She stopped. "Have you broken the pact?"

Nadine smiled. "No." They were back in front of the OEOB near the springtime trees. "The President's thrush in the President's tree," Nadine said. "I love it."

"Another example of how isolated the people are who run this government," Tot said.

"People here are more knowledgeable than anywhere else in the world."

"Psychologically isolated. Socially isolated. I'm new and I'm objective. The atmosphere around here is like living on a rich and powerful island of insiders, surrounded by a buffer of bureaucrats, ringed by a distressed populace."

"Tot!"

She was wound tight, caught up in herself. "Oh, it looks serene on the surface. But it's as stage-managed as any play. Morally, this town's in chaos. And it's as violent as Los Angeles." She shot Nadine a sudden smile. "Liberty, justice, security."

"*I'm* part of this city. You're talking about me."

"I didn't mean you," Tot said quickly. "But there's a complacency here, a disconnection from pain that I find very disturbing. Don't you feel it?"

"We're *not* disconnected. We're trying to do a good job." Nadine was upset and angry. "People really care about how this country is run."

"I didn't mean you specifically," Tot said.

Nadine knew different.

SEVEN

NADINE HEADED DOWN a corridor of the OEOB, passing two men arguing about limos—one of the perks of top executive staffers. She reached the administrative area presided over by Pamela Sewell and her staff. As the administrator for the section, Pamela controlled the in-coming and out-going mail, fax transmissions, and copying machines.

Pamela was Nadine's age and from a distance they looked alike. Up close, Pamela's features were not as lovely, her hair sandy, not blond.

"This was dropped off." Pamela pushed a dark blue folder across the desk. Nadine signed for it. "And here's something from your esteemed boss. He needs it first thing."

"What is it?" Nadine murmured.

"Do I know? If I know, do I tell?" Pamela replied with a faint smile.

One of the men from the hall breezed past them. "Rotten when you have to share a limo," he said, winking.

"Heartbreaking," Nadine replied. He disappeared down the corridor. "Who is he?"

"Colonel Chevack, one of Harper's new special assistants." Nadine rolled her eyes prettily. "Both of them are from your home state. We're turning into the California Suite."

* * *

A budget cap had been fixed on the decorating of all but the most senior offices. Nadine was a GS-15 with certain privileges, but her office was still furnished in Government Functional. Every week she brightened it with fresh flowers.

The chain of command at the National Security Council started with the adviser to the President, Norman Tate, and his deputy, Leo Townsend; next, the legal adviser, Adrian Anderson, and his deputies; below them, the agency was divided into program areas, such as legislative affairs, or African affairs, or intelligence policy.

Nadine was one of three deputy legal advisers to Anderson; she owed her job and her loyalty to him, but also to Leo Townsend. Her responsibilities were to give legal advice on contracts and statutes, write opinions, support Adrian and Leo in all things. If she pleased them, their political connections would help her realize her ambitions.

When she'd checked through the contract Adrian needed, making notes on a legal-sized yellow pad, she opened the dark blue folder that had been delivered from the West Wing.

It was a briefing paper. Something's out of place here, she thought: this wasn't her area. But the NSC staff of almost two hundred brought together specialists in various areas to handle a quagmire of issues. There was a lot of compartmentalization: some people knew one part of a program, others knew another. Only a few knew everything.

The briefing paper was a summary of an NSC program titled the Office of Public Information; the first page outlined the activities of a subcommittee on broadcasting. The second page was a list of names for potential consultants.

Nadine frowned: what was a briefing paper on OPI doing on her desk?

OPI's mission was to prepare guidelines to coordinate all government efforts in the area of domestic and international information programs. Its purpose was to disseminate the idea of democracy and to tell how democracy worked.

"Good," she mumbled, glancing out her window. A wind was shaking the budding trees.

The project was divided into public affairs, international political matters, domestic information programs, and domestic/international broadcasting. She went down the list of names on the second page and stopped at Della Izquerra. Someone somewhere had listed Della as a consultant to the OPI international television effort, whatever that was.

Her private telephone line rang.

"I'm glad I caught you," the cheery, Southern voice said. It was Claire Townsend, wife of the NSC deputy adviser. "About the party—"

"I hope we're keeping it simple?" Claire's parties were legend. She could tempt anyone to her table.

"Simple?" Claire said, appalled. "Big, splashy—that's what I'm doing. It's your fifth anniversary! I thought you might like Faye and Annie Ferray there."

"Great, Claire, but I don't know that either can get away."

"They'll come to *this* party," Claire sang out.

Nadine's door opened and Leo Townsend stepped into her office. "Guess who just came in?" Nadine said, astonished. "This is Claire, Leo." She could count on one hand the number of times Leo had been in her office.

At fifty-four, Leo had thinning hair and the compact, muscular build of a skier, a sport he followed as eagerly as football.

"I won't keep you from your dark bureaucratic deeds," Claire was saying to Nadine on the phone. "Call me back tonight on the guest list."

Nadine hung up. "How are you, Leo?"

"Couldn't be better." He'd stopped in front of her desk. Leo was a true professional and Nadine respected him. A Stanford graduate, he'd come from a wealthy California family. He was good-looking in an average way—except for his thin mouth and penetrating eyes, which regarded the world fiercely. Set under dark brows in his bland face, his eyes were the only feature anyone remembered.

"What brings you over here to the lowlands?" she asked.

"A couple of things with Adrian." Leo scanned her desktop and stopped on the briefing paper. "My word." He reached out, closed the blue folder, scooped it up. "A little premature," he said lightly.

"It's old information, Leo."

"How do you mean?"

"Della Izquerra is listed as a possible consultant, so it can't be that new."

"It needs major revisions."

"Hush-hush?"

"Nah."

She gestured at a stack of folders. "I have plenty of other things to do. But it sounds like a good project. I suppose you've seen Ryder's report about how misunderstood democracy is?"

"Misunderstood in which countries?"

"The U.S.A."

Clutching the dark blue folder, Leo walked briskly back to the West Wing of the White House. In his small office in the subbasement, he called out for his assistant, a man who'd worked with him for five years. When he appeared in the doorway, Leo pressed one finger against the folder on his neat desk. "Did you have these distributed this morning?"

"If that's OPI, yes."

"You're fired. Get out."

In her office, Nadine was making orderly notes on OPI for her day's work summary. This was a personal log to jog her memory if she needed it. Her private phone rang again. Claire again? Nadine admired Claire's social skills, but her incessant social focus put her off. The phone was still ringing.

It was her boss with a summons to see him.

"This place is leak-crazy."

Adrian Anderson III, the National Security Council's legal adviser, was thirty-seven, a bachelor who was invited to every dinner in Washington. He was descended from the Anderson family who'd seized on a commitment to government service after making fortunes from whaling and munitions.

"Another leak?" Nadine asked, taking a chair in his pleasant corner office.

"Didn't you see Bluestone's column this morning about Daniels?"

"Oh, our special assistant in Latin American affairs using the limos? Yes, I saw that."

"Someone burps at lunch, Bluestone covers it, and everyone here goes to general quarters. Chasing leaks is a bloody waste of time."

"Was he using limos for private business?"

"No, he wasn't," he said indifferently. Nadine smiled; she enjoyed Adrian. "But Leo came to see me about it. Everyone's in a flap over there." He waved a hand toward the White House, then smoothed his lapel carefully. Adrian was the smartest dresser in the OEOB, tending toward the Italians in style, which drew snickers from some of the military types.

"Adrian," she said abruptly, "do you think we're cut off from the public, maybe even from other parts of the government?"

"You've been talking to your husband again."

"I want to work on a plan to instigate a way to get regular feedback."

Adrian smiled. "When we want feedback, we will request feedback. Or I'll ask you and you'll give it to me."

Clearly, the subject was closed.

"Here's your contract." She put the folder on his desk. "Have you ever heard of a nonprofit outfit called CDEE? An environmental group?"

He started leafing through the contract. "Don't think so."

"I know I've run across it somewhere. My friend Della Izquerra got them a large federal grant."

"Doesn't ring any bells. You checked its incorporation, all that stuff?"

"Not yet. What's OPI?"

"Where'd you hear about that?" he asked her, his voice mild.

"I think a messenger delivered the file to me by mistake. I was asking Leo about it."

"Leo's had a busy day, hasn't he?" Adrian put down the contract and looked at her thoughtfully. "OPI's an information program about democracy. We subcontract a lot of the work out. Jay Harper, the new special assistant down on two, coordinates it."

"I don't know him. What's the international part of the project?" Nadine asked.

"The planning group's borrowed some specialists in Latin America, mainly Department of Defense guys and some new communications specialists."

"There is a domestic side to it, right?"

"Sure, they're supposed to introduce a full understanding of democracy and the free-enterprise system at home through grants and education or training to nonprofit organizations." He smiled. "It's a no-brainer program that's been around for a couple of years." Adrian glanced at her, lit a small cigar, and crossed his legs, flattening the sharp crease in his trousers.

"Why don't you quietly look into OPI?" he said. He sipped coffee from a china cup and puffed on the cigar. "Keep your eyes and ears open. There's something about it that doesn't feel right. It's grinding up legal work. We're spending a lot of time on it."

"Let's leave it alone until it bleeds," she said.

"No, it's our job to make sure all the *t*s are crossed properly in this office. But I want to tread lightly. Why don't you get to know Harper? I'm real curious about him. He's moved his phones and computers to another room downstairs and now he has two more assistants."

"What does Leo say?"

"Ummm, he's very protective of OPI," he said, choosing words carefully.

"He'll know the minute I start checking around."

"Yes, but for instance, your assistant's pregnant and you've been taking some of the load off her, doing some of your own copying, walking contracts all across the building. Are you and Pamela Sewell tight?"

"I wouldn't say tight. She gets the work done."

"Well, if you're in there copying, and if you see some paperwork on OPI, you could make an extra copy, or give it a good glance. Men stand out in a copying room; women look like part of the decor."

"Gee, Adrian, you're a peach."

"I'm speaking sociologically. You're one of the few women in here who isn't a secretary." The National Security Council was not an equal opportunity employer. Most of the staffers were men and upper-echelon advisers and assistants were all men; most of the clerical and administrative assistants were women.

Nadine felt uncomfortable, even though she knew other people cadged other sections' information when they could. Seeing Della's name on that list, Leo's haste in removing it from her office, and now Adrian's request alerted all her suspicions. "Why don't we do it by the book and I'll conduct an in-house investigation?"

"No, not yet. Just keep your eyes open. Be aware."

"I feel you're not telling me everything," she said.

He leaned forward. "I'm telling you all that I know. I'm just a tad uneasy about the program and I want to keep an eye on it."

Rob Ferray felt he was a happy man or ought to be: life had never done anything bad to him, he felt it never would. He'd once been a journalist with idealistic notions about the role of the press. Now, as Senator Drummond's press secretary, he fed reporters what he wanted them to know, encouraged them to cover what he needed covered, and he was, sometimes, their target.

In Senator Drummond's office in the Russell Building on Constitution Avenue, Rob was shouting at Harry, Drummond's administrative assistant. "It's television that determines what the Senator says and how he says it!" They were standing in the doorway between Rob's cramped quarters and the main office.

Harry was a brittle man of forty with quick gestures. "Then *you* talk to the guy. He's handling the subcommittee work for Mark."

Staff equaled power. Senator Drummond had four fully staffed offices in Washington and California, plus his subcommittee staffs.

"What's a new guy doing criticizing my work?" Rob said blandly. "Doesn't he know that TV *is* the political process? Warren Beatty said that," he said with a wink.

"He just thought the senator's comment could have been misunderstood."

"But Mark's only got ten seconds!" Rob cried.

"The guy's a budget man," the AA said. That meant he'd be a key player for the subcommittee the senator chaired: Treasury, Postal Service, and General Government, which kept an eye on executive branch expenditures, including the NSC.

"Okay, Harry, I'll talk to him," Rob said in his cheery, irreverent way. "I'll train the little bastard to give me ten-second bites."

Rob Ferray concentrated completely on whoever he was with and he gave his attention democratically—from the secretary in charge of the senator's mailing lists to a star television reporter. And to Claire Townsend.

At four that afternoon, Rob drew his nails gently along Claire's spine inside the opening of her unzipped dress. His tongue followed his fingers. Since December, the affair with Claire, ten years his senior, had progressed through the furious excitement of the hunt to the rapture of reward. Now it teetered at that junction where their sexual liaison would improve even more, or the connection would collapse.

Claire moved away from him and slipped out of her dress. She'd been a gymnast in her youth and she reveled in her firm, trained muscles. Rob felt her pride like a heat as her bra and panties hit the floor. She sauntered back to him, raised her arms imperiously, and pulled him to her. "You're addicted to women, Robbie," she said, stroking his chest. They lay down on the bed. "You feel so warm." He felt himself melting against her naked body. "Leo is so cold," she whispered against his cheek. "Has a heart like a pebble."

Even though Leo was Nadine's boss, Rob didn't know him well. He was a hard man to pick out of a crowd. Mr. Bland, Rob called him.

"Permafrost," she said.

"Claire . . ."

"Leo wouldn't think twice about keeping hostages in captivity for a year if it had elected Reagan. He's the kind of man who could do that."

"How loyal of you," he laughed.

She drew back from him slightly. "I'm loyal. We're a social and political team. I'm not endangering that."

"You are risking it with the party."

"Robbie! I declare, how silly you are. This party is—"

"—vindictive. Please cancel it."

"I'll do nothing of the kind. Where're your guts?" She kissed him, a challenge. "Do me."

He obeyed, pressing his full mouth to the mat of damp blond hair between Claire's legs, then urged her gently backward until her head fell over the side. Her throat arched, her arms dangled on the floor. Rob applied himself, kneading her waist with one hand while the other hand rubbed the crinkles deep inside her. Her body twisted, her orgasm shook both of them. Gently, he lifted her head and shoulders onto the bed like a prize. She shuddered and held on to him.

Pale sunlight slid under the drawn shades of the luxury hotel room. In moments like these, with Claire, with others, Rob felt released from the grinding routine of life in ways nothing else satisfied. He felt vital, at his best, in an intimacy that demanded much but whose conflicts were simple. Claire was more dangerous than his previous affair with the wacky network correspondent. He'd tried to break it off with the reporter, but she'd pursued him, threatening to make things mighty rocky, and for a while, that had scared the shit out of him. She'd moved on, but it was around then that panic had become one of his pleasures.

He leaned close to Claire, inhaling her fragrance, and ran his tongue over her lips. "I will drown in you," he murmured.

In Los Angeles, Cowboy heard the soft breathy voice and steeled himself against new demands.

"The woman went down to CDEE!"

"What woman?" Cowboy stalled.

"The one who was in the car with her."

"She went there?" *How would she know to go there,* Cowboy wondered. *What could Della have told her?* "It's probably nothing, let's keep our heads."

"I always keep my head," the man said.

Cowboy's anger swelled inside him. From habit, he gently scratched his elongated nail across his cheek. He was wary of this man who was unprincipled in a way Cowboy recognized but did not share. Cowboy tried a different tack. "The Friends are nervous, they have every right to be—after what happened."

"I do not like your friends' attitude. I'm in the game to stay and no one will push me out."

"No one's pushing you out unless you lose your head again!" Cowboy shouted.

"I am going to take care of that woman."

"No! You *scare* her off but you don't take her out," Cowboy said. "It would wave a lot of red flags. Are you hearing me?" The man laughed. "And use some imagination, she's no peasant."

The man hung up, still laughing. Cowboy opened his penknife and gently scraped it under an immaculate nail. Damned hicks. He never should have brought CDEE into the mix.

The reception in Washington that night, hosted by the Democratic Senatorial Campaign Committee, took place in an opulent old hotel that had been reclaimed from decades of neglect. Corinthian pillars lined the plum-colored walls, soaring to the arched ceiling. Towering floral arrangements splashed out of corners and sprouted from the buffet tables. Swarms of party officials from Washington and California jockeyed for drinks, food, or position, saluting Drummond and supportive members of Congress. The beautiful old furniture had warmed the backsides of public servants and lobbyists for a century.

Rob was in high spirits. A column in *The New York Times,* noting influential senators up for reelection, had named Mark Drummond as one of the top five.

"Rob!" Tot yelled. "Where's Nadine?"

"She went off to take a call," he said coldly.

"How about my interview with Mark?" she asked him.

"Soon. Have you been assigned yet to the California campaigns?"

"No, but an interview with Mark will help." The noise of the party was rising. "Rob, can't we be friends?"

"Friends? Are you a friend of my sister?"

"If Faye ever needed anything, I'd be there for her."

"I'll be sure to tell her that. You're really a prize, Tot. You were rotten to Faye, but now you want everyone to be friends again. Well, I don't forget."

"Nadine's forgotten it."

"She hasn't forgiven it, trust me," he said. "Friendship means something different to me, I guess, than it does to you. You and I are acquaintances in our work and that's it. We meet, we lunch—"

"I've heard about your lunches, Rob."

He pulled back, feeling a jagged streak of panic and excitement.

"I keep track of my friends and former friends' predilections," she said.

"Rob!" Nadine broke through the crowd. "That call was from the Wasp Queen!"

"How'd your mother track you down here?" Tot asked.

"She can find anyone. Tot, you want a scoop?"

"Am I human?" Tot said.

"Don't give her a scoop," Rob said.

Nadine hesitated. "Well, I think I will. She's my friend."

"How quickly you forget."

"Rob, that was two years ago," Nadine said. "Tot, the President's going to name my father to fill LaSalle's seat on the Supreme Court."

Rob was stunned. Buck Stern on the Court? A travesty!

"Wow," Tot said. She'd heard that Buck was on the short list because of his visibility and his long association with the President's father. But she'd rejected the idea he might be named because many thought Judge Ballard "Buck" Stern simply wasn't qualified. "Too bad Mark isn't on the Judiciary Committee," Tot said.

Rob was already calculating the advantages and disadvantages of the nomination for Mark's campaign. The press would have a field day.

"Are you excited about it?" Tot asked her.

"Yes, of course," Nadine said.

"Do you think he'll have trouble getting Senate confirmation?" Tot asked.

"Tot, don't interview me."

Tot gave an innocent smile.

"Dad never loses," Nadine said.

"Rob, care to comment on congressional reaction?"

"It's sure to be a controversial nomination."

"And Mark's reaction?" Tot pressed.

"Call tomorrow."

"Nadine, is the Judge in town?" Tot asked.

"No, he's home. Don't use my name, Tot. The announcement will be made at the President's California home, but it won't be public yet for a few days. Rob, Claire's canceled her party for us."

"How come?" he said, genuinely relieved.

"Because the Wasp Queen's giving a gala for Dad at the house after the announcement. We have to be there."

As Rob drove out Pennsylvania Avenue, toward their town house on Capitol Hill, Nadine was laughing about the leak craze in her office.

"I wish you worked somewhere else," Rob said. Somewhere far away from Claire's mischief. A sheet of Nadine's light hair fell over her shoulder. An image popped out of the darkness—Claire sprawled across a bed. He stroked Nadine's hair. "I'd like to see you in another agency."

"All right. I'll start the motions. Adrian's got a Yalie pal at the FCC."

Rob was astonished. "Honey, do you mean it?"

"I do."

"I mean, you never belonged at the NSC."

"I needed to get out of Mark's office."

"You took it to prove something to your *dad*! You don't have to! You're tops."

"It's moot now," she giggled. "No one can compete with a dad on the Supreme Court."

Rob let his hand drop to her shoulder. He remembered the day he'd first seen Nadine, a patrician California girl, but kind and just, too, as it turned out. She'd been sitting at the edge of a huge, midnight-blue pool, a pale, slender figure throwing back her head, her hair spraying drops of water on the baking tiles.

"Why did Gabe do it, throw away a good marriage like that?" Nadine asked. "It was so unlike him, deceitful. Why do men do that?"

Rob watched the image of her at the pool fade: he was back in the car. "Men have partners in their craziness, Nadine."

She moved closer to him. "It won't happen to us."

A sudden rain shower began. Rob flipped on the windshield wipers as he jockeyed around Union Station, heading out Massachusetts Avenue.

"I find myself thinking about Della a lot," Nadine said.

"I'm sorry about her and I know it's been absolute hell for Faye, but I think Della used drugs—or *some*thing—and it affected her mind. She saw plots everywhere."

"Plots? And what makes you think Della used drugs?"

"She had mood swings—"

"She lived passionately—just like Faye!"

"All right, all right," he said, placating her. Rob smoothed his curly hair back from his forehead. He suspected Della had been mixed up in something he didn't want to know about. He didn't want Nadine or Faye involved, either.

"When I last saw her," Nadine said, "she was talking about misappropriation of funds—by the organizations she funded." He turned off Massachusetts Avenue onto a winding, tree-lined street. "But unrelated to that, key project directors were being replaced."

"How many that you personally knew of?"

"Well, none."

"Boinnnng! Calamity!" He pulled into their small, underground parking area.

Inside, Rob began turning on lights, advancing into the yellow and gray living room. "So what about all this stuff with Della?" he asked with a bewitching smile that made Nadine giggle. "She thought there was misappropriation of funds? So some project directors were being replaced? Were *they* misusing the money? Who cares?"

She laughed. "I think she was telling the truth."

"Another plot!"

"Why are you so excited?"

"Because I love to debate you!" He swung around in the center of the living room and grinned at her. But his eyes were not laughing.

Nadine fell into his arms and kissed him. "Come upstairs, you," she said. "Maybe we'll get lucky."

In bed, locked against her, feeling the warmth and softness of her body, Rob tried to escape the feeling of having sex on order. Making love with Nadine had become permanently welded to making a child, as the work of kneading was connected to the making of bread. Rob wanted a child, but the certain joy of it was not real to him.

Nadine was trying not to wake Rob as she crept across the bedroom.

"What's going on?" Rob mumbled.

"I can't sleep. I'll do some work—that'll put me to sleep."

"Oh, God, I thought it was daytime." He rolled over. One of his charms was the way he surrendered to sleep. Childlike, he gave up his daily hassles, drew his pillow to him, drifted off, and he nearly always smiled in his sleep.

Nadine's head was throbbing from the wine. She went downstairs, turned on the hall light, and saw her briefcase.

The disk! She'd forgotten!

If it had been anyone but Faye asking, she would have let the disk sit until morning. Even so, she had no confidence in Faye's demands that they all "do something about Della." She went into the kitchen for a big glass of water, then into a tiny study off the kitchen and turned on her computer.

She inserted the disk and watched a line of dates and locations come up on the screen: San Francisco, Los Angeles, Seattle, Minneapolis. Some of the dates went back two years. Why had Della thought this was important? Nadine scrolled to the end of the list, about fifteen of them, then clicked into the directory for the disk. She found only one other file: OPI.

Nadine shivered.

She punched enter on the keyboard; the OPI file came up. The heading read "SUBCONTRACTS." It contained the previous list of cities paired with various corporate names.

She scrolled down to Los Angeles: CDEE.

Nadine shoved her chair back from the computer. CDEE was a subcontractor to OPI? Why? This was the last thing she expected. It didn't make any sense. CDEE dealt with environmental education issues. Why would OPI subcontract programs on understanding democracy to CDEE?

She keyed back to the first screen: the dates after Los Angeles on the first list showed 8/14/90, 9/15/91. Leo had lied to her! OPI was up and running.

Ignoring the ache in her head, she carefully rechecked both files on the disk. Why would Leo lie about OPI? Why was OPI subcontracting program work through CDEE? Why had Della hidden the disk in her sweater? When things didn't make sense there was always something worth looking for. She telephoned Faye at home.

Faye was reading in bed, trying to avoid sleep.

Nadine didn't say hello. "This disk is really odd. The government is subcontracting work through CDEE—and it doesn't fit. An agency looks for corporations or organizations that have experience in the field being subcontracted. CDEE doesn't have any specialty in broadcasting or political programs or the philosophy of good government, does it?"

"Not so far as I know."

"I have to do more checking. We can't just accept what's on some anonymous disk that Della may or may not have made. Faye, something else has come up. Dad's been nominated for the Supreme Court."

"Buck?" Faye said, bolting upright.

"The Wasp Queen's giving a party next weekend after the announcement. I hope you can be there, because I'll really need you."

After they hung up, Faye leaned back against the pillows and thought about the disk. Nadine was right: there was no proof Della had made it or was saving it for some purpose. She began reading the script again. She saw Buck Stern in the black robe of the Supreme Court. Good type-casting. Appalling politics. Mark Drummond and every political figure in California would be at the Sterns' home for the anointing.

* * *

Faye was swimming in the warm lake again, breathing water. This is so incredible, she thought, "breathing" water into her lungs like air, blowing it out in bubbles. She floated to the surface. Mist hid the shore.

"Della? I know you're around here somewhere." She dipped beneath the surface and swam, long slow strokes, eyes wide open in the dark gray water.

And there it was, the big, ghostly sea animal hovering ahead of her, buoyant, evil. The front of it was lower in the water than the rear, which curved up like a big shell. She thrashed at the water, trying to get away, reach the surface. It swept forward, moving fast.

The phone was ringing. Faye was flailing at the water, trying to get away. The phone kept ringing. She picked up. It was Della, screaming at her. "Get out of the car!"

"I'm not in the car! What are you doing to me?"

"Not me, *them*! Don't tell them you know!"

"I don't know anything!"

"Watch out, Faye!"

She awoke, panicked. Her phone next to the bed was really ringing.

"Hello?"

"Lay off Della," a voice whispered. "Lay off!"

The voice was smug, awful.

Faye hung up.

The phone rang again. She let it ring, but finally picked it up.

"We can reach you anytime. Lay off Della."

EIGHT

At National Airport in Washington, D.C., Senator Mark Drummond settled into a spacious chair on the private jet supplied by one of his wealthiest California constituents.

Around noon almost every Thursday, he and his staff raced to leave Washington and fly west. Thursday mornings were frantic—doors blowing open, interrupted meetings, aides waving folders, packs of assistants trotting down corridors with him, hefting briefcases and suit bags into elevators, down marble stairs to the waiting car, girls and boys all talking at once, all rushing to get him on his way west. And Mark was in the center, talking, laughing, listening, their magnet, buoyed by their boundless energy, wanting everything about himself to be as grand and generous as the image he saw in their eyes.

Throughout his career, Mark Drummond had usually won what he'd wanted—the education, the wife, the professional acclaim, the mistresses, the elections, the responsibilities.

But today, as the plane lifted off the runway, he wanted to be alone with his dad and talk quietly about where he was going. His dad had died years ago and now Mark rarely went anywhere alone.

Drummond unfolded his legs and rose to his full height

like a big golden cougar. At fifty-five, his golden-brown hair was graying at the temples. He surveyed the collection of former law students who'd become his main staff.

"Sir, can I get you something?" one of them said.

"A drink," Mark said, sitting down again. Rob was standing in the aisle near him. "You look worried, Rob."

"Only about Sparks," Rob said, "if he wins the primary."

Drummond laughed. "Maybe Langer will win."

The others laughed hard. Langer, a congresswoman, didn't stand a chance of winning the primary. "I don't know," Rob said gravely, "she might."

Drummond's campaign manager, to whom the nickname Smokey had stuck as a teenager when his hair went prematurely gray, was patting down his pockets, looking for matches to light his pipe.

"What are you getting on Sparks?" Mark asked him.

"Clean living. God and country. Home and hearth."

"Dig deeper."

"The environmental agendas," Mark's private secretary said, handing them across to him, "the revised weekend schedule, and next week's schedule."

"This is too close," Smokey said, waving the schedule.

"It'll work out," Mark said, glancing at the time frames between two meetings with major financial supporters in Sacramento and a rally in San Francisco.

Smokey leaned over Drummond's seat. "This time we've got to meet with Diaz, Senator," Smokey whispered.

Drummond shook his head. "No, no."

Smokey drilled in. "He can deliver the L.A. Hispanic vote, but he won't do it unless you have a one-on-one."

"You know where he came from, who he was," Mark hissed.

"It's completely deniable," Smokey whispered. "Diaz has a huge bloc vote and you don't have to do much to get it. If Sparks wins the primary, we'll need it." One of the aides passed Mark's drink to him. "I've set up the meeting today."

"Christ, Smokey—"

"I got him to come down to the Ramada Inn at the airport.

It's anonymous, it's convenient, and it'll all be over in a minute."

Smokey got up and left. Rob slammed into the lounge chair next to Mark. "This whole environmental thing is heating up and we have to handle it, come out on the right side of it," Rob said.

"Who wants what?"

"The *L.A. Times* wants a long interview this trip, and they're pushing for a debate."

Drummond rubbed a hand over his big-boned knee. Rob was his alter ego and his public face. "You set up what you think is right, Robbie, but no debates with Sparks. No free air time for him."

"I don't want to be a nag, but—Laura hasn't changed her mind on any of her appearances, has she?"

"No, Rob, she'll be on tap. My wife doesn't want to be the wife of a professor. She wants to be the wife of a senator. We're still in the same homes . . . we're just not together," he went on impatiently. "It'll all look fine. Quit asking about it."

"Okay. Tot wants an interview," Rob said.

Drummond nodded. "What's the slant?"

"How much it costs to campaign today for a series about campaign expenses and public financing. And, I thought you'd like to know Faye's on Herb Yount's entertainment committee."

"Tell Alice to put Tot into the schedule this trip." Drummond smiled his big smile at Rob. But he wasn't smiling inside. He was obsessed by money. He needed three million at least. Six months ago no one believed he'd be in a contested race with a major challenger like Sparks, who had plenty of fire in his gut.

"I need some time, Rob," he said. Rob rose and left him.

Mark Drummond felt light-headed; he wondered if he was getting the flu. He began each morning with his schedule for the day, neatly typed, a ton of messages, and a big reading file. He had no time for introspection. All day long he attended meetings, broken only when aides rushed in shoving papers at him, warning him of an upcoming vote, or by emergency phone calls from unexpected visitors. He taped interviews and made floor votes. In the evening, he usually attended some function. By the time he got home he still hadn't read the original file, and he still hadn't answered half the messages he'd been given that morning. Forty-five weeks a year, he flew to California on Thursday and flew back Tuesday morning. The campaign would only increase that pace.

Drummond sipped his drink, thinking about Royal Diaz. He'd force himself to stomach the endorsement meeting, but how had Diaz gotten so well financed and powerful so fast?

Vaguely, Mark Drummond knew he was losing sight of the reason he'd first wanted to be in the Senate. He was in the club and it was intoxicating, but he wasn't seeking new and better laws as much as he was forced to seek patronage and money. He'd faced the political realities. But in occasional moments like these, he felt fraudulent.

Faye found Detective Phelps in an Elysian Park coffee shop, near the Police Academy and the shooting range. Most of its customers, whether in suits or running shoes and sweats, were on the force. The walls were covered with the pictures of police graduates from remote times.

Phelps was sitting at the Formica counter, his sharp, concentrated face bent over a bowl of soup. The sound of distant gunfire played as constantly as the jukebox.

"I got a threatening phone call last night," she said. She told him about it.

"That's it?" he asked. "No gunfire, rocks through your windows, burning crosses?"

"Very funny."

"You've hit a nerve, Ms. Ferray. We can't do much except tap your phone and try to trace the calls—if there are any more." His sad eyes regarded her. "I'd advise you to quit asking questions of people like Ms. Izquerra's secretary."

"Oh, you know about that."

"And stay away from her dad, too. Just go about your business."

"They want to know what I heard, don't they?"

"Right. You think about some security."

Faye put a disk in front of him. "A computer disk I found in Della's sweater."

He put his spoon down. "What's on it?"

"A list of organizations."

He grimaced, pulled a napkin from the rack in front of him and blew his nose. "We'll take a look-see," he said, pocketing the disk. He picked up his spoon.

"Detective Phelps, I'm sure those names on it mean something."

His hacking cough came from deep inside. He sounded like a drowning man. "I'll let you know."

She watched him return to his soup. "This is very frustrating for me," she said, "and it's getting scary, and you just can't have any idea what that feels like."

He put his spoon down. "Ms. Ferray, give me a break here. If I could find out who put the explosives in your friend's car and why, don't you think I'd mention it?" His eyes were creepy, flat and full of pain.

"You don't have to be sarcastic."

"I'll be any way I want. You know how many murders there were in Hollywood alone last night? Nine. And there are two to three shootings an hour in this county—we don't even investigate them anymore." He coughed again.

Daily, Faye had relived the minutes she'd spent with Della as she died. Normally, she had a good memory, a trained memory. Somewhere in her brain, she'd stored what Della had said, but she was blocked.

Faye said, "Let's make a deal: when I remember anything more about what Della said, I'll call you. When you have something, you'll call me. Let's stop with the critical reviews."

"Fair enough," he muttered.

Washington was warm and damp. There'd been nothing in the press that morning about her father's nomination, but Nadine knew Tot wouldn't sit on it long.

Usually reserved, Pamela smiled widely at Nadine and whispered, "Congratulations." A few minutes later, Adrian came into Nadine's office. "Surprised about your father?" he asked. "He's a respected man. Don't forget it when the publicity hits the fan. C'mon."

"C'mon where?"

"Our semiannual meeting with the President," he said. "It's changed to the Roosevelt Room. I don't know how we're all going to fit in."

From her family, Nadine had learned early of the demarcated and exclusive levels of motion-picture corporate enterprises. Most employees—creative, developmental, or administrative—labored in their separate hives, buzzing to other workers at or near their level.

It was the same at the National Security Council. Most White House staffers, even those with high grades, rarely met with the President. They didn't lunch with the secretarial clerks, either.

"Sit over there by the wall," Adrian said. The heavy leather furniture in the room made it seem smaller. Adrian took one of the last remaining chairs at the table. The President was making a quiet round of welcomes, skirting the edge of the room between the plebes sitting at the sidelines, and the main players at the table. Leo was right behind the President, filling in names for him. "Nadine Ferray," Leo said as they came up to her.

The President took her offered hand. "Oh, I've met Nadine," the President said warmly. "This is Judge Stern's daughter," he announced, as if none of them knew her.

"You do my father great honor, sir."

"Well deserved," the President said. "You and your husband must come to dinner sometime."

"We'd be delighted, sir. He's Senator Drummond's press secretary."

"Wrong party, but bring him along anyway."

"Thank you, Mr. President."

"Are you interested in birds?" he asked suddenly.

"Yes, sir, but I don't know very much about them. Thrushes are common around here, aren't they?"

He brightened. "We're considering a program to stimulate interest in our native birds. Give people something to focus on besides drugs. If more people cared about wildlife, there'd be less drugs, I bet."

"Maybe so, sir."

He moved on. *I don't care what anyone says,* she thought, *I like him.*

Norman Tate, the NSC adviser and Leo's boss, opened the meeting. Nadine had only met him once; it was said that Tate was on his way out and that Leo really ran the NSC. But Tate's opening remarks were dignified and succinct as he led the group into the mainstream, summarizing for the President what his security council staff had been doing for the last months.

Nadine had not seen the President working with his major advisory group before. His enthusiasm surprised her. "I see!" he said several times, and "That makes sense!" Tate rowed gently into Soviet waters, touching on the tasks of reanalyzing the work, given the breakup of the Soviet empire and its mounting struggles. Then he paddled on to the Middle East, calling on the area experts in the room.

"Therefore, Mr. President, we'll be taking a much closer follow-up look at the recalcitrance of the leaders of Kuwait vis-à-vis the Saudis."

"Great. We shoulda blasted that Saddam Hussein."

Motion stilled. "Yes, sir," Leo said brightly.

"Him and his little band of Saudis," said the President.

"Iraqis," Tate said.

"Whatever," the President said.

"A related program on democracy and communication," Tate said, making a turn, "is the Office of Public Information."

"Mr. President, this program is in the thinking stages," Leo began, smoothing out his staccato delivery. "Its goal is to coordinate all public information as it relates to national security. Essentially, it's an education program to promote the precepts of democracy at home and abroad. We've borrowed some of our Latin American and Middle East specialists to help us get it in gear . . . Jay Harper is group leader. Jay?"

Harper had thick dark hair, a mustache, and a military bearing. Briskly, he picked up from Leo: "Mr. President, the program areas are: public affairs, international political matters, domestic programs of information . . ." From her chair against the wall in the peanut gallery, Nadine watched Harper lean forward, hitting his points hard.

"*We* know a lot about democracy, Mr. President," Leo cut in, "because we invented it, we live it, but how much does someone in Bangladesh or Angola know?—that's the heart of this program."

"Good, good," said the President.

Leo began drawing word circles, not once mentioning what Nadine now knew—the extensive domestic efforts of the OPI. Leo had left the "new" Office of Public Information behind in the backwaters, and sailed on to the Philippines. Leo's mouth worked as he spoke, but nothing changed in his face: his eyes didn't shift from the President's face, he didn't frown or smile, his head didn't move.

The President's eyes glazed over. Nadine watched the old hands in the room; they were taking the President's inattention in stride; newer people, like Harper, were gazing at the floor or looking around as she was, checking the room's climate. Adrian was staring past the President, his clever face a mask.

When the meeting broke up, Nadine trailed Leo and several of his aides down the hall. "Leo, a minute?" she asked as he was about to get into the elevator and shoot down to his subbasement quarters. "About OPI. Isn't that program more domestic than international?"

"No, the curve is international." His dark eyes regarded her coldly. The elevator door closed.

Nadine didn't move. She was shocked.

"Adrian, can we talk?" He waved Nadine inside his office. "The meeting just now. Disturbing." Adrian raised an eyebrow. "Does the President really not know Iraq from Kuwait?"

Adrian walked to his desk, carefully removed his Nipon jacket and hung it on the back of his chair. He smoothed the shoulder pads. He didn't sit down. "Well, he's not a hands-on manager, but *we* know where Iraq is and we serve him."

"Does he know what his ship is doing?"

"In broad outlines, I think we can say yes to that."

"Adrian, just five minutes ago, Leo told me point-blank that OPI's 'curve' is international, not domestic."

Adrian nodded as if he'd heard that conversation himself and agreed to her rendition of it. His bright eyes settled on her. "Perhaps he doesn't know."

"I don't believe that."

"Don't be hasty. What difference would it make?"

She hesitated. "Only to check his honesty."

Adrian nodded. "Have you been keeping your eyes open?"

She considered telling him about Della's list of OPI sub-contractors, but her innate caution stilled her. First, she would check them out thoroughly.

"Yes, I have. But I won't be a spy like some of the military types around here who spy for the Pentagon."

"Of course not. I think we'll be serving the President better if we look into that program more assertively. I'll handle any flak."

She was at the door when he said, "And, Nadine, don't go off on your own hook. Keep in touch."

Faye was driving west to Century City to meet with her lawyer when Annie called her. "Shoot's over, sis," she reported cheerfully. She lurched egocentrically into an analysis of the television movie to which Faye listened sporadically as she maneuvered onto the freeway. "Is Gabe still in town?" Annie asked.

"I have no idea. Why?"

"His name came up at lunch in Washington, did Nadine tell you? Tot was there. I suppose you know all this. Anyway, Gabe and Tot are not together."

"That's nothing to me, Annie."

"You got a hot date tonight? I'll take you to this great new spot near downtown—a club in a hotel that's packed with males who look like models and most of them are straight! There are three separate mood rooms—rock, jazz, and funk—or maybe it's reggae. You can tell me all about your movie."

Faye finally agreed.

Faye's lawyer, Karen Steiner, had thick, perfect black hair like a comic-strip coiffure. Karen was pleading with her to take Herb Yount's deal and forget *The Jungle Gym*. Faye flung herself into a fervent high-pitch, high-sell state, describing *Gym*'s action, themes, and characters to convince Karen it was the only film worth doing in California. She ended in tears. Karen put a comforting arm around her.

"This is so disgusting," Faye moaned. "I don't know what's the matter with me." She kept hearing the silky, smug voice on the telephone and it made her feel helpless and she hated that.

"You're suffering from the effects of a terribly narrow escape from death. If this movie is so important to you, you better try to make it. But your finances—"

"I know, I know. Make a deal soon, right?"

In a plain, ordinary room at the Ramada Inn at the Los Angeles airport, Mark Drummond shook hands with Royal Diaz. Diaz had brought along two associates, and Smokey accompanied Drummond. It took all Mark's strength to look Diaz in the eye and say, "Glad we could get together."

The handsome Latin man before him was no fool. Diaz's black eyes appeared lazy, a bluff. Mark had met him on several occasions, had assisted with an ambitious voter-registration program, and a day-care effort that became a statewide model. Della had helped set that up.

"Senator," Diaz was saying, "as you Americans say, it is teamwork that saves the day, yes?" He smiled broadly, displaying large, even white teeth.

Mark concentrated on him, looking for the needs inside the man, but listening carefully to the outside demands as they were stated.

"My people are entering into a new phase in a new world and we wish to be a total part of it. We want to offer you the support of the Hispanic community. I can deliver it." His associates stood behind him, hands clasped in front of them, legs slightly apart.

"I look forward to serving the entire community." Mark waited for the quid pro quo.

"And I need your support. I am not a famous senator with a war chest. I am a new arrival running, let's say, uphill. But it is the American dream that we all answer, yes? It is the desire to serve our people that makes us act."

That meant making appearances with him, but Mark would have had to do that anyway.

Smokey stepped in. "Judge Diaz, is it fair to say that you

would like the senator to appear at various functions in the Hispanic community?"

"*Sí*, certainly," Diaz said briskly. "But you and I, Senator, are from the same party, there will be many fund-raisers for you in Southern California." The big white smile broke onto his face. "I wish to be included."

"Financially?" Smokey asked.

"Yes, but more important, my people need to know they are electing someone who has a foot in both camps, who can respond in both camps—who is connected—that's what they need to see."

Mark Drummond felt the smile on his face and knew it looked forced. "The party decides on the joint appearances," Mark said, "but you and I see eye to eye, Royal."

Diaz was almost certainly going to be elected whether he was at a fund-raiser in Westwood or not. He wanted a higher profile. Maybe he wanted the Senate in six years. There were other, better Hispanic politicians in California, men and women of vision. Why hadn't one of them knocked this son of a bitch out of the box?

Faye pulled herself together, blew Karen a kiss from the doorway, and took the elevator down to the lobby of the Century City building.

"Faye!" Mark Drummond was standing at an express elevator in the high rise, his briefcase aloft, his jacket hooked over one arm.

"The man with the big personality," Faye said happily. "What a surprise."

Drummond let the elevator go. He grabbed Faye's hand. "Looking good," he said. She was in a red jacket, a dark skirt, and red Western boots.

Rob came around the corner, full tilt, balancing an open briefcase. "Robbie!" she cried, and leaned over the briefcase to give him a kiss.

"We just flew in," Drummond said to her. "Come up, meet the folks, have a drink. I have to change for a couple of meetings tonight."

Rob snapped the briefcase shut. "Mark, I'll see you at the meeting."

"Wait, Rob," Faye said, "how about lunch tomorrow?"

Drummond put a big hand on her shoulder. "Your brother goes where I go—and tomorrow that's Sacramento."

Rob waved. "I'll call before I leave the state." He raced away.

"Where's your entourage?" she asked Drummond.

"I ditched them." He laughed. "Get in this elevator." She did. "Actually, the bodyguard's upstairs and we're all meeting at the O.K. Corral tonight—the environmental shoot-out."

The elevator shot up forty stories to Mark's West L.A. Senate offices—a series of rooms opening off a conference room, which on good days gave constituents a view all the way to Catalina. Floor-to-ceiling windows faced south, twinkling lights, and way out there somewhere, the ocean.

"Great staff, Mark," she said, noting the emptiness. Light came from one of two back cubbyholes, but at seven o'clock, most of the office was dark.

"Ray!" Mark called out. One of the doors opened, framing a large man in the light. "In one hour." The man nodded, closed the door. Mark led the way to his private office—a comfortable, wood-paneled room furnished with his father's leather chairs and sofas straight out of the forties. The mahogany desk, too, was leather-topped.

"How long has it been since you and I had a chat like real people?" he asked, setting down his briefcase.

"A long time. Is it true that there are two kinds of people in Congress? Those who're unchanged by the experience, and those who're changed?"

He squared his shoulders, posed. "What do you think?"

"You haven't changed."

"Right answer." He smiled, opened his briefcase and tossed two files on the desk.

Faye stared at the sparkling nearby high rises, faceted columns shooting out of ground that used to be the back lot of Twentieth Century-Fox. She turned around. "How's Laura?"

"Fine, thanks." He raked a hand through his golden-brown hair, eyed her thoughtfully. "Wonderful you're working on Herb's committee, Faye. Above and beyond."

"Did you get the Hollywood Women's Committee invitation to come by for a talk?" she countered.

"I know all about those talks with the HWPC. You well-paid professionals get us old politicians in a cozy West Side mansion and you grill hell out of us."

"You want our money?" she asked, smiling broadly. "You listen to our concerns, answer our questions."

"Okay, okay." From a cabinet he took out a beautiful decanter and poured each of them a Scotch. "Single malt," he said, handing her a glass. She took off her boots, and sat on the leather couch, curling her legs under her. Mark was going through some phone messages, sorting and discarding. It was both exciting and comfortable to be around him.

He put down the messages and sat in a chair beside the couch. "What's happening with you?" he asked, turning his full attention on her. In the low light, her hair seemed almost black, not reddish-brown. "Anything I can do?"

"Has Rob mentioned the film I'm trying to get mounted?" He nodded. "It's a tough drama about corruption, but everyone says it's a downer. Even my own lawyer."

Drummond nodded and rose. "Tell me more. I have to change for this meeting." He walked to a closet at the far end of the room, opened the door, peered into the inset mirror. Mark started taking off his tie and unbuttoning his shirt. "You don't mind—?"

"Aw shucks, Mark, I'll lock the door." He laughed. "You laugh just the way you did in class," Faye said as he took a clean shirt out of a drawer in the closet. There *was* something different about him; Tot had been right. Had Faye worshiped him so much then that now any change toward the human shortened him? The rumors about Drummond in law school had been laudatory but dull: he'd had a sense of ethics, he'd never been rude or cruel in class, he'd had a stable marriage, and as far as Faye knew, he hadn't seduced any of the second-year students.

Mark was asking, "Are people out here as worried as I hear? That the industry's changing, cable's taking over, you're losing television markets in Europe, the networks are losing it at home."

"Yes."

"But Faye, what hasn't changed is that movies are this nation's best export! That's our culture out there seeding the world." He stood half in and half out of the closet, taking off one shirt, putting on another. His arms were muscled and tight, the hair on his chest gray-gold.

Drummond switched the topic to a proposed wetlands bill. "Don't you think we've got plenty of wetlands?"

"No! Gad, developers are tacking up wall-to-wall houses. Wetlands remind me of the beach. You know, I can't walk on a beach out here without getting flecks of oil on the soles of my feet."

"Terrible, yes, part of the price."

"Don't tell me you're for *more* off-shore drilling."

"We've got to have the oil, Faye."

"You wouldn't have said *that* a dozen years ago."

Drummond glanced at her. "This is the most important state in the nation. It's richer than most countries, and it's better managed, too. Sure, we have problems. I spend eighteen hours a day trying to get consensus on solutions. That's what government's all about—"

"You call what we have government?" She was suddenly furious. "I mean, look around—the dreadful housing, the homeless, the killings, the poverty . . . !" She stopped, breathless, surprised at herself. "I'm sorry, Mark." Where had her anger come from? She pressed a hand against her forehead.

"Nah, that's okay, you always get steamed up, say what you think. I like that." He pulled his tie tight against the clean collar, walked across the room and sat down next to her. Her face was strained and pale, her freckles bright. "Things are hard for you now—I heard about your father, and you're still grieving for Della."

"I can't get answers from the police, just a lot of 'it's under investigation,' and accusations that she was dealing drugs. Can you do better than that?"

"You bet," he said. "I'll get someone to look into it."

"Thanks, Mark." She leaned her head back against the couch. "It drives me crazy that I can't do anything."

"When anyone our own age dies," he said soothingly, "we feel acutely mortal."

"I'm so frustrated I even used my film, *The Jungle Gym*, as a way to get information."

"How do you mean?"

"A film is an entree. I went down to an organization Della spoke of on the pretext that I was looking for locations. They gave me a tour." She turned her head. His face, close up, was coarser, the white, brown, and golden hairs at his temple thicker, his nose bigger. "And I met this man, Diaz. He was at Della's funeral. You saw him there, too. Remember?"

Drummond rose, took her glass, poured more amber liquid into it. "Diaz?"

"Royal Diaz. Running for Congress."

"Oh, yes," he said, "but I don't know him well."

"You sure were looking at him hard."

"Probably trying to figure out where I'd met him. I question whether you should run around town asking about Della's death, Faye."

"I'm not doing that."

"Maybe Tot could find out something," he said. "Could you stand to call her?"

"No." She thought of Gabe. Had he thought he could just glue the pieces of their lives back together? She'd been right to back away from him. It didn't make her feel any better.

Mark was studying her. Diaz followed him everywhere. He began thinking of happier times, of Nadine, Tot, Della, and Faye, the quartet. He handed her drink back. "I often think of those early years. And the first campaign. We really took on the whole system, didn't we? Just crashed our way into it." He looked at her face as at a mirror. "You know, Faye, I can't imagine life without the Senate, without the work." He raised his glass. "Death to the invaders." His smile held hope.

When she rose to leave, he hugged her. She felt his solid energy and his big arms. She stepped away, but he held on to her shoulders, frowning slightly, gazing into her eyes. "You were always the mother to the group," he said, "you know that? You hang on to your ideals." His fingers tightened on her shoulders. "It's hard, but you hang on."

She rose on tiptoes to kiss his cheek, and as she reached up, her fingers grazed the hair at the back of his head. The intimacy of the touch astonished her. He reached up to disengage her arms as she was pulling away. His mouth opened slightly. His hands closed around her wrists.

His lips landed on hers suddenly. He dropped his hold on her. Shyly, one hand moved across her back, drew her to him. They stood together like survivors, holding on to one another. He nuzzled against her hair, swept his mouth against her temple, kissed her cheek. The comforting motions did not lessen what was happening. It grew. She put her arms around him, held on tightly, inflamed, starved. She closed her eyes; she didn't want to look at him; she was afraid of what she might see. He put a hand against her mouth, then slid it across her cheek. His body began shaking.

"Mark . . ."

"Shhhh . . ."

Suddenly, they were on the floor. Part of her skirt was hiked up, one arm outside her jacket; one side of him lay against her while he was pulling with one hand at his clothes. He entered her: she felt impaled and rushed to the act as he cried out, his breath gusting against her hair. His huge body covered her. They trembled together, locked and shaken.

Later, they lay against each other. "Mark . . ."

He did not move. "I've never done anything like this," he said.

"You may have wanted to," she said.

"No, not even that."

Somewhere a door shut. Faye stirred. Not looking at him, she reached out for her jacket and boots and put them on.

Mark sat up; his golden-gray hair was messy and damp. He tugged at his trousers. Her back was to him. He reached out for her shoulder. "Faye, how are you?" His tone was neutral, adult.

She turned. "I don't know how I am."

Faye walked along the corridor, taking deep breaths to calm herself down. She felt stunned, not so much by the act, but by the passion and the force behind it. She felt ashamed because she knew his wife, his children. What had happened in that office was too close a mirror to what had been done to her. She didn't want to understand the avalanche that had overtaken Gabe and Tot.

When she stepped into the elevator, she felt changed. The new feeling was forcing her to recognize her past in a different way. She pressed her back against the wall. She realized she wanted to go back into that room and lie down with him and do it again. Slower.

The elevator hurtled down forty stories.

NINE

AT NOON, DEEP in the Santa Ynez Mountains at his secluded California ranchero, the President announced the nomination of Judge Ballard Stern to the Supreme Court. About thirty members of the press, and Tot, who'd broken the story first, were firing questions at the white-haired nominee. They were told Ballard Stern had spent most of his life as an attorney, that he'd only been on the Federal bench a year, that he had little judicial experience, but he "knew right from wrong."

"What a relief," one reporter whispered.

"Well, sir, you do look like a judge," Tot commented.

"Yes, Tot, I look forward to the role," he replied.

The press yelled questions: Where did he stand on the right to privacy? On *Roe* v. *Wade*? On school prayer?

"C'mon, you know I won't answer those questions."

"Sir," shouted a television reporter from CNN, "what's your answer to critics who say you're unqualified?"

"It's a free country," he said.

As Faye made the three-hour drive along the coast north from Los Angeles, she wondered if Mark would be there. She hoped he would, she hoped he wouldn't. They had no future together, maybe not even as friends. She wasn't used to an affair with a married man, but it required no commitment from her. She wondered if Buck had information for her about Della's investigation, but she doubted the nomination had left him time. The nomination was big news: Ted Koppel was devoting Monday's *Nightline* to it; all over the country, advocates and critics were already debating Judge Stern.

Passing through the Sterns' gates, she drove along a winding unpaved road through oaks and juniper to the turnaround in front of the family's imposing Spanish-style home, El Contento. Standing in the middle of fifty acres of hilly land overlooking the Pacific Ocean, the house reminded Faye of the fun she and Gabe had had there, ridiculing the mansion's pretensions, making love in one of the imposing guest bedrooms.

Helena Stern had wanted the President's press announcement to be issued from El Contento, but when the Secret Service explained to her the physical remodeling necessary for the President's safety—added phone lines, a helicopter pad, the interior walls that would come down, the exterior walls and fences that would go up, the roads that would be blocked, Helena capitulated.

Faye recognized the Filipino butler at the door. "Mrs. Mittelman," he greeted her. He never forgot names, but she hadn't been called that one in quite a while. "You know the way, straight through to the west French doors."

It was a true California party on a bright, sunny day with the sea as a sparkling backdrop to the majestic garden. South of the house, just outside a grove of palms and oaks, a three-sided, striped canopy had been erected where caterers buzzed around a T-shaped table. Beyond, groups of white tables and chairs stretched across one level of the garden.

A mixture of guests from Hollywood and Washington were already present—national columnists, stars and celebrities, former and current members of the Cabinet, the CEOs of a network and two film studios, and a battalion of California congressmen. The costumes ranged from white "croquet" suits to cotton poplin dresses to silk gowns. The garden rumbled with chatter about the nomination, picture grosses, school prayer, the economy, and an antiabortion march in

Daytona that had turned into a riot.

Faye was poised in the Elysian fields between the terrace steps and the chatty party down on the lawn. Buck was at the center of one group, his hands carving descriptions; he was a fine storyteller, especially of early Hollywood lore. Helena, never far from her husband, was a stylish, angular woman with an indistinct, snobbish smile.

From the terrace, Nadine—next to Rob—saw Faye tip her white straw derby back on her reddish hair. Her sister-in-law wore a black and white pin-striped dress and was speaking with a man Nadine didn't know. Even from a distance, she could feel Faye's energy. But Nadine sensed that underneath, Faye was running from something: she was taking little half-steps backward, then planting her feet firmly as if to arrest her retreat. Faye's triangular face tilted toward the man, alert, listening, waiting. Faye spoke with intensity.

The man was listening coolly, then looked bewildered. Faye had probably said something irreverent. Unlike Nadine, she often spoke her heart before she thought—a form of boldness, even recklessness.

Spotting Nadine, Faye waved at her. Yet, even behind the wave, Nadine sensed a hesitation. "She's the only sister I'm ever going to have," Nadine said to Rob.

Faye stopped in front of them as Claire and Leo Townsend joined them. Nadine grabbed Faye's hand and squeezed it gratefully. Rob gave his sister a ferocious hug.

"I recognize you from the press," Claire said. She was an attractive woman in a knockout Versace dress. Leo false-smiled congenially. "Sam!" Claire cried in her lilting South-ern voice, moving her face past his in a flying air kiss.

"Claire . . . and Faye!" Sam Pike said, grinning broad-ly at one and all. Faye kissed his cheek; he smelled of peppermints.

"You know each other?" Claire asked.

"Sam's a good friend of my former husband's. I'm glad to see you again," Faye said, meaning it.

Rob, tugging at his collar, shot a look at Nadine and Claire. "How's the movie?" he asked Faye.

"It's the movie you'd like most to avoid."

"Looking for financing?" Sam asked.

"Beating the bracken with a shovel."

" 'Films are artifacts of light,' " Pike said merrily. "It's always hard to fund light beams."

"Who said that?"

"Gore Vidal."

"Did I really hear that name spoken in this house?"

A circulating waiter offered a tray of lobster and caviar canapé puffs to their group. Rob popped one into his mouth.

Nadine was in blue silk, her blond hair flowing from a wide-brimmed hat. "Adrian Anderson!" she called out, introducing him to Faye.

"I feel as if I've already met you," Faye said, looking into his lean clever face, shaking his bony hand.

"Do you?" Anderson said, pleased. "I've seen some of your films. *Roundabout* was my favorite."

As he drifted away, Nadine warned Faye in a husky aside, "The Wasp Queen."

Buck and Helena were advancing toward them. Buck seemed tall, but it was his air of noblesse oblige that lent him height. His mane of wavy white hair added to the illusion.

"Proud of your dad?" Helena said to Nadine, touching her lips to her daughter's cheek. "Of course you are, dear."

"Dad, of course I am," Nadine said catechistically.

Everyone in the group shook hands with the honored couple and celebrated the President's wise selection, though they also knew there were many who thought the nomination madness. Judge Stern shook hands firmly with Sam Pike.

"You're looking very pretty, Nadine," Buck said, "isn't she, Helena?"

"Nadine's always lovely," Helena said, fluffing up the back of her own blond hair.

Everyone began talking at once. "Faye," Buck said, drawing her away, "you asked me to look into a matter and I have made a few inquiries. The question's in good hands. The man in charge, Phelps, is one of LAPD's best."

"Bucky," Helena said, grabbing his arm. "I *am* sorry, Faye, but we have so many people to see . . ." Capturing the Townsends, the Sterns moved on.

Nadine whispered to Faye, "Whenever I see them I always feel like a ten-year-old begging for a seat at the grown-ups' table."

Faye ached for her friend, feeling lucky to have had her own parents. Then suddenly, she felt a chill, remembering one night sitting on the stairs, listening to Jerry crashing around in the living room, drunk and cursing and miserable. Had she consigned all those bad times to a void? To this day her mother wouldn't acknowledge Jerry had ever had a drinking problem. How much had that deception influenced Faye's own life with Gabe and inspired her mania for work, for talk, for good times at the expense of quiet introspection?

"Faye," Nadine said, "we need a minute alone."

"You've found something?"

"Yes and no."

Sam Pike shifted and Faye looked up to see Annie in pink chiffon, trailing a scarf, making an entrance on the arm of an actor from a television series. Faye and Rob waved. Annie sauntered over.

"Do you remember Sam Pike?" Faye asked her.

Annie looked charmingly blank. "I don't think so," she murmured. She offered her hand. "Mr. Mike?"

"Pike," he said, taking her hand. "But you can call me Sam." His wide smile wrinkled his cheeks. "Do you always look so ravishing, Miss Ferray?"

"Always, Mr. Sike."

"Pike," he said.

Faye laughed. "C'mon, quit kidding, you know Sam." Annie erupted into a fit of giggles.

Some distance away, Tot Jencks was chatting with Maynard Bluestone, the old-line Washington columnist, his thick body crowned by a large, bald head, his round glasses reflecting the setting sunlight. Bluestone's "Inside the Beltway" column was a savvy mixture of politics and gossip. His contacts were legendary. Government was his specialty, and his incisive comments elicited quick, emotional reactions from his thin-skinned prey.

In his hesitant, breathy voice, Bluestone was speaking to Tot as to an acolyte: "Politicians are more like entertainers every day, Miss Jencks. People say it's the money, but I know better. It's television, the people's corrupter. I don't mean reporters like you, my dear, I mean all those fictional stories on television where the good people always win, where everything's so simple and so easily solved."

He broke off suddenly. His eyeglasses reflected sunlight into Tot's face as he turned toward the terrace. Mark Drummond and his wife, Laura, had arrived.

Tot's shrewd cherub's face focused on Bluestone. "How do you see the California elections?"

Bluestone wheezed. "Going to be hot. Sparks has a lot of prehistoric friends in and out of court." His hand dropped on Tot's arm like an anchor. "It will be most exciting."

Faye hadn't seen Laura Drummond in years. She was a decorous woman with a PhD in economics; she shook hands, made small talk, and laughed at the right moments, but did not seem to be enjoying herself.

"What a grand occasion," Senator Drummond proclaimed, assuming command, speaking first to Buck and Helena, then to the immediate crowd around him. He quick-glanced at Faye, then turned, laughing, to Judge Stern and Leo. Faye remembered Buck was an old friend of Mark's. Perhaps Leo Townsend was, too, back in the old California days. She would ask her father; he would know.

Mark looked back at her. Sweeping a glass of champagne off a passing tray, she began to enjoy the moment. After all, nothing was forever and she did want to live fully. In that moment, she saw Mark's face as it was during their feverish lovemaking: suffused with desire. She felt her own deep hunger. They had used no protection; the wave hit them and they succumbed. Right behind the sharp memory, fresh desire for him arrived. Had Gabe been overtaken like that, too, she wondered.

Glad-handing his practiced way through the crowd, in moments, Mark was next to Faye.

"You didn't answer my question," he said in a deep low voice, gazing out at the waves breaking on the rocks below.

"What question?"

"I asked you how you felt about what happened," he said.

"I said I didn't know. I still don't."

He refocused his eyes from the Pacific to a bamboo grove behind her. "I want to see you again." His eyes settled intimately on her face. "I can't think of anyone or anything else—except you."

"I don't think so, Mark."

Again, he scanned the sea. He was courted so constantly he could hardly believe she was refusing him. "Would you consider making a film for the campaign? Smokey will contact you. He'd like to have that cinematographer who worked with Gabe."

"Campaign films are specialized work, Mark."

"Other producers have done it—look at Reagan's old team."

"Yeah, look at 'em," she said, cracking a smile. "I'll do some consulting for you, look at your TV spots, sit in on brainstorming sessions." She did want to make love with him again. It was nothing like being with Gabe—he was better, more attuned to her. But making love with Mark was liberating somehow.

"What are you doing Sunday afternoon?" he asked. "I'll still be in L.A. I *must* see you."

More guests were arriving, the lawn was getting crowded. "Mark, what happened between us, happened. But I've been on the other side of an affair, so I'm scarcely mistress material."

He straightened up. "I never thought you were."

The afternoon was waning, the sky was a deep, predusk red. A long table under the tent offered platters of curried mushroom strudel; golden mussels in their shells topped with a tangy sauce; Helena's famous Caesar salad. As soon as one boneless leg of lamb disappeared, another replaced it, served up with garlic purée and roasted red peppers.

The judge, eager as ever to establish a tone of conviviality, dubbed the supper a "camp-out," an image hard to sustain as a platoon of waiters served the food on china plates and snapped open thick dinner napkins across ample laps.

A Stanford man, Leo liked best to spin his conversation around sports metaphors. Government insiders joked that for Leo, football embodied the last bastion of the American spirit which his National Security bunch was charged to protect. His Redskins discourse was well under way when Faye took a seat next to Sam Pike. Mark Drummond and his wife sat down across the table. For the mushroom course, a waiter poured around a spicy dry Gewürztraminer.

"I hear you're writing a book about media and politics," Adrian Anderson said to Tot. Faye, surprised by his attention to Tot, realized her former friend, once a mere walk-on in broadcast news, had, without Faye's being aware of it, climbed to a different level. In truth, she missed Tot's surgical, aggressive mind and her snappy retorts. Tot was afraid of nothing and no one. Of all Faye's friends, Tot would not have backed away from an affair, casual or hot, with Gabe.

"Elections are America's pulse," Mark Drummond was sermonizing. "The greatest tradition in the world. Look at the globe—elections everywhere! And who did that? *We* did!"

Football to her left, Drummond in front, Faye turned to Samuel Pike. "Yes, just keep that wine coming, please, Sam," she said as he poured. "You're the perfect dinner companion because you have the best stories about the arts and you don't care a fig about sports."

"You're on Herb Yount's committee for Drummond, aren't you?" he said.

"Yes, but I don't want to talk politics, either."

"Did you ever read *The Education of Henry Adams*?"

"No. Was he related to the Adamses of early American history?"

"Yes. His book tells of a young man, around 1900, who was talking with the Speaker of the House, a cynical curmudgeon. Adams was singing of the ideals of the congressmen and their desire to serve—definitely a young man's position." Samuel Pike bent toward her conspiratorially. "And the Speaker replied, 'A congressman is a *hog*, sir. You must take a stick and hit him on the *snout*!'"

Faye laughed. Sam watched her with interest. "If you'd practiced law, what would it have been?"

"Civil law," she said, warmed by his jaunty eyes. "I would've been out there in the eighties trying to convince employers pregnancy was a sex-linked disability."

Pike raised his face to the dark sky. "I've always held the view that women are more powerful than they know—or *we* know." He placed his fingers gently against his bow tie. "But then, I like to think of power as information."

"Sam, have you ever heard of an outfit called CDEE?"

"L.A.? Nonprofit?"

"Yes. Is it well managed?"

"Why do you ask?"

"Oh, just something Della Izquerra said once."

He frowned, touched her arm. "You were with her that dreadful day," he said feelingly. "Did Della think there was something wrong?"

"Yes, but I don't know why. I went down there under the pretext of looking for a location," she said. "Oh, Sam, I just can't get what happened out of my head." She was very close to telling him about the anonymous phone call.

"I understand," he said sympathetically. "You'll feel better when you start making your picture." He sipped his wine. "It's amazing they can't find who did it. Didn't Della say anything before she died?"

"Yes, but I don't remember everything. She wanted me to watch her twins . . ." Sam seemed attentive, sympathetic, but an inner caution kept her from saying more. "Hard to make sense of it." She smiled at him.

"The mind works mysteriously." He patted her hand. "Today you can't remember anything, tomorrow the whole thing comes back."

"What kind of a person would blow up someone? It was like a power display, as if the killer wanted everyone to know."

"How can anyone know? We have to trust the people trained to deal with it. You mount your film. That's what you do best."

The governor of California had risen to make a toast from his seat next to the Sterns.

"We all know Buck and Helena," he began, "and all I want to do is wish them Godspeed. May you be confirmed with honor. We're all proud to know you."

Many stood and cheered.

Sam Pike whispered to Faye: "Justice Buck. Do you think that carries the ring of inspired jurisprudence?"

"Why, Sam, I think you're just a little amoral."

"Well, that does give me a bit more room to operate in."

The lamps in the garden glowed, lighting the trees, but beyond their cheery arcs, all was shadow. The sea was black. Desserts appeared, layer cakes with billowy white icing, French mints and chocolate truffles; coffee trays followed with gold-trimmed demitasse cups; decanters of golden dessert wine appeared.

Faye gave Nadine the high sign. They met in one of the guest bathrooms, a spacious chamber decorated with hand-painted antique Mexican tiles.

Nadine collapsed on a dainty boudoir chair.

"I'm getting threatening phone calls," Faye said.

"What?" Nadine sat up. "What kind?"

"A soft *awful* voice telling me to 'Lay off Della.' "

"Is that all?"

"That's enough!"

Nadine sounded unconcerned. "That's not a real threat because that's not how it's done. You want to threaten someone, you intimidate them, you sneer at them in the press, try to marginalize them, say 'She's that nut case who's always seeing conspiracies.' I mean, that threat's really out of date."

"I'm *so* relieved I only got an old-fashioned threat," Faye snarled. "It sure felt real."

"I'm sorry, Faye. Of course it's scary, but it does prove someone's afraid of what you heard, so—"

"Yes, yes, I know. What's on the disk?"

"I think it's a list of some of the government's subcontracting work done through private organizations like CDEE. But subcontracting's done all the time, so I don't know why Della was keeping track of it. The thing that bothers me . . ." Nadine stood up, peering at herself in the mirror, and pulled a compact out of her bag. "Della's list was primarily the subcontracting work of one new project at the National Security Council called the Office of Program Information. When I asked Leo about it, he lied to me. He said it was just starting up, but it's not new, and he said it was international. But all the places on Della's disk are in the States. I don't care if it's domestic or international, but why would he lie to me?" She powdered her face slowly. "It could be part of a security program I don't have the right clearance for."

"Leo," Faye said, "strikes me as the kind of guy who'd just say, get outta here, you don't have the clearance."

"Yes." Nadine began to wash her hands.

"What is subcontracting in this case?"

"Like it is everywhere else. The agency approves a program and budget, takes bids or assigns another outfit with expertise to carry out certain functions in the program, pays them to do it. It's very straightforward, Faye." Nadine reached for a linen guest towel. "I can't tell yet what it means or figure why she'd keep it secret. What with your phone threat, maybe we should just drop all this."

Faye's hand closed around Nadine's upper arm. "I will not be run off. Someone killed Della. I couldn't live with myself if I don't do something, if I don't at least *try*."

Nadine frowned. "Well, I agree but . . ." Her frown deepened.

Faye smiled. "You've got that look in your eye."

"What?"

"Like the one you had in contracts our first year of law school. Remember *Asselin* v. *Geller*? None of us could get it. You just kept sitting there with that frown. You wouldn't quit! You bird-dogged it until you were ready to drop. So get on this trail, Nadine."

"Why'd Leo lie?" Nadine murmured into the mirror. "Why'd Della keep those lists of places and dates?"

"Yeah, yeah, keep on thinking about it. You'll figure it out." Nadine was dusting powder on her beautiful face.

Warn Nadine to stay clear . . .

Faye blinked. She felt assaulted by Della's words, which until now she hadn't remembered. *Warn Nadine to stay clear.*

Nadine was stroking her lips lightly with pale pink lipstick. She gazed at Faye's reflection in the mirror. "You okay?"

"I just remembered something Della said that day." Faye's voice sounded hollow. Nadine stopped moving, one hand raised, holding the lipstick. " 'Warn Nadine to stay clear.' "

Nadine was stunned. "Why didn't you tell me before?"

"I just remembered!" Faye was close to tears. "Some of her words that day—it's like a concussion—I have blank spots."

Nadine reached out, squeezed Faye's shoulder. "I'm sorry. What did she mean?"

"I can't imagine. Why warn *you*? *I* was the one who was with her, *I* was the one she left her stuff for."

Nadine was still holding the lipstick. She capped it clumsily. "Are you sure she said that?" Faye nodded. Nadine snapped her purse shut. "C'mon, let's forget this for a while," she said shakily. "We'll go find Adrian. Don't you think he's great? He's not married." She ran a palm over her perfect coiffure.

"You said he'd never been married, Nadine," Faye said. She felt she was speaking from a trance. "He's probably gay."

"No he isn't."

They started down the carpeted hall that led to the foyer.

" . . . problems . . . can be handled." The intensity of Leo Townsend's voice coming from a study brought Nadine and Faye to a stop.

Another familiar voice: "Do you think I'm a fool?" It was Sam Pike's.

Leo said, "They wouldn't dare . . . they're up against California, not some hog state—"

Nadine grabbed Faye's arm. "What are they doing in there?" Faye shook her head.

Buck's voice: "I'm out of it now. You two handle it."

Leo: "I'm going back tomorrow."

Buck: "Sam, you go to Washington."

"Very well, but we're making a serious mistake about Mark," Sam said, nearer to the door.

All the voices began to talk at once.

Sam: "Listen to me and readjust: California is a *country*, not a state. What's won here is won nationally."

Faye and Nadine hurried down the hall, but as Faye passed the corner, she couldn't resist a peek back. Townsend, Judge Stern, and Pike were leaving the study. Sam, in the lead, waved to her. Faye waved back.

TEN

THE PARTY COLLAPSED in upon itself like a burnt-out star. Guests staying over disappeared into their rooms. The great house was silent.

Assigned to the Pink Room, Faye found a canopied bed and dormer windows looking toward the sea. It all felt familiar. During law school, it had been in this room that Nadine had confided to Faye she was falling in love with Faye's brother, Rob.

Faye undressed, pulled off the heavy spread, and sat in the middle of the bed, thinking of Della's words, *Warn Nadine* . . . What had Nadine said or done that would make Della say that?

She began thinking about moot court in law school when Faye had first realized how excluded Nadine had been from her parents' lives and how much she strained for their affection. The case she and Nadine had been assigned dealt with a man who'd been convicted of causing the death of an elderly Baltimore woman while robbing her. The woman had died not of injuries, but of a heart attack during the robbery. Was the defendant guilty of first-degree murder as convicted? Nadine and Faye had been handed the trial record to argue against the trial court's decision on appeal.

During moot court, Buck and Helena showed up. As usual, they hadn't told Nadine they were coming. After the arguments, everyone went out to a courtyard for wine and beer. Tot, Della, and other classmates had been there, but Nadine's parents stood back.

"I'll go get them," Faye had said.

"No, we go to them." Nadine was pouring two paper cups of wine. "I'm so excited I can't hold these." Faye took the wine and they walked over to Helena and Buck.

"I didn't know you were coming," Nadine said to them. Faye held out the wine to them.

"Oh, no, thank you, dear," Helena said, "I detest paper cups."

"How'd you know I had moot court?" Nadine asked.

"Why, dear, we didn't know. Daddy had to talk to Mark and since we were coming this way, we just dropped in."

"Serendipity!" Nadine said shrilly. "What did you think of the arguments, Dad?"

"How about that point of law he made regarding intent?" Buck asked her.

"Yes, but I got him back, Dad, didn't I?"

"Bucky, we have to move on," Helena said quietly. "We'll hit the traffic."

"Dad, what did you think of using *Bode* v. *Bush*—"

"Some other time, dear," Helena cut her off firmly.

Buck said, "You call me tomorrow, Nadine. I thought the whole thing was super." And off they'd gone.

Faye never forgot the look on Nadine's face: the skin seemed to press back against the bone, melding with it. Slowly, she poured the wine onto the brick paving.

"Robbery was an apt topic tonight," she said softly. "We shoulda argued the other side."

"What do you mean?" Faye had asked.

"Let them stand convicted. Let all appeals fail." She flung the cup to the ground and squashed it under her heel.

Faye left the canopied bed and went to the window. Why was she remembering that moot court night?

The moonlight shone on a cluster of palm trees. The boom of the waves blended with the sound of the explosion. Faye was smelling the smoke, seeing it pour from the canted car. What kind of person would blow up Della? Someone who was afraid of her, someone who wanted to make a statement, or to send a message. But to whom?

Warn Nadine to stay clear. Was she remembering it right? Yes, she was, Della *had* said that. Had she intended to give Nadine the disk? Had she been prevented? What would Della have said to Nadine about the disk? Here we have a bunch of subcontracting outfits and . . . what else? Faye didn't know. But before she'd died, Della had known the significance of those corporate names and dates. Otherwise, none of this made any sense.

Faye went back to the bed and stretched out under the covers. *Take it the other way around*, she told herself. Faye didn't know what kind of information Della had had, but what had Della known about Nadine that would have made her want to warn her? She'd known she was Buck's daughter, had gone to law school, was a good test-taker, had a fine analytical mind, and was married to my brother, Rob, Faye thought, reviewing the obvious. Della had known Nadine worked at the NSC, that she was a moderate Republican, and tenacious as a pit bull. Faye and Della always counted on Nadine to locate the perfect cite when everyone else had given up. But Nadine never did: she couldn't resist a good hunt.

That's why I've been thinking about moot court! Faye thought. Nadine couldn't resist a good hunt because she'd been chasing her parents' affection all her life! She was accustomed to the heat of the chase and Della had known that. *Della had also known I'd give her the disk and that Nadine wouldn't stop until she'd found out what it meant! Tot could chase things down, too, but I'd never have taken it to her. The disk had to end up with Nadine. Della knew she was dying; she was warning Nadine about a real danger.*

Faye was putting on her bathrobe before she realized she didn't know which room Nadine and Rob were in. She couldn't walk all over the house, knocking on doors. She'd have to wait for morning.

Faye felt even more afraid than she had after the phone call. *How long have I been afraid? What have I gotten Nadine into?*

* * *

Faye was the first down to breakfast, a meal in the Sterns'
manse that reminded her of old British movies. Sideboards,
silver salvers, eggs and meats and racks of toast, a choice of
newspapers, sunlight on antique linens.

She poured coffee and was checking her watch again when
Edward, the butler, came into the room.

"Good morning, Edward. Have you seen Nadine yet?"

"She left, Mrs. Mittelman. Very early. I believe she was
catching the helicopter down to Los Angeles airport."

"Oh." She sat down, calculating how soon she could reach
her in Washington.

Rob was in the doorway and he was upset.

"What is it?" she asked.

"Buck just got a call from Mom. Pop's had a heart attack."

Buck and Helena insisted Faye and Rob take their limo
and driver back to Los Angeles. Someone from El Contento
would deliver Faye's car.

"Pop collapsed after breakfast. Classic heart attack," Rob
said as the big car hummed down the long, tree-lined drive
to the highway.

"Jeez," Faye moaned.

"Pop's not going to die." Rob, who was almost never cross
or grim, set his jaw. "Don't even think it." Suddenly he was
weeping. He put his head in his hands. "God, I can't imagine
life without him." A moment later, he looked up. "I'm okay."
He opened the bar.

"Have some coffee," she said.

"He could be dying right now." A fresh tear rolled down
his cheek. He brushed it away. "I don't deserve such a great
father."

"What crap. How can you say something like that?"

He waved his hand, dismissing his words. Rob Ferray
didn't want to hurt anyone, but he felt like a fraud, leading
a sham marriage in a sham life. His father had not raised him
to live that way. How long could he keep pretending?

He opened a can of mixed nuts. "You starve when you
hurt," he said. "I eat."

"I thought Annie stayed over," she said to say something.

"She left with that TV guy." The constant dishonesty he had seeded through his life made him hunger to admit something true. "I'm glad she's not in this car right now."

"Yeah, she's trying, sometimes." She poured herself a cup of coffee from a thermos. "You were good to me when we were growing up, Rob—a real older brother."

He waved a hand. "It was you and me together," he said. "I tried to take care of Annie, too, but she—she never seemed like one of us."

"She's the person Mom never allowed herself to be."

"Yeah, maybe."

"You remember watching Mom and Pop on the sets?" Faye said. "Not so long ago they were young and healthy, and now . . . Pop's so sick. What's life about? We just start out and then . . . wham." She stared at the passing brown hills. "Della used to say that for you there were no bad guys." Rob kept silent. "You know what I remembered last night about Della's death?"

"Why are you pursuing this?"

"Because she was my friend."

"But she wasn't family, not like a sister," he said.

"She was my best friend, Rob, she was loyal. She let me be myself . . . she knew all about me, the bad and the good, and she still liked me, and we could talk about what we were afraid of, or what we'd done that shamed us, or the things we were proud of. I have the same kind of friendship with Nadine. Do you have that kind of friend? I don't think you do. Men don't."

"Men are different."

"Doesn't mean you don't need a good friend." She waited for him to reply, but he didn't. "Nadine didn't look well last night."

"She always gets upset around her folks."

"It'll be worse when they're living in Washington on top of you. When will the Judiciary Committee meet on Buck?"

"Probably not till summer, maybe earlier." He sighed. "It'll be a big fight. The nomination reeks of politics."

"Last night I was thinking about how Buck and Helena used to treat Nadine."

"They just never needed a child," he said. "They've got each other."

"Helena's more ambitious than Buck is."

"That's not true, Faye," he said, gobbling nuts. "They're *both* ambitious! Aren't you? Aren't I?"

"*Are* you?" she asked. "You never *seem* ambitious."

"Well, I am in my way."

Faye searched his sad face. "What are you ambitious for?"

"A good life full of pleasure."

"You're kidding."

His eyes changed. "Well, pleasure's high on my list."

"I would have said you believed in people's rights or good government or—"

"I'm not that altruistic, Faye."

They both stared out their windows, at the brown hills on one side, the sea on the other.

"Why do you think you're not worth anything?" Faye suddenly asked.

"Huh?" he said, jarred.

"You said you didn't deserve a dad like Pop." Faye's hair was pulled back, her eyes seemed chilly.

"I'm upset, Faye. Don't you feel that sometimes Mom and Dad are too good to be true?"

"No, they're real human. Pop drank too much and Mom protected him and denied it."

"How can you say that when he's just had a heart attack?"

"I don't love him less by seeing him honestly, Rob. I'm trying to do that. Maybe for a long time I didn't—none of us did. He's no saint you have to live up to!"

"I know that! Don't lecture me!" He poured more scotch into the tumbler.

"Rob, don't get drunk."

"Shut up!"

The hard edge in his voice was new, shocking. Faye realized she'd never examined Rob too closely—he was her brother and he was perfect. Now she saw the suffering deep inside him.

The big car charged forward, eating road.

He reached over the space between them and patted her knee. "I'm sorry, Faye," he said. "I'm being a rat."

"Are you mad at Pop for the way he was when we were growing up?"

"Mad? No." His face twisted. "I just don't want him to die."

But Faye, torn up by her father's nearness to death, was aware that she didn't know her brother or herself as well as she'd thought.

Jerry Ferray was snugly connected to machines in his hospital room at Cedars Sinai in Los Angeles. He looked thin and old; his prominent nose poked out of his face. Coo Ferray hovered by the bed. In her off-white muumuu, she resembled a nurse-priestess. Annie sat in a chair by the window.

As Rob and Faye entered the room, Coo raised her finger to her lips theatrically. Jerry opened his eyes. Faye leaned over him, feeling smudged and unclean.

"Buck sent us down in his limo, Pop," she said, knowing that would please him.

An oxygen tube snaked beneath his nose. "I'm not dying today. Tell Buck."

Rob was crying. "Pop," he said, stroking the back of his father's wrinkled hand. "Pop."

"Son, settle down," Jerry said. "I'm okay."

"We have very emotional children," Coo said. Jerry nodded and shut his eyes.

In the waiting room, a powdery cloud of Coo's fragrance enveloped her three children. They leaned toward each other, a vanguard against death and grief.

"Pop's doing very well, dears," Coo said, patting Annie's hand. "Just remember, his life line and his head line are long and unbroken. He'll be with us for years." Faye began to cry. "I know you're afraid, honey," Coo said. "We all are." Coo was reaching across Faye's shoulder to comfort her when Annie threw back her head and put a hand over her face. Coo turned from Faye to Annie; her youngest needed attention like she needed food. "We must be strong for Daddy," Coo said to Annie.

Faye patted her eyes with a tissue and straightened her shoulders. "Was his heart damaged?"

"The doctors are optimistic, considering," Coo said. "Besides, it wasn't a massive heart attack, just a little one. He's going to be back home very soon."

"Why are the doctors optimistic?" Rob asked.

"Because he's probably not going to die of a heart attack, I guess," Coo said, her voice shaking. "He's still got the leukemia."

That morning, Jerry complained of chest pains again, nurses charged in and out with machines, medicines were changed and injected. By evening, he seemed much better, but Coo slept in the next room anyway. The following morning, Faye stayed with her father until he fell asleep, then she went down to the cafeteria. Relief about him melted through her, her pace slowed and she leaned against the wall of the corridor. For the first time since Della had died, Faye hadn't thought of her, but now Della was near again, and Faye's fear came tumbling back. *Is it always with me now, like a second skin?* It wasn't like her fear for her father; *this* fear had penalties.

"Are you all right?"

Faye lifted her head. It was a nurse. "Yes." She went down to the main floor of the hospital to a double row of pay phones set into an alcove. Visitors lined the phones on either side of her in various states of numbness or distress. She telephoned Nadine in Washington.

"Pop seems to be doing well, Nadine. Rob'll fly out tonight unless there's a change for the worse. Listen, Nadine, I've been thinking about what Della said. About warning you. Have you thought about it?"

"Yes."

"I think we should pay attention." Faye felt silly, as if she'd performed somewhere, thinking it brilliant, only to find herself ridiculous. "Nadine, I don't want you to check into anything on that disk anymore. Just—just stop."

"Stop?" Nadine sounded amazed. "Faye, we're getting somewhere. You put me on the trail."

"I know. But I want you to stop. I couldn't live with it if anything happened to you."

"Has something else happened? More threats?"

"No. But I want you to stop. I feel—uneasy."

In her calm, tolerant voice, Nadine said, "Faye, Della was delirious, *we* don't know what she was saying really. Look, I'm having lunch with that Jay Harper who runs the OPI program and I'll call you afterward. I don't think he'll say anything to me, because all these guys' mouths were sewn shut at birth, but it's worth a try."

"No, listen, Nadine! I mean it, let's just—"

"I have to get to a meeting. Check back with that detective about the disk. Give Jerry my best love," she said, hanging up.

Faye stood at the phone bank listening to the callers around her and to the constant hum of the hospital. She deeply regretted involving Nadine. This was her job to do, hers alone.

Gabe Mittelman was standing at the elevators holding a bunch of tulips and the latest *Esquire*. His jeans were faded; he was wearing his favorite dark red corduroy jacket. His dark hair curled around his ears. Faye went up to him and touched his arm.

"Jerry's asleep, Gabe."

He turned; his gaze took her in fully. "Is he okay?"

"For now. It was nice of you to come."

The elevator arrived, passengers poured out. Gabe and Faye stepped aside. "Here," he said, "you take these tulips and I'll get more for him when I come back. You look all in. You need some espresso."

The sunny block was lined with a few immature palm trees that broke up the unremitting concrete. They walked past a torrent of cars and an ugly shopping emporium on La Cienega, and went into a chop house. It was limbo time, between breakfast and before lunch. They sat in a booth.

"Did you have breakfast?"

"Yeah, yeah." She nodded hastily.

"You didn't." He ordered poached eggs for both of them.

"What have you been up to?" she asked.

"Shlepping around town, meeting and greeting, reading scripts, getting ready to work again. I can feel the heat building." He smiled, creasing the vertical lines in his cheeks. "How about you?"

"I'm working on *The Jungle Gym*."

"With Herb Yount?"

"No. He doesn't want it."

"Is that the one about the whistle-blower—?"

"Yeah, a doctor and the congressman."

"The nerdy idealist? Why'd you go back to that?"

"It's a good story."

"Ah, Faye, quit screwing around."

"The movie's my way of saying good-bye to Della."

Gabriel had a way of looking at people that was completely frank. "Faye, stop already with Della. You've done all you could."

The espresso arrived. She watched his competent, handsome hands fiddle with lemon peels and sugar cubes.

"You're awful quiet," he said. There was something different about Faye, she seemed more grounded, but she also seemed more vulnerable. "Is Jerry really all right?"

She glanced at the man who'd once been her best friend. "It's a hard time, I'm not handling Della's death very well, and now Pop—"

"Doctors have written off patients before who went on to give them the finger and lived for years. You're a famous optimist—so be optimistic!"

"Della cured me." She fished the lemon peel out of her coffee and ate it. "I feel guilty that she died and I didn't."

"That's survivor's grief." He wanted to sit next to her, put an arm around her.

"I couldn't save her."

"Faye, let it rest."

"Oh, I know all that!" She lit up, intense, explosive hazel eyes sharpened—the Faye of old. "I went to see the detective, I saw some of Della's—"

"Faye, calm down." He seemed worried. He was retreating from her.

"I can't. Why should I?" She stopped. "There I go again. You always said it was hard to live with me."

"I think I said you're intense."

"You don't like intensity."

"I admire strong feelings, but not to the exclusion of all else."

The rubble of their marriage humped on the table between them. "Faye, maybe this isn't a good time, but I'd like to say something. It's about Tot."

"I don't want to hear about her."

"I want you to know how it all happened."

"I don't care. I thought I was pregnant, we had a fight, you disappeared. Fade-out."

"C'mon, Faye, things hadn't been good for you and me for quite a while. Remember when we went to Santa Barbara after we finished *Roundabout*?" His slow, warm smile reacquainted itself with his face, changing it. "After I finish a show, I just have to get back and listen to myself, but that wasn't possible with you. The fight that time, it wasn't your fault, I was an ass, I gave you a bad time, and now I can see it was—I should have taken time out by myself—away from you—long enough time to keep loving you."

"What we had—"

"What *was* that, Faye, what we had?"

"I loved you. I trusted you. We had a great partnership."

"True. Especially the partnership. But after a while, that's all we had, the town's hot team, seen everywhere, always talking film, even at night, you and me. A limited partnership."

"We had more than that."

"I never saw you except in crowds," he said softly. "You were always working, talking, running."

"Weren't *you*? Just what do you think producers do—wait for the money to blow in through the windows?"

"I wanted a different kind of marriage, Faye."

"Oh, I knew you were drifting away," she said, "that's why I took on more work. I couldn't talk to you about anything except work. We made love and I could feel you thinking about the crane shot the next day."

"Why didn't you ever say anything?"

"I tried . . . oh, maybe I didn't. But I did the best I could," she said fiercely. "That time in the cabin in Santa Barbara? I came back and you were gone. I don't want to fight it through again, Gabe. That was only a symptom. You know what I resented? Your manner, as if you were laying down some ancient law to me: 'It was going to be this way or the highway. Baby next year, not this year.' "

"I know it might have sounded like that, but I didn't mean it. That night in Santa Barbara, after our big argument about children and life, I went back to L.A. and bumped into Tot and we started talking."

"I'll bet she was very understanding."

"She was a good friend to you, she took your side. It just hit us a few weeks later and once we were in it, well, it was very heavy. Neither of us wanted it. But *we* were responsible for it—no one else. We weren't captives. You know, I could sit with Tot for an hour and not say anything?"

"Well, terrific," she said.

"When's the time you and I were just *being* together, Faye? We were always *doing*. It wore us out, it burned out something critical."

Her knees were shaking. She reached for her handbag and knocked it to the floor. Gabe watched her scramble for her wallet, makeup, papers. When she'd collected everything, she was on the attack: "I can't imagine why you'd leave wonderful old Tot!"

He'd meant to clear the air, to say what had not been said, to remove barriers, to find out what, if anything, was left. But there was too much wreckage and he was angry all over again.

"Tot and I weren't in love, but she's stubborn, she didn't want to face it, she held on longer than I did." Faye was clawing through her bag again. "Are you listening?"

"Yes!"

"We both pretended longer than we should have—the divorce was already in motion, you were being a shit, talking through that stupid lawyer you had. It all got completely out of hand." He stopped, testing his words in his head. "I remember when I knew. I was on a set, talking to Mel Page in *Tenth Mile,* in that restaurant scene where he's with his pal, talking about their wives, and Mel had a line about when you know you're in love."

Faye closed her eyes; she felt tears brewing in her chest, she knew her nose was getting red. She didn't want to feel the pain again, but she couldn't leave.

"The line went, 'It's not that you can't stand to be without her for a minute, it's that you *can* stand it if it's best for her.' Not an earthquake line, but it was basically honest, and at that moment I knew I wasn't in love with Tot—I cared for her, respected her, I'd been attracted to her—Faye! Open your eyes, look at me!"

Her eyes popped open. She was crying.

"I'm standing there on the set," he said, his voice trembling, "and something's wrong with the lights that'll take an hour to fix, and wardrobe is yelling at someone, and Mel's being a prince, and Jake's lost something like all the original film—I mean, it was hell—and I knew that *I'd* lost everything—you, the marriage, the partnership, and most of my old friends. Everything."

She was touched, but something hungry and perverse in her stifled the feeling. "So you left," she whispered.

"I went to Maine, yes."

"I heard Tot was with you there."

"She came up once. We both saw it wouldn't work. She went on to Washington. I went to Europe."

"I don't know what you want from me."

"Faye, don't push me away. I'd like us to be friends." She didn't answer. "Then what was happening between us at Nadine's cabin?"

"Nostalgia."

"No, it was more than that. I wanted—"

"You want to come back and pick up with me as if nothing had happened."

"Not true. I went up there because I thought maybe we could get together, be friends." He grabbed her arm. "You did, too! Faye, this isn't coming out the way I wanted—"

"The whole marriage didn't come out the way I wanted. I thought you were a decent man, Gabe, I don't know how you could do something like that. I had my own part in it, I'm not denying that, but this is all past now, let's just say adios."

She got up and left. A minute later, the eggs arrived. He dumped hers into his bowl and broke the golden yolks. His hand shook, he couldn't eat. He put down his fork. He sat in the booth, grieving and angry.

Their marriage had ended in Gallup, New Mexico, site of their last shoot together, *The Tenth Mile*. He'd always felt Gallup was an appropriate ending, a jumble of low buildings, short junky streets surrounded by desert and bureaucrats. When they'd finished the shoot, Gabe had told Faye about Tot.

He finished his espresso. Faye focused on her work more than on living. But he hadn't improved her living, he hadn't improved his own, either. Why had he picked a woman like that? Because he admired her. Because she was fascinating. Because she brought her mind and her heart into love. Because she challenged him.

What had made him think he could repair his relationship with Faye? He'd blown it years ago. If she'd gone off with another man and then tried to return, to start up again, would he have leaped at the chance? He leaned back in the booth, controlling grief.

As he left the restaurant, he remembered the tulips. He went back inside. Faye had taken them with her.

ELEVEN

JAY HARPER'S OFFICE was two flights down from Nadine's in the OEOB. She met his secretary, Tawny, in the hall.

"I'll be back in a sec," Tawny said in a confidential voice. She was one of those big Rose Queen beauties with tumbling hair and slender hips. "He's expecting you." She whisked away.

Tawny kept a neat shop. Books and reports were aligned, there were no loose papers about, in and out boxes were empty. Nadine tapped at Harper's inner office door.

"Come."

The small windowless room was jammed with an impressive array of secure computer terminals, cables sheathed to prevent electronic eavesdropping. A high-speed printer was disgorging yards of paper into a receiving bin. Harper, behind a vast desk, was on one of his several phones. When he saw Nadine, he heaved his weight forward in the large high-back leather chair and clapped his hand over the receiver. "I'll see you outside." Nadine nodded and retreated.

"Yeah, Los Angeles, damn you," Harper barked into the phone. "You're a bunch of cowboys out there. It won't work like that."

Nadine shut the door and sat down in a blue federal-issue

chair in the outer office. As a deputy legal adviser, tracking down facts was part of her job. What Adrian wanted, he got. Her investigation into OPI had expanded. She'd checked into CDEE, going through the Securities and Exchange Commission, and then through a friend of hers who was an officer at the NSC's bank. CDEE had been incorporated in Delaware like a million other companies; its corporate officers were California residents. She had not yet checked the other companies on Della's list.

Harper came out of his office. His suit was wrinkled and covered with the fine dust from the printer. He slapped at it. "You've come at a good time—no flaps!"

"Pretty sophisticated setup," Nadine said, nodding toward his inner office.

"Yeah, we're fully computerized now."

They went to a little French restaurant. Jammed into the basement of an old building just off Seventeenth Avenue and H Street, it was dark and homey with open brick walls and a back garden for pleasant days.

Though Harper had a military bearing, he was boyishly upbeat and easy to like. "What's your branch?" Nadine asked.

"Air Force," he replied, studying her. He crunched his big white teeth into a piece of baguette and swallowed it down. "But I know all about you. You ask everyone to lunch! You got some kind of OEOB social agenda?"

"Well, we're all in our separate niches over there and last year I thought lunches would be one way to get to know some of the staff, but I don't have that much time to pursue it." Nadine smiled warmly at Harper and shrugged one shoulder. "Leo thought—"

"What a great man," he said. His sharp eyes scouted the room behind her.

As their orders of pot-au-feu were arriving, Nadine said, "In our meeting with the President, you gave a report on the Office of Public Information program—do I have that right?"

"Yeah. We've needed something like that for a long time," he said. "No one has ever tried to harness—to categorize all the information programs the government funds." He made a molding gesture with his hands.

"How did it start?"

"I believe," he said, choosing his words, " . . . it began as a way to educate and control what people knew about government programs and to coordinate all government communication projects. Two-edged."

"I understand OPI began in eighty-eight."

"Eighty-nine. The great thing about the plan is it does away with duplication—keeps two or three agencies from collecting the same data." He glanced at her, pleased. "I'm big on controlling waste. Big on thrifty democracy."

"I understand you like poetry," Nadine said.

"Oh, you've been reading the official bios?"

"When you were reporting the other day about the OPI, I was reminded of that Carl Sandburg poem about democracy. 'I am the people, the mob, the crowd, the mass. Do you know that all the great work of the world is done through me?' " she quoted.

"Right, right," he said, enthused. She couldn't tell if he actually knew the quote or not.

"I always thought the poem was also talking about the power of the press."

"I believe in the free press," he said, hunching forward with a boyish grin. "I believe in using the press." He laughed.

At the front of the noisy restaurant, Leo Townsend caught sight of Nadine's shiny blond hair. The back of her companion was not distinctive, but when he shifted in his chair, Leo knew who he was.

Cowboy was eating a salad at his wide rosewood desk.

"We have problems, Cowboy," Leo said on the speakerphone. "I just saw Nadine Ferray in a restaurant with Harper."

"Ah." Cowboy raised his pale eyebrows. "Romance?"

"Hardly," Leo said, nettled. "She's curious about OPI."

"I do hope not. Is Harper okay?"

"He's no problem. Harper's a believer. Works twenty hours a day and considers it an honor."

"And so do I, Leo," Cowboy said. "Consider it an honor, that is."

"This all started when an OPI briefing paper was sent to her by mistake."

"Unfortunate," Cowboy said, hearing the agitation in Leo's voice. "But I'm more concerned about Faye Ferray than misrouted briefing papers. Della Izquerra must have said something to her, because she went out to CDEE."

"Oh, Jesus."

"It's being handled."

"I'm putting a telephone tap on Nadine."

"Well, you're always resourceful, Leo." Cowboy's voice held doubt, but Leo was too annoyed to detect it. "How's the operation on your side?"

"All the new computer links are in place," Leo said proudly. "I'm expanding my area in the NSC."

Cowboy heard the boastful note. "Good man."

"Just consider it, Cowboy. Not ten years ago, the NSC had almost no modern communications abilities."

"I thought the high-tech military communications in the White House maintained batteries of secure phones."

"Oh, sure, but it wasn't until the mid-eighties that the NSC even initiated its own computer system. It collected all the government's foreign policy information in its own central bank from State, from the CIA, the Pentagon, NSA. Someone called it a 'technological coup d'état,' and, boy, was he right! Put that sucker right over the goal line! That's what made the Iran-Contra operation possible.

"Now we've enlarged the network to track domestic programs. They're fully adapted to OPI's needs. Beautiful system. Harper can tap into any data bank dealing with national security in the government, and now he can pop in and out of any domestic-agency budget as well."

"The Chief will be delighted." Cowboy smiled. All people, no matter how powerful, wanted strokes. Leo's voice shot on, but Cowboy was thinking how unfortunate it was that Faye Ferray had been with Della that day. How much had Della said? How long could he, Cowboy, keep a tight rein on Leo and the others?

"Harper's got a secure line direct to me, so we're sealed tight," Leo was saying.

"Leo, you're a master."

"I've managed to keep the size of the staff under wraps, borrowing personnel from other agencies—even Harper. His salary's paid by the Air Force."

Cowboy smiled to himself. Leo had forgotten it was he who had first suggested Harper.

"So, although my operation is technically part of the White House NSC program, no one knows how much I'm spending—or toward what end," he whispered.

"And how about the head of the NSC—?"

"Tate. He's resting comfortably in the dark."

"A permanent location, I trust. Keep in touch, Leo." Abruptly, he hung up.

After her lunch with Jay Harper, Nadine went back to her desk. She had checked every firm listed on Della's disk against public information from the Securities and Exchange Commission. She sat back, amazed. Adrian had been right: something was wrong. Without Della's disk, she might not have found it. The trails were converging.

Seventy-three percent of the companies on Della's disk shared some of the same officers listed for CDEE—interlocking boards. Some, but not all, showed up on the National Security Council's list of subcontractors to the OPI program even though it appeared few of the companies had any connection to OPI's stated goals. Instead, the companies on Della's list dealt in environmental concerns, insurance, computers, legal aid, and a lot of other areas.

One of the first friends she'd made in Washington had been a Senate investigator. If he had run down the OPI and CDEE trails to this point, finding the same people on different corporate boards, she could hear him asking, "How and where did they meet each other? What had they been involved in five years ago or two years ago and what made them converge?"

But Nadine was not a Senate investigator. She had career realities to consider, like the costs of continuing the chase. Outside her window, trees bloomed delicately. She got out a legal pad and began summarizing what she knew. Should I go on? How will it affect my career? Adrian? Leo? I need them to get ahead. If I continue the search, she wrote, can

I maintain my good relationship with Leo? Will Adrian continue to support me?

If I learn what the OPI program is really about, will I be believed? Will I be told to back off? If I do, will I be able to live with what I know? Should I continue my search? She underlined that.

She turned to a fresh sheet and started another list. If I go on with the search, how do I protect myself? What steps can I take without prejudicing myself? She made a list of all the people in executive authority who might have something to do with OPI and its subcontracting. What are their connections, if any, to corporations on Della's disk? Trace people with review authority and who they deal with. Decide the order of approach. What kinds of questions can I ask without revealing my real motives?

She stared at her notes. Going on from this point was tricky. Leo had brought her into the National Security Council and she was indebted to him. He'd lied about the OPI program, but whatever she discovered would affect him. And what affected Leo, affected her career.

If I go on, she thought, I'm going to need help. She buzzed Pamela Sewell.

When she arrived, Nadine asked her to shut the door.

"How's everything going with you, Pamela?"

"Good. My daughter's in a special class—a gifted program."

"Wonderful. I want children so much," Nadine said.

Pamela had worked with Nadine for two years and knew of her desire for a child but had never discussed it privately before. "You will. You need to relax, that's a lot of it. My husband and I were married for three years before our first was born."

"Yes? That makes me feel a lot better."

"Then the second one came along right away, almost too soon! I felt so overwhelmed." Pamela grinned wryly.

Nadine smiled, longing to be overwhelmed with children. "Pamela, Adrian's asked me to look into the OPI program and I think you can help me."

"Me?"

"I had lunch with Jay Harper today. Have you heard anything about what he's doing?"

"People kinda wonder what's he running down there," Pamela said. "They think he's carrying out, you know, some special charge."

"Like a private operation?"

Pamela didn't bite. "It's authorized or else he wouldn't be doing it, would he?"

"Would you say Harper keeps a low profile?"

"I don't think it's really low," Pamela hedged.

"Can you be more specific?"

"We got backed up while you were in California. The main copier went out. So I took some of the most urgent stuff down to two. People were streaming in and out of his office. I asked one of the clerks what was up. She said she didn't know, but he started early and ended late. Then she said, 'Some high mucky-muck business on the information program.'"

"I need some help from you, Pamela, and it won't interfere with your workload."

"I don't want to get in trouble, Nadine. You know what my situation is, I'm divorced, my kids—this job is all I have."

"No, no trouble. Adrian's authorized this, but we don't want to make an announcement that we're doing a little digging. If you see some stuff float by your operation about OPI, just let me know. I'll do the rest. You'll be well out of it, and I won't forget your cooperation."

Gabe eased open the door of the hospital room. Jerry Ferray, thin and pale, was alone, stretched out on his bed. The morning light shone brightly against the walls of the white room.

Gabe hadn't seen his former father-in-law in a long time. It was hard to imagine Jerry was so ill. He'd been a dancer, he'd spent his life exercising—the best medicine. But he'd been a heavy drinker. Even so, drunk or sober, Gabe had always liked this slender, erratic, decent man.

"Gabe, what are you doing here? Seeing some other guy on Charon's canoe?"

"Nope, just you." Gabe's bashful laugh was more of an audible smile. "How's the ride so far?"

"Choppy." Jerry eyed his former son-in-law. "Hear you

weren't nominated for an Oscar."

"Well, I don't take that Oscar stuff too seriously."

Jerry hiked himself up to a sitting position. He was feeling better, but he knew it was only a brief reprieve. "Bullshit. Don't ever underestimate the awards. They can light up a career."

They chatted about fishing and traveling, vying with each other through exotic lands they'd visited. "You went to Morocco?" Jerry said.

"Yup, last year. Jer, you look tired. I won't stay."

"Don't go yet, Gabe. You mind telling me why you divorced my Faye? Just tell me to go to hell if—"

"I didn't want it, she did."

"Why'd you cheat on her? Why'd you get involved with Tot? Just tell me now, because I might not be here tomorrow and I want to know."

"I regret it all."

"Faye deserved better!"

"Yes, Jerry, she did."

"I know she's opinionated and stubborn," Jerry said.

"But she's compassionate, too. Geez, she cries in movies, sometimes at the news! She cried for an hour when Terry Anderson was released." Gabe remembered seeing a movie with Tot. He'd been moved by it. But Tot had come swinging out of the theater saying, "Sentimentality is wrecking American culture." Then she'd leaped into a sharp, funny synopsis of the film. He'd thought at the time that if he'd been with Faye, she would have been wiping her eyes and hanging on his arm.

Slowly, Gabe moved to the foot of the bed and put his hands on the rail. "Jerry, all I can tell you is that sometimes madness takes over and all we're left with is regrets."

"If that's what you're living with, you deserve it." Jerry was shaking; his cheeks were bright pink.

"Jerry, please, this isn't good for you," Gabe said, deeply upset.

"Good for me? Nothing's good for me. I'm dying, man, and I'll damned well do or say whatever I please." He drew deeply on the oxygen tube under his nose, fingering it delicately. "Fucking body, lets you down when you need it.

Coo and I always thought our problem would be Annie. Rob had Nadine, a wonderful woman, and our Faye was all settled with you. Annie was the loose cannon, having a kid, getting a divorce, bam-bam like that, everything messy. Then after seven years of marriage, *you* decide to plow one of Faye's best friends." He leaned his head back against the pillows and breathed deeply. "I always liked you, Gabe, never figured you to throw it all away."

"Now, Jer, that wasn't all that was going on."

"Fuck you, don't patronize me."

"I really don't want to talk about this—"

"Then get out. That's all I'm interested in—my children. That's what it comes down to." He reached for a glass of water. Gabe tried to help. "Get away. I don't need your fucking help." He drank through a straw. Gabe retreated to the foot of the bed. "Are you going to try to mend the marriage?" Jerry asked.

"Faye doesn't want that. I'm not sure I do, either."

"Have you asked her?"

"Jerry, Faye doesn't want me back in her life. She knows she can call on me for help, but—"

"Oh, shut up, for chrissakes. Once in a coon's age you get a real partner in life. All the work you do together is five times as good as the work you do alone. That's what Coo and I had, so I know what I'm talking about. You wrecked it. You haven't done anything since you and Faye broke up and you don't know what you're going to do—"

"Jerry, I've *chosen* not to work."

"Then you're as dishonest with yourself as you were with Faye. Oh, I guess you read the scripts, take the meetings, have lunches, but you can't visualize the script, am I right? You don't get any of those butterflies that make it possible to work creatively. You don't have any joy."

Gabe felt a chill shiver his spine.

"My girl can't get it together, either. She's got no joy in her life. She's diddling around with a movie she can't mount and she's got half her heart cut out, thanks to you. Just when she starts getting her life back together she sees her best friend blown up . . ." Jerry shut his eyes, breathing hard.

"What do you want me to do?" Gabe asked softly.

"Give her some support, help her get over Della."

"Ah, Jerry, she doesn't want to talk to me. Give me a break here."

"Never, you bastard. No breaks from me. You're both so zeroed in on running away from each other, hurting each other, you can't see how much you're hurting yourselves." Jerry fell back on the bed like a cut log. "Get outta here."

Outside the hospital, Gabriel passed a travel agency. He gazed at the posters of Czechoslovakia and let them woo him. He went inside, and started to ask questions about Prague and Bratislava. Suddenly, he stopped. "Sorry," he said, "never mind." He walked out. He'd always run. He couldn't afford to do that anymore. He started walking fast, choked on his frustration. The most frustrating part of it was that he was glad Faye had such a loving and loyal dad.

Gabe could barely remember his own father, he'd died so young. After that, came a succession of show business underachievers his mother had known. She'd married two of them. Between husbands, she'd worked in wardrobe at one of the studios. One of Gabe's earliest and most deeply rooted memories was of his mother's beautiful laughter from a distant room. He had adored her and hated her.

He'd been raised in two worlds, Jewish and Christian, the former overcome by the particular fate of his parents, and by the smothering omnipresence of Southern California Christianity. The world he came to be a part of was run by Jewish men, but it produced immensely popular cultural artifacts about the white Christian world. He learned to keep his most deeply felt emotions hidden beneath a calm, warm surface, a face that promised much and held back more.

By age ten, Gabe had always been in trouble. The rabbi at his temple had taken an interest and he'd helped, but it was Sam Pike who'd made the real difference. Sam had been on the board of a youth organization similar to Big Brothers. He'd helped pay for Gabe's bar mitzvah, he'd found donors to put Gabe through a private arts school, he'd helped him through college, he'd introduced him to Buck Stern, who'd put him up for his first job as a lowly assistant to a producer.

The sound of a horn right next to him made Gabe leap. "Watch where the hell you're goin'!" a man in a car bellowed.

Gabe found himself standing in the middle of the street. "Sorry," he said, retreating. But the man went on shouting. "Have it your way," Gabe yelled back. "Up yours!"

Gabe stopped on the curb. He wasn't moody or uncertain; aside from his addiction to travel, he was solid. He wasn't upset by what Jerry had said about Faye—Gabe would expect no less from Jerry. But it showed him the measure of Tot's power and Gabe's own needs. Otherwise, he would never have sacrificed everything on so many levels with Faye.

Gabe saw Tot slowly peeling off her clothes for the first time with him, her rounded arms lifting her blouse over her head, her tiny body squirreling into his arms. Tot's face was shiny with the mystery of passion and her need to see inside him. "We can't go back, Gabe," her look had said, "not after this."

Behind that look came the tormented months. He remembered Faye turning in her fingers a spiral shell she'd found on their honeymoon beach as the dreaded words about Tot had dropped out of him. "I *do* love you, Faye, but . . ." Had he really said it was hard to live with her? Had he said he and Tot had something quite different? *Stupid platitudes—that's the way we talk to each other,* he thought, embarrassed.

The funeral had brought him back to L.A., but he'd come back for more than that. He'd come looking for himself.

Now, standing on the curb, he faced it: he'd sundered his life and he'd spent years avoiding it. Jerry was right. Creatively, personally, his life was shit.

Gabe found Keith Llewellyn stretched out on the lawn in his Santa Monica backyard, a script tented over his face. His dog, Bob, a golden retriever, was barking loudly at a much smaller dog, who seemed to be holding her own. Keith, a screenwriter, was one of his best friends. They were about the same age, had worked together, and shared common interests in planning real or fantasy travel itineraries, sitting for hours over a beer at nondescript bars on Wilshire, doodling on napkins.

Keith gave Gabriel a beer. "You're just in time to give this little dog a home," Keith said.

"Not me," Gabe said. They sat down in canvas chairs beside a round redwood table.

Keith had a pleasant manner, dark straight hair, and green eyes. "This little dog's been trained, but abused," he said. Gabe steeled himself for the sob story. Keith was always finding dogs. Everyone who worked in the business had been given the opportunity to take one of Keith's foundlings. "She was locked in an airless car parked next to mine in a Glendale shopping center. I worked at that door for twenty minutes before I realized the car was unlocked. I just picked her up and took her away."

"Illegal as hell."

"Criminal, leaving an animal to fry in a car like that."

The dog was skimpy but alert—short-haired, bony, piebald markings. Bob towered over her.

"Sorry. I really don't want one of your dogs, Keith. Besides, Bob seems to like her."

"What brings you here?" Keith asked.

"Felt low. Just saw Jerry Ferray in the hospital. He was giving me hell about Faye—I would have done anything to have a dad like that." He watched the dogs. "Going to see Jerry—I don't know why I keep trying to be part of the family."

Keith sipped his beer. Bob crouched down in front of the little dog and studied her with his golden eyes. "You still in love with Faye?" Keith asked.

"Nah, nothing like that." Gabe looked away. "All we do is fight or scowl at each other, but this Della business scared the shit outta Faye. It bothers me, too. Feels bad."

"Yeah. She called me," Keith said. "She wants rewrites on *The Jungle Gym*. She was pretty tense."

"I want Faye to be okay. Jerry doesn't think she is."

Keith snorted. "How could she be?"

"She ought to stay out of it. Let the cops handle it. Whoever blew Della away has to be worried about Faye, because Della didn't die right away. Faye can't recall what Della said. You know her—she won't back down till she's got it right. Faye's talked to the cops, she's even got Nadine checking Della's files or something."

"Man, you always stay too long at the party. If you can't talk Faye out of playing investigator, and you don't want to join her in the good fight, you'd better get out or get working."

"I think I'll stick around and work."

TWELVE

THE STRETCH LIMOUSINE was stifling.

Herb Yount dialed up the driver in the front for the second time. "How about that air-conditioning?"

"Still dead, Mr. Yount. Sorry. We'll be down there in about ten minutes."

"Your company's not getting a cent from my company for a ride in an oven," Herb snapped.

"What's going on with our weather in this town?" Sam Pike asked merrily.

"Ozone," Herb said, "we're all going to fry in the next century."

"We're frying now."

The last of March had come roaring in like a furnace. "Maybe it's the rain forests," Gabe said.

"The weather's like box office reverses or heart disease," Herb intoned. "It's God's way of humbling us when we reach too high."

That shut everyone up for a while. Herb had planned a more convivial ride, stocking up on champagne, iced caviar, vodka, and pâtés. Five of his studio's pictures were up for various awards, including a few for Gabe and Faye's last picture, *The Tenth Mile*. But as the temperature climbed, Herb's mood plummeted.

The limo was plush. Gabe Mittelman was sharing a love seat with Matilda Sayers, a costarring actress from *The Tenth Mile*. She was a real beauty whose attention to her career was as fixed as the tides. Gabe had invited Sam Pike, who sat across from him near Annie Ferray and her escort, the producer from her first television series. Herb Yount and his wife commanded the head divan.

Annie wanted to smoke a little dope, but couldn't in front of Herb. She saw a wall, thick with red and blue graffiti, go by. "Where *are* we?" she asked.

"The Ramparts," Gabe said. "High crime and the best carnitas in L.A."

"He's kidding," the producer reassured Annie.

"But why aren't we taking the freeway?" Annie asked.

"Wall-to-wall limos heading for the Oscars," Gabe said, laughing. "Our driver's trying to get us there before we suffocate."

Doors locked, windows up, the great white gull-wing stretch limo was gliding through the DMZ between Hollywood and downtown Los Angeles, a gang-warfare district of destitution and sudden death. They streaked by crumbling buildings encrusted with aggressive graffiti codes. It was another country on the planet L.A., inhabited by an inflammable mix of Latinos, Koreans, Cambodians, Filipinos—as distinctive and, to Gabe, as vibrant as the Lower East Side of Manhattan had once been, but far more unstable.

Ahead rose gleaming high rises. The limo pulled out of a stop at Sixth and Beaudry, rolled across the overpass, dove into the forest of fifty-story buildings, and turned north on Figueroa toward the Music Center. At First Street, before the turn into Hope, they encountered a logjam of limos.

"I thought they solved this problem," Annie wailed, stripping off the shimmering stole of her skin-tight gold lamé dress. Her jouncy breasts bulged over the low-cut neckline. Herb poured everyone more champagne.

The great white limo nosed forward, stopped. In the distance, at the Music Center entrance, the screams of fans wafted on the air, rising and falling. Gabe loosened his tie. His hairline felt damp. His full, slightly cynical smile tilted his features up. He punched his long legs into the space between his seat and Sam's; his feet baked in his elkskin cowboy boots. The car inched forward.

"You, Sam," Gabe said, "are the only person in this car who doesn't look hot."

"The pleasure of the Oscars," he replied, "as American as apple pie."

"You don't look down on Oscar?" Gabe asked.

"Never—I live for Oscar." Sam laughed playfully.

Annie asked Herb for more champagne and rolled down the window next to her. There was no breeze.

"The champagne will make you hotter," Sam said.

"But happier," Annie shot back with a broad smile. Pike noticed little tears of perspiration on her forehead. Her hair was twisted up and out from her head like sculpture. She raised her plump, fleshy arm and barely touched a column of curls, testing them.

The giant car rolled forward twenty yards, bringing the rising and falling a cappella screams of the fans slightly closer.

"Faye coming?" Sam asked pleasantly.

"She's meeting us there," Herb said.

"What's she working on these days?" Sam asked.

"A dog," Herb muttered. "I tried to talk her out of it. Gabe, you talk to her—you know the score. I wanted her to do *Lights Out*. But would she? No."

"She refused?" Matilda exclaimed. Herb nodded.

Annie said, "That Judy character in *Lights Out* is a honey."

Matilda watched Herb narrowly but he did not react.

"How silly we are! Let's open the top," Annie said.

It was peeled back to reveal a rectangle of blue sky. Annie stood up through the opening. "God, there's a thousand limos ahead of us," she reported.

Pike stood on a fold-down seat and poked his head and shoulders through the roof. Annie was waving to a man in the limo behind them who was also getting some air.

"He's that studio vice president who's under investigation. Well, people *say* he's under investigation, something about a missing twenty thousand."

"Stealing twenty's tawdry," Pike said. "Stealing a million at least has some dignity."

Annie hooted. Out of sight of the others inside, she ran a hand down his cheek. "Matilda's a really cold bitch, isn't she?" Annie whispered to him. "We should use *her* for air-conditioning."

Sam Pike put his head close to hers. "You know Tony Valdi?"

"Yes, I've met him. I think Faye knew him in college."

"He's at BeverCo, an independent production company with plenty of money. Tony was telling me the other day how much he liked your work." The limo oozed forward another ten yards. "He'll be at the Governor's Ball later tonight. Maybe you can convince him to finance Faye's film with you in the lead."

Annie grabbed his shoulder. "What a brilliant idea!"

"You'll have to get a script of *The Jungle Gym.*"

"But I've already got one!"

He grinned at her. Annie clapped her hands and started to lean down into the limo. Pike took her arm. "Don't tell Faye or anyone yet. Let's just see what happens."

Inside the car, Gabe remembered other Oscars with Faye . . . he thought of the slow dressing in the afternoon with the sense that the town was on a sudden holiday, and the only people working were hair stylists, publicity flacks, and the party planners, busily producing the separate parts of the industry's celebration of itself.

Traffic thinned, time slowed, the town tilted toward the old downtown streets as they filled with fans crowding into the bleachers around the Music Center. The pregnant mid-afternoon lull embraced champagne cocktails, tranquilizers, evening dress, naps. He and Faye had made love in the sunny, sweet afternoon before their first Oscar party, clambering around a bed strewn with their dress clothes, drinking champagne out of one glass, trading it from mouth to mouth, kissing, kissing. Then they dressed fast, dashing for the limo, her hair flying, he carrying his cummerbund and tie, she trying to put on her necklace as she tumbled, laughing, into the car for the holiday shared by only a few thousand people in one tiny spot in the universe.

The screams from the fans were ear-splitting.

"My God, we're here!" Herb cried.

The limo door opened. They emerged, sweating and forcing smiles, landing on a red carpet in the baking sunlight. They were in another line, inching their way toward reporters and cameras, and once past them into a lounge area where hundreds milled about, faces damp, the women's brocaded necklines smudged with streaky makeup.

When the inner doors finally opened, everyone rushed inside, opening their arms to the air-conditioning. More champagne was passed around on trays. Gabe had four glasses. People talked incessantly without any eye contact at all. At last, he, Sam, Matilda, and the others hurried down a long corridor that resembled a cattle chute into the auditorium to sit for hours under the sweep of the cameras.

The Tenth Mile picked up a few respectable awards, and lost others. After the Oscars, the Governors' Ball was the official party around whose sun spun smaller, noisier, more "in" parties all over town.

The sit-down dinner at the ball was served by white-gloved waiters: lobster and pheasant, baby vegetables, huge carved chocolate roses floating in a sea of sparkling Amaretto.

After dinner, though the band played on and some celebrants were still drinking and screaming to be heard, many were lifting the table favors and the bouquets, and trying to leave to find their limos, get to a more "important" party, to make connections, be seen, prove they were part of the main tapestry.

Faye did not sit at Herb's table, but Gabe finally saw her with Annie in a clogged group near the ballroom door. She looked cool in a sleeveless, low-cut blue sheath. He shouldered through the crowd.

"This whole night is like being in Russia—waiting in line," Annie was saying. "Faye, you need to do something exciting with your hair."

"Her hair looks great," Gabe said. "Simple and classic."

"Simple and drastic," Annie said, giggling.

"Well, what we see is only illusion," he said, rephrasing a quote he was too drunk to remember.

"Faye," Mark Drummond said. "Gabe!"

"Enjoy the show?" Gabe asked, shaking his hand. Drummond had a tight dry grip. He was wearing a beautifully cut tux. The crowd surged around them. Mark put his hand under Faye's elbow. Faye smiled at Mark. *Is she with him,* Gabe wondered, stirred. *Where's Mark's wife?*

"I had hoped *Tenth Mile* would have been nominated for Best Picture," Drummond said.

Gabe bowed to Faye. "Madam's movie."

Faye realized Gabe was drunk.

"Guess that's it," Gabe went on, "the last cord between us has been cut. *Tenth Mile* was our last film," he explained to Drummond. Annie watched her sister and Gabe with frank interest.

Drummond, never at a loss for a comment, rested his palm on Gabe's shoulder and said, "Part of life. It's all part of the same road." He turned his golden-brown head toward Faye. "Laura and I just wanted to say hello, Faye, can you spare a moment?"

Gabe watched Faye squeeze Mark's arm as they stepped into the jabbering crowd jamming through the door.

"That's the way it goes, Gabriel," Annie said.

"Yes, Annie. Consequences."

Faye and Mark were outside the ballroom in the corridor. "My staffer here told me the police are seriously stumped on Della's death," Mark said, "but they haven't given up on it."

"Thanks, Mark."

He led her around a combative couple doing an exhibition Lindy in the hall and pressed through the swinging glass doors.

"Isn't this a hoot?" Faye's voice climbed over the din of cars and laughter. Limos were lined up all the way down to the street. "Bet you don't have scenes like this back East."

Mark laughed and took her arm. "We have our own version. Did I tell you about the time the majority leader clobbered the minority leader with a hat rack?" He dropped her arm. "Faye, I have to go. I want to see you again. I need to see you again." He squeezed her hand and went back inside.

Faye saw Herb and waved. A couple near Faye were arguing drunkenly. Suddenly, the woman seized the man's

crotch and squeezed. Astounded, he grabbed at her crotch.
A grim test of strength that went on and on.

"God," Faye said, appalled, "Herb, let's get out of here."
Herb gaped at the couple. He quickly checked for photographers. The man yelped and dropped his hold on the woman. Herb was moving Faye smartly down the crowded walk.

"And a good time was had by all," Faye murmured. "I
really don't like it out here anymore."

Norma Goldstein, Herb's VP of development, had joined
them. At the Y of the driveway and the street, two limo drivers were blocking traffic into the hotel and pounding each
other with their fists. The doors to their cars were open, horns
were honking, other drivers were shouting at them.

Blinding lights flared: a television reporter in a paper hat
started a stand-up in front of the camera with Dudley Moore.
Herb was shouting at Faye over the racket, but she couldn't
hear him. People were coagulating around them, shoving and
laughing.

A distinctive, low voice close to Faye said, "Lay off
Della."

She spun around. Norma, in a long crimson dress, her
back bare to her tailbone, was inches away with an executive
from Fox; next to them was Dudley Moore, the glassy-eyed
reporter, and Gabe, stumbling slightly, just outside the circle.
Herb touched Faye's shoulder. "Are we singing off the same
page, Faye?" The group around Moore burst out laughing.
Faye felt cold and crazy. Had she really heard "Lay off
Della"?

A limo roared up the driveway. "Here's our car," Herb
called out. The driver was battered and bruised, his eye
was swelling, his tie was gone. "Christ," Herb said, "what
happened to you?"

"A fight, sir, to get into the driveway. I won."

Herb laughed gleefully. "Way to go!"

Herb's limo dropped Faye at her home at three in the
morning. Standing on the lighted porch, she reached through
the open front door for the hall light switch. The limo honked
softly and drove away. She waved and fumbled at the switch.
The light inside did not go on. The hallway seemed cold,

unwelcoming. A jolt of fear shot through her. Had someone cut the electricity? Should she go back to the street and use her car phone to call the police?

Ridiculous. She strained for calm and stepped inside. But she didn't shut the door. The porch light lit her way to the living room where she turned on a lamp. She went back to the hallway and tried the switch again.

"Burnt out," she muttered.

She felt like a jerk, imagining someone had cut the electricity. But she picked up the hall phone to make sure it was working.

She wanted to talk to Nadine about the voice at the Oscars, but it was only six A.M. in Washington. She went downstairs and flipped the hall switch at the landing. No light. It worked off the same switch as the upstairs hall light. She felt her way to her bedroom doorway. Had she locked the front door, put the chain on it? She went back upstairs. The front door was wide open. She secured it. She went to the front windows and locked each one, then through the kitchen to the back door. It was unlocked. Damn! So careless. She'd done that before. Her legs felt weak. She sank down at the kitchen table. The sharp, peculiar voice cut through the dense silence, "Lay off Della."

I will not let this run me, she thought. She turned out the lights and went downstairs.

Without the hall light, she was groping her way across her bedroom to the bed table lamp. A faint, reflected glow from the city below came through a tall window. Faye was reaching for the lamp when she realized all the scripts and magazines that usually took up one side of her bed were stacked on the floor by her feet.

She had not done that.

She glanced at the bed and felt her chest contract. She jumped away.

There was a man in her bed.

She tried to scream and could only croak. She backed out the door into the hallway, her heart thudding. Who was he? In the dim light from the doorway, the man looked like Gabe—dark hair, a long chiseled face. His eyes were closed.

She forced herself toward the bed and, shaking, leaned over the prostrate form. Beneath his chest, the covers sloped off in a funny, bumpy shape. Slowly, the sensation took root in her that he wasn't asleep. But she was reaching for the quilt and pulling it back. Her eyes traveled down his chest. At first, she refused to take it in. Then she recoiled.

Below his rib cage, his body cavity was open like a pocket. Inside . . . inside . . . what were those still objects inside him?

Dead pigeons.

He was stuffed with pigeons! Bumps and bumps of them, beaks and claws and wings, some pushed up inside the rib cage, some shoved down into his groin, some spilling out over his legs.

She vaulted away, slamming into the corner of her bureau with such force bottles flew from it, breaking. Faye pushed away for the door, hit the frame, socking an elbow against it, felt the impact but no pain, took the stairs two at a time, hanging on to the banister. She grabbed the phone, dropped it, tore open the front door and dashed for her car. Panting and shaking, she finally unlocked the door, reached for her car phone.

It wasn't there! Before the Oscars, she'd taken it inside. She dashed back into the house, clawed over surfaces, found it and fled to her car.

After locking all the car doors, she was trembling so hard she couldn't punch in a number. 911, 911, she finally punched in 911. After she'd gasped out her name and address and screamed "Body!" she leaned back against the seat, puffing. She willed herself to calm down. She didn't want to go through this alone. Rob was in Northern California. Phelps. She should call Phelps. She opened the glove compartment and started hunting for the card he'd given her. Everything fell out—car insurance, registration, matches, tissues. She'd never find the card. She dialed 911 again and left a message for him.

She waited in the car. She choked back nausea; the waves came again. She pushed open the car door and vomited in the street just as the headlights of her neighbor Boyd's car lit up the yard.

"My God," he drawled from his car window, "drunk *again*?" By remote, he rolled up his garage door and surged forward. The door slid shut behind him.

She rested against her seat, seeing the man who didn't belong in her bed.

She dialed Gabe. The phone rang and rang. "What?" he said, groggy.

"It's Faye. I need you."

Faye was sitting in the kitchen, listening to men's voices downstairs in her bedroom—Phelps, other officers, and Gabe. Sometime later, Gabe came into the kitchen. His face was pasty. He went to the sink, splashed water, and drank out of his hands.

"Who is it?" she asked.

"They don't know, maybe a derelict." He wiped his face with a tea towel, sat on a stool beside her, took her hand. But he could not erase the picture of the pigeons in their grisly nest. It was a terrible theater of intimidation.

"Ms. Ferray," Phelps said, coming into the kitchen, "the man's been dead a while. He didn't die here." He watched a shudder shoot through her body. "I'm not going to . . . fool you about anything—this is a serious threat. We'll be opening an investigation. Do you know anyone who would do this?"

"You mean, a disgruntled agent, an out-of-work actor?" She hadn't seen Phelps standing up before; he was almost as tall as Gabe.

"I'm not kidding," Phelps said. "Hollywood people *are* kinda unstable, they do crazy things. You see a lot of actors and such you don't know well—"

"Don't you get it? This is connected to Della!" she yelled at him, charging off the stool. "How dare you ask me about my coworkers? It's all linked to Della!" Gabe grabbed her. "Get him out of here," Faye snarled. "I want him out of my house!"

"Faye, c'mon, sit down here."

"I don't want to sit down!" She wrestled away from Gabe.

Phelps was looking at her thoughtfully. "You're right, Ms. Ferray," he said softly. "It may be connected to your friend— but I didn't want to alarm you."

"I'm plenty alarmed."

"You said something else happened tonight."

"I heard a voice in a crowd telling me to lay off Della. The same message as before, the same voice."

Phelps stroked his cheek. "Did you remember anything else your friend said?"

"Just what I told you—about warning Nadine in Washington. What was on the disk, or haven't you had time to play it yet?"

There was a long pause. "Our men haven't found a connection to your friend's murder."

"Bullshit!" Faye yelled. Phelps stared at her boldly; his look wasn't judgmental and he wasn't intimidated. "If there's no connection, why would Della have hidden it?" she demanded.

"Maybe she just forgot it, left it in that sweater."

"No, she left it for me."

"How about some protection?" Gabe broke in.

"I don't have enough men to assign, but I can suggest a security service."

"A body's left in my bed, split from its throat to its groin," Faye said, "and you can't free up a couple of men?"

"I'll see what I can do tomorrow," he replied remotely.

"Someone's after me!"

"Someone wants to *scare* you," Phelps said. "If they'd wanted to kill you, they would have."

"Now that *is* comforting," she said nastily.

"Ms. Ferray, get some security. Don't tell the world what happened here tonight—go about your business. Don't go charging off to Della's friends or associates, don't even talk about Della. Act like you've got the message. You 'lay off Della.' " He moved a hand across his mouth.

"That's it?" she asked, incredulous.

"There's not much anyone can do about a stalker," Phelps said. "Please cooperate with us. Whoever did this is worried about what you might remember."

Sam Pike was a light sleeper. He picked up the telephone on the first ring. "It's Gabe, Sam. I have some trouble." Sam listened carefully. "I mean," Gabe was saying, "a body with a load of dead pigeons stuffed into it, it's grotesque, it's mad."

"Tell me exactly what happened." When Gabe had told him, Sam said, "Serious."

"Here are the security guys the detective suggested," Gabe said, ticking off the names.

"Good, but this one's better." He searched in a small address book on the bed table, and read off a number. "You tell them I suggested you call. Are they putting a black and white on her at least?"

"He said someone would keep an eye on the house."

"You'd better, too. Don't underestimate the lunatics out there, Gabe. This one sounds dangerous."

THIRTEEN

FAYE DIDN'T HAVE to act like she had the message. She *was* scared. She went to her office the next day, but felt absent. Sleeping in the bed that had been host to the body revolted her, but she didn't want to unnerve Jerry and Coo by asking for refuge, so she moved into a hotel near her office. She took her assistant Steve into her confidence, and Rob, who was so appalled she had to restrain him from telling the world. She put him in touch with Phelps. She did not tell Annie. Trim, big security men with flat eyes were installed. "Don't be nervous," one of them said.

"I'm not nervous," she said. "I'm scared to death."

That first day, she called Nadine every hour. "She's still on the Hill," the woman said.

"This is extremely important," Faye repeated.

Faye's other line was ringing; outside, Steve picked it up. When Faye hung up, Steve rang her on the intercom. "That call was from Anthony Valdi," he said. "In charge of production for BeverCo. Says he wants to talk about *The Jungle Gym*."

Faye was thinking of the pigeons. The phone was ringing again. She picked it up. "Faye, it's Mark," he said.

"Mark?" She felt disconnected from everything that had

happened before Oscar night.

"Have I caught you at a bad time?" he asked.

She started to laugh. "A bad time?" Bad time now, for her, took on new meaning. "No, Mark, I—it's a great time."

"My staff's been filling me in on everything you've been doing for the fund-raiser. I'm grateful, Faye."

"Nada, Mark." Fund-raiser. What had she been doing on Herb's committee? She couldn't remember anything about it.

"Faye, my interview with the Hollywood Women's Political Committee is Friday night. I thought we could have dinner after the bear-baiting?"

"Irreverence about the HWPC will get you nowhere."

"Mixed with my respect. How about dinner?"

"No, I can't. Maybe some other time, Mark."

After they hung up, she sat at her desk, flipping a pencil back and forth between two fingers. "Steve! Call up a furniture store and get a new bed and bedding delivered to my place—it's full of security men, they won't have any trouble getting in."

"Yes, ma'am."

"I'm not going to live like a prisoner. I'm not going to be run out of my own house! Did Tony Valdi really say he wanted to discuss *Gym*?"

"Yes, ma'am."

"I think I went to college with him." She called Mark back. "You're on. Friday."

Nadine returned her call at three o'clock that afternoon. "I want you to go outside to a pay phone and call me from it," Faye said.

"W-what?"

"Please, just do it."

Nadine hung up. Faye waited. A half hour later, Nadine called. "All right, I'm in this phone booth," she said, cranky.

"Give me the number." Faye wrote it down. "I'll call you back."

"Faye! What are you—"

Faye hung up, went down the hall and out the front of her building into a brick courtyard. The guard kiosk divided the area between the busy street and the door of her building;

rows of cars were on either side. A phone booth perched at the corner of her building across from the kiosk. She called Nadine back.

"Everything's changed for me out here," Faye said to her. "Now, just listen." She told Nadine everything that had happened. "Don't you think it's possible our phones are tapped?"

"My God," Nadine said, shocked. "Yes, yes I do."

"Then we have to take precautions."

"Who—who was he?"

"They don't know. It was very gruesome, Nadine. Someone's afraid of what I heard from Della."

"Do you think there's more—to remember, I mean."

"Yes, I do. There is something," Faye said in a thin voice, going back to the moments after the explosion. "Something between the time she said to warn you and . . . and when the paramedics arrived. I haven't had that awful dream in a while. . . ."

"Faye, I can hardly hear you! Have you got security?"

"Yes."

"Do you want to come out here, stay with me?"

"No, I want to get back to a normal life. Nadine, we didn't take this seriously enough before, but believe me, I do now. And I don't want you in any danger. You *have* stopped looking into the stuff on the disk, haven't you?"

"Oh, yes," Nadine said. "You speak, I obey."

In Washington, Nadine replaced the telephone receiver. It was almost seven, getting dark and chilly. She left the phone booth and walked back the half block to her office. She would have to find other telephone arrangements; she couldn't keep running in and out of the OEOB.

Inside, the quiet was one of emptiness, not serenity. Her high heels echoed. The distant hum of a power printer and a ringing telephone sounded behind doors.

With Pamela's help, and through her own investigation, she'd discovered OPI had many subcontractors, and some of them were on Della's list. Subcontractors often dispersed parts of the work to "consultants." But so far, she hadn't found anything beyond the way the government normally did business *except* for the kinds of companies on Della's disk: they didn't seem to have the expertise managers of the OPI program would be looking for in subcontractors.

How much money was flowing out of the National Security Council through OPI to these subcontractors? How were they using that money? How could she get access to Harper's files? She caught herself: she'd leave that to Adrian.

Nadine was almost to her office when she heard the phone ringing. She hurried, hoping it was Rob back from Northern California. But when she snatched up the receiver, no one was there. She put down the telephone. Her hand was so damp it left a palm print on the receiver. The building suddenly seemed even emptier. Her lamp sent a skirt of warm light across her desk, splashing against the near wall.

Hastily, she gathered up all the papers connected to Della, shoved them into her briefcase, snapped off the light and left.

She drove home too fast in the rain, but once there, she felt better. She took all her papers into the kitchen and spread them out again on the table, looking first at the printout she'd made of Della's disk. Were all the company boards on the disk interlocked? How had the board members met? What interest did they share? She wondered if she dared call one of the subcontractors listed on the disk.

No, she thought, too risky. She began putting the papers back into her case, pausing at the printout of Della's list for which Pamela had supplied addresses and phone numbers. If she made one direct call, she didn't have to identify herself. Her desire to know how the other companies on Della's list were connected to OPI was overwhelming. She decided to risk it—and then she'd really quit, as she'd promised Faye.

She frowned at the telephone. Would her home phone be tapped? No, she didn't believe it. Faye was the person they wanted. She selected a company in the West where the business day was still going on.

"The Narwell Corporation," a woman's voice said.

"You're listed as a subcontractor to the Office of Public Information in Washington," Nadine tried. "Could I speak with the unit that handles that contract?"

"Huh?"

The conversation deteriorated. The receptionist had no idea what OPI was. Nadine finally rang off, then called another, and got the same response. Gee, she thought, if she called Northrup, they'd sure know which unit was handling the B-2 bomber. Della's list wasn't working; it didn't seem to have anything to do with OPI. Good, she thought. Or, the connection with OPI was so covert, no one on these levels knew anything about it.

"I'll stop after one more call," she said, out loud. She chose a New York outfit listed on Della's disk.

"Yeah? Citizens for Mock," a man's voice said.

"I was calling Eastern Media, Inc.," Nadine said.

"We're one unit of them, but they're closed. I'm the only person in the office. What can I do for you?"

"I wanted to inquire about a subcontract with OPI."

"Yeah? Is this Tawny?"

"Yes." Oh, God, she thought, Harper's secretary, deeper and deeper.

"How's every little thing, sweetheart?"

"Okay." Nadine didn't know what to say. "Ah, there's a minor hitch out here. I have a record of the transactions on April 4, 1990, and September 15, 1991, but we have no receipt of delivery—"

"Huh?"

"And no report on your progress on the project."

"Huh? I don't get it. We made the deposit through the consultant as always."

"But we have no record of it."

"It's in the bank. You don't get no record. What the hell's going on?"

"Oh, well, probably just clerical," Nadine said, switching gears, hearing the alarm in the man's voice. "How's the program going?"

"Program? Who *is* this?"

Nadine hung up. Her hand was shaking. She sat quietly in the bright kitchen, listening to the rain pounding outside.

FOURTEEN

ANTHONY VALDI WAS tall and hefty, with thick brown hair, a neatly trimmed beard, and a soft determined voice. His huge hand swallowed Faye's. "This is a real treat." His arm swept toward three white sofas circling a marble table.

BeverCo was a new and aggressively independent production team that had hit L.A. two years before with plenty of money to spend on action-adventure pictures.

"I hear you're working on the Drummond committee," he said. His smile was engaging.

In college, she'd thought Tony Valdi was kind of dumb, but at thirty-five he'd grown into himself, a man who seemed sunny and smart. He was pouring coffee from a silver pot into china cups. His movements were economical and precise.

"Faye, I'll get right to it. I'm crazy about *The Jungle Gym*."

Faye smiled distantly. "Gee, Tony, great. Dare I ask where you got a copy of the script?"

Tony stopped moving. "I thought you knew I had a copy."

"No."

He shifted, tugged at one of his cuffs. "I guess we have an irregular situation here, but let's put that aside for a minute. No one's trying to put anything over on anyone; it came in here and I read it and I loved it. I want to start off with you from a position of goodwill. I'm not a stranger, right? Our people know each other, right? Now, I know BeverCo's been doing some real main-fare pictures, *good* adventure flicks, and we always make a profit, though our quality, as far as you and I're concerned, might leave something to be desired."

He paused and smiled engagingly. "Faye, I've been brought into BeverCo with orders to upgrade the product. We like *Jungle Gym*. We believe in its moral and critical values. I want you to give us a chance to show what we can do because we got a lot to offer and we can pay a first-class tab, too."

There was another shoe about to drop. She could feel it. "I'm glad you like it, Tony, but the only way I'd do it is on location in Washington—"

"Right," he said amiably. "It needs the vistas, the sense of really being there."

"And there's a lot of interior set construction, plus tank work. Expensive."

"No problem." He nodded pleasantly. "You can't talk me out of this."

"And there's the abortion scene."

"It's well handled," he said. "It doesn't say abortion's right or wrong."

Faye stared at him. "And the crack sale."

"Gee, I don't recall that scene, but—hey! done all the time."

"Final cut."

"Of course, expected." He smiled again. "I know you think I'm putting you on."

He wasn't acting like any exec she knew. "Are we talking a TV movie?"

"Oh, no. Feature all the way. See, over here we're planning a whole range of films. Now, I'm looking for the creative people we want to hook up with. I've always admired your work, and Gabe's, too, natch. *Gym* really turns me on. Faye, I want to see this picture's made with that touch, that honesty you have, and that humor, too." He sipped his coffee.

"We do have some casting ideas. We think it needs a surprise in the lead, someone you don't expect, but someone who can carry it, too." Tony stirred, a mountain shifting from deep internal tremors. Then he smiled broadly. "We're seeing Annie in that role."

The other shoe. "Annie?"

Tony was nodding happily. "Yes, yes. Surprised you, huh?"

"I guess I know who gave you the script."

"Let me explain our position because I want you and me playing on the same team. You're on my short list of producers we'd like to work with. We've been looking for something to do with Annie, and I put it together in my mind—presto."

"Annie's a terrific actress, but she's not right for this role—it's cooler, more cerebral. Annie's not complicated, she's right out front like Bette Midler."

"I like casting against the grain," he said loudly. "Just think about her with the right costar, the right director!"

"Look, Tony, I'm not here to run down my sister, but Annie? I'm not even sure she could pull off the part."

Tony tented his big hands. "I'm afraid Annie's a nonnegotiable element."

"What?"

"There's a lot of support here for *The Jungle Gym*, Faye. We want to make it with you. It'll be your production outta our shop. We'll line up major distribution—I'd like to give Herb Yount first crack at it."

"Herb's already passed, and I can't see how he'd ever go for Annie in the lead. But I can see some ways the script could be changed for her. How about the 'Congressman Joe' role, do you have someone in mind?"

"No. Everything else is entirely up to you."

"Everything?"

"Everything." Their eyes locked. "Casting Annie does change the role but it also makes it exciting, a bold, energetic, earthy heroine who speaks her mind and isn't afraid to throw her weight around, and who still has that come-hither look in her eye. Personally, when Annie mentioned you were trying to mount the film, I was absolutely delighted, because I couldn't think of anything better than for you to make a great film with Annie with a wonderful costar, wonderful director. Annie broke a few rules, but all in her enthusiasm for the picture. She really wants to work with you. *Please* think it over."

Faye put down her cup. "I will, Tony," she said, rising.

"That's the spirit," he said genially. Getting to his feet, he walked around the low table between them and took both her hands. "I've always admired your work, Faye, sort of worshiped you from afar, I guess." He dropped her hands. "I really want this movie to happen."

It was the moneyman's pledge to the creative toiler in the vineyard. There were more sophisticated execs, but Tony Valdi brought it off better than most.

BeverCo's offices were on Sunset Boulevard, a wonderful junk heap of buildings, rich and tawdry, faddish and fun. The traffic never stopped and at this hour, eleven o'clock, it was jammed, a four-lane grillework grin of BMWs and Ford Broncos and Jags. There was no horizon except the buildings jumping up the hill across the street.

As soon as she was in her car, Faye was right back in her own precarious reality: Oscar night, the body, fear and nerves. Trailed by a bodyguard, she pulled out of the parking lot, joined the throng, skated through a hole in the traffic and came to a stop at a light. She felt cut off from herself, as if she'd just seen a scene on TV between Tony and some woman who resembled her.

Everything seemed unreal: she had a sudden "go" on the film to which everyone else had said "stop." Instead of being furious that Annie had shopped her script, she found it struck her as funny—but strange, too. What in Annie's experience would have made her think of Tony and BeverCo?

She checked her rearview mirror—had she seen that blue BMW before? Was she being followed? Was her new bodyguard there? She was watching the traffic behind her so intently she almost hit a pedestrian on Horne Street.

She wilted over the steering wheel, shaking and sweating as the woman shouted at her, also frightened. People behind her honked; she drove on. Since the Oscars, Phelps's investigation had been unable even to ID the body. She was doing what Phelps had said, but her inaction and her confusion frightened her. It was only in meetings with other people that she could forget for a while. The horrid dreams had returned, saturating her nights.

That evening, Faye reread the script of *The Jungle Gym* and tried to picture Annie playing the role of Celia. It *was* interesting casting. But could Annie, who had only done television, carry a film? More important, would she behave or would she create difficulties during filming? By breakfast, Faye could see how *Gym* might be changed for Annie. By noon, she was beginning to see Annie as creative casting.

Herb Yount called. She went to see him and was once again reminded that principal casting was the real use of power in film.

"Have I got a surprise for you," Herb said, steering her to a sofa. "You know how crazy this business is, we all have to be flexible, keep our eye on what's important, right? Guess who's read *The Jungle Gym* and loves it? Roger Reynolds!"

"Reynolds?" She'd never hoped for a star of Roger's caliber or reputation in the picture, nor had she ever made a film with a star whose name was right up there with Sean Connery's or Kevin Costner's. Roger was stratospheric.

"He wants to play the congressman!" Herb shouted. "Think of the box office."

She was. Her films made money, but Roger's name sold a picture to the world. This news was career-changing, this was a move to another level of moviemaking—the big time. She began laughing. "I guess *The Jungle Gym*'s a good picture now."

"I always liked it, Faye." Herb started pacing his carpet. "Roger's good casting for Congressman Joe, he's got just that right amount of nerve and idealism—"

"Character," said a voice that sounded like hers.

"Right! A tough sweetness. Bite. He's got bite. He *is* Congressman Joe! And you know what's really great? He's always wanted to play a member of Congress! See? When these things fall into place, they fit big! You can handle him. Sure, he's got his perks and retinue and his attitude. But, hey, the work comes out terrific on the screen!"

Faye was so excited she could barely speak. "Dare I ask about scheduling?"

"He's got room if you start right away. I've spoken to Tony—he sent the script over. He loves Roger."

"The world loves Roger."

" 'Course, Roger won't do it unless Gabe directs."

"Gabe?" She was stunned. "Gabe?"

"They're pals, *you* know. What's the diff? You can work with Gabe. Can't you?" he added, irritated.

"Yes, yes, Herb. I can work with Gabe."

Faye returned to her office, spinning.

Gabe was standing beside Steve's desk in her outer office. "What are you doing here?" she asked.

"Just wanted to know how things are going for you."

Steve was holding a life-sized tarantula. "Lots of calls, Faye," Steve said, putting down the big rubber spider.

Faye went into her office. Gabe followed her. He shut the door behind him. "Got time for dinner?" His eyes smiled. He'd styled his hair so it curled below his ears; he wore a white shirt, dark jeans, and cowboy boots.

"Can't today, Gabe."

"Are you okay? Are you taking Phelps's advice?"

"Yes. I'm not talking to anyone about Della. I'm keeping my head down. Phelps calls daily. Gabe, I really appreciate all you've done. The security guys are great. I thank you."

"You moving back into your house soon?"

"Thought I'd give it a try tonight."

He nodded, glanced at the painting of the Royal Rosarian, at the sly, knowing glint in the man's face, shaded by his ludicrous umbrella. "Are you doing some work for Drummond's campaign?"

"We've spoken about it."

He nodded, put his hands in his jeans pockets. "He was always fond of you. How's that wetlands bill? Is he behind it?"

"As far as I know, Gabe," she said softly.

"Faye, a while ago I trashed *The Jungle Gym* and I'm sorry. I didn't mean to do that. Any project you're interested in has got to be good, and I—I spoke out of turn. It's been bothering me."

Faye tried to hold in the impulse to laugh, but she couldn't.

"What's funny?" he asked.

"Because—well, everything's so cuckoo. Someone puts a body in my bed and things I once found funny now seem scary and things that used to upset me seem funny." She put her briefcase down on her desk. "You really move fast!"

"What do you mean?"

"How'd you know about the deal?"

"Deal?"

"Tony Valdi! Herb Yount! The deal!"

"I don't know anything about any deal."

"Tell me another." She leaned against her desk and folded her arms. "And I suppose you haven't spoken to Annie."

"No, not since the Oscars." Gabe touched his mustache and shifted his lanky frame uncomfortably. "I mean it."

She weighed what she knew of Gabe against what she felt at the moment. "Okay, you didn't hear about it." She lifted her chin; one wing of her hair trailed across her cheek.

"So you have a deal?" She nodded. "Why aren't you glad?"

Because you and Annie are elements, she thought. She shrugged and moved around her desk. "Life's different now, bodyguards, everything."

"But you're moving forward. Right?" She nodded. "Are you going to take the offer?"

"I'm thinking it over."

"Work will be good for you. I'm happy for you, Faye."

In that moment, she knew that he really hadn't known anything about BeverCo, Herb, Roger, or the deal.

"I brought you some protection," Gabe said, opening the door. "Okay, Steve."

Steve came into the room carrying a small dog. He handed it to Gabe. Gabe handed it to Faye. She couldn't remember when she'd last held a dog. She put it down.

"Is this your idea of a guard dog?" she asked.

Gabe laughed. "Maybe more of a companion."

Keith's foundling was about fifteen inches high with slender black legs, a tan spot over one eye, perky ears, a busy tail.

Steve was snapping his fingers at the dog. "What kind is it?" he asked.

"Who knows?" Gabe said. "Do you like it, Faye?"

"Gabe, where the hell is your head? I'm not a big animal person."

"It might bring out a different side of you."

"She looks like one of those dogs in the circus," Steve said, "the ones that run around on their hind legs and wear cute hats."

"God, a hat!" Gabe said. "I shoulda thought of that!"

"Where'd you get it?" Steve asked.

"Bought it off an abusive owner."

"Gabe, what am I going to do with a dog?" she said, laughing.

"Dogs can go anywhere," he said offhandedly. "I've spent some time on this dog, she's housebroken, she's been to dog school—she's trained to walk three paces behind you. Sit," he commanded. Instantly, the dog sat down and watched Gabe. "Okay!" The dog went over to him, wagging its tail. He patted its sleek little head. "She's smart, Faye."

"Gee, why not a rottweiler?"

"This one has a big bark."

"Well, I'm touched," she said. Gabe looked up at her skeptically. "No, I really am."

Gabe started to the door. "Good luck on the picture," he said. "Remember, I'm on your side, Faye." He left.

Faye thumped her anklebone against the leg of her desk chair. Cursing, she fell into it.

"Ten minutes," Steve said.

"Or what? We die?"

"The meeting with the people about Drummond's fundraiser."

Faye put one hand to her head. "Lord." The dog barked. She sounded like a toy. "Big bark," Faye muttered, "who's he kidding? Steve, you have to take this dog."

"No, no." He waved his arms, backing out of the room. "No, no."

In Washington, the file bound in red lay open on Leo's desk. He was reviewing the latest security telephone transcripts on Nadine Ferray. The code on the top page indicated the date and time of the call under surveillance, the location of the caller, the location of the receiver of the call, the date and time of the transcription, the names of the parties under surveillance.

The pages resembled a script. The calls covered all of Nadine Stern Ferray's calls, which dealt mainly with the routine of her daily life. The transcriptions were precise. Leo opened the manila envelope he'd just received. Embedded in a batch of calls was one from Faye Adair Ferray.

FAF: "Nadine, I want you to go outside to a pay phone and call me from it."

NSF: "What?"

FAF: "Please, just do it."

"Shit," Leo said. "They're on to the taps." He'd have to tap nearby phone booths. "Shit," he said again.

But the next transcription showed Nadine had used her home phone that same night at 19:12.

NSF: I wanted to inquire about a subcontract with OPI.

Citizens for Mock: Yeah? Is this Tawny?

NSF: Yes.

Mock: How's every little thing, sweetheart?

Leo clamped his jaw together. Then he quickly scanned the call.

NSF: . . . there's a minor hitch out here. I have a record of the transactions on April 4, 1990, and September 15, 1991, but we have no receipt of delivery . . . no report on your progress on the project.

Mock: Huh? I don't get it. We made the deposit through the consultant as always . . .

Leo slapped the transcription down on his desk. He was sitting erect in his chair, his arms bent at the elbows, resting on the desktop. He stayed like that for a full minute.

FIFTEEN

CARL REEVES WAS the bodyguard Faye liked best. He was a big man with red hair and warm brown eyes. As Mark Drummond's driver pulled up in front of Faye's house, Carl climbed out of his car.

"It's okay, Carl," Faye said from her car as she drove up behind Mark. "He's a friend. We'll be going to dinner shortly."

Up close, Carl recognized Senator Drummond. Faye parked her car in front and slammed the door. From inside, the dog barked and scratched on the window. Faye opened the door; the dog bounded out.

"I love dogs," Mark said. "New friend?"

"Temporarily."

Carl smiled at the dog.

"What's with the security?" Mark asked as she unlocked her front door.

"The police think some nut's connected to Della's murder. My mom and dad insisted." That was what she was telling everyone.

Inside, her house didn't feel like home anymore. Faye put the dog down. Mark strode around the living room, filling it. He loosened his tie. He was going through the motions of relaxing, but he was tense. So was she. Her house was strange to her. So was Mark.

"How do you think it went?" he asked about the Hollywood Women's Political meeting they'd just attended.

"It went well." The dog was trotting around sniffing the furniture. Faye felt like inspecting everything, too. "I mean, everyone knows you're not part of the old Hollywood left, more in the center. But you seemed different, Mark."

"We all are." He shrugged. "But how do you mean?"

How *did* she mean that? For days, she'd felt disassociated from her brains. During the meeting that night, she'd again slipped away from her fears and the odd sense of living a double life, shut it all away in a corner of herself. Now, back home, the mutilated corpse was still lying downstairs. She forced herself to speak. "Being in the Senate separates you from the rest of us, the way we live."

"You think your friends tonight know the way the rest of the country lives? Do you?"

"The people we saw tonight are trying to use the power they *do* have for good."

"So am I."

"Mark, I'm not faulting your motives."

"Thank you."

She was moving around the room without purpose. "I fault the institution."

"Congress? Oh, Faye, you have no idea what it takes to govern this country, the compromises we all must make, the views that have to be accommodated, the contesting needs, the thicket of special interests—all coming from *citizens,* people who really believe the right to abortion is murder, that prayer in the schools is right, that guns are as much a part of our heritage as the Constitution, that jet bombers create jobs . . ." He shook his big head. "I don't want to talk about the Senate." He folded his arms over his chest. "I want to talk about you. I'm thinking of you a great deal."

"Mark, so much has happened since Della died, I haven't stopped to find out how I feel about so many things . . ." What did she feel about him, about them together? "I think— adultery is deceitful. Let's not start something."

"It's already begun."

"Then let's just cool off."

"I can't."

"There must be real trouble in your marriage."

"Was there trouble in yours?"

"Yes. Only I didn't know it. I spent that last year working, not seeing."

"I'm not Gabe, you're not Tot," he said. "Yes, there is trouble—my wife and I are virtually separated. She lives here and she'll be with me at important functions during the campaign, but I live in Washington, alone."

"No divorce, though."

"Probably not." He moved across the room, stood in front of her. "Do you think I'm toying with you? I'm not. Do you think I do this often? No, never." His eyes settled on her. "I can't stop thinking about you," he said softly. "Every time I look up, I see your face. I'd like to get back to the kind of focus I had before we—"

"—fucked on the floor of your office."

He put his hands on her shoulders. "You can't push me away. I want to stop thinking about you, but I can't. I've never been a passionate man, except about issues, helping people, until now." His shy glance seemed honest, and it hit her hard.

"Would you like a drink?"

"Just some soda water. Then we can go somewhere quiet, have a little dinner."

He followed her into the kitchen. "How's your dad?" he asked.

"Better, amazingly enough." She dropped ice into his glass, poured in some soda, and poured herself a glass of red wine. "Rob saw him a couple of days ago . . ." For an instant, she let in some of the panic she'd felt when she'd last been in this house. She pushed it away.

In the living room, a silence widened between them. In it, she felt a craving for honesty. Maybe she could ride that back into the life she'd once had.

"I think I'm in real danger," she said.

Mark put down his glass.

"In danger of losing my feelings to the thought police," she said, "of letting what happened with Gabe and Tot ruin me. I didn't realize until Gabe came back how much I'd let what happened run me, how bitter I was. When Della was killed, it was like something was sheared away, separating me from what was past. I began measuring everything from that day with her: everything before was like a mirage life. Everything after was real, and now . . ." She imagined the bedroom below and the body in the bed with its hideous stuffing. Each shock cut away another part of her past.

The dog jumped into her lap. "Yikes!" Faye yelled, surprised. The dog leaped away, sat down, staring at her.

Faye leaned forward. "That time in your office, Mark, that wasn't like me."

"Me, neither."

"Yet, here you are in my life." She remembered riding down in the elevator from his office and seeing herself from a distance as if she were watching someone else. "You've brought a lot of feelings to the surface that I've tried to forget. They weren't gone, merely submerged. Rob says I'm rash. I'm trying not to be." She felt edgy, not confident.

"There are times when emotions can't be controlled," he said. He touched her hand. "You're so lonely. Just you and your principles." He put his big arm around her. She leaned against his shoulder. "I'm lonely, too. I didn't feel it until that night with you in my office. Maybe you lost track of yourself for a while. I did. It's easy to do." He rubbed his knuckles against her cheek, a joke caress.

She was facing away from him. "There are things I can't handle . . . but, oh, I can feel how much I need you."

She turned and rested her head against his shoulder. She touched his hair, feeling again the surprising, jolting intimacy. He locked her against him, then lifted her head and pressed his lips hard against hers, bending her body.

A few minutes later, downstairs, she stood in the doorway, looking at the new bed. Mark said, "Would you prefer to go out, have dinner?" She shook her head. The dog stepped warily into the room.

Faye began unbuttoning her blouse. Mark was taking off his shirt. She sat on the edge of the bed, feeling hungry for protection and affection. But those needs couldn't blot out what had happened in the room.

"What's the matter?" he asked.

"I can't make love in here," she said.

Mark's driver picked up a five-course Japanese dinner and drove them to a little house in Brentwood. "This was the first house I ever owned," he said. "I use it when I'm in town, but Laura prefers to stay up north—in the place we had when I was teaching."

Faye's mood changed. They laughed and ate. Outside the doors, sunlamps bounced warm rays off a small enclosed pool. The air was steamy, comforting. They played in the water like children. His arms around her, she scooped water in his face and plunged away. He grabbed her leg, his hand slipping down to her ankle. She flipped around, but he wouldn't let go. He was underwater, hanging on to her. She tried to shake him off. He popped up beside her, water streaming from his hair, beading in his lashes. She embraced him, climbed up his body, water flowing across her freely, touching the planes and creases of her body, a lavish release. She flung herself on her back, he dove beneath her and came up the other side. She perched on his hips, half in, half out of the gleaming water. Standing, he clasped her tightly; his lips trembled. His eyes warmed her. He began walking deeper into the pool, and she rode him until they were in the deepest end, connected, sinking, and flattening out, rising. The water blazed; she felt secure.

Mark Drummond had no idea when it ended. He was beside her on a bed, her head resting sweetly on his bare shoulder. "I want to go home soon," she said. Neither of them moved. Later she said, "Tell me you don't love me."

He drew her closer. "Be quiet, Faye." He felt utterly safe with her.

Faye was so tired and sleepy when the car took her home, she was getting into her new bed before realizing it was in that room of the body, the violated room. Turning on a lamp, she saw the little dog sitting at the foot of the bed. She wondered whether to encourage that, but was glad the dog was there.

*   *   *

"Della? Della? Talk to me! I know you're here." Faye was swimming in the warm lake again, breathing water. She floated to the surface; mist eclipsed the shore. She swam on, trying to see into the dark water.

The swollen, ghostly shape thrust up right in front of her. Its front did not seem as solid as the arching, rising rear of it. The part Faye faced was separating and swaying. Terrified, she clawed at the water, trying to reach the surface, but the immense figure rose with her. Then, she recognized it.

The thing was a giant nautilus. Protruding from the front of its bulging spiral shell, tentacles as thick as trees whipped through the water, reaching for her.

Faye was sitting up in bed screaming. The panicky dog was dashing around the room, barking.

Slowly, the nautilus receded, moving away, its undulating tentacles vanishing into the air and the walls. Trembling, Faye sank back against the pillows. The dog jumped back on the bed, whining. Faye's harsh breathing gradually subsided. A nautilus. The only nautilus she could remember was the submarine from Jules Verne's *Twenty Thousand Leagues Under the Sea*. But this dream was not about any submarine.

She turned on the lamp and went to the bookshelf where she kept a tattered paperback encyclopedia. She doubted nautilus would be described, but it was. A nautilus was a sea creature with a coiled spiral shell. As it grew, it secreted larger shell chambers, sealing off the older, smaller ones like secrets, living in the newest addition until it, too, was outgrown and a new one produced. At its front end, around its mouth, were scores of tentacles that captured prey and stuffed the meal inside. The thing lived in very deep waters. It was a carnivore.

Oh, God. She lay back on the bed, controlling her breathing. Finally, she turned out the light.

The dog cocked its head and ears toward the bedroom door. Faye heard it, too—a strange uneven noise from upstairs.

The dog growled, a weirdly deep sound for such a tiny body. The intermittent sound went on. Faye got up, frightened. The dog skittered off the bed and stalked stiff-legged toward the door, still growling ominously. Faye crept to the foot of the stairs and looked up. Deep dark filled the stairwell. She heard the unnerving sound again.

A slow step at a time, she went up.

The dog trotted before her, cutting across the living room, stopping beside a small four-paned window near the back door in the kitchen. Faye turned on the light. The dog rose on its back legs, trying to reach its front paws onto the windowsill.

A brilliant yellow canary was trapped between the torn screen and the pane.

When Faye opened the window and reached for it, the bird fluttered frantically, battering itself against the screen.

"Selections," Della had said. She was in the car, murmuring, her eyes staring. The tenor's voice was sailing across the intersection. *"Tia . . ."* Della had said. "What about 'tia'?" Faye had asked. Della had sputtered, *"Bigger . . . bigger than I said."*

What else had she said about "tia" or "selections"? Faye forced herself back to Della's dying, trying to remember, trying to hear.

"Tia," Faye said out loud to the dog. "Selections."

The canary flew up, opening a wing, then fell back onto the sill.

SIXTEEN

SINCE CHILDHOOD, FAYE and Rob had held "sessions." They began the Christmas they were nine and ten while Jerry and Coo were on location, making a musical about farming in Iowa. Without any help from their housekeeper, whom they disliked, Rob and Faye wrote letters to Santa and made a list of what to give their parents. Part of the fun had been talking about Annie's gift while she'd sat beside them, age two, not understanding a word. When they were older, they'd expanded the sessions to discuss problems or to make pacts. Annie was never quite a full member, being only ten when Faye and Rob were in their late teens.

Faye called a session. *The Jungle Gym* was a fact, but Faye didn't want Annie to know that until she got some assurances from her. If Annie went into production feeling she'd made it happen by herself, she'd be impossible to work with. Rob would be Faye's witness.

Mark Drummond had won the California primary and was pitted against Sparks, which brought Rob into town for strategy meetings. He met Faye and Annie at Harry's Bar near Mark's Century City offices. They sat in the back room in a corner banquette.

Rob was laughing. "Isn't it ironic, Faye, that now people are trying to talk you into doing this film when only a while ago *you* were trying to talk *them* into it?"

"Really," Faye said, glancing again at one of her bodyguards, sitting at the bar. They had become part of her life.

"I thought I was helping!" Annie said. "I just met Tony at the Oscars. He read it practically overnight."

"Annie," Rob said, a warning. The only rule in a session was to speak honestly, without acrimony. Annie often ignored rules.

"You do not send my projects around," Faye said.

"But they want to work with me. And I love that film."

"It's my film, not 'that' film, and it's just as likely that BeverCo wants to work with me. What I need to know from you is why you took it to Tony."

"My agent knows him," Annie said, mixing truth with fiction to cover Sam's role.

Faye couldn't tell when Annie was telling the truth, when she was lying, or when she was playing dumb.

"I didn't mean to do anything wrong." Annie fiddled with a corner of her turquoise scarf.

"Annie, you submitted a property that wasn't yours to submit."

"That script's *been* all over town. And they want *me* in your movie. I'm thrilled! Aren't you? Don't you want good things for me anymore?"

"Of course I do," Faye said.

"You can't stand not being in the driver's seat, that's it, isn't it? Well, right now, I'm in the driver's seat."

"Oh, Annie, this isn't good," Rob said.

"You think you're better than I am," Annie said to Faye, "but I put this deal together. I've *saved* your film!"

Faye rubbed her forehead with her fingertips, struggling to find a way to take the deal and feel comfortable with Annie in it. I should have let my lawyer handle this, she thought.

"This is such a hot potato," Faye said, "and I don't want it to come between us, Annie. You and I used to be close. I'd like to feel that way again, but this film might not help that. Rob, you understand."

"Don't you *want* to work with me?" Annie cried out.

Ah, there it was. Faye sighed. But she didn't duck. "Annie, one of the reasons you've had difficulty getting more offers is your professional attitude."

"Well, I have a passionate nature!" she drawled, tossing her scarf over her shoulder.

"That's not all. You like confrontations. You battle cameramen, directors, hairdressers. But on *my* production, I won't stand for any of that."

"You just don't want me to have this role," Annie growled, looking slit-eyed at her, abandoning all childish pretense.

"Not so. But I do want to find a good way to work with you," Faye said, weighing her tangled feelings about Annie.

"Faye, please do it with me," Annie said softly, her eyes pleading. "It won't hurt you and it'll help me a lot. I promise I'll be on time, I won't argue, I'll follow direction. You'll be proud of me."

"Rob, you're my witness," Faye said. She could feel herself believing Annie—a dangerous feeling.

After Faye left, Annie threw herself into Rob's arms for a hug. "She's going to do it, Rob, I can feel it."

Although Rob was fond of Annie, he had no illusions about her tyrannical side. "If she does, she might wake up in the middle of the night and curse you."

Annie pouted and her cheeks sagged prettily. "No, Robbie. She knows she owes me."

"How come?" he asked, taken aback.

"Because we all ought to stick together," she said brightly, "that's how come." But she knew her most promising currency would be guilt and hope: Faye hoped they could be close again and felt guilty that they weren't.

Rob chewed his lip. "Annie, how did this all come about— you getting this outfit so wild to do this film?"

Annie relished story-telling. She sailed into an account of the Oscars, set the stage for Sam Pike's introduction of Tony Valdi, his interest in working with her, about sending the script to him. "See, Robbie, what's different is that I'm taking charge of my own life. And I made it possible for Faye to get her financing." She grinned at him.

"You're jealous of her."

"I'm not." The pout again.

"Don't you dare go into this to humble Faye."

"I wouldn't do that! Besides, she doesn't humble."

"Okay, but . . . wow, I have to catch a plane." He jumped to his feet. "Don't you press Faye, sister, this is no game."

Annie was amazed and injured. "Wouldn't dream of it, Robbie. Everything's up to her from here on."

Rob did not have to catch a plane for hours.

He drove east on Santa Monica Boulevard, heading to the recently opened Royale Hotel in Beverly Hills. Leo and Claire were in town and Leo was tied up in meetings.

In the car, he began thinking about Sam Pike. Why would he be so interested in helping Annie get a part? He had a reputation for professional generosity, but helping Annie's career seemed like a real wild card. Was Sam sleeping with Annie? Rob tromped on the brake at a stop sign as he imagined Sam Pike, twice Annie's age, climbing over his zaftig sister. He shut down that image, and accelerated. Whatever was going on, the result was Faye had a deal.

He skipped to other thoughts: he had meetings with the campaign's media handlers, who chattered about sound bites, constituencies, and electronic democracy; with the primary over, the summer would roll into the campaign corridor, and Rob would be setting the stage for positive TV coverage. Bad luck Mark wasn't on the Judiciary Committee, because July or August would bring Judge Stern's confirmation hearings for the Supreme Court. *Those* senators would be on the tube every day, all day, on C-Span.

Rob stayed out of the campaign's back-room machinations, which always involved bargains, compromises, blackmail, and tides of money it was best not to know about. Smokey and his guys dealt with all that. Rob kept the candidate's face in front of the audience and helped put the words into his mouth. Which wasn't at all hard—Mark was a natural; reporters liked him, cameras liked him, voters liked him.

Still thinking about his father-in-law, Rob cut through the giant intersection of Santa Monica and Wilshire. Not in all the years he'd known the Sterns had Buck once taken Nadine's part against Helena, nor had he ever seen Buck actually take a stand in an argument. He spoke in generalities, floating above obstacles, telling anecdotes. Buck seemed to remember the most obscure facts—legal cites, a subparagraph in some film deal, old jokes, old political contests. He had no idea what Buck stood for beyond his unswerving allegiance to America's free enterprise system. Rob couldn't imagine growing up with a father like that.

As his thoughts returned to Sam Pike, Rob was pulling into the Royale Hotel valet parking stand. There was something shifty about the man. Maybe Sam wasn't helping Annie, only going through Annie to help Faye without her being aware of it. He was doing it for Gabe! Now *that* would be like Sam Pike.

Feeling better, Rob got out of his car jauntily, tossing his keys to the valet, anticipating Claire.

Faye was driving west to meet Gabe for dinner and to ask him formally to direct her picture. With Roger in it, he'd need no convincing. She was the only one who needed convincing. She passed up the valet and pulled into a lot half a block from the restaurant on Santa Monica Boulevard. Walking back, trailed by her bodyguard, she ticked off all the other kinds of work she could have chosen. Jazz dancer led the list, lawyer next. She could have married that nice guy in college, what's-his-name; today, she'd be a mother living in Encino.

She was at the door of the restaurant, late; Gabe, always on time, would be inside. She had not really thought about what it'd be like doing the picture with him, day in, day out. She spun away from the door, and started up the block.

"What's up?" asked Carl, the bodyguard.

"Just a walk, Carl." *The Jungle Gym* was the biggest picture she'd ever started and the prospect of producing it thrilled her. This was a story for Della, the only thing Faye could do for her. No matter how tough things got during the shoot, Della and the secret meaning of the film would sustain her. *Keep your eye on the ball*, she ordered herself. So what if Gabe's directing? She could put up with him—and with Annie. Della was at the core of *Gym*. The movie was going to have a big car explosion, too.

She turned around and went into the restaurant.

*   *   *

"I just have a different vision of the script, Faye. You asked for my opinion and I say emphasize the comedy."

God, she thought, *preserve me from the director's vision.* "There isn't a lot of comedy in *Gym,* Gabe."

Gabe and Faye were well into their blue-corn tamales and shrimp appetizers.

"But it is a bit wacky in spots. Those could be heightened."

"A movie's very delicate," she said. "We start screwing with this script, we'll lose the baseline ideals. We'd be doing something dishonest with it. Audiences have to feel we're being honest with them."

"Yeah, yeah, I've heard that creed before. 'It's easier to make truthful movies.' ".

"Can you really see Annie in the Celia role?" Faye asked.

"Well, she changes it some, but in an odd way, it's really interesting casting—*if* she'll follow direction and *if* she really wants to do it."

"Oh, she wants it, all right, but the director will have to keep her in line." Faye nibbled at a tamale. "I'm afraid of working with Annie."

"Well, now we're down to it."

"What punishing God stuck me with a such a talented and temperamental sister?"

"Ah, you both are."

"See, I'm scared Annie and I will end up total enemies."

"Maybe you already are."

"Not yet, but I'd like us to remain . . . at least decent to each other."

"If Annie's sufficiently inspired during the shoot, she'll behave."

"Gabe, Annie initiated this deal in a backhanded sort of way. She believes *she* made it all happen."

"So, let her. You know it's your picture. And I do, too. Who wants Annie so much anyway?"

"BeverCo."

"No room to move around?"

"None."

He stroked his index finger under the edge of his mustache.

"Must be a hell of a deal or you wouldn't touch it. What's going on?" He sipped his beer.

"I want you to direct."

He put down his glass. His long face brightened and he laughed. "C'mon, Faye, *you* don't want me. Who does?"

"Herb."

"Well, I'm good, but I'm not box office. Who else?"

"Roger Reynolds."

Gabe whooped. "I'll be damned. You got a big picture here! Is Roger available?"

"Yes."

"Geez, a movie with Annie and me and Roger. You get to work with everyone you want to avoid."

"I don't want to avoid Roger!"

"How do you feel about working with me?"

"Great, how do you think I feel?"

"Pressured."

"A little, but I know what's important here." She wanted to put new people in her life, not step back into the old rut, but inside her new feelings for Mark she'd begun to find leniency toward Gabe. Or maybe it was the corpse in her bed and Gabe's speedy response to her call that night. "We could make this film, Gabe, I mean, if it was like the old days, we'd be crazy about this picture, we'd be up late, thinking up ideas, and planning and—well, what else are you doing?"

"What's going on with you?" Gabe asked. "Has anything else happened?"

"No, nothing."

"How about Phelps—has he got anything yet?"

"The man's been identified. Some homeless soul from Texas."

He tabled all the questions he had about the picture. Something was different about her. It wasn't the fright she'd had, or Della before that, and it wasn't the prospect of a film, or her tension. There was something deeper. Seeing her like this was almost like getting to know a new person, someone who reminded him of a woman he'd known a long time ago, but who wasn't quite like her. The skin was stretched tight around her wide mouth and over the bridge of her nose. Her thick hair fell around her face, making her look pale. "Are you getting enough sleep?"

Her hand fluttered, a dismissal. She saw the nautilus hovering in the gray water. "No, I'm okay."

"Well," he said, not entirely satisfied, "what's the budget?"

"B.R.—before Roger—it was about twenty-four. How do you feel about working with me?"

He was about to lie. "Doable. The idea of shooting with Roger in Washington's a real turn-on. And Annie and Roger—that might be some combo." Gabe saw her try to smile, one of those public smiles Faye never quite got the hang of. "If you can't do this comfortably with me," he said, "you ought to get another deal, Faye."

"I can do it."

Gabe was frowning at what was left of his blue-corn tamales. He plucked one from the plate with his fingers and ate it, keeping his eyes on her. "I saw Mark Drummond at a dinner the other night. He asked how you were doing, sang your praises, seemed almost indiscreet." Faye's pale skin couldn't hide a blush. She's sleeping with Mark, he thought, that's one thing that's different about her.

Gabe looked around for a waiter. "Mark's so full of himself. He stands there listening to people—and he's really hearing them—but it's just a way to feel important." He was avoiding her eyes. "You want dinner?" he asked her.

"No." She sipped her wine. "I feel I'm losing control of the picture even before it begins."

"Why?"

She lifted her shoulders with a vague acceptance quite unlike her. "Fate. This picture is fate. But I'm going to make it the best way I know how even if it means working with you and Annie! Are you on board? Are we, as Herb says, singing off the same page?"

"You bet!"

When they left the restaurant the sky was a luminous orange purple, glowing, but dimming fast.

"How's the dog?" Gabe asked, glancing at Carl, who was strolling alertly behind them.

"I decided not to give it away. She tracked down a bird in the house."

"See, I was right about that dog. Besides, you need it to balance all the technology in your life." Carl was ahead of them now. "Where's he going? Where's your car?"

"In that side lot next to the hotel." She stopped. "Back into harness, right, partner?"

From habit, his hand reached out for her face, detouring abruptly and landing on her shoulder. "Right."

The light was going fast. The sky was streaky with low clouds, tufts of black palm fronds swaying against it. Faye was setting her tape deck. Across the lot, people were coming and going around the hotel. Alone in her car, she felt the shroud of the night wrap her. The nautilus was rising before her, its powerful tentacles whipping the water in long sweeping strokes. Where within her did this foul apparition come from? She stared at the bright lights of the hotel marquee and the purple sky behind it.

That day, she'd broken her silence and called Izzy from the pay phone in front of her building. "Did Della have an aunt?" she'd asked. No. "Isn't *tía* aunt in Spanish?" Yes. But she'd had no aunt. "Uncle? *Tío*?" No. "She'd talked about *tía*, Izzy."

"Faye, you have to stop doing this to yourself," he'd insisted.

"She talked about 'selections.' "

"Faye, stop this."

Detective Phelps had telephoned, his regular checkup call. She'd kept the conversation neutral, not telling him about "tía" and "selections." Remembering was tied to the monstrous nautilus dream. She'd call him from a pay phone tomorrow, even though remembering fragments like "tía" couldn't compare to the body in her bed.

Carl was looking at her from his car. "Any trouble?"

"No," she called back, "just relaxing."

On the far side of the lot, a car had pulled in and stopped. A man got out. His gait looked familiar. Faye saw a woman emerge, stretch like a cat and fall into the man's arms. They kissed, screened by the lengthening shadows against the hedges, then walked across the lot toward Faye's car, their arms entwined around each other's waists, heading toward a Chrysler not far away. Faye watched them, remembering what it felt like to walk that way with someone she loved.

The couple stopped beside the Chrysler as the parking-lot lights went on. Rob. With Claire Townsend.

Claire got into the driver's seat, Rob leaned down and kissed her, then stepped back as she started the engine and rolled away.

Faye was out of her car. Carl started from his.

"Rob!" Faye called out.

He whirled around. "Faye?"

"What—what's happening?"

"Nothing." He was moving toward her.

"Nothing? That was Claire Townsend."

"Who are you, the mother superior? Get off your high horse!"

He was in front of her, tieless, his jacket caped over his shoulders.

"Get off *my* high horse? You—you're having an affair with Leo's wife?"

"Lay off, little sister," Rob said coldly. "This isn't important for you to—"

"Not important?"

"It's not serious, Faye, these things—they're part of life."

She lurched back as if he'd slapped her. "I can't believe you of all people are saying this."

"You always overreact, Faye. Shut it down, for chrissakes, and don't give me any of your puritanical bullshit. You could be married and making pictures with Gabe right now if you'd kept your head."

"Are you nuts? Is this *you*? Nadine's bound to find out and when she does—"

"Nadine's a lot cooler than you are."

"It will *kill* Nadine—"

"We have a very open marriage."

"I don't believe that."

"It's really none of your business, is it?"

"Quit acting like this, this isn't you!" She grabbed at his arm.

He shook her off. "Stay out of it!"

SEVENTEEN

ACROSS TOWN, LEO Townsend was being driven west on a tree-shaded street in Beverly Hills. He sat in the back, talking to Cowboy on the car phone.

"We've spoken about this before, Leo," Cowboy was saying. "It's natural they'd talk about Della. If we stay cool, it won't amount to anything."

Leo was not feeling cool. "Nadine's taken on her own OPI investigation, and she's no amateur. What if she takes it to the press?"

"That would be a serious problem," Cowboy said. "But I don't think she's going to do that."

"She's done worse and you know it," Leo snapped. "She called our subcontractors. I sent you the transcription."

"Keep the lid on, Leo. We've got bigger problems. I hope they get a full airing tonight."

"What do you mean, 'bigger problems'?" Leo snorted.

"I'm sorry I can't be there with you," Cowboy said, "but I'm going to recommend that we pull back for a while."

"It's an election year! We can't pull back!"

"Nadine's only a symptom, Leo. You should give her some time off. She could fly out here and be with Rob awhile."

"I want her out permanently," Leo grumbled.

"Not a chance," Cowboy said decisively.

Leo's car pulled up in front of an English-style brick house well shaded by dense trees. "I'll be a few hours," Leo told the driver.

In a spacious oak-paneled study, a small gathering of men laughed and bantered like old friends who knew where the drinks were and could help themselves: a former governor of the state, a nine-term congressman, a former state attorney general, and the CEO of an insurance conglomerate.

The elderly man known as the Chief thumped a brass paperweight on an end table. The room quieted. The chairman's features relaxed, but remained watchful.

"We're going to start in a minute," he said, "as soon as we get Cowboy on the speaker." The state-of-the-art device sat on a Duncan Phyfe drumhead side table.

"Cowboy," the Chief said, "can you hear us?" His personality was forthright, his eyes and voice moderate but commanding.

"Yes, Chief. Sorry I can't be there." Cowboy was sitting in his private office. From beyond the locked door he could hear the murmur of the guests at his reception. "Go ahead."

A few minutes later, the Chief was saying, "But our situation is under control since the unfortunate incident with Ms. Izquerra."

"I suggest we cut off all funds to CDEE," proposed a short, round man with a bushy mustache.

"They won't take that lying down," said the former DA.

The Chief seemed shocked. "We're in charge, and we'll handle them."

"Don't be dramatic, Bob," said the former governor. "The subcontractors don't even know who *we* are—"

The former DA's gaunt face hardened. "I *meant* that CDEE group is run by a vindictive asshole. We'd do better to dribble money at him till we can take him out."

A calm silence wafted through the room.

"You hear all that, Cowboy?" the Chief said. "We need to keep everyone in line here, right?"

"Yes, indeed," Cowboy responded over the speaker.

"The program's not in trouble," Leo said. "It's going great." With his usual rapid-fire, fifty-caliber style, Leo walked them through OPI's sub-rosa program goals. Thanks to Leo's adept bureaucratic skills, OPI's budget had been doubled.

"We can increase *that* figure by the next term," Leo was saying. "Harper's quarterbacking those terminals, so start getting your wish lists together for two years from now."

Cowboy, in his office, grimaced. He was visualizing the mine fields that could blow up the *current* plan. "We're rushing ahead too prematurely," he said. "I spoke about it last year, but we decided to enlarge anyway. Now, we should dig in and consolidate." He wanted his current operation to run without hitches. He hoped Harper could be trusted, but he didn't know for sure. He also hoped Nadine Ferray would go on the road with her husband and the senator, but that was unlikely. He hoped Faye Ferray really had been scared off, but he didn't think so. "There are factors that can rise up and bite us in the ass. Let's avoid them and expand later."

"We've got total support," Leo put in, staring hard in turn at each man in the room, not at the speakerphone.

"We're going to have some problems," Cowboy said softly.

"They can be handled," Leo shot back.

"Cowboy, what are you saying?" the Chief asked.

"Before we expand we should go all the way through the current level of programs—from the agency to the subcontractors, their consultants, the candidates, the banks—everything. If we expand, we'll have to take on more personnel. Word will get out, more than it already has."

"Is something out?" the DA asked.

"No, no," Leo assured him.

"There *is* informal, in-the-know awareness," Cowboy said firmly, "that Harper's quarterbacking a special program."

"So what?" the former governor demanded. "There's always a scent in the air. We've nothing to worry about."

The DA coughed an interruption. "What would we do if something did leak?"

The men in the room stared at him.

"Retrench." Cowboy's sharp voice came over the phone. "Relocate." *If we had enough warning,* he thought. He heard Leo over the hubbub: "That will not be necessary!"

Cowboy fingered his gold penknife and did a private assessment as he pictured the men in the room and heard their voices on his phone. The plans were in full advance, everyone was obsessed with the prospect of success, of pulling it off, and though most of them knew all the risks, knew the plan's chance of continued success was decreasing for a number of reasons, not one spoke a word about that. They badly wanted the ultimate goal to be true and real, they suppressed all doubt. Doubt made waves and that made them feel less omnipotent. Cowboy hung up in disgust.

That night, Rob fell back against his seat in the plane, ordered a drink, and tried to pull his thoughts together, but all he could see was Faye's angry shocked face. He took the drink from the flight attendant, ripped open a bag of peanuts and poured them into his mouth. It was tragic Faye had seen him with Claire. He didn't think she'd tell Nadine, but it diminished him in Faye's eyes. And, there was nothing he could do about it now.

His hand was closed so tightly around his glass that he had to consciously unwind his fingers. He had to believe it would all work out, that he could skate through it without too many bruises or too many fractures.

Nadine had felt queasy that day and stayed at home to make preparations for Rob's homecoming. But he was late. She was asleep on the couch when the front door slammed.

"Honey," Rob called out. He came into the living room, holding a bouquet of white and yellow roses. He struck a pose.

"Oh, Rob, you are heavenly." He strode across to her and rubbed the rosebuds against her cheek.

"Just mortal, but terrific." He kissed her. "You want to go to an all-night club?"

"Rob!" she laughed. "It's one in the morning. We have to work tomorrow."

"Screw work—let's have some fun!"

The idea was exciting, like the old times with Rob. As she took the flowers to put them in water, she noticed his sleeve. "Where's your other cuff link?"

"Oh, Lord. I guess I lost it. Maybe they'll find it on the plane. I'll go give them a quick call."

He went upstairs to use the bedroom phone. It was ten o'clock on the West Coast. He telephoned Claire.

Claire answered. "Can you talk?" he asked. "Is he still gone?"

"Why, yes. Where are you, naughty boy?"

He ignored her question. "Claire, I left a cuff link. Check your rental car, but it might be in the room we had."

"Oh, honey, who cares about some old cuff link?"

"If it's in the room, they might mail it to me and there's no reason for me to be staying in that hotel. If it's in your car, Leo might find it."

"He won't know it's yours, you silly goose."

"They're engraved from Nadine."

"Oh, well, sweetie, I suppose you're right. When do I see you again, Robbie? I sure do miss you, honey lamb. My arms are jes' aching for you."

"Yeah, mine, too," Rob said, listening for Nadine.

"Let's set a date, Robbie."

"Next week."

"Well, my week is jes' chockablock with engagements, except for Tuesday afternoon."

He sighed. "Tuesday." He hung up, hearing Nadine coming upstairs.

The next morning, Faye met Tony Valdi for breakfast at Il Fornaio, an airy eatery in Beverly Hills.

"You know what I'd rather be doing today?" he said as they sat down at the small window table. "Riding a horse along Malibu beach."

"You like to ride?"

"More than taking meetings—except this one, of course, I hope."

"I would have thought you'd plunge right in and mix it up at meetings."

"I didn't say I wasn't good at them," he said, smiling. He brushed his palm thoughtfully against his beard, ordered cappuccino for them, and placed his big hands palm down on the table. "So. Where are we?"

Deal consummation was treated either as a solemn ceremony at elaborate lunches, or like pillage: explosive, reckless glee from the victor, no pity for the victim forced to cave in.

"I'm ready to go if you are," Faye said. She sat back as their coffee arrived.

Tony extended his hand across the table. "Great!" he said triumphantly, grinning broadly.

She shook his hand. "There are a lot of points we have to talk about, but one is Annie, *your* casting choice, remember." If there was trouble later, who picked her would be the first thing everyone would forget. "There're some things about Annie in the role that intrigue me, but I can't command her best behavior. So far few have."

Tony's bushy eyebrows drew together.

"If she gets very naughty, I can shame her before Gabe and the cast, which I don't want to do. Or I can fire her. I need you to be ready to pay her and let her go if it doesn't work. She can't hold up production."

"You got it. What else?" Tony asked.

"My lawyer will call your lawyer."

"Oh, boy, Faye, I'm really looking forward to this," Tony said eagerly. "I'm aware of your concerns about Annie, and different ones about Gabe, and Roger can be a pain in the ass, but you're a pro—it'll all work out. There's just one thing, Faye. The start date's three weeks from now."

"Can't be done! Too fast! Even Roger—"

"Got to be," Tony said in his "tough love" voice.

Faye drove to Bel Air to visit the star of her film.

Roger Reynolds had heat. Compelling physically, he couldn't be ignored in a crowded room. She wondered if he'd exuded heat at eighteen before anyone knew Roger Reynolds.

"Faye Ferray," he said, sticking out his hand, "I've heard of you." He had merry blue eyes. "C'mon out on the patio." He was a short, compact man with quick mobile expressions on a broad face that mirrored his mercurial inner currents when he wanted to reveal them.

The patio decor was out of a sixties Roman film—sculptures popped out of the grassy expanse around an enormous aqua-blue pool. They sat in the shade of an oak tree as a Chinese butler served iced tea in tall, frosted glasses garnished with sprigs of fresh spearmint.

Roger critiqued the script ably. His questions were based on his "character," by which he meant the character of Roger as star. Faye tried to put his concerns to rest, but was not entirely successful. Like most big stars, he had a remarkably objective image of himself, as if he stood outside, looking at the star he'd become from the point of view of his fans. He'd do nothing to endanger their perception of him.

His stunt man and double, Craig, arrived and they all talked about deep-sea fishing, Craig's sport when he wasn't working for Roger. Roger's masseur showed up. Then his business manager.

"It's all going to be wonderful," Roger said, rising. "I have the utmost confidence in everyone. Let's just pound this script into place, right, Faye?"

The Jungle Gym started at a dead run. Faye expanded her office space, the phones never stopped, the days blurred: the process was called preproduction, a charged atmosphere dominated by script rewrites, casting, location and transport arrangements, crew hiring. Faye called it the best time in the world. She suppressed Della and the threats, and pared her bodyguards back to the minimum. She reshaped her life in a form she recognized.

"Hire anyone who can read!" Faye was yelling at Steve that morning when Keith Llewellyn popped into her office. "Come on in and shut the door," she said. "Keith, I want your word that the conversation we're about to have is confidential."

"Sure."

"No, not 'sure,' swear on your mother's heart."

His eyebrows bobbed up and down. "Okay."

"I need you to write a whole new scene for me to be shot out here when we finish in D.C. Here are my notes. You can be flexible with the dialogue, but it has to include these lines."

He looked at the paper. "What's the big secret?"

She narrowed her eyes.

"Okay! Okay! My lips are sealed!"

"Zack!" she called as Keith was leaving.

Zack was forty-five, an experienced production manager who'd worked all of Faye's pictures, a tough saint with encyclopedic knowledge. "Find me the best explosives guy with cars. I'm adding a scene to the script. This is just between you and me, so don't check with anyone else about it."

Zack nodded. Faye's way of working on this film already had him worried. On the way out he met Julie Prescott, Faye's associate producer.

"This show's really going to be something else," he mumbled.

The long tables held laptops, cassettes, papers, maps, and clipboards. Faye was sitting at one end with Zack and Julie. Gabe and his assistant director, Dino, sat on the couch. All morning Steve and others had burst into the room with calls that couldn't wait, insurance papers that couldn't wait, Tony's latest casting suggestions. Outside, the late L.A. spring weather was balmy and sweet.

Annie never just walked into rooms, she "entered" them. Today she was in purple jeans and shirt. She ignited her biggest toothy smile. "And who belongs to that?" She pointed dramatically at Faye's little dog.

"I do," Faye said.

"Looks like the Normans' dog across the street, you remember? When we were kids?" She sat on the couch beside Gabe.

They were going through the script. "This scene still isn't working," Gabe said, "in fact, this whole sequence isn't working."

"Oh, I see," Faye said, "now that we're rolling and Herb's signed on for distribution, the one thing that brought us together is being doubted!"

"C'mon, Faye," Gabe said, "I'm talking about tone, about what I hear and see from it."

"*This* draft wasn't part of the deal," Annie was muttering, flipping pages.

"Movies aren't about deals!" Faye said. "We don't shoot deals here—we shoot scripts—*this* script."

Zack and Julie glanced at each other. Annie pouted. She hooked one leg over the other, straining her already too-tight jeans. "The scene at the monument," she said. "Celia's lines don't express what's going on, and I think she ought to be more open with him about what's troubling her."

Faye calmed herself. Her sister wanted more lines. "Annie, the script's being rewritten to suit you and the character. Celia is now a bold, warm, controversial sort of doctor, and Congressman Joe is a hard-driving legislator who has a sweet side and a way with women."

Annie smiled smugly at Gabe and Faye. Faye knew she wouldn't look that way long. With Roger on board, the script would steadily shift to satisfy his demands at Annie's expense.

"I really feel," Gabe said, "we should substitute the Vietnam Memorial for the Lincoln Memorial."

Everyone started to talk at once. Annie was outshouting everyone. "Gabe's right! My character wouldn't connect with the Lincoln Memorial—she'd only know Vietnam!"

"Annie, pipe down," Faye said. "Vietnam for Lincoln. Done."

"Emmet's got to find some other locations," Gabe said, "because these pictures, they just aren't what I see in the script." He smoothed out a series of location photos the production designer, Emmet Greenleaf, had sent back from Washington.

Gabe was changing into his forceful director mode, claiming his view of the picture. Faye had seen him do it before as a way out of his retiring nature. What she hadn't seen was the loneliness underneath. Faye remembered a time when she and Gabe had talked of nothing ordinary, while living totally in the moment with each other. That had been a long time ago, a different life.

"We're real short of time here," Faye said, "but I do want a sense of Washington's duality—half Northern, half Southern, power capital of the world, murder capital of America."

Gabe put down the photos. "Yeah, duality. Good."

"It's a realistic film with plenty of tension, but without special effects, without fantasy," Faye went on. "Julie, what do you have?"

"We're doing preproduction on the L.A. setups while we're shooting in D.C.," Julie said. "That tell you anything? We got big problems." Julie Prescott, thirty-eight, was a problem-cruncher. A Midwestern African-American, she'd worked on films in New York and Washington before moving to Los Angeles. She was the perfect associate producer, hard and sweet.

"The location economics tell us," Zack said in a measured voice, "that we've got to shoot all the important interiors, except for the two establishing scenes in Congress, here on sets. All the important exteriors will be shot in D.C. The crack den and the lab can be shot here."

"Faye, I want to shoot the chase out there alongside Chesapeake Bay," Gabe said, petting the dog as it wandered under the table.

"We'll try, but the insurance people aren't going for it," Faye said. "They want it shot here in the tank."

"Lonny will be disappointed," Gabe said of his director of photography. "He wants to shoot Annie in the bay."

"Yes!" Annie cried. "Yes!"

"But what if we lost you in the bay?" Faye said.

"Sorry to break in," Steve said, breaking in. "This just arrived from Tony's office." He gave Faye a gaily wrapped box. "Your start-of-production present."

She unwrapped it. "Oh, great!" she cried, lifting out an electronic translator.

"Just give her anything technological," Julie said, "and she's a happy woman."

Faye was already punching in "dailies" and "overtime." Zack glanced at Gabe, who had shut down, his arms folded against his chest, eyes sad.

"There's a note about us in Smith's column," Julie said. She stabbed a long nail into the newsprint. "All about the Washington shoot." Julie was an avid reader of trade and news columnists. Zack began listing the motels and hotels he'd lined up for cast and crew in Washington. Annie was trying to attract the dog. Gabe stared out the window.

"We got more art direction problems," Julie said.

"I know. We'll get to those after lunch—"

"Lunch!" Annie shrieked. "I'm late!" She flew out.

"Gabe," Faye said, "when you have script problems, talk to me, not the whole office."

"I'll talk to whoever I want whenever I want."

Everyone in the room started going through files and making notes.

"Of course," Faye said, "but the less dissection of the script in front of Annie, the better." She jumped out of her chair. "Casting! Boynton's reading for Celia's son."

"Boynton's *reading*?" Gabe said. "When did he condescend to do that?"

"For me."

"Boynton's trouble. I don't want him."

"Let's just look at him," Faye said.

"Aw, Faye, get real . . ."

They went off, arguing.

Zack leaned back in his chair. "Well, actors love Gabe," he finally said. "He's never cruel."

"But he can be cold," Julie said.

"She'll use the big rush of this shoot as a way not to communicate with him. Otherwise, they'll be at each other's throats."

"No, they won't. They still love each other," Julie countered.

"Who cares? Can *we* get through this? That's the point."

EIGHTEEN

IN WASHINGTON, A special messenger delivered to Leo the transcripts of the security phone-tap surveillance of Nadine Stern Ferray. He began reading quickly and thoroughly. Twenty minutes later, he stopped, stunned. The page in front of him was a verbatim transcript of Rob Ferray's call to Claire Townsend from Nadine's home phone.

"My arms are aching for you . . ."

Leo's staff assistant was buzzing. He ignored it. Rage and something close to acute pain uncoiled inside him. His control suppressed it. His tense mouth thinned. He would do nothing. He would wait.

Tot was in Washington, watching rough-cut tapes of the California senatorial race on a console monitor. It was part of an irregular series of specials on the California elections, which were heating up. Larry, Tot's editor, sat beside her, punching buttons on the console. He had a pudgy, quiet face. When the phone rang he reached for it and passed it directly to Tot.

"I thought you'd be in California," Nadine said.

"Just got back."

"I need to see you, Tot."

"Oh, can't today. I'm editing all the California stuff."

"Please, it's really important."

"Nadine—I'm in *edit*ing. I have a *dead*line."

"I'm coming over."

When Nadine was shown into the immaculate editing room an hour later, Tot was struck by the tension in her friend's face. "What's up?" she asked, reaching out to clasp Nadine's arm, then swiveling back to the bank of monitors.

"I've been working on something, and I need advice." Nadine sat in a chair behind Tot and the editor.

Tot pointed at a monitor. "That's the shot, Lar." She swung around. Nadine was smiling fixedly, like a mannequin. Her eyes glittered. She seemed exhausted in a deep, interior way. "In about half an hour, we'll go across the street. You just sit tight and look at the pretty politicians."

Shots of Mark Drummond were intercut with interviews with the other candidate for the Senate seat, Howell Sparks.

"I feel so out of touch with California," Nadine said. "Did you run into Rob on the trail?"

"No," Tot said, watching the monitors, "I was with Sparks this time."

"How's Mark doing?" Nadine asked.

"Good, but Sparks is strong."

The footage rushed by. "Faye has a deal on her film," Nadine said.

"I heard. I'm glad."

"I hope nothing goes wrong. Do you know this Tony Valdi?"

Tot laughed. "Anything could go wrong, Nadine. I hear Valdi cuts a few corners, but he cares about movies and moviemakers." She smiled up at the monitor. "Larry, take it up to where he says 'What's wrong with profit?' "

"Faye's going to be out here shooting in a few days," Nadine said. It was only when she mentioned Faye that Nadine remembered she'd called Tot from her office phone.

Spring was evaporating into the heat of summer. "This way," Tot said, fanning herself with her hand. The coffee shop was a grimy retread from the forties, and it was packed. She and Nadine got the last table at the back. Tot flagged a harried waitress and ordered two cups of tea and a donut. She put her stubby hands on the table.

"How's your work going?" she asked. "Got any big scoops over there in mole-land?"

"Yes."

"Really?" Tot said, surprised.

Nadine contemplated Tot. She reached out; her pale, immaculate fingernails plucked a paper napkin from the metal container on the table. "I want everything I tell you to be on deep background."

"Okay. You got it."

"You remember at the cabin when Faye wanted all of us to try to find out more about what Della was working on?"

Tot nodded. The waitress set down cups, metal teapots of tepid water, tea bags, and the donut.

"I started checking for Faye, looking into that L.A. outfit, CDEE—the one Della mentioned?" Nadine told Tot briefly about Faye's finding the disk and her own efforts to check out its list of names and dates.

"A disk, huh?" Tot said.

"It seems so long ago. Anyway, around that time, Faye remembered more of what Della said just before she died."

"Like what?"

"Della talked about warning *me* to stay clear."

"Weird."

"Well, not really. Della left the disk for Faye, but she knew Faye would give it to me, and she knew I'd find out how the organizations on it were connected to the NSC."

An icy calm settled over Tot.

"When Faye remembered Della's warning to me, it spooked her and she told me to stop checking the disk. She was very direct about that. So I agreed." She nudged her tea bag into the teapot with her fingertip. "But I didn't stop."

"You didn't?"

"No, I couldn't," Nadine whispered. "Then Faye was threatened—I told you about that awful—thing—in her bed—" Tot nodded. "I made one last move." Nadine pushed a folded sheet of paper across the table. "This is a memo I found. I think the NSC is creating fake subcontracts to organizations like CDEE."

Tot took the memo.

"We have a program called the Office of Public Information—it's supposed to teach democracy. The real conservatives at the White House are very high on it. And in some ways, it's a good program. But I think it's been subverted. The man who's administering it is Jay Harper. This memo came out of his office. It's not that incriminating, but it is if you know some of the background."

"So, what's going on?"

"I think Office of Public Information, the OPI, is a shell to convert millions of government dollars into corporate funds through subcontracts, which are then wire-transferred into offshore banks."

"What's the money for? What happens to the money?"

"The memo mentions upcoming elections in Africa. Maybe the money's used to influence those elections."

"Not the first time," Tot said. "Too bad the money's not going into someone's pockets here—that's always news."

"I don't know. I think Della was on to it. She knew CDEE's normal work, so she might have seen a lot of money rolling in and out."

Tot could barely contain herself. Could this be the reporter's dream? Was it just being handed to her? She immediately distrusted it because Tot believed all success came from hard work. She was not about to get carried away.

"The NSC can set up and fund any old propaganda program it wants, Nadine."

"Sure, but they don't have the right to fund their own private State Department."

Tot stared at her. "You can't peg that sort of thing on one memo. And, what's an outfit like CDEE got to do with elections in Africa? Nothing, I'll bet. No, the money's got to be used in some other way in this country."

"I really don't know. I'll give you what I have, but it's not *that* much." She told her about the calls she'd made to the "subcontractors" organizations on Della's list. "And then I hit one outfit in Ohio—a woman who was either very new or just plain dippy. I said we'd discovered a minor error in the contract and we needed a fax of what they'd received."

"Pretty thin, Nadine."

"Right, but—" Nadine laughed. "She faxed it to me. I couldn't believe it!" She pushed another piece of paper across to Tot.

"This is very general . . ." Tot read, " 'OPI hereby . . . subcontracting the work listed below . . . an information program on the use of media in a democracy . . . ' "

"There's an open secret at the NSC—you know the way information floats around from one department to another— people know something's up on the OPI program. If a reporter started checking around, some people might talk because they know Harper's running something special that might not be completely kosher—the way people knew Oliver North was running a special program for Reagan. But you have to promise me something."

"What?"

"You won't relate anything I've told you, or might tell you, to Rob."

"What's he got to do with it?"

"Nothing. But I don't want him—or anyone—to know where you got this information. You've got to leave me out."

"I promise. But why stop now?"

"What I do affects other people, Tot. Leo Townsend, who brought me over there—we used to have a good working relationship but now I'm being deliberately cut out of information I ought to have access to. And I don't want to hurt Adrian, our legal adviser, to say nothing of my own career."

"Well, sure, but—"

"I'm pregnant, Tot. For the first time in my life, I'm pregnant."

Tot couldn't think of a more knowledgeable and reliable source than Nadine. If Nadine thought the NSC was turning OPI into its own Big Brother program with defrauded government funds, something like that was probably going on. But how were they using the money?

Tot didn't want to share the information prematurely with her assignment editor or her producer. She wanted to check it out first. Maybe it was nothing. But if it was big, she wanted to stamp it as hers before anyone else got wind of it.

She rushed back to the station to tape the stand-up to wrap around her California footage for air later that night.

"Tot!" Her assignment editor, Maury, a thickset balding man, greeted her. "Good piece on California." He draped a heavy arm around her shoulder and steered her into his office. "Lloyd and I want you to work with him on a piece on how the government is spending taxpayers' money—agency and department budgets."

"Great! Great!" she said. Now she had a perfect cover to investigate Nadine's allegations.

"Yeah, well, calm down, it's not a prime-time piece yet. I thought you liked doing the California reports."

"I do, I want to do more of them—you know me and the number stories. Which agencies are you talking about?"

"Start with HUD and the FCC."

"Shouldn't we have something from the executive branch?"

"No. We're assigning you a fact-checker and a film crew."

As soon as she finished the wraparound on Drummond and Sparks, she went to the closet the network called her office, which she shared with two other people. She sat down at her table and snapped on her laptop. Then she carefully reread the memo and the fax Nadine had given her. She left a message for a reporter she knew who covered the White House and was well versed in NSC matters. Then, despite the limitations of her new assignment, she used it to set up appointments with the NSC adviser, Norman Tate; his deputy, Leo Townsend; and Adrian Anderson.

"A gift for you, Pop, because you cotton to birds . . ." Faye held up a cage. The recuperating canary was inside, looking frisky.

Los Angeles was warm and muggy. Jerry Ferray was on the deck where he spent every afternoon "until the gloaming."

"Thanks, honey. And who's that?" He pointed at the dog.

"That's the canary's pal, Pop."

"Is that the dog you tried to give your mom?"

She nodded. From habit, she glanced around the deck carefully, and in the kitchen windows. There had been no new threats and the expense of the bodyguards had seemed unnecessary so she'd let them go.

"I'm going through some scrapbooks," Jerry said. He held up a picture of Coo at twenty-five. "Dazzling, ain't she? Personality to match."

"It must have been easy to fall in love."

"*Easy?* It was impossible not to love her." He put down the picture. "And here's you and Rob and Annie." Faye, about twelve, was sitting with her brother and sister on the edge of a set under a brute light. The picture seemed so innocent and remote from her life today.

"We're starting to build the sets for when we get back," she said.

"Build big sets," Jerry chortled, "get the money men in over their heads and *pray* for a box office bonanza."

"I'm changing the script again and adding some special effects."

"You look positively sly. What're you doing, a movie within a movie?"

"Sort of."

"You devil. How is it working with Gabe again?"

"He's good at what he does, but it's not easy." She sat down. "Pop, if you knew that the husband of a good friend was having an affair, would you tell your friend?"

"No. Don't you have enough problems?"

"I don't know what to say to my friend."

"You must know the philanderer, too," her father said.

"Oh, yes, I know him."

"Stay out of it."

"I knew you'd say that."

"What do you think about Buck on the Court?"

"Can't see it."

Jerry cackled.

Faye thought back to the night of Buck's party at El Contento, to the voices in the study that she and Nadine had overheard. "Is Buck an old friend of Sam Pike's, Pop?"

"Pike? Oh, sure, he and Buck—and some other native son, I can't remember—"

"Leo Townsend?"

"Maybe. Can't recall."

"He's Nadine's boss."

"Yeah? I forget a lot up here on Olympus. Anyway, they go back to the George Murphy Senate race in 1964 when Barry Goldwater was running for President. Buck was a fresh young attorney, up to his eyeballs in politics. It was a time like—it was like Lucifer had been released from his chains! An' there was George Murphy, doin' a little soft shoe and carrying the spear for every California nut! Hot damn, what a time.

"Buck was kinda a middle-of-the-road Republican. I think Pike was an Independent, verging on a Republican." The canary started to sing. "Nice tone," Jerry said. "When do you leave for D.C.?"

"Tomorrow, for three weeks—if we stay on schedule, doubtful—then back here."

"Are you ready to shoot? Seems like you just got the deal."

"We're shooting without benefit of planning—just firing from the hip and praying we don't hit the soundman."

Jerry laughed weakly. "What fun. I remember a couple like that."

She broke her rule and asked him how he was feeling.

"I'm not feeling a lot worse, just a little worse."

"The doctors say your white count's better."

"What do doctors know? I'm awful sick of feeling sick."

"Yoo-hoo!" Coo sang out from the far end of the deck. A warm breeze blew her periwinkle-colored muumuu around her chunky body. She was carrying a plate of cheese and crackers. She leaned in to kiss Faye, and spread around her powdery cloud of fragrance. "We didn't expect you," she said in her direct way. "Stay for dinner?" Coo's small ruby mouth turned up hopefully.

Faye put her arms around her mother and hugged her tight. "Gee," said Coo, surprised, pleased, "what's gotten into you?"

"I don't want you to feel ignored, Mom. You're very special to me."

In Washington, it was seven in the evening. Another file of security surveillance reports had been delivered to Leo. He opened the folder and read rapidly until he came to the fifth transcription. He punched a button on his secure telephone. In California, Cowboy's assistant answered. "He's in Washington, Mr. Townsend, at the Jefferson Hotel."

Leo dialed the hotel. When he came on the line, Leo said, "You do get around, Cowboy. We have to meet."

"Bite-the-bullet time," Leo announced.

The night was warm. Cowboy set a fast pace as they walked around Lafayette Square behind the lighted White House grounds. Sculptures commemorating foreign military leaders who'd aided the American Revolution tacked down the corners of the park.

"I was right all along," Leo said, as they passed the statue of Lafayette near the Treasury building. "Nadine's off the reservation. You wanted to wait, even though she was calling the subcontractors—"

"She's a terrier, all right," Cowboy said admiringly.

"I got a house full of them. Adrian, too—he'll be in lockstep with her unless we yank his chain. Nadine's gone to Tot Jencks. *Not* a social call, Cowboy, it was a demand that the reporter meet her." They were coming up on Briga-dier General Thaddeus Kosciuszko, the Pole who'd built the fortifications at West Point and Saratoga. "And today the Jencks woman calls me with an interview request." Leo's mouth tightened. He shoved his hands in his pockets.

"Oh, hell, Leo, she doesn't know anything—none of them do."

Leo stopped walking. "I don't operate like that. I assume everyone knows everything until I find out otherwise. It's safer. This problem's not going away. We have to move."

Cowboy was gazing up at a lofty flowering chestnut tree. In some ways he was more worried about Leo than about Nadine. "Are you suggesting some medicinal releases—a 'leak' that affects Nadine?" he asked.

"Of course I am! She has to be discredited!"

Cowboy struck out for the next corner. "Buck Stern won't like it."

"But *she'll* back off."

A break in the foliage afforded Cowboy a view of Andrew Jackson in the center of the square. "If there's going to be press releases, I'll handle 'em."

"I've got a few ideas that'll make her—"

"You cannot ride roughshod over her." He watched the shadows on Leo's face. Leo had a right-wrong, north-south mentality. He was not adaptable. "I'm concerned about Stern."

"We have to shut their water off!" Leo insisted.

With a sudden movement, Cowboy seized Leo's lapel, bringing his face close. "You are a rash sonofabitch, Leo," he said softly. "I'll help you cut the ground out from under Nadine, but it'll be done my way, and you'll be a perfect gentleman. Don't do anything crazy, or we'll both have to deal with Stern. Are you reading me?"

Cowboy dropped his hold. Leo straightened his jacket. He was very angry. His thin lips had disappeared; his eyes were slits.

Together the two men began cutting diagonally through the square.

"Your emotions are engaged in this Nadine business," Cowboy said. "Am I wrong?"

"Definitely wrong," Leo said, rattled, furious.

Close to the Jackson statue was the Bernard Baruch "Seat of Inspiration" park bench. "I'm going to sit here and clear my head," Cowboy announced. Leo cut away from him without a word.

Cowboy eased onto the bench where Baruch had supposedly thought over world affairs before giving advice to his friend Franklin Roosevelt. Cowboy wouldn't stay long. Washington wasn't really safe anymore. Washington was a city at war with itself. But he wanted to seek inspiration. He regretted the interference of Buck Stern's daughter and wondered how much she really knew. He wondered how much she'd told Faye Ferray. At least *she'd* been scared off. He thought about Leo, who'd been very useful. They would never have been able to operate without him or without a complaisant President. But Leo was not being straight with him. Leo was cracking.

NINETEEN

THE CAST AND crew of *The Jungle Gym* came swinging into Washington, D.C., spinning and gyrating. They set up shop eight blocks from the White House in a small hotel on a tree-lined side street.

Additional office space had been rented next door in an old brick building. In it, technicians appeared, met, muttered, disappeared; assistants were scrawling out signs to identify areas for extras, permits, catering, casting, vouchers, publicists; fax machines popped out messages and printers ground out script changes delivered by modem from the coast. Zack, the production "father" who'd ultimately meet everyone's needs, was eyeing the posted sheets for the Name-the-Dog contest. The day was soggy. Every talent and film hustler in the nation's capital was banging on the door.

Ground Zero was the second floor of the hotel where Faye was enthusiastically hunched forward on a couch in the main room of her suite with Julie and three assistants. The double doors to her suite and Gabe's across the hall were wide open, and the staffs flowed through, back and forth, like schools of fish.

Gabe was sitting at a table with Lonny, his director of photography; Dino, his assistant director, and the local location manager. He could see Faye as he spoke to her on the phone; it was an odd sensation. "I had a delegation of African-American locals this morning," Faye was saying, "about staffing on our shoot. Julie is now our liaison with the city." The dog barked. Gabe could see her sitting on the couch, wearing a dressy collar from Julie and a matching harness from Zack. "The bad news," Faye went on, "is that Roger doesn't want to sit around and he's made a deal with Herb: no waiting."

"How can he do this to me?" Gabe said. No waiting meant shooting all the scenes with Roger first, and then returning to shoot pickups, angles, other characters. It would cost a fortune in time and money. He hung up, disgusted.

"Group all of Roger's scenes and give me the damage," Gabe said to Dino.

This became known as "The Roger Problem." Scene breakdowns were usually plotted for location, not for the convenience of the actors, because moving people and gear from one location to another was costly and time-consuming. It paid to stay in one place until everything connected to it was shot. Dino's assistant had just finished sorting all the crowd scenes to make full economic use of the extras.

"I don't think we have the time," Dino whined.

"Don't tell me, tell *her!*" Gabe flung an arm in Faye's direction across the hall.

He was sitting at a table looking at the latest photos from Emmet, the art director. "We've got to find a space with more trees, thicker trees," Lonny, the cinematographer, was telling them. He was about forty, short and round with curly black hair and passionate black eyes.

"Bushy trees! Mature trees!" Lonny said. He was an excitable man.

"Mount Vernon, Arlington Cemetery, the Arboretum . . ." the location manager was reciting.

"We've been there!" Lonny snapped.

Everyone was frazzled by the haste and the increasing strain between Gabe and Faye. "This is a problem with a solution," Gabe said. "Maybe Emmet's people will make trees."

A tubby, chirpy woman with a clipboard bounced into the room. "Catering," she called out. "Special orders."

"No heads," Dino said immediately, "I won't eat any food that's come from something that once had a head on it."

"No fats," said Lonny.

"Anything," said Gabe. "And a lot of fruit."

She scratched notes on her clipboard and clucked at the production rush as she left.

"Nadine!" Gabe heard Faye yell. The two women embraced, and sat down together on a couch. Nadine was talking with her hands, unusual gestures for her. "She's awfully excited," Gabe said. An assistant location manager, a production assistant, and a secretary began gathering in the hall, blocking his view.

"Communications," Lonny said, going down his list.

"We're going all cellular on this one," Gabe said. "God, look at the line forming while those two women chat. Ever notice the way women talk? They lean close to each other as if everything's a secret."

"Here are the costs so far," Lonny said. Gabe barely glanced at them. "You okay? You seem real distracted." Lonny knew Gabe was a stickler for getting the best gear for the least money, but on this shoot Gabe didn't seem to care how much was spent.

Gabe mumbled, "Can't tell if I'm going forward or backward. This could be three years ago, or now."

Lonny nodded as if he himself had worked shoulder to shoulder with a former wife. "We've got two days around Congress," he said, "two days around the vets' memorial, and then the Tidal Basin."

"Won't work, man. We gotta shoot all of Roger's stuff off the top."

Across the hall, Nadine was saying, "Rob doesn't know yet. He's still in California and I don't want to tell him on the phone that he's going to be a father."

Faye was caught between delight for Nadine and dread. She kept seeing Rob and Claire in the parking lot and it filled her with apprehension; it made her feel separated from Nadine when she most wanted to be close.

A shout of laughter went up from Gabe's suite. "Look at them," Faye said to Nadine, "bellowing and whooping. It's all a game to men, have you noticed? The dears," she added.

"Can you take a break?"

"Stick around, we'll have a bite to eat." Faye beckoned to her waiting staff; they poured into the room. "Isn't this heaven?" Faye yelled, startling the dog. "Don't you all love chaos!"

Eight blocks away Tot was interviewing Norman Tate, the NSC adviser. He was cordial, noncommittal, a little vague. While he gave little away, he clearly enjoyed being interviewed.

Leo Townsend's office had told Tot the deputy "does not grant interviews." She tried again before she left the White House, got the same answer, and went across the street to the OEOB where she was shown into Adrian Anderson's office.

"Do you remember me, we met at Judge Stern's?" she said.

"Yes, I do." Adrian had a pleasant smile and he was wearing a wild tie. "Didn't you go to law school with Nadine?" She nodded. "You did that piece a while ago on the economics of an oil spill in Japan. It was good."

"Thanks. Adrian, I just came by to say hello, I don't want to waste your time. I'm doing a budget piece—how the money is spent in government—and I'm talking to various agencies, but we also wanted to cover executive offices, like the Office of Policy Development or the NSC, so I stopped in and talked with Norman Tate. I just need some background, off-the-record information."

"Shoot." Adrian enjoyed her. She wasn't cynical or negative or aggressive.

She asked him about programs in Latin America and how they were developed, run, and budgeted. He answered briefly and referred her to the special assistant in charge of Latin American affairs.

"Maybe Nadine can give you some background on all this."

"I'm going to talk to her." She gave him her widest, most innocent smile. "One of the things people are concerned about is how funds make their way through Congress, into agency budgets, and out again into a program. Can allocated funds for one program be shunted off into another?"

"No. Money allocated for a program gets spent for it—otherwise, we'd have all kinds of congressional problems. Oversight is stiff. Why, Appropriations and the Office of Management and Budget would be down our throats in a second." He stroked his beautiful tie.

"The Office of Public Information is a new program here, I understand."

He stared at the ceiling. "Yes, comparatively. But I'm not in the program area. I'm the legal adviser."

"One person characterized OPI as a rogue program."

His smile faded. He knew she wasn't nearly as dumb as she sounded. "We don't have rogue programs here." He looked at her without animosity. "What do you really want to know?"

"A source has suggested that executive branch programs are being clandestinely rerouted in this office. Do you have any comment?"

"None."

The drizzle had almost stopped when Nadine and Faye left the hotel. The street sparkled, the trees dripped lightly, and the gravid air smelled of earth and grass and summer. Since she'd spoken with Tot, Nadine had felt freed. A taxi was swishing toward them.

"You want to ride?" Faye asked.

"No," Nadine said, "expectant mothers need exercise." They set off down N Street. "I feel as happy as I can remember being in my life. Rob will be happy, too. I'm going to quit my job and the elections will end, and next February I'll be a mother. And soon, Rob'll be home for a week!"

"I'm so happy for you," Faye said. Was this what Rob needed—a child?

"I recommend this, Faye. Your biological clock is ticking away, too."

"Who would you suggest I mate with?" Faye said, her happiness for Nadine dislodging her anxieties about Rob. "It's a problem finding a single man or a man who already has children but who's interested and willing to have more."

Nadine squeezed her friend's arm. "Adrian's single."

"We didn't exactly hit it off."

"Maybe you didn't try hard enough. Would there be any reason for that?"

"Well, as a matter of fact, there is." The street was getting crowded as they turned onto Connecticut. "I'm seeing Mark Drummond."

Nadine stopped. "How far has that gone?"

"Pretty far." She grinned.

"Tell all. How is it?"

"Powerful, bewildering, anxiety-making."

"How long's this been going on?"

"Not long."

"But *Adrian*'s single. Mark's not going to leave his wife."

Instantly, Faye was sorry she'd mentioned it. She'd forgotten the mirror it threw up: Rob and Claire and Nadine, Gabe and Faye and Tot. "It—it just happened," Faye said, urging Nadine to start walking again. "It won't last. I didn't want to get involved—no, that's not true, I did want it once it started. I could have stopped it and I didn't."

"Do you see him a lot?"

"No."

"Does Rob know?"

"No."

"He'll find out, Faye."

"Maybe, maybe not."

"How do you feel about Mark?"

"I feel—I'm attracted to him, physically. It's released me from a lot of bitterness about Gabe."

Nadine tugged Faye to a window displaying toddler clothes. They stood together, pointing. "Isn't this sweet," Nadine said, "talking about babies and sex like normal people, not about poor Della or OPI or anything like that."

They moved back into the swirling crowd. "I never had an affair with a married man," Nadine said.

"It's dishonest," Faye said. "It rips up the trust."

"Well, yes, in most cases. Gabe and Tot—that was a betrayal." Nadine broke away from Faye to make room for two children bumping along beside their mother. "But you're not close to Laura the way Tot was to you . . . and Laura and

Mark haven't been married except in name for years."

"It's still a form of betrayal," Faye said. "I'm ambivalent about Mark, and then I feel all those good feelings in my body again. Nothing lasts forever. I call him up and just spin with desire for him. And then I get involved in the production and forget all about him. I hope we go our separate ways before anyone's hurt."

"My God," Nadine said, suddenly realizing the connections. "If this got out during the campaign, it would be disaster. How discreet—?"

The man hit Nadine in the breast with a force that buckled her. She felt something catch on the pocket of her jacket, another hand take her elbow, and someone else grab her arm.

"Nadine!" Faye cried. Nadine was on her knees on the wet pavement. Faye dropped down and put her arms around her.

Nadine could hardly speak. "He punched me in the breast," she gasped.

"Honey, that guy really slammed you." A gray-haired woman in a Chanel suit hovered over them.

"Can you stand?" Faye asked, trying to help Nadine up.

"I won't miscarry from a blow in the breast," Nadine whispered.

"The son of a bitch just kept right on walking," the smartly dressed woman yelled. "Did he take anything? I saw the whole thing. That's what those fuckers do," she ranted, gripping her Fendi bag.

"I'm all right," Nadine said. The pain shot straight through her chest like a hot poker. She put her hand out; Faye steadied her.

"Get a cab, will you?" Faye asked the woman.

"These goddamn streets," the woman caroled, eyeing Nadine, "it's open season on taxpayers! The police can't protect us and don't care! This used to be a safe town." She stepped off the curb and waved her bag imperiously at a taxi.

In the cab, Faye said, "Take us to the nearest hospital."

"Oh, don't overreact," Nadine pleaded. "Let's just get to the Anthony and have something to eat. I haven't seen you in months."

"But you might have a broken rib."

"No, let's just go on."

"We can't! Someone ought to look at you!"

Nadine breathed in deeply. "See? No broken ribs. I'm fine."

The taxi was pulling in front of the Anthony Hotel. "I've got it," Faye said. "Just give me a dollar."

Nadine was rummaging in her pocket when she found it.

The note was handprinted in block letters: "NADINE STERN FERRAY, BACK OFF OR YOU'LL REGRET IT."

Nadine began crumpling the note.

"What's that?"

"Nothing, nothing." Faye reached over and took the note from her. "It's nonsense," Nadine protested.

"Driver," Faye said, "take us back to the Winthrop Hotel on N Street." He heaved his shoulders in silent protest against the capriciousness of women; the taxi started moving.

"Oh, don't get excited, Faye. Driver, stop."

The taxi stopped. The man ran his hand through his hair.

"I am not excited," Faye said. "Driver, let's get going."

"Ladies," he said, "which is it?"

"To the Winthrop," Faye said.

"It's an easy walk," he said.

"No, just take us there." The taxi drove on. Faye opened the note and read it. "Nadine, what's going on?"

Nadine folded herself back in the seat, one hand pressed against her ribs. Her suit was wrinkled, part of her blouse had pulled out of her waistband, her hair was mussed.

"I lied to you," Nadine said, after a moment. "I couldn't stop checking."

Faye shut her eyes.

"You got us into all this, back at the cabin. You sent me the disk."

"I asked you to stop."

"I'm sorry, Faye."

"Good, stay out of it!"

"It's so big," Nadine said respectfully. "I can feel it buried under all that paper and bureaucracy. No wonder Della was scared. But I can't get a handle on it, it needs someone checking from the outside now. I've told Tot everything."

"Oh, Nadine, no! This message—" She shook the note. "*This* is serious."

Nadine lowered her voice. "Yes, but there *is* a connection between Della's list on that disk and OPI. It's real, it exists."

"I don't want to hear about this!" Faye shouted. "Driver, stop!" They were one block from the hotel. She paid the taxi and they got out. "I can't talk to you in that cab," Faye said, rattled. She took Nadine's arm. "You don't know what you're doing! You don't know how bad things can get! Didn't you believe me about the possibility of being wiretapped?"

"Yes, I'm careful." Except for the Tot call, she thought.

"Whoever's doing this to you and to me is sophisticated and dangerous. You just have no idea what it's like to find a body in your bed!"

Nadine started giggling. "I'm sorry, it's just 'body in your bed' struck me as—"

"You're very silly to discount this, Nadine."

Nadine stopped and pressed a hand against Faye's cheek. "We're out of it—I told Tot that. She'll do her reporter thing and if she finds something, fine. And if not, well, that's it."

The telephone was ringing when Nadine got home that night. It was Maynard Bluestone, the Washington columnist.

"Ms. Ferray, I'm calling to let you know that one of my columns will be covering 'leakers' on the staff of the NSC. My sources have named you."

"What?"

"They've linked you intimately with a Washington reporter." He named a reporter Nadine knew slightly. Nadine gasped. "Do you have any comment?"

"None of that's true, it's outrageous, it's libelous! I'll sue if you run anything like that."

"Are you referring to the reporter or to the leaks?"

"Both! I mean it—I'll sue!"

"Thank you, Ms. Ferray. I'll include your denials."

Nadine immediately telephoned Rob in California, but he was out and not expected back until late. She telephoned Tot, and reached her answering service. She felt trapped.

The interconnection of government and the press—especially the crowned heads, the columnists—was powerful: what they said about the White House, the President, the executive staff, or Congress was widely read, and always elicited quick, emotional responses. The press could make or destroy careers.

She was staring at the pattern in the carpet. This was the opening shot; this was retribution for OPI. And now that it had happened, she wondered at her sense of invincibility all those weeks that she was checking the companies on Della's disk. She cast back to the President's meeting with the NSC staff when she'd caught Leo at the elevator. She'd thought he was lying to her about OPI's being new, but Adrian had thought Leo might not have known much about it. She could have complained privately through channels to Leo that she thought Harper was overstepping his mandate. But she hadn't done that. And now someone had leaked what sounded like a skillful mixture of truth and falsehood to Bluestone. Someone wanted her out of the NSC, maybe out of government. Leo? Norman Tate? Could she have misread Adrian?

She stared at her telephone. She would have to go out to the drugstore to reach Rob. And whatever Leo's role was in all this, she had a duty to level with him and to alert him to Bluestone's column. Leo was her boss and her father's friend.

Faye couldn't breathe water anymore. She was desperately trying to reach the surface, she could feel it up there, but no matter how hard she swam, it was always beyond, above, ahead.

Her arm broke into chilly air. Below, a loose, wet rope hit her knee and snapped around it. Her face popped out of the water; she breathed air! Another rope wrapped around her waist and snatched her beneath the surface.

She looked down. The nautilus. An undulating mass of tentacles beneath her, pulling her deeper. Horrified, she opened her mouth. Water flowed in, choking her. The speed of the descent increased, the coils were wrapping her in a package. Beneath her she could see the giant mouth opening to receive her.

Faye awoke screaming and couldn't stop. She didn't know where she was. The room made no sense to her. She was on the floor beside the bed. Her forehead was pressed against the carpet. A dog was barking, high-pitched, continuous yips. There was someone pounding on a door, yelling. She flattened her arms on the carpet and let her body follow.

It was Gabe's voice. "Faye! Goddammit, Faye!"

She crawled to her knees, then to her feet, tottered to the door and opened it.

"Faye, for God's sake!" he gasped, plowing into the room, staring wildly around. "What the hell's going on?" Faye was backing away from him, one hand pressed to her forehead. Her thick hair was jumbled, her pajama top was open and twisted to one side. He went into the bedroom, stripped the spread, and put it around her. She backed into a chair and sat.

Julie was standing in the hallway with Zack, looking in. "Faye, are you all right?"

"It's okay," Gabe said. "Take care of the management if they come running up here." He shut the door, leaned against it and stared at Faye, huddled in the spread. The dog sat on its haunches between the sitting room and the bedroom.

"Who heard?" she mumbled.

"Everyone."

"I've—I've been having dreams . . ."

"You call that a *dream*? I thought you were being butchered."

"What time is it?"

"About two."

"Three hours to wake-up." She raised her head and pushed some of the hair out of her face. "It's only a nightmare, Gabe. I'm all right."

He was worried, ready for action, but frustrated. "Are you going to be able to work?" She nodded and clutched the spread around her. "How long have you had these nightmares?"

"Couple of months. Three months. Well, since March." She drew herself up. The dog, calmer, began to advance into the sitting room.

"Before the Oscars," he said in the code they used for the "body in the bed."

"Go back to sleep, Gabe. I really don't want you to keep rescuing me. I'm really all right."

He was uncertain. "What if you have it again? Does Julie just tell management the producer is loco and has these little problems at night?"

When she stood, holding on to the back of the chair, he said, "Sit down" and tapped her on the shoulder. She sat. Gabe went to the portable bar and broke out two airline-sized bottles of brandy. "Tell me about the dream."

"I really don't feel like it, Gabe."

"That's tough. Talk." He handed her a brandy. "You got half an hour."

"I'm in water and being dragged down by a monster, a nautilus, with big tentacles."

"A what?"

"A nautilus. It's a creature with a shell and tentacles sticking out the front end and a mouth and the—the tentacles stuff food in the mouth. The first dreams weren't scary. In fact, Della was in some of them—she'd phone me—you know, in the dream—talking normally, sounding strong. She tells me about the twins, tells me to . . ." Her face squeezed together. "To—look after Nadine. I feel so responsible."

"Why?"

"Because," she replied angrily, "I was the one who insisted we had to find out what happened. I got everyone going— even Tot! None of us knew what Della was involved in. Then I found a computer disk in Della's stuff. Nadine figured out what was on it, government subcontracting."

"Hold it, just let me track this."

"I remembered some of what Della said as she—was dying. That was a big beef between me and Detective Phelps, the remembering. After the Oscars, I got really scared, but Nadine was already digging around, using the list on the computer disk. I asked her to stop, she said she would, but she didn't, she was into the chase, and *she* wasn't being threatened, no one was leaving bodies in her bed. And then, yesterday, when Nadine and I went out to eat, she was knocked down on the street. We found a note in her pocket—"

"Note?"

"He put it there when he punched her!" She held the spread around her like a cape as she went for her purse and found the note. Gabe took it.

"A definite message," he said.

She saw the calm, gentlemanly expression on his face. "You're going to be analytical," she said.

"I was going to ask you what Nadine has found that would make someone punch her out on the street."

"Just one punch. Nadine thinks a program run by the government is pumping millions of federal money out of the country into foreign elections."

"Yeah, it is. It's called State Department," he said gently.

"Or, the money's going into domestic companies, but she doesn't know why."

He swallowed the last of his brandy and sat down beside her. "I don't discount what's happened to you, I saw that dead man in your house, I saw Phelps's reaction, how seriously he took it. So did I. But—"

"Nadine gave what she found to Tot."

He leaned forward, putting his elbows on his knees. "Faye, I don't know how to help you. Let's just get this picture finished, Annie and Roger might do something special together—maybe you'll have a good movie. Okay?"

"Okay. Thanks for not ridiculing me."

He opened the door. "See you in two and a half hours." He shut the door.

Faye sat in the chair, seeing the mouth of the nautilus, its tentacles and the blackness below. She concentrated on a picture on the wall to make the tentacles go away.

The door opened. "I'm glad you weren't being murdered," Gabe said softly. Faye was hunched in the chair, crying. "Oh, Faye . . ." He went over to her, put his arms around her.

"I don't care about what some strangers are doing in the government—I only care about Della, about what happened to her, and now about Nadine . . . I'm trying to be brave, I'm trying to do what's right, but I can't stand it anymore." She pressed her face against his shoulder as he knelt beside her.

"You don't have to do anything." But he knew nothing he could say would help. She had exhausted herself.

He stayed an hour, got her talking about the production and some of his ideas for tomorrow, got her into bed. And finally, she fell asleep. He watched her until it was time to shower and meet his crew. He left reluctantly. He hadn't realized how much he wanted her safe. Knowing that again felt new, not old.

TWENTY

The Jungle Gym began shooting the next morning in front of Union Station, not far from the Supreme Court on Capitol Hill.

The white marble station had been designed as the front door of the nation's capital when rail was the way to get around. Zack had secured the permits to film at the front portico and in the little plaza a few steps from the front of the station around the Columbus Memorial fountain. Cables snaked across the sidewalk, connecting all the gear eighty people were tending so three minutes of action could be preserved on film.

The scene was organized disorder at eight in the morning. Reporters thronged the station, scanning for Roger Reynolds. When his stretch limo pulled up on a side street, they surrounded it. He stepped out with a wave, fully costumed in a three-piece suit and carrying a leather designer attaché case. His quick, mobile face slipped from disdain to tolerance for the opening ceremonies.

"Roger!" Gabe said. "Good ride in? You look great."

"Had a little work done around the eyes," Roger replied. "No, just kidding. I see you're up to your old tricks—Day One publicity glut." Roger's entourage drew around him protectively. Gabe was greeting them by name when Faye appeared looking amazingly zippy in a floppy red hat, red jeans, and a red shirt. Roger hugged her, and introduced the men around him.

"Oh, I've met Craig," she said, kissing Roger's double. "How's the deep-sea fishing?"

"Where's the trailer?" Roger asked. Faye pointed at the station's big parking lot, which held the equipment vans, generator, nurse's station, portable toilets, actors' trailers, and the all-important caterer's van. "Security?"

"Loads of it. The first few days are pretty public, but then we'll be off on side streets."

"Gabe, are we ready to go?" Roger asked.

"Soon as Annie gets here." Roger's retinue folded around him. "And here she is," Gabe said, relieved.

Annie's limo glided to a stop. She stepped out, accompanied by her makeup man, hairdresser, maid, and a gofer.

"The battle of the entourages," Faye mumbled to Gabe.

"And you thought you had nightmares," he whispered.

Annie and Roger met in the middle of the roped-off street, their attendants circling around them, each group eyeing the other. Photographers jumped about.

"Roger!" Annie cried, opening her arms.

"Miss Ferray," he said, taking one of her hands, pulling it down, kissing her fingers.

Instantly, Annie's manner changed: she became demure. "You're so charming," she said. She too was fully made up and costumed. "I remember when I first met you—" she began. But Roger was turning away and his staff was folding around him again.

Dino started shouting, the press was urged back.

"My fans," Annie said to Faye, sweeping her arm toward the sizable crowd behind the police cordon. "Aren't they great?"

"They're extras for the background demonstration in the scene."

"But they look just like my fans."

"Well, then, I'm sure they are!" Faye said.

All morning, they shot around the press and the crowd of onlookers. During breaks, Roger disappeared into his trailer with his friends; Annie stayed out with "her fans" and talked to the press.

"Lunch!" Dino shouted. Tables had been set up in the parking lot, and actors, extras, crew streamed forward to the buffet, laden with breads and meats and salads and fruits.

Gabe was trying to catch up with Faye, who was walking swiftly past the buffet, talking on her cellular phone. "Delighted, Mark," she said, stopping to lean against one of the catering trucks. Gabe stopped beside her. "Mark, we can meet there . . . Yes, me, too," she said softly, ringing off. "I invited Mark over tomorrow."

Gabe pushed off the truck. "Always a pleasure to watch our senators in action," he said, shrugging.

Julie, a bright scarf wrapped around her curly black hair, picked up a bullhorn. "Attention, please! We have the jury's final result on our Name-the-Dog contest! Faye, bring what's-her-name over here!" Faye held the dog aloft. "And the winning name is—Cricket! Zack, take a bow!" Cheers, hoots, applause. Zack bowed.

Faye laughed. "Cricket? Who was on this jury?" She put Cricket on an empty table so people could see her. "Here's my dog's trick," Faye said. She gazed into Cricket's eyes and frowned. "Growl."

Cricket instantly gave out a surprisingly low, ugly growl. The crew clapped, went back to their lunch.

"Have you seen this?" Julie asked, putting a copy of Bluestone's column in the morning paper in Faye's hand. "It's a hoot. Isn't your friend in the NSC?"

Faye took the paper. The column outlined the dangers of unstable personnel working in security positions. Without naming Nadine, but drawing a clear bead on her rank and job description, the column ticked off "one executive branch staffer's severe marriage problems, which could affect judgment in a sensitive position." It asserted that "this person has been intimately linked with a Washington reporter. The NSC has long been troubled by its security leaks, but it hasn't seemed able to act with dispatch. Pillow talk takes on no new meanings here. If the NSC can't protect its own security, how well can it protect ours?"

"Ohh, God," Faye groaned.

* * *

The White House was seething.

"I was literally on my way here to tell you he'd called last night," Nadine was saying to Leo in his office, "but I had no idea it would be in today's paper—"

"The column's incredible!" Leo yelled. "It's asinine." His outrage was convincing.

"Leo, I'm not the cause of the leaks all these months."

"I'm sure you have nothing to do with them," he said.

"I mean, this has to be about someone else, talking about pillow talk and marriage problems, that's not me!"

He drew his thin lips into a line. "I'm very disappointed in you. You've been looking into the OPI program. The attorney general and the President authorized that program."

"Leo, I don't know what's going on here."

"Given everything that's happened, you'll have to be interrogated on this leaking business—"

"Interrogated? All of this is completely untrue—"

"We'll have to play by the rules. We'll get Adrian to handle the investigation."

"Investigation?"

"And when that's all done, you and I will have a private meeting strictly through channels on whatever complaints you have. Do you have any objection to a lie-detector test?"

Could she possibly pass it? She'd just given Tot everything she knew. But she wasn't *the* leaker they were looking for— she could be truthful on that score. Leo's eyes were on her. "I'm shocked that you'd even suggest such a thing to me. Lie-detector tests aren't even that accurate."

"You know the procedure, Nadine," he said. "If we don't follow it, your position will be worse."

"I am not guilty of these leaks."

"Let the test confirm that. Then this can all be over." He smiled and his eyebrows lifted.

"It's against all my better instincts, Leo."

As soon as Tot read Bluestone's column, she insisted on seeing her assignment editor. Lloyd was at his desk, sipping a Diet Pepsi through a straw and going through a stack of newspapers.

"Not now, Tot," he said.

"Now! I've got a source inside the NSC for a story I've been looking into. It's a lot bigger than Bluestone's leakers." She outlined it.

"That's pretty hard to believe, Tot," he said deprecatingly.

"But what if I'm right?" she pressed. "Do you want to be the man everyone points to and says, 'He had a jump on Watergate II and he passed'?"

When Faye got back to her hotel room that night, she had messages from Nadine, Herb, Tony, Steve, and Detective Phelps. Assistants flowed in and out, cellular phones clapped to their faces.

"A Mr. Pike wants to come out to the shoot tomorrow," Julie said to her.

"Sam Pike?" Faye asked. "Fine." She was dialing Detective Phelps before she realized it and stopped. "I'll be back in a minute." She went down to the lobby and called Phelps from the pay phone.

"I called, Ms. Ferray," he said, "to suggest you get some more security. An informant came through for us. The man who made the bomb that blew up your friend's car has been found, but unfortunately he died of gunshot wounds last night before we could talk to him. The informant said this man also put the derelict in your bed. We believe someone's stepping up the pressure."

"Who was he—the man who blew the car?"

"Used to be a pro, but he had a big smack habit. We think someone's cleaning up loose ends out here. You get some security and stay alert."

Still on the pay phone, Faye called Nadine. "Can you call me back at the usual number?"

Nadine sighed. "I—okay."

Faye made production calls from her cellular phone while she waited for the pay phone to ring.

"How are you?" Faye asked when Nadine called back.

"I'm not used to being stared at and whispered about," Nadine said. "And this phone business is really a pisser."

Nadine almost never used rough language, which told Faye how tense her friend was. "The column didn't name you."

"I'm the suspect who fits the description, Faye, except for the marriage problems. It's a small town."

"The L.A. police detective called me. They found the man who bombed Della's car, but he's dead. I've got to get more security. Phelps thinks someone's tying up loose ends."

"Then get a bodyguard. Listen, Tot's with me. She wants to speak with you."

"No," Faye said.

The next voice was Tot's. "Faye, there must be more than Nadine thought or Bluestone's column wouldn't have said what it said. Someone's doing a number on her."

"I realize that. I'm sorry she involved you."

"Why? It might be a good story."

"Because I don't want anyone else hurt," Faye said. She glanced around the hotel lobby; the only people there were production people and a pair of elderly tourists. "Is Nadine going to lose her job?"

"Probably," Tot said carefully. "I just thought you'd like to know this isn't all for naught. Besides, she's going to be a mommy."

"It's one thing to take a pregnancy leave, quite another to lose a career."

"Yes," Tot said. "Listen, it's chilly in this parking lot. Here's Nadine back."

"So now what?" Faye said.

"Before I left the office, I packed my briefcase full of my files and my notes. I want them close to me."

"Why?" Faye asked, seeing Gabe come into the lobby and head upstairs.

"I don't know. I'm nervous. I'm being interrogated tomorrow."

"Interrogated? My God, does it never end?"

"The National Security office is a special case. Leaks are zealously investigated, and properly so. I have to take a lie-detector test—"

"A *lie* detector? What are you supposed to have given the press, for God's sake?"

"Anything, if proved, will do," Nadine said. "Or even if unproved. They're looking for a leaker. We're advisers to the President. You can't conduct or plan international policy if half-formed, unapproved working papers are handed out to the press. I'll either pass it or I won't."

"You're not the leaker they're looking for, isn't that some protection?"

"I hope so. I doubt it." She exhaled a little puff that carried over the phone. "I feel like a failure."

"Oh, Nadine, don't. We'll get through this, we will. Why don't you come over here, watch us work all night?"

"Tot's staying with me."

"I don't think that's smart, Nadine."

"I don't think it really matters anymore."

TWENTY-ONE

IN THE CORRIDORS of the OEOB the next morning, people greeted Nadine as usual, but she felt the currents underneath and they reminded her of Tiber Creek bubbling under Constitution Avenue.

Nadine reached out to open her office door. It was locked. She turned. Someone ducked into an office. A door closed. Pamela was coming down the hall. She seemed embarrassed and a little afraid.

"What's happening?" Nadine asked her. "Am I really locked out?"

"Yes. I tried to call you."

"Can I see Leo?"

"Well, Nadine, he telephoned, he said he couldn't see you until later today. You're supposed to see Adrian." Pamela pursed her lips; her large blue eyes blinked.

"Don't worry, Pam," Nadine said softly, "you're not involved."

Nadine went into Adrian's office. "Reporting in," she said.

"Please shut the door and sit down," he said. "Leo has charged me with the investigation. He spoke to you yesterday about it, right?"

"Yes, but Adrian, why am I locked out?"

"I couldn't stop it. The guys found some files connected to CDEE in your computer, along with some charts listing monetary payments, apparently to you."

"Impossible! They're plants!"

"Your bank account is being investigated. It'll be a really bad sign if we find similar amounts in it."

She stared at him. "Whose side are you on?" she demanded.

He was running a finger along the corner of his desk. "There are times when there are no sides," he said, "just areas."

Lively reactions to Bluestone's column appeared in the morning paper and on television.

For the second day of the shoot in front of Union Station, the damp summer heat promised to come in hard and melt everyone's will. The crowd was larger and Julie had put on more security. One enterprising local news program had summarized the *Jungle Gym* story of a government whistle-blower and interviewed members of Congress. It was a soft-ball question; the legislators commented predictably about the movies, freedom of speech, and the arts; the President, when asked to comment, had talked about the movies he'd loved as a kid. Senator Drummond defended the rights of all filmmakers everywhere.

Julie was worried the shoot was already breaking down, but she couldn't put her finger on the cause. Gabe and Faye bounced between being alert to each other or totally indifferent. Faye, for instance, wasn't picking up on the way some cast members checked her with their eyes when Gabe gave an order. Faye was distracted by the innuendos about Nadine in the press. Gabe bewildered Julie. He was kind, but he'd been ordering Lonny about like a sergeant. Lon, quick to take offense, was working slower, his manner truculent.

A special unit photographer was snapping pictures of Roger again. "Please turn this way, Mr. Reynolds . . . Oh, thank you . . . Yes, and if I could just have one more . . . Oh, that's great." Roger was patient but that wouldn't last if he had to wait more than five minutes for Lonny to solve a lighting problem. Faye was usually on top of situations like this one that could flower into little disasters. But she was tinkering with the portable fax attached to her cellular phone, trying to get it to receive.

The constant attention to Roger made Annie seethe, but she was also trying to flatter him and be engaging; her act was not attractive.

"How's everyone today?" Sam Pike asked, looking cheerful and dapper in a fresh cotton cord summer suit and a straw skimmer.

"Hi, Sam." Faye noticed the photographer was still groveling in front of Roger. She instantly went over to them. "I wonder if you could take a few pictures of Annie and our other costars?" she said, clamping her hand on his camera arm.

"Oh, sure, sure," he said, but kept on shooting. Roger gave him the finger. The photographer grinned widely—a thousand-dollar shot.

Roger, disgusted he'd fallen for it again, turned on Gabe. "Can we get going?" he yelled.

"Five minutes, I swear," Gabe promised.

Fifteen minutes later, Gabe began shooting an aggravated Roger and an unmollified Annie. The shot was terrible.

"Good," Gabe said, adjusting the panama hat he wore whenever he shot, rain or shine. The atmosphere was charged, but Gabe was polite to everyone. He didn't even seem to be directing, letting the actors play the scenes any old way, as if they were in some curious and public group exercise that had its own shifting and unspoken rules. Usually, he softly suggested which action or tone seemed best.

Not today. "Annie, don't tug at Roger as if you're asking him for a handout. Take hold of his arm with authority." Annie's eyes slid toward Faye. "And take off that necklace. I don't like the look."

"But Faye—"

"Take it off," Gabe said.

Everything exploded at once. "I can't light this," Lonny said. "This look is shit. I told you last night, Gabe—"

Roger threw up his arms and started stomping back to his trailer, followed by his attendants. "Just give me a buzz when you get it right," he said nastily over his shoulder.

Annie had had enough, too. She waved at her makeup man. "Everything's melting!" she pouted. Faye was finally receiving her fax from the insurance people regarding the Chesapeake Bay scenes. Sam Pike ducked out of her way as she headed for Annie.

"Who got the financing?" were the first words out of Annie's mouth when Faye reached her.

"You made a promise," Faye said in a low, hard voice. Annie had added two more gofers to her attendants and had demanded her agent fly in an underling to take care of her business to prove she was bigger than Roger Reynolds. No one was bigger than Roger.

The makeup man was trying to powder Annie down, whisking at her nose and chin with his brush as she gestured at various people or props. "None of us would be here, except for me!" Annie cried, building her irritation into a first-class tantrum.

Faye put an arm around her billowy waist and drew her away from the makeup man. "Annie, if you make the Alps out of this ant hill, I'll fire your ass so fast you'll be standing outside your hotel looking for a cab because there won't be any limo."

"You won't!" Annie shrieked.

Still smiling, Faye ground in her ear, "Try me."

Annie reared back. Gabe looked up from his huddle with the camera crew. Roger and his double were talking behind their hands. Both men started laughing.

Sam Pike was standing right behind Faye, looking delighted and eager. "Faye, could you spare Annie for a coupla minutes? I brought Annie and Roger some champagne and something from Air Force One. Gabe, can I have five minutes?" Gabe waved and went back to his huddle.

Sam moved Annie away. "You and I got a date in a limo." Julie heard Sam say as they passed her. "Faye'll fire your sweet ass. Don't think she won't, honey."

"I like the pages," Faye was saying to Keith on her phone in her trailer. "I just have a couple of changes." When she'd finished with him, she called Steve about the sets being built in L.A. "Faster, they have to build faster!"

Nadine opened the door to the trailer as Faye was hanging up. "Who's the tough guy sitting outside your trailer?"

"New security. How are you?"

"I've just had my interrogation and a lie-detector test," she said. She threw her bag on the couch. "I've been locked out of my office." She sank into a chair and checked her perfectly combed hair with a shaky hand. "I feel like I ought to protect myself, but I don't know who from."

"If we stick together, we'll be all right." But Nadine's manner disturbed her. "How did the test go?" Distantly, she heard Dino calling the lunch break.

Nadine went limp, one hand dangling over the arm of her chair, her eyes flat. "I did leak information to Tot," she said. "So, I probably didn't pass the test."

"But you're not *the* leaker," Faye said, "the one they've been looking for. Emotionally, you knew that, so maybe you did pass."

Nadine, flaccid, surrendering, only nodded.

"When's Rob getting back?"

"Tonight. We've managed to miss each other on the telephone ever since everything broke. Now I'm locked out and he can't fax me, so he sent me a telegram! I thought telegrams had gone the way of the 45 rpm record. His wire said to remember Bluestone is a snake and that the staffer with a bad marriage didn't describe me." She sighed with longing. "I bought his favorite wine, I've ordered a catered dinner at home, and we'll sit there in the candlelight and I'll tell him he's going to be a father."

Julie opened the trailer door. "Senator Mark Drummond."

"Oh, God," Faye said, "I invited him to lunch."

Nadine perked up. "Let's get him in here. Let's talk to him about what's going on. He's on the Senate Appropriations Committee—the executive branch budget watchdog."

Mark Drummond was making the rounds of the cast and crew, shaking everyone's hand, chatting and laughing his big laugh, everyone's friend and supporter. When he sat down in Faye's trailer with a plate of food, Faye ran a hand across the back of his neck. "Mark, there's something Nadine wants to discuss with you."

"Of course, of course." He instantly fixed his eyes on Nadine, ready to listen and solve.

"Mark, I'd like you to consider a Senate investigation into a program called Office of Public Information being run by the National Security Council."

He frowned at her, amazed. "What is this?"

"I want to clear my name, Mark," Nadine said. Her voice was tight, her earlier exhaustion gone.

"Nadine, I know this is a painful time for you, but the press will fade—"

"What if publicity has been created to divert attention from what I was doing?"

"I don't understand."

"I was looking into the OPI program for the NSC's legal adviser. At the same time a disk Della left for Faye gave us the names of companies that were getting subcontracts from our office. So I was working from both ends, you might say. It's common knowledge over at the NSC that OPI may be going beyond its original goals. This whole mess with Bluestone, being locked out of my office—it's a setup! All I did was look into a program no one wanted examined. I don't leak information to the press."

Mark rearranged his face, glancing at Faye. "You're under a lot of pressure, Nadine. It's always a shock when you're the butt of rumor. It's easy to see ghosts, plots, where there are none. The power of the press can be very intimidating."

Faye was astonished. "Don't be condescending, Mark—"

"I'm not!"

"This all started with Della. Tell him, Nadine."

She launched into tracking down the list on the computer disk, but the deeper she got into describing the subcontractors and the interlocking boards of directors, the more incredulous Mark Drummond became. "It's a giant swindle of government funds," Nadine finished.

Drummond was shocked. "Oh, Nadine, this sort of thing isn't like you."

"Mark, didn't we learn anything from Iran-Contra?" Faye asked.

"We learned life goes on, Faye, and there are a few bad eggs," he said, annoyed. "If Nadine makes a charge like this, she'll only look like she's trying to save her own skin, that what they're saying about her is true. I'm sorry, Nadine, but I haven't heard enough for me to call for an investigation. My God, you can't even get to your own files."

Faye said, "The timing is wrong, huh, Mark?"

"What?"

"Campaign first, reelection first, everything else second."

"Well, I can't do much for her if I'm not in the Senate, can I?"

Nadine opened her briefcase. "Here," she said, handing over the disk and a file folder of notes. "This is Della's disk. These are my private logs of everything I found, step by step, when I was trying to figure out why Della kept the disk. Now, you get a Senate investigator on that and you'll have something."

"All right," he said, smiling. "I'll look at what you have." He rose and bent down to give Faye a public kiss; his hand pressed into her shoulder. She felt the warm pressure like a memory, of something good that had once happened to her, but was not happening anymore.

When Mark Drummond returned to his office in the Russell Building, he summoned Harry, his administrative aide. "Dig up everything you can on some program called Office of Public Information out of the NSC."

A half hour later, a staff assistant who worked for Drummond on the Senate Appropriations Committee came in with some information. "I thought I remembered this one, Senator. It's an information program created by some of the people around Leo Townsend in the White House."

"Information about what?" Mark grumped.

"Democracy."

"What's its budget?"

"About a hundred mil."

"Getting up there. You say it's Leo's program? Where's the head chief—Tate—in all this?"

"Same as always, carrying Leo's canteen."

*   *   *

It was quiet in the trailer after Mark Drummond left.

"Maybe I should get a lawyer," Nadine said. She felt loosed from moorings she'd depended upon all her life.

"Have you spoken to your father?"

"No," Nadine said. "Not yet."

Julie stuck her head in the trailer door. "There's another problem with Annie," Julie said, "and Zack has major hassles with the Maryland Film office—"

"You stay, Nadine, and rest," Faye said. "And if you want to make any personal calls, go in and use a pay phone in the station."

Judge Stern was on the ground floor of El Contento in his study, a large room with heavy burgundy leather furniture and a window that looked out at the Pacific.

"Is Bluestone talking about *you* in his column?" Judge Stern asked his daughter on the telephone.

"Yes, Dad. He called me for comment."

"You'd get more support from your people at work to fight these accusations if you'd stop interfering," he said. His hand gripped the receiver tightly. "I heard from Leo. Can you imagine how silly and ridiculous you're being?"

"Dad!" she cried out. "The legal adviser himself asked me to look into the program!"

The pain and the shock in his daughter's voice cut straight through him. He steeled himself against it.

"When I think of my daughter spinning stories like some television writer—my God, if I were Leo and one of my people went behind my back, I'd fire her on the spot. Leo's courtesy to you and to our family in this thing is magnificent. He's protecting you, he's trying to protect me, and all I can wish is that you go to Leo and apologize."

"Daddy, please, just listen—"

"Now, you get yourself together and maybe we can all put this behind us. Stop talking about programs running amok, and start behaving like my daughter! You take your medicine and move on. You do that, you'll find other people will, too. No one likes to see careers ruined, yours, Leo's, mine, maybe Rob's—these things spread, Nadine. Stop behaving like a child. Drop this foolishness." His knuckles were white.

Buck Stern hung up, unwound his fingers from the receiver, and let his hand drop to the surface of his desk. He knew exactly what he had done to her, the enormity of his deception, his fraudulent outrage. He'd done it for *his* good, not hers. Bluestone's column had shocked him deeply; he didn't understand how it had come about or how his daughter had ended up in the middle of everything. But he, Judge Ballard Stern, had to remain outside all of it.

He felt lonelier than he'd ever felt: he'd betrayed his daughter, he'd done it instantly, without a second thought.

He pressed the button on his intercom: "Edward, call for the car. I'm going into town."

"Buck, old man," Jerry said. "Didn't think surprise visits were your style." Jerry was stretched out on the living room sofa, reading *The New Yorker*.

"You're looking good," Stern said. "I mean it."

"Feeling good. I've got a reprieve for a while." He eyed Buck. "Help yourself to the bar and get me one of whatever you're having."

Stern felt like a martini. There'd been years when he and Jerry had lunched at Chasen's and they'd laughed and eaten everything they never ate anymore, washing it all down with martinis, but so had everyone else. He took out the shaker and stirred up the power drink.

"Wicked, Buck. You here to corrupt me?"

Stern sat in a wing chair near the sofa and immediately began a conversation about the U.S. Open. When that played out, he poured more martinis. "How's Faye doing? Hear she's back in D.C. on a big shoot with Roger."

"She's the light of my life," Jerry said, feeling the martini melt his veins.

"Bet she's not as stubborn as Nadine," Stern said. "Faye used to dance and sing around like a little Tinkerbell."

"Tinkerbell?" Jerry said alertly. Something was wrong with Buck. He never talked children. *Jerry* talked children. He remembered the morning Nadine had been born. The nurse had said, "It's a girl!" and Buck had scowled. "Just a girl?" he'd muttered. But he'd grown fond of Nadine, at least Jerry thought he had. "How's Nadine? She running the government yet?"

Buck nodded gamely. "Yes, sir, you do seem better, Jer. You'll lick this, I know it. Lotta people from the old days, they're rooting for you. I was thinking about—" Jerry waited, saw him change his thought. "I was thinking about the old days when right was right and wrong was wrong, and our kids had the whole world in front of them, well, shit, *we* had the whole world in front of us, the kids were just babies. You remember that time on the boat—where were we? Arrowhead? Christ, I can't remember these things anymore. It was a Sunday during the Goldwater campaign, wasn't it? What were we *doing* out there? How did Faye get over the side, for God's sake? Sank like a damned rock. What was she— four, five, six?"

It was a revealing moment. Jerry searched Buck's face, looking for the reason he recalled it now. "You were the first one in the water, Buck."

"It was easy to pull her out, I was always a good swimmer. But I no sooner get back on that fuckin' boat with your dripping kid than Nadine jumps in—she fuckin' jumped in. What was she proving?"

He peered at Jerry. "Did she want attention? Did she think it was a game?" He shook his head in an exaggerated motion. Slowly his smile faded. "Don't we always want the best for our kids, Jer? We want them to think well of us, don't we? And sooner or later they get on to us, don't they? They see the cracks and the flaws and I guess after a while they just put up with us."

The image of Nadine at some future moment standing in front of him with the full knowledge that he'd thrown her into the pot as a sacrifice sobered him. He drained his glass, climbed to his feet, went directly to the bar and mixed up another batch of martinis.

Jerry watched him uneasily.

"We want our kids to think the best of us," Buck said, "but, shit, is that a practical hope? You used to get loaded and yell at Rob, and I'd be thinking how screwed up he'd get . . . 'Course, he isn't. He's a nice guy. I guess they survive us." He returned with the martini pitcher.

"Buck, is something wrong with Nadine? Is Rob okay?"

"Sure they're okay—I didn't come over here to tell you they'd been hit by a truck. Nadine's having some problems on the job, she's getting some heat from a columnist— her first real taste of just how hot the fire can be from our Fourth Estate." He sipped his drink. "Aw, screw 'em. Bottoms up, pal."

"Don't kid a kidder, Buck. What's up?"

Buck swept a hand over his white hair and tugged at his tie. "We can't be all things to all people, can we?"

"You just learning that?" Jerry laughed and sipped at the gasoline in his glass.

"But what if we have to choose, Jer?" Buck whispered. "What if our kids prevent us from making our way and we have to make a choice?"

Now Jerry was thoroughly aroused. "Is the President withdrawing your name? Are you losing your dough?" He made his voice light and mocking. "Is someone blackmailing you for all those election high jinks?"

Buck's face softened, eased. "Ah, c'mon, Jer, that was just politics." Jerry scoffed. " 'S true, Jer. The other side always makes mistakes. We capitalized on 'em. Look at ol' Drummond, sashaying around as if he's already elected; it comes outta his pores, but he's making mistakes. Voters won't like it."

"You're supporting Sparks, the little home builder."

"Damn right—well, I would, if I could. I'm out of it for now. Keeping things clean for the high court." The high court seemed far away on this day. Very far. Every stone on the street leading to it was imprinted with Nadine's pretty face. "That court . . . I want smooth hearings, I don't want a damned carnival. These things . . . so delicate. Least little wave can capsize 'em."

Jerry did not have the kind of relationship with Buck that allowed him to comment about how distraught he seemed. But that is what Jerry was thinking when Buck said, "Jerry, have you ever felt guilty about one of your kids?"

"Yes, I have," Jerry said slowly. "About Rob. He got the brunt of the bad times. He was a kinda happy-go-lucky kid, not a lot different from Faye, but he was the son, so he took the heat. I didn't see it then, but later, I remember watching him play some ball in the park and I realized a lot of the cheerfulness he'd had inside was pasted on him."

"I feel guilty about Nadine," Buck said quietly.

"Why?"

Buck tossed down the rest of his martini. "Girls. Girls are hard. They look up to their dads, don't they? It's so hard to be what they want—well, you know all about that." He was so close to telling Jerry what was going on that it scared him. "I got a meeting in Century City with a bunch of old-timers who think they're really running the country but they have to turn up their hearing aids to catch the sound of a siren. Good seeing you, Jer. Take care of yourself." He walked out of the house as if he hadn't a care in the world.

TWENTY-TWO

IN WASHINGTON, EARLY that evening, the Lyndon B. Johnson oak tree threw a long shadow across one end of the President's Park. Leo Townsend was letting Nadine sit outside his office while, inside, he smiled at the results of her lie-detector test. They weren't all he'd wanted, but they were enough. He could discredit her if he had to. "All right," he said to his assistant, "send her in."

He was standing at his office safe, a sheaf of papers in neat files, and a tape in his hand. He gestured at what he held. "The results of your interrogation and your lie-detector test." He tossed them in the safe, closed the door, spun the dial. He sat down at his desk, clasped his hands in front of him, and stared at her. "You failed."

"Oh, God, Leo, I couldn't have. I'm not any leaker—"

"It says you are."

"My God, I'm not going to just sit by and be convicted of something I didn't do—I'll take responsibility for what I did do—I was looking into OPI, but you know why— you've read my interrogation—I don't just leap to conclusions—"

"You're a sneak and a traitor," he sneered coldly. "And I know Rob's in it with you."

"That's—preposterous, Leo! You know me! You know Rob!"

Leo's expression was glacial, his eyes boring into her. His lips had all but disappeared.

"You and Rob will stop at nothing to bring me down."

"What's Rob got to do with any of this?" she demanded.

"Rob would do anything for intelligence on me. He's even sleeping with my wife—been going on for months—and you condone it!" he yelled, knowing Nadine had never heard of the affair. His tone was just right, outraged, injured, accusatory. Nadine looked ill. She was sitting way back in her chair. He pressed a button on his phone console. His office door flew open, a marshal stepped into the room.

"You're dismissed, Mrs. Ferray," Leo said. "The marshal will escort you out."

Nadine was walking up the shaded street toward her home. The night was sultry. Nothing she'd once believed about this night was going to come true. She'd hoped she could skate through the lie-detector test and she hadn't. She'd hoped she could save her career and she hadn't; she'd hoped her news of the baby would renew her marriage. She felt duplicity all around her. She felt vulnerable to Rob for loving him, vulnerable to her parents, vulnerable to her physical state and the need to protect her child.

She reached the town house on the little hill. The lights were on. Rob had come home. She leaned against the bottom of the stone steps.

Nadine played by the rules she'd been taught at home and in law school, and so did most of the people she knew. The rules were out there like guideposts, perceivable, definable. When someone knocked down a post, Nadine had always been able to scan the horizon and confidently recite the rules. But now the rules and customs by which she'd lived had dissolved. In their place was emptiness, immeasurably threatening.

When she got inside, Rob was in the kitchen on the telephone. He waved in his open way and blew her a kiss. She walked heavily across the tile, took the phone out of his hand, and hung it up.

"I know about Claire. I know everything."

"What are you saying?" he asked, stricken. "Know what?"

"Don't make me say it!"

"I don't know what you're talking about!"

"Your affair with Claire Townsend!" she screamed.

"Nadine, come off it—this is silly!" His eyes moved desperately away from her and in that moment, she knew that what Leo had said was true.

"Don't lie!" she screamed.

"I'm not lying! Honey, who's telling you—"

"Leo! Leo's telling me. Then he fired me!"

Rob leaned against the drainboard as if she'd struck him. "This can't be happening," he said. "None of this is true."

"It is true. I can see it in your face. Give me credit, you bastard, I'm not blind. You've betrayed me—God, you're no better than my father!"

He reached out for her. She dodged away across the kitchen. "Honey, I've always loved you—you're my rock, you're everything—"

"Hardly everything. Clearly not enough!"

"You can't take Leo's word over mine!"

"I don't want to, but he wasn't just firing me—he was getting back at *you*!"

Rob felt his mind go into paralysis. He'd always thought that if anything came out, he could convince Nadine it wasn't true. "Listen to me, Nadine, Leo's conjured this up—this is politics!"

"Stop lying!" she yelled at him. "It makes me sick!" She turned away. "Is everything a lie? Has our whole life been a lie?" She started out of the kitchen. "I want you out of this house—now!" She didn't even think about telling him she was pregnant.

Nadine woke Faye up early the next morning. "Can you come over here?"

"I'm in the middle of a shoot, remember?"

"It's Sunday, you're not shooting today. Please."

It was a warm, gloomy summer morning, raining off and on, the low clouds rolling in the sky, their bottoms dark and dirty.

Nadine was on the telephone when Faye and Cricket arrived. "I wish you'd stay off the phone," Faye said.

Nadine covered the mouthpiece. "Who cares now? They already know everything about me! Adrian!" she said into the phone. "You've thrown me to the dogs! You're a cad!" She waved Faye at the extension in the other room.

"A *cad*?" Faye mouthed. A *cad*?

"You're *not* supporting me, you're burying me," Nadine said to Adrian.

Faye held on to Cricket's leash and picked up the extension phone. Adrian was saying, "I'm in charge of this investigation, Nadine, and it's not over yet." He lowered his voice. "People in Harper's office are shredding, there's a rumor the Justice Department may step in, which means the press will be sitting at the door, screaming for sound bites."

"What's going on?"

"Bluestone's column! He practically accused the NSC of security leaks. Tate's wild. It's come home to him that he hasn't been minding his store. He's out for revenge, but he's blowing the influence of the column out of proportion!"

"And OPI . . . ?"

"OPI? No one's talking about that."

"Then why is Harper shredding?"

"I don't know. But Nadine, if anyone here helped you in your perambulations through the OPI files, you tell them to keep their heads down till this passes."

Nadine put down the telephone. "Pamela . . ." she said. She dialed her, but there was no answer.

Faye was standing in the doorway. "Adrian didn't sound so bad," she said.

"No, I think he's okay."

"Who's Pamela?" Faye asked.

"A staffer in my office who helped me."

"You don't look good, Nadine."

Nadine pushed the hair back from her temple in an automatic gesture. "I know. Rob and I—" What could she say— the marriage was over? Was it? Did she want a divorce? She didn't have any answers, just pain. "I have to try to catch Pamela. Come with me."

"Nadine, I really can't," Faye said. "We're not shooting today, but—"

"Please."

"Sure, okay," Faye said.

The squeal of a car's brakes was followed instantly by the crash of metal against stone, something thick and ungiving.

"Not another," Nadine said. "They come around that turn at the top of the street so fast." She was putting on a raincoat and hat. "Let's go."

Outside, they heard a shout. Cricket barked and strained at her leash. Up the street, a battered pickup truck had struck the concrete wall that edged the turn and separated the street from a hillside of trees. A knot of people was gathering around the truck. The driver's seat was empty, the door open.

"Let's go in your car," Nadine said.

Faye started slowly up the street. People were leaning from windows, staring down at the scene. Faye picked up the car phone, driving with one hand, watching the road, trying to remember the number to reach Julie. She punched it in with her thumb. She slowed to a crawl as she reached the knot of people around the pickup.

"Stop! Stop!" Nadine suddenly yelled out. Faye stomped on the brake and Cricket barked.

The hood and bumper of the truck was crushed against a figure in a red raincoat, pinning it to the wall.

Nadine was getting out of the car. "Where are you going?" Faye asked. A car behind her honked politely. The street was narrow; there was no way around Faye. "Nadine!" But Nadine was walking toward the catastrophe. The car behind Faye honked again.

A hard rain began—a summer downpour. Some people darted back across the street to their homes; others remained. Faye realized she was still holding the car phone; sounds were coming out of it.

"Who's this?" Faye asked faintly.

"Julie!"

"I'll call you back." She replaced the phone.

"Hey, honey, can we get movin' here?" A man in a Navy-issue rain jacket was standing by Faye's window.

"I'm sorry," she said, watching Nadine stop beside the pickup. "My friend—I'll get her."

"Ye-ah, because no ambulance can get in hyar if you all don't move it."

Faye jumped out of the car. "C'mon, Nadine . . . oh, God . . ." The woman was pinned, her body collapsed forward, her cheek pressed grotesquely against the hood, her sandy hair soaked by the rain. Her vacant eyes were open.

"Let's get out of here," Faye whispered. Nadine didn't move. "C'mon." Nadine was transfixed. Faye pulled her arm. Nadine stepped back. The man in the rain jacket opened the passenger door of their car; Nadine slid inside. Faye put the car in gear and crept around the corner and down the slope. They had gone several blocks when Nadine said, "Pull over," in a strange voice. Faye swerved into a parking spot. Nadine stared out the windshield, her hands locked in her lap.

"What?" Faye asked.

Nadine let out a low moan. "Back there. That was Pamela."

TWENTY-THREE

THE SUMMER RAIN pounded on the roof.

"I liked Pamela, she was a nice person. She helped me," Nadine was whispering. "Oh, God, oh, God, this is so awful . . . She helped me and look at her now . . ." She covered her face with trembling hands. "Jesus, what's in that program that they'd kill for? First Della, now Pamela . . . ! They'll do it, they'll get us, too!"

"No they won't!"

"That was me!" she cried. "She was mistaken for *me*! I'm next!"

"No, Nadine, that's not going to happen."

"You don't know that."

Faye tried to calm her, conscious of the irony: Nadine had always been the serene one, she the excitable. "We're just going to sit here in this anonymous production car and use our brains. No one knows where we are—"

"Where was the driver? He would have seen us!"

"There wasn't any driver there—" She felt nauseated and wished she had some water.

"He could have been in the crowd!" Nadine said. She was frantic.

"No, he'd want to get away. We—we are not going to be victims. We're going to find out who's doing this because—

Nadine, are you listening to me? We've got to find out who's doing this so they *won't* get us."

But Nadine wasn't listening. Her face was stretched taut, even her eyes seemed attenuated. She wasn't afraid only for herself, she was horrified by Pamela's death and the manner in which she died. "I can't stand this—I feel hunted!" She opened the car door.

"Nadine!" Faye flung herself across the car seat and grabbed her. "Don't leave!" Nadine wrestled with her, but Faye got her back inside the car. That's when Nadine started to scream so loud Faye thought the car was rocking. She slapped her hard. All sound stopped except the pounding rain.

The window was rolled down, but the car was still hot and damp. A half hour had passed. Faye was staring at a tear of water rolling down the side of the windshield. She was more scared than ever before.

"Think of your child, Nadine."

"Yes." Nadine was listening to the rain on the roof. She was back in Bennett's class in law school, hearing him call her name and feeling the jab of fright. She knew she was in the dim, soggy car but felt exactly as she had back in that classroom: overwhelmed, cowardly, desperate to flee.

"Aren't you afraid?" Nadine asked Faye.

"I've been scared for months."

"I can't deal with this. I mean it."

"We can't give up." Faye's voice was shrill and tight. "Let's think about where you can go for a while and be safe. Maybe my security men can help."

"I don't trust anyone we don't know."

Faye reached for the car phone. "Is Rob on the Hill?"

"Rob . . ." She could see him standing in the kitchen, she was yelling at him, he was lying to her. "This is unreal," Nadine mumbled.

"You're going back to the Coast with him," Faye said, trying to remember how to reach Rob's office.

"No, I'm not," Nadine said.

"But we have to call Rob."

"No!" Nadine snatched the phone from Faye. "I don't want him to know."

Faye was stunned. "Why not?"

"You just have to accept that. Do you?" Faye was staring at her, amazed. "Do you?" Faye nodded. Nadine put the phone back in its cradle. "I don't want him to know where I am right now. And California's out—that's where they'd expect me to go."

Faye didn't know what to do. "We can't just sit in this car all day."

"I can't go back home, or to friends here, either," Nadine said.

Suddenly, Faye had an idea. She picked up the car phone and called Julie.

Faye, Nadine, and Julie were in Faye's hotel bedroom with Hester, makeup for the production, and Lewis, the hair stylist. Nadine was sitting before a mirror, a sheet draped around her. Hester was making her up, describing the aging accents she was using, darker shadowing here, lighter there. Faye watched from the bed with Cricket.

"Is this what you want, Faye?" Lewis had cut Nadine's hair short and dyed it black. Faye peered at the makeup. It was subtle; only someone close to her could tell it was makeup. Nadine looked ten years older. Lewis put a pair of out-of-date spectacles with heavy plastic rims on Nadine.

"The Wasp Queen wouldn't know you," Faye said.

Nadine stared at herself in the mirror. She was wearing an outfit from wardrobe: a skirt that hit her calves, a Peter Pan blouse, and a light jacket.

"Wonderful, guys," Faye said. "Thanks." She'd worked with Hester and Lewis for years. "It's going to be a great gag, but don't tell anyone. Got it?"

"Sure, Faye."

After they left, Faye said, "Julie, this is not a gag."

"Okay," Julie said, "I'll bite. What is it?"

"I'm putting Nadine into the production as an extra. You show her what to do so she doesn't stand out. No one's to know."

"Whatever you say, Faye."

"You get me a contract and put her on the call sheets. She'll be staying with me at the hotel."

"Are the cops involved?" Julie asked at the door.

"No. It's not like that." After Julie left, Faye turned to Nadine. "My movie's going to be your camouflage. If we're careful, no one will know for a while. It'll give us time to regroup."

"This isn't going to work."

"Yes it is."

"Faye! It won't."

Faye whirled on her. "What *else* have we got?" She felt tight, wretched. "You call Rob. He'll be worried."

Nadine turned away from the mirror. "We had a big fight," she said in a flat voice. She began walking around the room: the posture was Nadine, the style of the woman was not. "Leo fired me yesterday. He told me how Rob was involved in the leaks, how Rob and others on the Hill wanted him out, and then he said Rob was having an affair with Claire." A strange new look crossed Nadine's face. She sat down on the bed. "Rob hasn't done anything to Leo, he's only been unfaithful." The dog jumped up on the bed next to Nadine; she petted her. "Cute, huh?" she said in an unnatural voice.

Faye, torn between her brother and her friend, could only whisper, "An affair?"

Nadine nodded. "And with Leo's wife, of all people." Suddenly, she was out of control again. "How could Rob do that? Do you think it's true? Tell me! Oh, never mind, I know it's true, I saw his face last night. It's true. Oh, Jesus, poor Pam," Nadine moaned, gripping her knees, folding over them. "I said I'd protect her, I told her everything would be okay." She straightened up. "Her eyes are staring at me. Who's doing this? Who's doing this?"

Later, Faye went downstairs where Gabe was rehearsing Annie and Roger. As she neared the door, Gabe came flying out. "Gabe, there's something—"

"Not now, Faye. Sorry."

"It's important."

"I said, not now!"

He started down the hall in a hurry. She turned and walked in the opposite direction. His boots clattered down the back stairway. Gabe couldn't do anything about Pamela, or about Nadine. But he was the only person she trusted.

*   *   *

There was no chance to talk to him the next day, either. The filming moved to the Vietnam War Memorial in the park near the Lincoln Memorial. Faye and Julie were moving along the polished black granite walls that swept out of the sloping ground like giant wings in flight. "Here," Julie said. She pressed her long fingers against a name among the thousands carved into the stone. "My brother." Cast and crew kept their voices down, some ran their hands along the carved names, finding a name, others stood back in silence, holding their gear or their props.

Gabe and Lonny were beside the camera when Gabe suddenly swung around and stared at Faye. "Are you all right?" he asked. "You don't look good."

"I'm fine, fine. Maybe we can talk later."

"Has Phelps called? Is there—?"

"No, nothing to do with him."

In the movie story, Celia and Joe are feeling vulnerable to the forces that don't want the lab frauds exposed. Their anxiety blows away their mutual dislike, a big surprise to both of them. The scene at the memorial brings them together for the first time: they care about each other. Gabe called it cliché, but Faye liked it.

Roger was late and that worried Faye. He was capable of retribution for rehearsals he hadn't wanted to do on Sunday. Roger was like a young tiger—impulsive and violent. But he wasn't young, he was experienced, and that made him even more unpredictable.

This was the day that would test how well Faye had hidden Nadine. In her role as an extra, a "mourner," she stood near the wall with another "mourner." Annie was complaining about a picture of her in an article. She'd been copying Roger's professionalism, but she was also picking up ingenious ways to make self-involved demands.

When Roger finally arrived, they began shooting. "Annie," Gabe said, "just come on down the path here, don't hang back."

"It's like an open tomb. It's spooky," Annie said.

"You weren't in Vietnam," Gabe said. "You weren't old enough to have experienced any of it."

"Neither were you!" she shot back.

But he'd been twenty as the war wound down, and though he hadn't known anyone who died there, it had been the drumbeat of his teens. He had been surprisingly affected by the folly of government and the dignity of life that these granite slabs captured. It *is* tomblike, he thought, and it was crowded with echoes for him. "Annie, *use* the spookiness," he said. "Relate to Roger that way. It's done all the time."

The second and third takes were worse. Roger and his men began smoking, looking at their watches, and eyeing the press, which was out in force. Tot was with them.

"I can't find Nadine," she said to Faye. "Rob even called me, which shows how upset he is. What do you know?"

Faye moved Tot slowly toward Nadine in her "mourner" masquerade at one end of the memorial. "How'd Rob sound?"

"Strange."

The thing about Tot that was so helpful to her as a reporter, and so annoying to Faye, was that she gave little away: she'd state what she knew and then she'd shut up to see what people said.

"Could you elaborate, Tot?" They were almost up to Nadine.

"He's worried about Nadine." Tot glanced at the two extras, then moved on, running her fingertips over the carved names on the wall.

"Nadine and Rob had a fight," Faye said to Tot. "Rob's been having an affair with Leo Townsend's wife."

Tot whistled. "Oh, no." She blushed.

Dino came up to them. "Gabe wants to move people around." He went over to Nadine and her companion. "Ladies, twenty feet west, please." He looked back to check with Gabe.

"Remind Gabe that Roger's sitting in his trailer counting the minutes," Faye said, watching Tot. She had not recognized Nadine.

Gabe wiped the inside band of his panama and put it back on his head. "Faye says Roger's counting minutes," Dino reported, loping up to him.

"Roger's not running this shoot," Gabe snapped, watching Tot trying to keep up with Faye, who always moved fast. Then Faye stopped, stood with her feet slightly apart, head up, her red-brown hair pulled back with a clip. Two crew members were asking him questions; he ignored them, watching Faye. "Okay, Dino, go get Roger for the take."

When Nadine came into the trailer, Faye was reading a tiny article about the accidental death of an executive branch staffer, Pamela Sewell.

"You're right, Faye, switching hats is like switching personalities."

Faye glanced up at her. Nadine had been sick that morning, and worried about her appointment with her ob-gyn in a few days, but now she seemed desperately cheerful. Faye didn't trust the big changes in Nadine's moods.

"We have to talk to Tot," Faye said. "She'll be here in a while."

"Whatever you think, General."

"Rob's calling me."

"I won't talk to him."

"I didn't say you had to."

"You, of all people, should know what I feel like now," Nadine cried, breaking into sudden tears. "Or is it too much to hope that you'd take my side over Rob's?"

"Nadine, please don't. I'm in the middle. You and I are in real trouble. Pamela—"

"I can't talk about her now," she said, crying. "Did you know she had children to support?"

"We need more muscle on our side. How about your dad?"

Nadine started laughing; it was not a cheerful sound. Her eyes were still damp with tears. "I called him, remember? Back when I thought I was in trouble?" she said brightly, running a finger under her eyes. "I didn't know what trouble was, did I?"

Tot opened the door. "Faye?" She saw the black-haired woman. "Oh, sorry. Is this a good time?"

"There are no more good times, Tot. Come on in."

Annie was cutting across the parking lot to Faye's trailer. "Faye's not going to make me wear this shit." Susan, of wardrobe, trailed her, carrying a suit and dress over her arm. "Drab, drab," Annie was muttering.

At Faye's trailer, she heard Nadine's voice: "I'll be your Deep Throat . . . who's getting the money and why? Money's going out of the country . . . then it comes back in . . ."

"You can go," Annie said quietly to Susan, taking the clothes from her. Susan went off gratefully. Annie sat down in the chair by the door. She heard Tot's voice. "I haven't found anything . . . like every other reporter . . . we're being stonewalled." The voices dropped. Then Tot said, "Pamela's death has brought out the 'conspiracy' columns . . ." More mutters. Annie started counting voices. "Just assume your phones are tapped . . ." Tot said. "Yes, yes," Annie heard Faye say, impatiently. "Remind Adrian . . . about the tapes in Leo's safe . . . Did I flunk the lie detector? . . . Only Leo's word . . . Tapes might exonerate me . . ."

Annie opened the door. "Hey, you can't—!" Faye yelled. "Oh, Annie. I'm busy now. Come back later."

But Annie was already inside. "It'll only take a minute." Faye and Tot were at a table with another woman. She looked around for Nadine. "Hi, Tot," Annie said. No one introduced her to the other woman. "Faye, I have to see you about wardrobe. This isn't right." She held out the suit. "See? My character wouldn't be caught dead in this. It's dumpy, it's beyond awful. *This*"—she held up a teal-blue dress—"is what she'd wear."

"It's what *you'd* wear, Annie. But Celia is the administrator of a research lab—"

"That doesn't mean she has to be a cluck!"

There was something about the way the black-haired woman smiled. Annie held the dress up in front of her and bent the waist in with her arm. The woman swept a hand up against her temple.

"Nadine!" Annie cried. "You changed your hair!" She studied her critically. "I'm sorry, but I think it makes you look older. Now, don't you agree with me about this dress?"

Faye put her head in her hands. "Annie, Nadine's taking a little time off and she's going to be an extra for a few days. But it's a secret, don't tell anyone."

"Why?"

"She and Rob had a fight."

"You don't want Rob to know?"

"No," Nadine said, coming around the table toward Annie. "But why?"

"I'm talking to him later, Annie," Faye said. "Nadine doesn't want to see him until she cools off. But if you can't keep the secret, say so now."

Annie gazed at the three women. "Well, sure. Gee, are you giving her lines, too?"

That night, Faye, Gabe, and the others watched the dailies of the first day's filming at Union Station. Dailies with Gabe and Faye had always had an air of "let's look at what we've got and how we can do it better." Some directors demanded silence in dailies; Gabe encouraged comments. But dailies could be tense: some actors basked in their own on-screen brilliance, others cringed.

As the footage rolled on, Faye's attention divided. Nadine's days inside the production were numbered: Annie couldn't keep a secret. But Faye needed time and Nadine wasn't doing well. What were they going to do? She had to trust Tot. How ironic. As she watched a take of Roger walking out of the station being accosted by Annie, Faye realized she did trust Tot in this. She had no idea about the footage she was watching—it could have been *All About Eve*. *I should be so lucky,* she thought. The dark room was full of friends, but Faye needed more allies and a new plan. "Maybe a new life," she mumbled.

"You shrimp!" Celia was shouting at Joe on the screen. "All you guys think about are your perks and your elections. You aren't lawmakers! You're thieves!" She had just the right tone, Joe registered just the right amount of surprise, dislike, and outrage. Gabe had been right. Annie and Roger had chemistry. The angle and the light on them were perfect. Behind them towered the Beaux Arts station, and in the reverse angle, the Capitol dome.

"Julie, I've got calls to make," Faye said. "If my brother phones, tell him to come by tomorrow. Tell him not to worry."

Faye reached the street and felt no less abnormal than she had in the stuffy screening room. Nadine was a basket case and Faye felt something had shorted out inside herself as well. She knew she wasn't really coping—just giving the appearance of it.

The air smelled sweet as she stood outside the old brick building on the little street. *I better call that klutz, Phelps,* she thought. But she didn't move. *Oh, Lord, what is this trip about?*

Nadine was waiting for her when she got back to the hotel. "Pam's funeral is tomorrow. I'm going."

"God, you can't!" Faye said passionately, all her fears reigniting.

"I am going." Nadine's hair was neatly combed, her bathrobe pressed, its sash perfectly tied. She was at peace again.

"I know you know where she is," Rob said. There were deep shadows under his eyes, his mouth was tight, his jaw set. His jacket looked as if he'd worn it a week.

"Let's not fight here," Faye said, leading him away from Nadine, still costumed as a mourner. Rob didn't even look at the cast or crew as Faye headed up the path beside the granite wall of the memorial toward the parking lot.

"I'm so sorry for you, Robbie," she said, as they stepped inside her trailer in the lot.

"This isn't your business. Just tell me where she is."

"Nadine made it my business, you're my brother, we're all family."

"She isn't at home, she isn't at work—she's been fired, I suppose you knew that. I went back home, she didn't take any clothes . . . Buck's worried sick! You can't imagine the pressure I'm under from that man." He ran a hand over his jaw, stumbled against a bench, and sat down. "Please, help me."

"She doesn't want me to tell you anything."

"How can I fix this if I can't talk to her?"

"It isn't something you just fix!"

"I didn't mean it like that! Faye, you gotta help me!" he said, rising from the bench.

"I want to. I can't."

"Damn you!"

"I haven't done anything except try to help my friend!"

"How about helping your brother?"

"I don't want to be in the middle of this—it's too painful."

"She's in trouble—I could help her."

The phone rang. "Okay, I'll be there right away." She switched off the phone.

"Yeah, right, go to your production. It always saves you from real life, doesn't it?" He swung the door open, slamming it against the side of the trailer. "No wonder Gabe left you." He stumbled, going down the first step, and grabbed the doorknob.

"Rob, I love you, don't say things like that."

He was at the bottom of the steps. He took her arm and tugged gently, patted her face with his hand. Then he left.

"Who *are* those guys?" Gabe asked Zack, pointing to two grips at the top of the slope by the memorial. It was late afternoon and they were wrapping for the day.

"Jim and Jonathan are sick," Zack said. "They sent a couple of local subs. It's cool."

"Where's Faye?"

"Up the path. Said she wanted to see Lincoln."

Faye was standing inside the Lincoln Memorial when Gabe found her. She was holding Cricket on a leash and gazing up at the huge sculpture of a weary Lincoln, his hands draped over the arms of the chair.

"That's just how I feel," he said, slipping his panama back on his head. "We only got half of what we needed today."

"Do you think this is really a great country," Faye asked, "with a great people?"

"Not today," Gabe grumped.

Faye gazed out at the Mall over which Lincoln sat sentinel all the way to the Washington Monument. "A place like this is a reality check," she said softly. "It's easy to forget that some people really believed in this country. I find it very moving and it makes me proud, and I don't feel proud of this country all that often."

Gabe put an arm around her waist. "You are really the

biggest softie I know," he said. They stood together in the silence. "Let's take an hour in Georgetown before dailies," he said.

"Warm out here," Faye said.

"If you'd left the dog, we coulda sat inside."

They were on a terrace crowded with umbrellas and tables, overlooking the Potomac. "Did you catch that act of Sam's at the station?" Gabe said, watching her carefully. "He took our Annie right in hand, didn't he? He should have been a producer. Think they're sleeping together?"

"She wants to sleep with Roger." They ordered another plate of clams.

"Faye, there are two new grips on the shoot."

"So what?"

"They're not grips."

"What do you mean?" she asked.

"They're ringers. I think Nadine should leave."

She stared at him, astonished. "How did you know about Nadine?"

"Can't fool old directors and you can't pass off a sister-in-law as an extra."

"Tot didn't tumble."

"She's not an old director. What's going on?"

"Nadine's been fired, she found out Rob's having an affair, and a coworker of hers was killed."

"Killed?" he repeated, shocked. "How?"

"By a car."

"Accident?"

"Maybe, but Nadine doesn't think so. She's better now, but she didn't feel safe, so I dyed her hair and put her in the production. Sue me."

"She could have gone to her folks, to friends—"

"Gabe, I know this is hard to take in, but she was terribly afraid, she wasn't reasoning, she didn't want to be where people might expect her to be. She was incapacitated. I saw the accident and it was—horrible."

Stunned, Gabe stared at the river. "Okay, I'm behind the curve and catching up. But Rob should take her back to the Coast."

"Didn't you hear me? *Rob*'s been having an affair with her boss's wife." Their eyes met.

"Sorry," he said.

"Nadine won't even speak to him."

Gabe glanced back at the river. "All right, but Nadine shouldn't stay here," he said.

TWENTY-FOUR

THREE DAYS BEHIND schedule, they were wrapping up at the Vietnam Memorial. It was a beautiful summer afternoon; some of the cast were sitting on benches, smoking and drinking coffee as the grips hauled the equipment out to the parking lot. Julie sat down next to Faye in the sunlight. "You look really relaxed, Faye."

"Yup, feels good. What's up?"

"Dailies tonight are set early—a lot to go through. Where's Nadine?"

Faye's phone buzzed. "She's gone out to California to visit her folks," she said, clicking on her phone. "Faye Ferray," she said.

"This is Billy Radigan."

"Oh, good—the famous Billy Radigan who rigs explosions?"

"Yes, done a few gags," he replied, referring to jobs.

"As long as you didn't do *Twilight Zone*," she said.

"Cars, mainly."

"Billy, I need a car blown up, and part of the building next to it, but I don't want the car demolished," Faye said, watching Gabe talking to Roger at the far end of the parking lot, his hands moving, describing a shot. The contest she'd felt between herself and Gabe had died. When had that happened? Gabe broke away from Roger and was heading toward her with long strides, panama hat tipped back. "Thanks, Billy," she said, "I'll call you in a couple of days." She clicked off, but kept the phone to her ear. "I'd love to, Mark, when?" Gabe slowed his pace. "Mark, thanks! That's great. Yeah, bye-bye." She put the phone down.

"But I wanted to say hello to my senator," Gabe said.

"You did not."

Sam Pike was standing in Annie's hotel suite, holding a bunch of pink roses. "You are full of surprises," she said, pushing her face greedily into the flowers.

"I'm flying out in three hours. Do you have cocktail plans?"

She shimmied her shoulders. "You pour while I scrub off this makeup, and get into something more revealing."

"Good day's shoot?" Pike asked, selecting a bottle of Merlot.

"Good from my point of view," Annie sang out from the bathroom. "Roger's a sweetheart. Faye worked something out with Herb and Tony which is giving him more time before his next picture starts."

Sam was watering his wine. Annie came back wearing a flowery silk dressing gown; her peachy face was shiny. She curled up next to him on the sofa. "I'm glad the film's going well. It must take Faye's mind off her friend."

"Friend?"

"Della Izquerra." He didn't notice the alert, interested look on Annie's face.

"Della?" Annie said, puzzled.

"Yes, yes, the woman who died," he said. Annie clocked Sam. He'd answered too quickly. "You yourself said Faye was obsessed."

"Why do you care?"

"Only for Gabe's sake, my dear. They are in the production together."

"We're all in it," she drawled.

"I was talking to Buck Stern yesterday. He's worried about Nadine, can't reach her."

"Oh, she's all right," Annie said. "She had a big fight with Rob. I overheard them talking in the trailer."

"Who?"

"Tot, Faye, and Nadine. Nadine had learned something secret at her job about Della, I guess, I don't know, but she was telling Faye that. And get this! Nadine was so scared Faye disguised her and put her in the movie as an extra!"

Sam Pike blinked. "She said that?"

"Of course not. Faye said that Rob and Nadine had had a big fight and Nadine needed a break—all a big fib."

"She's in the production?"

"Yes, playing one of the tourist extras." She sipped her drink. "Isn't that a hoot?"

"Maybe you can tell Nadine to call her dad."

"Well, she hasn't been around the last couple of days." She drained her glass and snuggled closer to him.

"How did all this come about?" he asked.

"Well, I was outside Faye's trailer when she and Tot and Nadine were all talking about Nadine's work, I guess it was her work, sounded like it, and when I walked in I pretended I didn't know anything, but I did know I'd heard Nadine's voice. That's when I realized Nadine had changed her hair and all."

He put an arm around her. "What were they talking about while you were outside, sweetie?"

"Oh, some gobbledygook about offshore banks. Someone's friend had died. Oh! And about a lie-detector test!"

Sam put out a chuckle. "Sounds like your movie."

She giggled and slipped her hand inside his shirt.

"What *is* your movie about?" he asked her.

"My character blows the whistle on a government agency. She finds out they're hiding the results of tests which show a drug is dangerous. She takes the information to her congressman—I mean, she takes it other places first, and ends up with this congressman. They immediately dislike each other, but when her life's threatened, they start teaming up. Then, all the evidence of the lab notes that she first spotted on the drug disappear—"

"Wait a minute," Sam said. "This sounds like Della

Izquerra's situation. Faye mentioned something to me at Buck's party a while ago . . ."

"Oh, yeah, I guess it is like Della. Do you think she's been making her story all along?"

Sam laughed and ran his hand along her throat. "Come closer."

Adrian strode angrily out of the White House. He'd just come from Leo's office where he'd asked for the tapes of Nadine's interrogation and the results of her lie-detector test. But Leo had refused to give them to him for his investigation. "The Justice Department's handling that," Leo had said. Adrian knew the Justice Department wasn't yet interested and hadn't investigated a thing. "Stay out of it," Leo had said.

"Stay out of it? You directed me to conduct an investigation."

Leo had calmed down, but he hadn't given an inch about the interrogation tapes or the test. Adrian had threatened to take it to Tate.

"She failed the lie detector," Leo had shouted.

"Fine. It's evidence. Let me see it."

Leo had refused.

Adrian was jogging up the steps of the Old Executive Office Building. He believed Leo had just wanted Nadine out, and if he didn't watch his step, he, Adrian, would be out, too. He hooked a right inside the building and collided with a woman. "Sorry!" he said. "Ms. Jencks!" She was holding her elbow where his briefcase had hit it. "You all right?"

Twenty minutes later they were in a coffee shop just off Pennsylvania Avenue, and Adrian was confirming to Tot what Nadine had told her about OPI—off the record. "You tell Nadine to stay in her foxhole," he said. "Have you seen her?"

"No," Tot said. "Did you know Pamela Sewell?"

"Yes, I did. That accident was so shocking," he said.

"Everyone think it was an accident?"

"Yes. Hit-and-run. That corner's infamous. Pamela was working with Nadine, did you know? This is all off the record," he repeated.

"I don't double-cross people," she replied. "Nadine hopes her lie-detector tests will exonerate her."

"I thought you hadn't seen her."

"I lied." Tot smiled sweetly at him, and she felt the smile deep down, warming her.

Adrian said, "Did you see Bluestone's column today?" She shook her head. "He had a brief, but telling item announcing that the 'leak at the NSC' has been plugged, quote unquote."

"I'm not interested in those leaks," Tot said.

"I am," Adrian said, "because I haven't finished my in-house investigation of the leaks."

In the hotel lobby, Faye was talking to Nadine. "You sound great. Where are you?"

"Leaving Albuquerque on the Southwest Chief. This was really a good idea, Faye! I don't even have any morning sickness."

"When do you hit Los Angeles?"

"Tomorrow. I'll call you when I get in."

"Call me tonight, too, at the pay phone." Nadine had called regularly, and each day she sounded more like her old self. "Can I tell Rob you're all right, Nadine?"

"Yes, but I don't want to see him."

"C'mon, just talk to him. He's suffering." Silence. "Nadine?"

"Yes, I'm here. I'll call him from Los Angeles. You can tell him I'm okay."

It was a step.

Upstairs in her suite, Faye had changed her clothes and was about to go to the production office next door when Tot called from the lobby, wanting to come up.

"I ran into Anderson," Tot said, flopping down in a chair in Faye's bedroom. "We have progress. He confirmed a lot of what Nadine's been saying. Where's Nadine? We have to talk."

"She's gone, Tot."

"Gone?"

"Not here. Hasn't been here for more than a day."

"Where is she?"

"I don't know."

"Do you mean to tell me you just let her go off?"

"She's a grown woman."

Tot was on her feet. "Christ, this is terrible. Where do we start?" She was pacing back and forth with short, agitated steps, her hands clasped together, all the innocence erased from her face. "This isn't like Nadine to just disappear!"

Faye was astonished by her reaction. "Tot, she'll be all right—"

"All right? How can you say that? You know as well as I that Nadine wasn't herself, and you went to all those lengths to help her. I really took my hat off to you for that one—and I was really worried about her, about her mental state, let's say it plainly. Weren't you? She's my oldest friend, I care about her. Now, for some stupid reason, you just let her go off. Jesus! we don't even know where she is."

Faye couldn't stand it. "Tot, Tot! Nadine's okay!" Tot stopped pacing. "I put her on a train. She's going to California."

"What the hell are you doing, jerking me around like that?"

"Tough. I didn't want anyone to know."

"How could you lie to me?"

"And you've never lied to me?" Faye said.

Tot slowly lifted her head. "I guess it's always going to come back to that, isn't it?"

"Probably."

"So," Tot said quietly, "how is Nadine?"

"She'll call later tonight. I felt it was safer that she not stay here. The day she left, she was coming back to her old self or I would never have let her go, and she's sounded good when she's called. She calls twice a day."

"Why didn't you tell me? Don't you think I'm close to Nadine? That I'm concerned?"

"I guess I forgot," Faye said.

"You didn't forget."

"Oh, of course not," Faye said, angry. "I admired you for sticking to her so faithfully. I wish *I'd* had more of that from you."

"I didn't steal your husband! It became . . ." Tot groped for words. "It became a—a terrible personal defeat. It's amazing to me that we've all weathered it as well as we have, that we're all functioning, speaking, trying to get along."

Faye gripped the edge of a bureau. She had no anger left in her. "The costs were high, and, yes, it is amazing we've come out of it. I've missed you as a friend. I've wished—many times—that it had been anyone but you with Gabe. I'm numbed to it now, but there was a long time when I wasn't. It was petty of me not to tell you about Nadine, but I'm not sorry."

Tot folded her arms across her chest, then let them drop with a sigh. "I've wanted to say something to you, Faye, but nothing seemed . . . adequate. Lots of women chased Gabe, he's that kind of guy, and he is a director. But I wasn't one of those women." Tot scooped up her handbag. "Someday, I'd like to be friends again. Is that possible?"

"I don't know." Faye let herself down in a chair. "Let's just concentrate on Nadine's situation. Is there any scuttlebutt about Pamela's death?"

"The coroner's report had nothing surprising. It's an accident, she was walking on the sidewalk as the truck skidded and went out of control. They're searching for the driver. The pickup was stolen."

"Okay. Let me tell you about the phone system Nadine and I are on in case they're tapped."

Nadine did not call that night, nor did she call the next day.

They were filming in downtown Washington around the Treasury Building, a pile of sandstone and pillars. The weather was bright and hot, the production was plagued with breakdowns. Annie fled, weeping, to her trailer, demanding apologies from the child actor who was playing her son; Lonny fought with the art director's assistant, calling him sheep's balls; the camera broke down; lights blew; the prop assistant broke his ankle.

Faye's phone rang. It was Rob. She put a finger in her ear to hear him in the crush of the production and the street noise. "I don't know where she is, Robbie. Can I call you back? Where are you?"

She hung up and trotted around the corner to a pay phone

she'd already staked out. "I hate pay phones," she muttered, wiping sticky soft drink off the receiver. When she reached Rob, she said, no preliminaries, "She's on a train for California."

"So you did know!" he shot back. "God, my own sister, lying to me!"

"She made me swear not to tell, Rob! Let's have some slack here, okay?"

"Why a train?"

"She thought it would be less noticeable. She was supposed to call me, and she hasn't. Why do you think I'm breaking my word to her? I'm as worried as you are. Are you going to stay in town for a while?"

"Yes. Mark and I are rehearsing for the debate with Sparks."

"I gotta go." She hung up and trotted back up the block toward Gabe. Out of the corner of her eye, Faye saw a man who was familiar, but she couldn't place him. He was unremarkable, in a suit and a hat, and carrying a briefcase. Then she realized that he'd been at the memorial shoot, too.

"Generator's out," Dino said to Gabe.

"How can one day bring so much bad news?" Gabe demanded of the world at large.

Mark Drummond was in the Senate's media studio, standing at a podium, under the lights, preparing for the debate with Sparks in L.A. It was senatorial showtime and his staff, media consultants, and coach sat in the "journalist's" chairs, tossing questions.

Faye watched from the back, then threw in a question of her own. "Senator, have you reconsidered calling for an investigation of the NSC?"

"Hey!" Smokey called out.

Another man jumped out of his seat. "Who *is* that?"

"Senator, you chair an Appropriations subcommittee," Faye shouted, "and it has oversight of Executive Branch offices—" One staffer had reached her, ready to remove her physically.

"Okay, everybody, five minutes," Mark said easily. He

ushered Faye into a small room off the studio. "Now, what is this?"

"Nadine's missing. She was on a train to the Coast, she called me every day, then the calls stopped."

"She can't have been gone long." He hooked a big arm over her shoulder, but it didn't feel comfortable, just heavy.

"Mark, I don't know who else to ask to help me." She reminded him of the threats Nadine received, of Nadine's investigation at the NSC. "Please, Mark, investigate this."

"I'm very sympathetic, Faye—"

"Can't someone on your staff look into Nadine's notes and Della's disk?"

"Investigations can backfire," he replied.

"Senator," his aide said impatiently. "We haven't got much time."

"All right, Faye," Mark said, tucking a hand under her arm. "I'll talk to my colleagues. How do you think the material for the debate sounds?"

She was reaching up to give him a kiss. His eyes were on her, waiting, expectant. She lowered her heels and stepped back. She couldn't remember what he'd said in the rehearsal.

"Give it more fire, Mark, like the old days."

Both doors between the suites were open that night, people were plunging back and forth, taking faxes, talking on phones, making lists.

"We've got to make up the time," Faye said to Gabe.

"We're not that much over," he called out. "Any word from Nadine?"

She came across the hall into his suite. Cricket bounded after her. "No. But the train's in L.A. This is so unlike Nadine, not to call." She lowered her voice. "For a while there, I thought we'd won. I felt so confident. Now I just want to get back home. I don't feel safe here anymore . . ."

The local location manager was sitting at a table, phoning. "Would you excuse us, Ken?" Gabe asked courteously. He followed him to the door, slipped on the Do Not Disturb sign, and shut it.

"I have to get going, too," Faye said.

"You saw Mark today."

"Yes, Nadine asked him to look into some of this."

"What is Mark to you?"

"An old friend." She started out.

He looped an arm around her waist. "Care to sit down a moment?"

"No, I've got calls to make."

"Please stay."

She pulled away. "What's come over you? I don't want to relive what's already been lived." Yet, there was a strange newness about him. She moved away, but stopped at the door.

"Am I different?" she asked.

"Yes. So am I. What is this between you and Mark?" he asked.

"An affair."

"I'm sorry to hear that." Gabe walked over to her. "I love you, Faye."

"Once, once you did. Don't, Gabe. I mean it."

"You can't have anything worth having with Mark. He's only interested in himself."

"Don't you even speak about this," she said. "You're intruding, it's awful of you."

"I *was* awful once. Don't you think I know it?"

She stopped. "What?"

"C'mon, Faye, I know what I'm doing, I was aware of what I did. I hurt you very badly once, and now I feel I'm doing something equally awful."

"Gabe, I don't have the faintest idea what you're talking about. I really have to . . . do some work." She picked up Cricket and left, shutting the door behind her.

He swept scripts and files off the couch and threw himself on it.

She opened the door. He lay on the couch, staring at the ceiling. "Tell me, Gabe."

"I feel swamped."

"What?" she asked, still standing by the door.

"I'm finishing the shoot and then I'm going east. You edit. I can't work with you."

"*You* can't work with *me*? Where is all this coming from?" she demanded, amazed.

"There isn't anything you can say to me that I haven't said before and more often. There's something sick about leaving your wife for one of her friends and then wanting your wife back—I hate that image of myself," he said to the ceiling. "You know why I made this picture? I knew I'd find out what I felt for you and what I did not feel. I didn't expect to learn what, besides anger, you felt for me, but I've faced *my* part of it—the blame I'm due, my mistakes, my virtues, too, if you like. I'm far from perfect, and so are you."

"Gabe . . ."

"One of us can't put us back together, maybe two can't, either." He turned to face her. "I'm very sorry for what happened, but you are so angry—I don't blame you, but I don't want to see you that way anymore. And I don't want to feel this way anymore. And I won't." He sat up. "So, Faye, we've reached an end. I'd hoped for better."

She leaned against the doorjamb. "You said you don't want to feel 'this way' anymore, that it's one reason you're going. Feel what way?"

"I'm going to miss you all my life, but I don't want to miss you anymore while I'm with you—*that* way." He paused. "Get it?" he added roughly.

"Yes." But she couldn't get past the memory of the pain of their separation, as fresh, almost, as when it occurred. It was in her eyes and Gabe saw it.

"I didn't know it was a mortal wound," he said. "At Nadine's cabin, after Della's funeral, I thought enough time had passed, that we could forgive, maybe be together again. I really thought that."

"Did you take what I felt for you so lightly?"

"No."

"Or what you felt—for me or for Tot?"

"No! It was deep, what you and I had, that's why I thought—"

"Honestly, Gabe, you 'thought'?"

"Spare me the sneer, Faye," he said, rising. "*You* felt the same way for a moment, up at the cabin."

"The arrogance of you guys—it slays me. You make me feel so lonely." She picked up Cricket again. Gabe lay back on the couch and put his hands behind his head.

"Was anything you said to me true?" she asked angrily.

"All of it." He shut his eyes. "Get out."

The hall was empty. Faye was trying to get her key in the lock when Cricket barked, and kept on barking. "Shhh," she said, opening the door. Cricket dashed through the first room and into the second; Faye followed, turning on lights. The second room had a door to the hallway; it was just closing as she entered. Cricket was standing on her hind legs, her front paws trying to reach the knob.

Only Julie had a key to her suite. Faye picked up the phone and called her. Julie answered immediately. "Are you awake?"

"No." Julie's voice was clogged with exhausted sleep.

"Did you make a copy of the key to my suite?"

"No!"

"Okay, go back to sleep."

Faye sat down in a chair, thinking about Gabe, thinking about endings and beginnings.

TWENTY-FIVE

The Jungle Gym production had reached juggernaut phase: by eight the next morning, sixty-five people and twelve tons of equipment were all back in front of the Treasury Building, snarled in metastasizing problems. The heat was murderous. At noon, the backup camera jammed. Lonny exploded. Zack, next to Faye, muttered, "This is sabotage, Faye. Got to be."

"Yes," she said quietly, "I know."

"I can nose around," he said.

"No, you let me do that." She patted his shoulder.

In her sightline stood the man she'd seen for several days, the stiff bureaucrat type with the balding head. "What the hell is that guy doing there?" Faye said. "If he works for the government, I'm not paying his salary to stand around my shoot!" She broke away from Zack and accosted him. "Who are you?" she demanded.

"Isn't it okay to watch?" he asked, startled.

"You've been here for days."

"I work in the Treasury," he said. "I've never seen a movie shot before."

He seemed utterly harmless. "Sorry," she said, "stay as long as you like."

I've been stalked too long, she thought. The Treasury Building offered no comfort or beauty; it was massive, cold, unrefined. Andrew Jackson had directed it be built in this spot because it would block his view of Congress from the White House. For Faye, it blocked out hope. It was like a big, terrible *thing* looming over her shoot. "Who picked this location?" she demanded as Zack passed her.

"You did," he said.

During the lunch break, Faye told Zack, Gabe, and Julie that the Chesapeake Bay shoot was out, mainly because of insurance. "Not to worry," Faye went on. "The contingency plan has already been developed, and the set's under construction in L.A. So we can wrap here in a few days."

"The set?" Julie said. "No tank?"

"Celia and our congressman are going to have a narrow escape, but it doesn't involve water," Faye said.

"All right, people," Gabe said with a lightness no one else showed signs of. "Plan R!"

"Have we really reached R?" Zack muttered as he left.

"What's this contingency plan?" Gabe asked.

Faye's cellular phone was ringing. She held up a hand. "Yes?" she said into it.

"Dear, it's Coo."

"Oh, Mom, what's wrong?"

"Can you come back? Daddy's in the hospital again. The doctors are being very glum. It's not a heart attack, but the remission's over. He's having transfusions."

An hour later, Faye and Annie were walking in Pershing Park near the Treasury. Annie was holding her voice down, but her gestures were extreme. "*I* need time off! What will Mom think when I don't show up at the hospital?"

"Mom understands shoots!"

"You ought to have more respect for *my* feelings, I got this movie started," Annie cried, slashing a tissue at her tears, ruining her makeup. "Without me, none of *this* would be out here!" She flung her arm at the traffic snaking past the cast and crew and gear scattered around the Treasury.

"That is the tenth time you've reminded me," Faye said. "You completely discount my own efforts. You're being selfish. Pop's in a hospital and you're talking about what Mom'll think if you don't come running. You don't mention Pop, or me or Rob and what we might be feeling. You know how worried I am about Nadine, but do you ask about her? No! Do you ask what I've been going through? And now you start talking about this production as if you single-handedly pulled it out of a hat!"

"I *have* wondered about Nadine and where she is, I *do* think about other people! How can anyone be an actress if they don't have a real understanding of people?" Annie said in Faye's face before she strode away.

"Tot, do you have the pay phone numbers I can reach you at, just to be on the safe side?" Faye asked her. They were standing in the ornate lobby of the Willard Hotel.

Tot handed her a card. "I'm sorry to hear about your dad, Faye."

"Here are the pay phones I used with Nadine. It's a real nuisance, let me tell you. See, I've coded them." Tot looked at the list of three phone numbers: each had a letter in front of it. "That way I can say, call me at B."

"So, when I want to talk to you, I call you at home or at the office and you tell me which pay phone, right?"

"Yes."

"How's the shoot going to run without you?"

"Better," Faye said. "We're almost wrapped. I'll see Herb and Tony, get us set up and ready to go on the lot."

"Are you going to have some bodyguards out there?"

"Oh, sure," Faye said. "Tot, everything Nadine did here, everything the three of us have talked about—it's in your hands now. Don't drop it, don't give up."

Tot was surprised. "I won't. And I hope it's a great story, too."

Faye wondered if she'd ever be able to look at Tot and not see her with Gabe. Their friendship was mending, like a broken bone, but in strong light the fracture would always be visible. Would the break with Gabe ever be healed? She could feel her need for distance from him. "Last night, Gabe said he's leaving right after the filming's done. Do you know anything about that?"

"No, nothing, Faye."

"He said something that really bothered me—well, he said a *lot* that bothered me. He said he hadn't known until this shoot that our separation, his and mine, had been a mortal wound."

"To you?" Tot asked. Faye nodded. "No, Faye. He was probably talking about himself. You've got a lot of life left, with or without him." Tot's gaze was shrewd and honest.

Nadine had left the train in the grand old Los Angeles station on Alameda Street. A damp chilly wind slapped against her. Balmy paradise had turned raw in the middle of summer. She gripped the collar of her jacket, carefully looked up and down the stilled train cars. Only then did she walk across the platform toward the shelter of the station. The wind shifted, gusting at her back: she felt she was on the run.

Her feeling of being followed had started about a day ago. She'd changed trains in Chicago to the South West Chief, and had felt safer for a while. Now she did not. The truth was she no longer knew what was true, and she was afraid.

She entered the domed L.A. station and glanced behind her. She felt she'd been catapulted outside normal life, riding a plateau where time was unlocked, space unlimited. She should have stayed with Faye in Washington.

Low clouds were slung across the sky like bunting. The dismal streets around the train station seemed war-torn: many buildings were boarded up. She hadn't been in downtown Los Angeles for years. Ten blocks away, gleaming dully in the smog and rain, skyscrapers and new hotels rose up. They'd been built with the hothouse money of the eighties while she'd been in Washington. Everyone stayed there or in the new clubby places on the West Side. She'd be easy to find there. She also thought she'd be easy to find at the cabin, where Faye expected her to be. She had to make a new plan.

She began walking south, past Temple Street. She remembered the old safe days of childhood. The Hotel Alvin rose before her like a derelict ship. When she'd been a child, the Alvin had served tea and sandwiches. The lobby had been a place of old-fashioned potted palms and pillars; antique tables with white cloths had marched in front of her as she'd hung on to the hand of a ready aunt. The Alvin had been her grandmother's rest stop for tea, and she could still remember anticipating the arrival of crusty old relatives who never spoke of the present or the future, but only of the past.

But as she approached, the Alvin seemed flinty and uncharitable. The graffiti on its corner wall spelled out a word that looked like "SEIZE." Its once gaily striped window awnings were gone, as if the hotel's eyelids had been surgically removed. The marquee was still there but part of it was torn, one edge lifted obscenely by the gusty winds.

She was numbed by the rainy chill. She cast around for a cab, unsure of anything. Picking up a cab on the street in Los Angeles was impossible. She should have taken one at the station. A newspaper skated across the sidewalk. She turned back to the hotel. It would do; no one would look for her in such a place. She would call Faye.

The wind thrust her into the lobby and her entrance rustled the elderly residents like autumn leaves. They turned in their faded chairs and stared at her through rheumy eyes. An elderly clerk stopped stirring his coffee. The potted palms were gone, an air of passive disenchantment hung upon the room. A loud TV set was tuned to an afternoon news show. She had a vision of a million old people like these thin-necked aging cranes watching the news, then telling each other what they'd seen and heard, spreading falsehoods.

On the fourth floor, the wide, uncarpeted halls and the ornate woodwork around each solid, outsized door were the only real echoes of the hotel she remembered. Inside, the room was sparsely furnished but clean, a relief. Long ago, someone had painted it apple-green. She tossed down her purse and bag, and locked the door. She ran her fingers through her short hair and felt tears bunch in her eyes.

She yanked the window shade down but failed to notice the rotund man pulling down the earflaps of his waterproof cap as he leaned against the brick wall across the street.

Nadine eased down on the old bed. The springs tipped her into the middle. She surrendered, resting there in the trench.

* * *

She awoke at nine that evening, climbing up from accusatory dreams. She had to call Faye. She rummaged in her briefcase for her appointment book.

Footsteps outside her door. She froze, one hand inside her handbag. The steps came up to and passed her door, disappearing down the hallway.

Across the street, the man in the earflaps edged off the wall to shake hands with the worried, but expensively dressed man who approached him.

"You Stern?" the man in earflaps asked.

"Who are you?" Buck Stern demanded.

"Bostram, sir."

"How'd they find her?"

The man in earflaps shrugged and smiled shyly. "I've been with her most of the way."

"Which room?"

"Four oh one."

Stern glanced distastefully at the old hotel across the street. There was something in his eyes, sad and hard, that made the man in the earflaps turn away.

The water exploded percussively out of the tap as Nadine rinsed off her face. Her black-dyed hair still disconcerted her. She rubbed a towel over her hands and face. She was hungry. She picked up the edge of the shade and looked out at the dim street. It had stopped drizzling.

There were no footsteps and the knock at the door was gentle. "Nadine. It's me, Dad."

Below on the street, a buckskin-colored Lexus drew around the corner and stopped up the street from the Alvin. The man in the earflaps walked up to it, and leaned down at the open rear window.

TWENTY-SIX

"POP, IT'S ME, Faye."

Jerry lay beneath a sheet, his nose arching, the skin of his cheeks clinging to the bone, tubes attached to his arms, machines beeping.

He opened his eyes. "I'm not as dead as I look."

Faye's chin began trembling. "Mom said you were having transfusions."

He shook one wrist, feebly disturbing a network of tubes. "This is breakfast. I'm improving. I want to go home. Put a pillow behind me so I can see you." When he was sitting up, he said, with no strength, "Bet you're glad to be back in L.A."

"Yes, Pop. Gone long enough to have forgotten my car phone number."

"Tragic. Rob flew in. He's a wreck over Nadine. Like she vanished. Poor Robbie, he says he's to blame."

"No, he's not." A kind of peace settled over her with her father in the quiet white room, a sense that whatever was going to happen had already been set in motion months earlier.

Jerry pulled his bony hands out from under the covers. "Buck came to see me a while ago, all in a dither, sorting something out . . . talking about the old campaigns . . . about you kids . . ."

"How odd."

A faint smile crossed his lips. "Yeah . . . Buck never seemed to notice you kids when you were little, now he's rambling about all of you. Remember when you fell in the water and he pulled you out?" She shook her head. He sighed. "I swear . . . the things kids don't remember . . . I always figured that's where you got your fear of water."

"Pop, I'm not afraid of water."

"You were, too. You refused to take swimming lessons."

"I did?"

Jerry was fiddling with the IV in his arm. "Damn thing is irritating as hell," he said. "Yeah, ol' Buck was in a stew all right."

"When did you see him?"

"Two weeks maybe. Go see your brother . . . talk to him."

"I have to see that detective about Nadine."

"Rob's already reported her missing." He sighed deeply. "Terrible . . . Nadine disappearing. Buck has everyone in California looking for her . . . That canary you brought me . . . ? Sings like all get out . . . a winner."

A steep wind had swept Los Angeles clean. After Washington, the rugged city seemed clear and green and easy-going to Faye.

Her second day back, Faye checked into her office where Steve welcomed her with flowers, production books, phone messages, and obvious delight. She left a message for Buck and Helena and went off to lunch with Tony Valdi at the Ivy in Beverly Hills. In an absentminded way, Tony extolled the dailies he'd seen as if *Gym* were someone else's film—not hers, not his. Faye described the breakdown problems that were forcing her to ask for an additional week in the L.A. schedule.

"Iffy," Tony said.

"Iffy? We've got to have it. We're halfway through the picture. Let's bite the bullet and finish it right."

Tony changed the subject.

* * *

In his downtown office, Cowboy was reading a newspaper article noting that filming in Los Angeles was on the rise. Faye Ferray's picture was cited as one of several returning "home" for completion. A small blurb on the next page was about an unidentified woman's body being found in a hotel tub. The apparent cause of death: suicide.

Faye found Detective Phelps at the Academy Cafe in Elysian Park. At four in the afternoon, the cafe was not as crowded as before, but the gunfire from the range kept up the same continuous, uneven blare. She sat down next to him at the counter. He was eating apple pie and ice cream.

"You're into cholesterol, I see."

"Why not?" The fatalistic look in his eyes chilled her.

"Why do you do this work, Phelps?"

"I thought we were on the side of law and order, Ms. Ferray." He went back to his pie.

She watched him eat. "And now you're not sure?"

"When there's no respect for the judicial system because citizens think it's not evenhanded, then trust is destroyed and respect for law comes next. After that, only brute force can keep order. And there's not a police force in the world that can do that. Remember the riots—the insurrection? Want some coffee?"

"Sure." For the first time, she was aware of him as a human being. "What's your first name?"

"Sebastian."

Her coffee arrived. "What do people call you for short?"

"Phelps."

"Been on the force long?" She sipped her coffee.

"Twenty years. I've been married and divorced twice, got a grown daughter. I'm retiring in December at age forty-six and I'm writing a novel."

"What about?"

"What do you think? A civilization out of control."

"Control isn't everything."

He turned his head toward her. "Let me put it another way. A civilization cannibalizing itself."

He was forking up the last of his ice cream–soaked pie with delicacy and precision. He was a neat eater. "Maybe I misjudged you," she said.

He raised his head slightly at an angle and gave her a look of intimate recognition. "Yeah, you did." He turned all the way around to face her, put an elbow on the counter, rested his fist against his mouth, and considered her. Then he went back to his pie. "So, what can I do for you, Faye?"

"I'm looking for my sister-in-law, my friend, Nadine."

"Her husband and her father have been by, but she's a missing person—and that's another department, not mine."

"This is all part of the same string," she said, irritated again. "Nadine was checking that disk you said wasn't any help. She found something and her coworker in Washington was killed—maybe by accident, the one I called you about. Nadine and I both have been followed, we've been threatened." He was listening closely but his face showed no expression. "This is not a movie, Phelps."

"You couldn't make the movie I live every day."

The hard misery in his eyes stunned her. A cry of frustration and sympathy welled up her throat. "I—I don't know what to do anymore."

"C'mon," he said, putting a hand under her elbow, "out to the range."

He led her to the shooting gallery. From an upstairs walkway, they looked out at men and women firing away at the targets. Over the din, Phelps said, "If people don't want to be found, it's damned hard to find them. I told your brother that when he came to see me. She'll probably turn up the way people do—people who haven't done anything, that is."

"What do you mean?"

"She hasn't broken a law, has she? She's not running from the law?" Faye shook her head. "It's probably that she wants to be alone, be off somewhere. She'll turn up." His dark gray eyes examined her. "*You* were threatened, but here you are."

"But I don't feel safe."

"When did that start again?"

"When I didn't hear from Nadine."

"That's natural after the experiences you've had. You keep your security out here and I'll put a car on your house, too."

"Thanks. How about Pamela Sewell?"

"I called the D.C. force—like you asked me to," he emphasized, "and it was a straight up and down hit-and-run. Couldn't she have been coming down that hill to see your sister-in-law and been run down by accident?"

"I just don't believe that. She knew what Nadine was looking into, she helped her, and she's dead and Nadine's missing. When I let it, I feel so—undone by everything, I just don't know where to turn . . ."

He reached out for her arm and pulled her toward him. Her shoulder nudged his hard chest. She leaned lightly against him.

"I'll look into it," he said, moving her gently away, one hand still gripping her arm.

It was after four-thirty when Faye left Sebastian Phelps. He'd become a man, not a hostile cardboard detective. She wondered if his novel was any good, if it was about oppressed cops or oppressed civilians. Maybe it was a raw detective story that matched his eyes. She took surface streets to Herb Yount's offices to meet with him. But all the way over the hill, she felt the look that had slid out of Phelps's eye—a communion, an acknowledgment, a challenge.

"Spoke to Gabe," Herb said to Faye, "he's wrapping up. Leaving the second unit to shoot whatever, heading back here tonight or tomorrow. What's this big street set being built?"

"The revised ending. Keith Llewellyn wrote it."

"I didn't get the pages."

"Sure you did. We couldn't get the insurance to cover the car crash in the Chesapeake Bay. Billy's doing the explosives work."

"Explosives?"

"It's a terrific ending, Herb. Roger loves it. I'm going to invite a lot of press out to see the fireworks. Maybe we'll ask Mark Drummond if he's in town, whaddya say?"

"Are you coming to the review of his new TV spots?" Herb asked.

"Oh, yes," Faye said, dimly recalling it. "Herb, what do you think of the dailies on *Jungle Gym*? Aren't they great?"

"Good, good, Roger saves it—hot damn, I love that guy."

"What do you think of Annie?"

"She surprised me. She's got a real quality. Full-bodied, rich, but like she might go off the deep end any minute. Gabe's done real good."

"Thanks, Herb. I appreciate that."

Herb caught himself. "You, too, goes without saying."

Faye went down to Celia's laboratory and office set. Near it, carpenters were erecting the congressman's office. She talked with the construction foreman and the scenic painter, then went outside and walked in the black-edged sunshine to the back lot where the "intersection" was being finished. The buildings facing it were two-dimensional, propped up from behind.

"That window in that storefront," she said to the construction coordinator, "it's got to be bigger." A greensman was hauling a tree into place in front of the window. "Strike the tree. There are going to be people behind this window that the camera has to pick up. Get it?"

"And it's got to be armored, too," a voice behind her said, "because there'll be civilians behind it and we're going to blow out those windows over there." It was Billy Radigan, special effects tech.

"How do," Faye said, shaking his hand. He was a short burly man with a goatee. "Any problems with the plans?"

"Nope. We'll have quite a blast for you. Those windows in that building will go and these over here, too. Boom."

"Great, but don't destroy the car—big noise, little damage."

He scratched his beard. "That might be—well, a car isn't very big. A charge can blow it up, take the fenders, hood, all that, right off it."

"So what if it didn't?"

"Dud."

She nodded. "Ever thought of doing police work? I should've talked to you months ago. Let's take a little walk, Billy." They talked about the armored window to protect the viewers, about arming the car, about keeping the time down. "It's crucial," she said. "The sequence is in three scenes—preblowup dialogue, blowup, and postblowup dialogue. We got to run this like a live show."

"I can't let actors drive a car that's armed."

"Okay, Billy, but arm it quick because I have to keep people in that window watching. And I want a big boom."

"So dub the sound in later."

"I will, but I need a big sound. We're shooting film, but this is also like a live stage show."

Billy went away mumbling. She looked at the storefront window and imagined the faces behind it. She breathed in deeply, satisfied and scared at the same time. She had no idea if what she was planning would work, or what the outcome would be.

In Washington, Adrian was at a small bar in Chinatown with Paul, who'd run Nadine's lie-detector test.

Paul was a florid man in his fifties. He sat on his chair as if he'd been flung there, one arm flopped on the table. He seemed inattentive and looked sloppy, but Adrian knew his work was careful and accurate.

"Very out of school," Paul said.

"Yes, we could say that," Adrian said.

"Read the report."

"I just wanted your impressions."

Paul's big eyes roamed to the ceiling, around the back wall, and down. "For my money, the test showed no indication Ms. Ferray was lying about the leaks that have plagued your offices. She was telling the truth as she knew it about *them*. So"—he sighed heavily—"in my judgment, she wasn't the source of *those* leaks. But she was asked a couple of questions she lied about."

"What?"

"Mainly about divulging anything to anyone."

"And that was in your report?"

"Yes."

Therefore, Adrian thought, someone—probably Leo—released false information to the press about Nadine and the leaks. "Thank you."

Paul was rising in a shambling, uncoordinated way. He said, "Never saw you, pal."

Adrian nodded. He waited fifteen minutes. Then he called Tot. "Are you free for dinner?" he asked. "I think we should compare notes."

"How's the campaign going, Mark?" Sam Pike asked pleasantly. His hands clasped behind his back, he was standing in Mark Drummond's private office in Los Angeles.

"Great," Mark replied, his standard answer. He sat down in a brown leather chair. "What can I do for you?"

Sam glanced curiously at the room. His sandy hair was combed straight back from his brow, accentuating his sharp, straight nose and high forehead. "I have an offer I think will interest you, Mark. Want to take a little walk?"

Mark laughed. "You don't trust my office?"

"I don't trust any office. Just a little stroll. You won't be disappointed."

They walked in the plaza between the Century City towers. "Those Sparks TV spots are killing you, Mark."

"They're tough, but nothing we can't handle."

"You've lost the initiative to define the issues. All you're doing is reacting to Sparks." Pike strolled on, hands clasped behind his back, letting his words sink in. "But isn't it all about how we often must create *cause* to achieve *effect*?" Pike pronounced "often" with a hard *t*. His pale blue eyes twinkled happily.

Mark Drummond was uneasy and impatient. "What do you mean?" He eyed the master political consultant.

"Sparks has a series of four spots—the 'tough ones,' as you call them," Pike said. "But only the first one's on now. I can make sure the other three never hit the air."

Drummond was aghast. "How?" A quick smile from Sam Pike. "Why would Sparks's people cancel effective spots?"

"They're not Sparks's TV spots, exactly. They come from a private group funding television spots under independent expenditures for communications," Pike said, naming a legitimate category of campaign funding. "Might be as effective as the Willie Horton spots—remember those? They were created and funded by an interested group outside the Bush campaign."

"Why would an independent group outside Sparks's campaign bag their spots?"

"Because I have a certain influence with that group," Pike said.

"Why would they switch from a Republican to a Democrat in the middle of a race? That's unheard of."

"This group supports candidates in both parties—not unheard of—and they're helping out with the spots. As you know, commercials made from independent expenditures aren't like other campaign contributions because they have no money limit. They're a campaign's mother lode," Pike said cheerfully.

"Sparks's people won't yank spots that are hard on me."

"Oh, I rather think they will. It could be in their interest, too."

A small crowd was gathering around a mime who was juggling balls. "Yes, sir," Sam said, "those contributions for Sparks's TV spots are going to dry up if you give the word."

"What's the deal?" Drummond asked bluntly.

"You bury the NSC investigation."

Drummond stopped walking. So far, there wasn't any investigation, he'd only talked to a few colleagues to sound them out. But he'd heard whispers from the NSC—there were problems over there—these things were never secret.

"It's damned hard to pull an investigation back once motions have been made," he said.

"Not that hard. You can do it." Pike smiled. "Let me tell you about the rest of this deal." He clasped his hands behind his back again and began walking. "People know about your dalliance with Faye Ferray. Tapes and pictures. Not too good in the middle of a hard campaign."

Mark forced himself to continue walking beside Pike. "No one cares about that shit anymore."

"Oh, yes they do. A respected man like Mark Drummond, husband, father, well-known wife—economist, isn't she?— making out like a teenager in a pool with a divorced film producer. That won't play at all well down in Orange County or in those logging counties up north, either."

"I'll be goddamned if I'll sit by while you do a job on my reputation," Mark boomed.

"*I'm* not doing it! Good Lord, Mark." Pike touched the knot on his tie. "But it *is* the truth."

"Truth, that's rich coming from you. You don't give a rat's ass about truth, Pike. But my relationship with Faye won't look anything like the truth once the media savages it."

"Yes," Sam said, regretfully, "the great engines of lies do seem to begin in the media. But, then, that's all part of the system."

"I wouldn't touch your deal with a stick—"

"Hold on, Mark, I don't think you've understood me clearly. This is strictly quid pro quo. And it's a today-only offer. I *can* deliver my part, believe that. And I can get you the best people for new spots—"

"I have the best already."

"You have *good* people, Senator, you *don't* have the best. What I'm offering you is win-win—no leaks on Faye and a brand-new spot campaign at no expense to your campaign. And it's all legal."

"Where's the money coming from?"

"Private sources. Substantial private sources."

"Not good enough, Pike. I have to know who the group is."

"America Today," Pike said, "that's the group, and they're all legitimate U.S. corporations interested in making democracy work."

"I want to see the list," Mark said.

"I'm afraid you're in no position to bargain."

Drummond was heading across the plaza back to his building. "No deal."

"I didn't know you were so impetuous, Mark," Pike said. "The group I represent has plans for you."

Mark turned.

"They feel the time will be right to support you for a run at the Presidency in the next election two years off."

Drummond was stunned.

"See?" Pike said. "Isn't that good news?" His smile was like a delicate wave curling across his face.

Drummond swatted at the air with his big hand. Condescending son of a bitch, he thought. "You're mighty proud of yourself, aren't you, Sam?"

Sam Pike was genuinely surprised. The old horse's ass had a few good instincts after all. "I have to admit, Mark, the overall picture does have its agreeable aspects."

With a tactile sense of the game, Sam laughed warmly at Senator Drummond. "Believe me, if you play your cards right, in two years you'll be sitting in the Oval Office. The Veep won't make it. You will." Pike turned to admire the plaza view of Century City. "I like that slogan Smokey's got for you this year. 'If you can't believe in Mark Drummond, you can't believe in anyone.'"

TWENTY-SEVEN

FAYE'S NIGHTMARES CUT an interior channel beneath her days. She'd had none as bad as the one in the Washington hotel, but the dreams were still frightening—the water was deep, the tentacles powerful, the nautilus malevolent and sly.

This night, Faye dreamed she was inside the shell of the nautilus, sliding from segment to segment, each smaller, more slippery. The marine air was fetid. There was someone or something behind her and she was desperately hunting for a way out.

She woke suddenly. The doorbell was ringing. It was nine in the morning. She'd overslept. She nearly tripped over Cricket as she went upstairs, wrapping her bathrobe around her. "Who is it?" she called.

"Gabe."

She glanced at herself in the hall mirror. She opened the door. His face shocked her. He was ashen, unshaven. "I got in late last night." He put an arm around her waist. "Let's go in and sit down."

"No," she said, backing away from him. "What's wrong? Tell me."

He held on to her arm. "Nadine's been found dead."

Faye didn't say anything, just kept backing away from him.

"Sam called me." Cricket bounced around Gabe's legs, jumping up and down. "Buck called him. Let's sit down." Gabe's hands stretched toward her. She shook her head, backing through the archway into the living room. "Buck identified the body. Oh, Faye, I'm so sorry. She committed suicide."

"No, no." She was trembling. He reached out again, she slipped away. "It's my fault, I got her into all this." She was headed toward the windows but veered away.

"That's not true!" Gabe said.

She turned and bumped into him, dodged, kept going. "I did this . . ." She turned toward the kitchen, her arms tight against her sides. "God, no, no!" She lifted her hair, scrubbing her hands up the sides of her face. "This can't be happening." A sob shot out of her like a fountain. "Not Nadine, not Nadine." She bent in the middle, then slowly sank to her knees.

Gabe went to her.

She felt vacant. She was lying on the sofa, Cricket was curled beside her. Beating and sizzle sounds came from the kitchen.

"Comfort food," Gabe said, bringing a plate to her.

The pancakes steamed. "Gabe's tranquilizers," she murmured.

She tried one. Gabe was a good cook, but the pancake tasted like Pablum. "Great," she said.

"Fair." He poured syrup on her plate. "Someone has to tell Rob."

"I will." She winced at the prospect.

Gabe was sitting listlessly in a chair, staring into space. Faye dialed Mark's headquarters, but Rob was in San Francisco and wouldn't be back in L.A. till that evening.

Faye's hazel eyes were puffy slits; her mouth was pale, the two freckles dotting it like periods. "First Della, then Pamela, now Nadine," she murmured. "Me next?"

"She wasn't killed," he said tonelessly. Faye was reaching for the telephone. "Don't call anyone until you feel better."

She punched the number wrong, redialed, wrong again,

redialed. "Helena," she said, "it's Faye." Gabe got up and walked away. "Helena, I just heard. It's so—ghastly . . ." She heard Helena's muffled voice, then Buck came on the line. "Buck, I want to come up, see you."

"I'm sorry, Faye, we don't want to see you right now."

"But, if it helps—when I was with Nadine—"

"It doesn't matter now."

Faye began crying. "I don't know how she could have committed suicide."

Judge Stern's voice broke in, strong and determined. "I have the coroner's report. She was found in a wretched hotel. She was overwrought, her mind deranged, and I blame your brother for this!" His voice rose, picked up speed. "She called me from Washington, she told me about his disgraceful affair. We don't want to see you or him."

"Oh, Buck, we—the services . . . ?"

"Nadine's being cremated. We'll have a memorial later. That's all I have to say. Helena and I are leaving for Washington—the hearings."

"Buck, how could she have done this?" Faye wailed. "She was pregnant!"

She heard Buck suck in his breath and let it out. Gabe spun around, astonished.

"Pregnant?" Buck whispered.

"Two months. She was ecstatic."

The line went dead. Faye turned, shocked. "He hung up. He hung up! What's wrong with those people? Do you know what they're doing? Cremating her!" She started sobbing, gusts of broken sound. "We won't even have a chance to say good-bye . . ."

Gabe folded her into his arms. There was a kind of nobility in her terrible grief, the way she surrendered to sadness and joy, anger and sensuality with the same heedless force. Holding her, he saw her standing on a set in a rage, elbows out, feet apart, saw her on a bed, arms above her head, her face shiny with pleasure, and he saw her now, tormented. He held her, prizing her. She went on crying. He looked at the half-finished walls, the old plaster fireplace, and thought about Nadine, the beautiful aloof friend who hadn't had a very happy life.

* * *

Detective Sebastian Phelps saw them enter his office and knew they were both grief-stricken. Faye's face was waxy and unnatural, her hazel eyes staring in the way of people who are looking inside.

"This is my—my former husband, Gabe Mittelman," she said. The men shook hands.

"I'm extremely sorry to hear of your sister-in-law's death," Phelps said. "Did you get your security?"

"Yes. Phelps, help me. I want to see the coroner's report."

"I don't have it. It's not my case."

"Can't you get a copy? Whatever's happened to Nadine is connected to me and Della." She collapsed in a chair. "Wouldn't the autopsy show if she was pregnant or not?"

"Yes, but—"

"If she wasn't pregnant, it'd show a recent abortion?"

"Yes."

"My sister-in-law was pregnant and I don't understand why she'd—commit suicide."

"Faye thinks Judge Stern might have identified the wrong woman," Gabe said.

Phelps eyed Gabe, a good-looking man, who seemed as beaten by the news as Faye. "Fathers don't make those kinds of mistakes." His gaze settled on Faye.

"Please, Phelps," she said. She felt exhausted, as if she were about to float outside her body and only Phelps's eyes moored her to the chair.

"If an autopsy'll put your doubts to rest, I'll get you a copy."

Faye knew when she saw Rob that he'd already heard. He came through the terminal doors of the Burbank airport with two aides, and she put her arms around him. He tolerated it.

"I don't want to talk, Faye," he said. Rob was drunk. The aides backed off, shifting the bags in their hands.

"I'm your strongest ally, Robbie," she said. "Nothing will ever change that." But he was moving away from her. She went after him. The aides followed, glum and wary. "Rob, Nadine—I have a lot of questions—"

"Oh, Faye, what do you know, what do any of us know?"

"She was pregnant."

Rob stumbled. An aide steadied him. "All right," he said to the men. "You two go on. I'll see you tomorrow."

Faye drove Rob out of the airport, heading for Ventura Boulevard. Rob was having difficulty focusing. "Pregnant?"

"Yes. I need the name of her ob-gyn."

"Pregnant . . ." he breathed. "Pull over here." He gestured at a bar and knocked his knuckles against the car window.

"We're going home."

"Mom and Pop's? No way. Pull over!"

"No!"

He grabbed the door handle, opened it. She pulled over.

They went into a neighborhood bar in the Valley, full of people in jeans and colorful shirts and expensive haircuts. They found a place at the end of the bar. Rob ordered a double scotch.

"We were a bad-luck pair," Rob was saying. "Maybe she just thought she was pregnant, she wanted to be so much . . ."

"Rob," Faye asked softly, "what if that suicide victim wasn't Nadine?"

He twisted his head toward her. "What are you saying—she's alive?"

"I'm just trying to look at all the possibilities—"

"You aren't! You're just pushing my face in it! You want to hear it from me?" he said, his voice rising. People at the bar stared, then glanced quickly away. "I'm ashamed. You satisfied? She might have been dying while I was out in some podunk farm town, feeding the local papers, or when I was—" He slammed his fist on the bar, holding back his tears with enormous effort.

"Let's get out of here," she whispered.

"I know what you think of me," he said.

"No you don't."

"When everything blew up, I called Claire and . . . that's over. I got back home and Nadine was gone. You knew where she was, Faye, you didn't even give me a chance to make it right with her."

"You can't make things like this right overnight. She'd had

a whole load of shocks that day, being fired and you—"

"People like Nadine don't get fired—"

"C'mon, Rob, Leo found out about you and Claire—he probably wouldn't have fired her for everything else—it was because of Claire! It was because of you!"

Rob was asking for another drink. "Nah, she was playing some damned game with those fuckers at the NSC. She went off the deep end with Mark's people once, too, checking things out, going after obscure files, gathering testimony, all that shit lawyers do—"

"Robbie, it was Claire—that's all Leo needed." She took his arm. "C'mon, let's go home."

"No." His new drink arrived.

"Rob, this is tearing me apart, too."

Her brother was staring at his drink suspiciously. His hand approached it, wrapped around it, fell away. "I've fucked up my life."

"I really feel she wouldn't kill herself—"

He turned fully around on his bar stool. "You are really something, you know that? Her own father identified her. What do you want—that someone killed her? Is that better? She's dead! Buck saw her!" His voice was rising dangerously; people were now staring at them avidly.

"Why do you do this? It's cruel. You don't know what you're talking about, Faye, you just think you do. And you've got a real attitude that pisses me off. You think you got *Jungle Gym* on your own? You didn't! It was Sam Pike. He got it for Annie. Actually, probably for Gabe." He leaned forward. "God, you should've seen our own little Annie after you left Harry's Bar that day. She was so sure she'd get the role. And I wondered why because if there's anything the ol' Ferrays know it's that casting's a bloody roll of the dice."

"Sam?" Faye said, shaking his arm.

"He and Annie have a thing together," Rob mumbled. "You ask Annie."

Faye rolled Rob out of her car and into Coo's ready arms about nine that evening. "He's a little tired," Faye said, which was the family code for "drunk as a skunk." Coo knew what to do.

"Faye, dear," Coo said, "you come inside, too. You look awful."

Faye stared at the warm lights in the windows of the house. "Can't. I have to see Annie."

She took Coldwater Canyon over the hill and plunged into Beverly Hills. Driving in darkness felt like traveling in a chamber. Time and space were honed into new shapes, the road itself seemed altered, and any act was permissible. She thought about Phelps's hand falling onto his desk when he realized—what? That it wasn't over? That there was something else to do? No, no. He had felt helpless. He had felt pained.

Annie was dressing to go out. "Roger's asked me to a big party at his house," she said, letting Faye in. "Daddy isn't worse, is he?"

"No, Pop's fine. I wanted to tell you about something else."

"Come back here," Annie said. "Faye, you look a wreck." She led the way down the hall.

Faye had forgotten how lacy and contented Annie's bedroom was. The large makeup mirror was lit, jars and pots and brushes scattered on top of the dresser below it. Annie sat down and examined her face for changes on the walk from the front door.

Faye sat down on the corner of the white satin bedspread. "Nadine's dead. I just saw Rob."

Annie spun around. "Dead?" She opened her eyes wide. "How awful. What happened?"

While Faye told her what she knew, Annie turned back to the mirror and finished outlining her eyes. She felt uncomfortable. She'd never told Faye the whole truth on any subject, but usually when she'd given her word, she'd tried to keep it. Coo was very strong on keeping one's word. Annie finished her face, rose, and slipped out of her kimono. "I just have to get dressed," she said with an air of repentance.

"Annie, tell me something."

"Sure," Annie said brightly. She felt her stomach muscles tighten as she went into the closet and took out a luxurious and richly decorated dress.

"Rob was very upset, so he might be exaggerating. You've often said that you got *Gym* mounted by taking it to BeverCo. What made you take it there?"

Annie stepped into the dress and pulled it up and over her hips and breasts. "Don't you think I pay attention to the trades?" She zipped up the dress without asking for Faye's help and sat down at her mirror.

"I just want to know what the steps were," Faye said.

"You aren't the only person who knows people," Annie said.

"Rob said Sam Pike was involved."

"Sam and I are good friends."

"More than that maybe?"

"Maybe." Annie smiled coyly. "Sam might have mentioned BeverCo was looking for material, but anyway I sent them the script. And they liked it. The rest is history." She was flicking a small brush against a curl of her hair.

Something worse was settling inside Faye. "Did you tell Sam about Nadine being in the shoot?"

"Of course not," Annie said.

"You did, didn't you?"

"I wouldn't do that!"

"Who else did you tell?"

"I didn't tell anyone!" She threw down the brush, jumped up and went to a bureau. She yanked a drawer open.

"Annie, this is important—"

Annie whirled around. "Well, what if I did tell?"

"Sam?"

"Yes. Just Sam. I overheard you all in the trailer, Nadine was sounding weird, talking about her job and finding out something about Della. I just mentioned she was in the movie because it was all so wonderful and silly, and I, well, it seemed to me—"

"Is everything 'I—I—I' with you?"

Annie seemed confused and injured. "What do you mean?"

"You are *the* single, most self-centered human being I've ever met."

Annie narrowed her eyes. "You never liked me, did you? You've treated me like a foster child, not like a sister, but I didn't know until this minute how little you cared about me.

I've stopped trying to make you like me. I'm only looking out for myself now."

Faye stared at her sister. If it hadn't been so painful, it would have been funny because there she was, accused of being self-involved, and talking about herself! Faye put her hands on Annie's shoulders. "I do care about you, Annie, but I don't like you very much. And there is a difference."

Annie pulled away. Her chin was trembling. "We don't have to be close; where's that written? You're cold, Faye, trying to paste failed relationships back together, letting your career go to hell, trailing around Gabe, and he's a joke! He just up and left you two years ago. He could have made a lot of money, he was on a roll, but oh, no, he wants to hide out in Maine. He could have been famous."

"Gabe doesn't care about money," Faye said.

"Oh, sure, it's all for art."

Faye collapsed on the corner of the bed. This woman, her sister, had nothing in common with Faye, and if Annie wasn't an enemy, she certainly was no friend.

Annie was fixing her hair.

"So Sam had the pull at BeverCo, is that it?" Faye said.

"They wanted me!"

"*Sam* wanted you. Wake up. You're good at reality."

Annie frowned into the mirror. Had it all been something else? She remembered Sam saying the movie would keep Faye busy. That had always struck her as such an odd thing to say, as if it had just slipped out of him and he'd regretted it. Had he had some other interest in the *Jungle Gym* deal? But what of it? She didn't care.

"Well, Faye," Annie said, adjusting a lock of her pretty hair, "the upshot is that I have a good costarring role with Roger Reynolds, and you have a movie. So what's the diff?"

Faye drove home. Carl, her favorite security man, was on duty. "Mr. Mittelman's in there," he said. "That was okay? He had a key."

"Yes, okay." But she wanted to be alone. Inside, Cricket jumped around her. Faye fed her, went into the living room and fell onto the sofa and closed her eyes. She wished Phelps were in the living room; she wanted to talk to him.

She opened her eyes. Then she went downstairs. Gabe lay on her bed, watching television.

"Sorry, I didn't want you to come back to an empty house." He got off the bed.

"Oh, stay a while. What's on?"

"Campaign roundup, our own senator," Gabe said, sitting on the edge of the bed like a visitor. His face was drawn, the lines in his cheeks deeply scored.

"Did you eat?"

"Not hungry."

"Me, neither."

Mark was giving an interview to reporters at the Los Angeles airport. She sat on the other side of the bed. "I can remember the first real conversation I had with Nadine," she said. "We were in high school and all the jacaranda trees were in bloom, which makes it spring. The blossoms were all over the sidewalk. We were talking about Kent State, which had just happened—it was the first time we felt, as students, that we weren't automatically safe." The telephone rang.

"Yes?" Faye said.

"Phelps. I'll have the autopsy report tomorrow. How are you doing?"

"Okay." Gabe was staring at the TV set, his face vacant, miserable.

"Call if you need anything," Phelps said.

"Yes, thank you. Bye." She hung up. "That was Phelps."

"Television's changed everything," Gabe mumbled. "Mark's a good actor on the campaign stage. And he's getting solid Latino support."

Faye remembered the look on Mark's face, fear and dislike, when he saw Diaz at Della's funeral. She'd known it then but she hadn't let herself take it in, she hadn't pressed Mark about it. What else had she not allowed herself to know?

"*Tia*," she said.

"What?"

"That's what Della said that day, '*tia*' and something that sounded like 'selections.' "

Mark was in the middle of an exchange with a reporter about offshore oil drilling. "You know my record," Mark was saying. "But my opponent will have oil drills lined up along our coast like parking meters."

"Maybe Della wasn't saying *tia* but *pia* or *dia*—that would make more sense, *dia*."

"Do you have a Spanish-English dictionary in the house?" he asked.

"Upstairs."

Gabe returned with a battered dictionary and two Cokes. Faye was sitting cross-legged on the bed with Cricket.

"Maybe Della didn't say 'selections' but 'defections,'" Faye said.

"Or 'affections'?"

" 'Elections'? There's a hundred words that'd fit."

Gabe sat down on the edge of the bed again and turned off the sound on the TV set. Watching Mark on TV in Faye's bedroom was almost too painful. "I got to go, Faye." He handed her the dictionary.

"Just help me with this a moment. If Della was talking about God, what would God have to do with 'defections' or 'selections'? It would have been more like 'affections,' right?" She started thumbing through the dictionary.

"*Dio*," Gabe said.

Faye tilted her head. "Close, but not . . . quite. Aha, dio is spelled *Dios*. I think I heard sibilance at the end. *Tío* is uncle . . . *río* means river, *ría* is an estuary."

"*Río, Dio,* is there a *pío*?" he asked.

"It means 'pious' or 'dappled' or 'chirping.' What did I hear that sounds like *tío* or *tía*?"

"Keogh?"

"A retirement fund? No."

"Keyhole?" Gabe tried again. "*Ría, tía,* maybe *día*?"

"*Día,*" she repeated. "That means day."

"*Buenos días,*" Gabe said. Then he saw Faye's face.

"Ye gods. Días. *Diaz!* Royal Diaz! Gabe, that's it! That's what I heard!" She leaped off the bed. "If it's 'Diaz' then it has to be 'elections'!"

Gabe put an arm around her. Her elation was infectious; he felt the smile lift his face. "Now what?" he said, getting up.

"Talk to Phelps! Now I've got something!" She reached

for the phone, but Phelps was not there. She left a message.

Gabe tightened his grip on her waist. She let herself be pulled closer. "You feel different."

"Been working out. So, tomorrow, we're starting early. Stage nineteen?" She gazed at him steadily. He didn't flinch.

"Where have you been?" he sighed, sweeping his arms around her. "Where have I been?"

"We've been away." *Am I still away from him?*

He pressed his cheek against hers, then kissed her very slowly, testing her lips, brushing against them, knowing that if she kept still she'd feel the calm of being loved again.

They stood together in the room full of interrupted tasks and mute television news, and they each listened. Gabe turned out the light, stretched out on the bed beside her. "I feel like I've been ill for a long time and I'm getting well," he said.

She propped on her elbow. "Maybe we're both getting well."

But she wasn't sure.

TWENTY-EIGHT

"WE'RE ALL REAL sorry to hear about Nadine," Julie said the next day on the set. "We all liked her."

"Thank you, Julie," Faye said. "How did you hear?"

"Annie mentioned it."

"Um." Faye flicked on her laptop.

"The office set won't be finished in time for the new schedule," Julie said in a low voice, "and Roger doesn't like his suits."

Faye had awakened that morning, wanting to be alone again, but Gabe had been on the far side of the bed. She'd left another message for Phelps; one of his people had called back asking if there was trouble. "No, no," she'd said, "just have him call me later."

Faye was on the sound stage but she wasn't. Nadine's death had stunned her, she was swimming again, waves of awareness and denial. Nadine couldn't have committed suicide . . . unless she'd been more unbalanced than Faye had thought. "Do we ever know anyone?" she said out loud.

"Nadine?" Julie asked.

"Yes."

"She didn't seem the type to . . . commit suicide."

"No, she didn't."

They were getting ready to shoot a brief scene between

Celia and her Supervisor when Tony Valdi appeared on the laboratory set dressed in a handsome Bill Blass suit. He waved at everyone, tossed compliments, and slapped Gabe on the back. Faye watched him: hearty executives on the set were not a good sign. "Tony!" she said, giving him a big hug.

"Faye, let's talk." They walked outside and stood in the alley beside the stage. "These look like hands," he said, holding them out, "but they got thumb screws attached. No more extra time. We gotta come in on schedule. In fact, if you could come in early . . . ? Money's tight." There was an edge in his voice.

"How tight?"

"Come in on schedule and we'll be okay."

"I can't do that—we have three days on this set, then the intersection stuff, then—"

"Cut the intersection! Get another ending!"

"Are you nuts? It's built, it's crucial!"

"Then cut the lab stuff. Faye, you're five days behind and I can't cover them." His show of joviality was gone.

"Five days is nothing!"

"We're out of money."

"Right now?" she asked, aghast.

"Some of our investors, offshore money, got caught—their savings and loan failed. I'm keeping you going by raiding another production we got that I shut down yesterday. Sorry, Faye, you gotta wrap this up pronto."

Faye watched him strut away, knowing why he'd driven her to get the movie done in a millisecond.

"Hey, you." Keith Llewellyn was standing at the open doorway, his hair ruffled, his square open face peering inside. "How goes it?"

"Armageddon was easier," Faye said. She stepped into the production trailer-office beside the sound stage.

"New pages," he said, handing them over. "The explosion scene. Okay if Bob comes in?" Faye nodded, scanning the pages.

Cricket had been sitting under a counter. Now she jumped up, wagging her tail. "See? She remembers," Keith said.

"You know Cricket?"

Keith looked sheepish. "Ah, shit, I blew it."

"That whole story, buying her from some abusive—"

"I found her and gave her to Gabe." Cricket and Bob were going around in a circle, smelling and pawing each other.

Faye smiled. "Well, there was a time when I would've handed her back, but not now. I love her. Listen, I need some more rewrites, got to compress a couple of scenes."

"I'll do what I can, but I'm really pressed."

"Thanks. And Keith, don't tell Gabe I know about Cricket and his little deception. I'll spring that on him myself at the right moment."

"Oh, now, don't be hard on him—"

"Me? Hard?" He was at the door. She didn't want to be alone in the trailer. "Wait a minute, Keith, I'll go with you." She was dialing the phone. "Just want to call Herb." Herb wasn't expected back until late afternoon. She picked up the list of press and other guests she was inviting to the set later that week. "Keith, come to the explosion scene," she said as they left the trailer. Filming explosions and other dramatic stunt work were treated like staged happenings for the benefit of the press and top executives.

"You bet! I love explosions," he said. "Are you gonna have helicopters and child actors like *Twilight Zone*?"

"Don't be grim, Keith."

He left her at the entrance to the sound stage. She paused at the opening. Inside, the lights were bright, the sounds of hammering, sawing, and crew yells were comforting. She'd had second thoughts about her arrangements for the explosion scene, but now that she'd remembered Della had said Diaz's name, it was even more important to go ahead. The scene was the only way she could end what had begun the day she'd lunched with Della. But inside, she felt detached. Nothing could bring Nadine or Della back.

Gabe, behind her, slipped a hand down her arm. "How are you?"

"Tony says he's running out of money. No extensions."

"Aw, shit, what's going on?"

"He suggested cutting the intersection scene—"

"Can't do that."

"He suggested a new, cheaper ending."

"Never let the money guys pick the ending! It's always wrong." He saw Dino passing the trailer. "Dino!"

"Of course it's wrong," Faye muttered. "I made this movie for that ending, the intersection *is* the movie!"

Gabe was talking to Dino. "What?" he asked Faye.

"Nothing."

"Dino, get someone with Annie—she's rotten on those lines." He turned back to Faye. "Tony's not pulling the plug on Roger!"

"Of course not—he thinks he'll get his money back with Roger."

"C'mon, Billy's waiting."

Faye scooped up Cricket, they climbed into an electric cart and rode off.

"Here's the invitation list for the explosion scene."

"Looks long," he said. "How many press you asking?"

"Tons. Plus others, like Tony and Herb, Mark Drummond's a maybe, Rob, Buck, but of course he won't be there, Tony's staff. I asked Sam, too. Keith's rewriting the dialogue in the scene just for Señor Diaz."

"You *asked him*? Faye, that's crazy, that's dangerous. No, no way!"

She hiked a shoulder. "Well, he probably won't come." But she was trying hard to get him there; she'd even called on Rob to help deliver him.

"You better fucking hope he doesn't. You're setting yourself up."

"I have my guards and there'll be people everywhere. Gabe, this is—well, it's closure for me, probably the only one I'll get." Gabe made a sound under his breath. "Too late! I mailed them this morning."

"That's the dumbest thing I ever heard!" They were at the intersection set. Cursing, Gabe leaped off the cart and started talking to Billy, who was with one of his powder men and a county fire inspector. Faye followed them over to the car. The men got down on their hands and knees and peered into the car, muttering to each other, then walked back to the cart. Cricket barked at Billy; he patted her head.

"Billy," Gabe said, "here's the way we do it: we'll shoot Roger and Annie at the car just as he steps back and she pulls away. Then we'll follow her as she drives down through there and stops at the intersection. We'll cut there. Annie gets out, we'll arm the car, put the dummy in, film the blowup. Cut. Same setup, Annie gets back in the car, we get the extras out there, Roger comes into the shot, reaches the car, they have their dialogue, paramedics arrive . . ."

"Lotsa cameras, huh?" Billy said, looking at sketches of the camera setups.

"We have to do this in one day."

"Right-o." Billy went back to his men.

Gabe was staring past the storefront window. "Don't look now, but there's Detective Phelps." He was getting out of his car on a side street.

Phelps had an easy, muscular walk. "I haven't been back here before."

"Was she pregnant?" Faye asked.

Phelps stopped. "No."

"Ha!" She grabbed Gabe's arm. "See? Was the body's hair black or blond?"

"Blond." Phelps's features shifted, took on a relaxed, attentive look. In the bright daylight, Faye saw his eyes were dark gray.

"Dyed blond?"

"No. Natural."

Faye leaned against the cart. "I'm so . . . relieved," she said softly, tears springing into her eyes. "It wasn't Nadine!" She suddenly clasped Phelps with both hands. "See? It wasn't Nadine! Gabe." She hugged him. "It couldn't have been Nadine," she went on to Phelps, "because her dad didn't know—or someone didn't know—she'd cut her hair and dyed it black, or that she was pregnant."

Phelps's eyes slipped toward Gabe.

"I didn't know she was pregnant," Gabe said, "but she sure changed her hair for the production."

Phelps wanted to believe Faye, but was cop-skeptical. "Why would a father pretend his daughter was dead?"

"I don't know," Faye said. "We have to find that out." Phelps nodded, watching the men clustered around the car. "You are *truly* the most contained and hidden person I've ever met, Phelps."

Phelps laughed, a ripe, rolling sound, easy and warm. It astonished Faye. "What are you filming out here?" he asked.

"Big scene with explosives on Wednesday—I want you to come." They started walking toward the storefront. "What do you know about Royal Diaz?"

"Prominent Latino guy," Phelps said.

"Della named him, I heard that name." Faye told him about the decoding of "tia" into "Diaz."

"Just naming him," Phelps said, "that's not much. She didn't say 'Diaz blew this car up,' did she?"

"No, but I'm sure she said 'Diaz.' CDEE, his outfit, is on her disk."

"I remember."

"Oh, so you did look at it. That's what Nadine was working on and that's why she's gone."

Phelps put up a hand. "Don't think she's alive. We don't have any proof of that yet."

"Faye's invited Diaz to witness her re-creation of Della's death scene," Gabe said. "I think you ought to talk her out of it."

Phelps surveyed the intersection. "Not smart, Faye. Gutsy, but not smart. You better get lots of extra security." Phelps jammed his hands in his pockets. "I'll need the name of your sister-in-law's dentist for her dental records."

"Judge Stern told me they'd had her cremated."

"Oh, now, that is a bad sign," Phelps said, staring at the hills rising behind the lot.

"He's right, you're making a dumb move," Gabe said, driving back to the sound stage. Cricket sat between them, alertly facing front.

"Why would Buck identify a body as Nadine's?"

"You're not even listening to me!"

"Could Buck have been fooled by someone? Maybe he was being blackmailed," she said. "Maybe it had something to do with Leo. He's the only one who wanted Nadine out of the picture. Maybe there's a connection between Buck and Leo."

"But *you* said they've known each other for years! Sam, too!"

"Some *other* connection," Faye said. "I wish I could talk to Buck. I'll speak to Jerry." She thought of Buck's party at El Contento when he'd just been nominated for the Court. "Nadine and I heard them talking in the downstairs study. It seemed so odd, them huddled in there with the party going on full blast on the lawn."

"Sam, this Leo, and Buck?"

"Yes. I don't remember what they were talking about, something about Mark."

"Naturally, the senator who's everywhere."

"You have no reason to be jealous of Mark."

"Good," he said, squeezing her knee.

Something had happened to her. She felt completely cut off from Gabe. What had changed? "I saw Annie last night. She and Sam have been having an affair."

He hit the steering wheel, grinning. "I'll be damned, that old so-and-so!"

"She told Sam about Nadine being in the production."

"Well, so what? Who's he going to tell?"

"She said it was Sam who suggested BeverCo to her." She turned so she could see Gabe's face. "You'd have thought Sam would have called me."

"Not necessarily. If you'd made the contact yourself, would you have hired Annie? Not in a million years."

"Gabe, why would Sam do all this?"

"Sam likes to be useful, to make connections. He's always been like that and you know it. He'd see it as a way to help Annie—maybe she asked for his help."

"Maybe he really wanted to help you. Did you know about the movie—I mean, before it happened?"

"No," Gabe said. "What difference does it make?" He pulled up in front of her trailer.

"Oh, none, I guess. I just feel like a prop being moved around."

"Oh, if only you were," he exclaimed, "how much easier life would be!" He kissed her cheek.

"Gabe, come inside. I have a minor addition to the explosion scene." When he heard what she had in mind, it was not minor. "You're loony," he said, "brilliant, but loony."

Faye watched him move off. But she was alone again in

the trailer. Hastily, she gathered up what she needed and walked up to the parking lot. Buck and Leo. If more than old friendship connected them, might that also be true of Sam? Could Nadine's investigation of OPI be the link? But how, and why? OPI came out of the federal government— it didn't have anything to do with California foundations, Sam's world, or California politics, Buck's world.

Faye didn't really care about OPI or budgets or programs. She only cared about Della and Nadine.

"Faye!" It was Susan from wardrobe. "I was trying to find you. Annie and Roger were supposed to come in for wardrobe fittings, but I can't find them. I sent Roger's jackets out to his home."

"I've got new pages for her. I'll check her trailer on my way out."

"She's not there," Susan said sourly.

Faye's phone rang. "I'll take care of it," she said to Susan. She clicked on her phone. "Yes? This is Faye."

"It's Tot," she said. "Faye, I'm so upset about Nadine, I can hardly function." Her voice was tense and grieving. "Call me back on B."

When Faye reached her from the pay phone outside the commissary, Tot said, "I've found out the famous leak release was a setup to discredit Nadine, and I've found a second source on the lie-detector material. We're going to air it! Adrian's been helpful but I need more corroboration. Nadine could have done that . . . I need those notes Nadine gave to Mark, and the disk. Can you get them back?"

"I'll try. Listen, Tot, I remembered what Della said!" Quickly, Faye told her.

But Tot was back on the campaign-financing assignment. "I'll be out in California at the end of this week."

"That's far away from Nadine's story," Faye said.

"Yes. There's nothing I can do about that, but I won't give up. I swear."

Faye knocked at Annie's trailer. Muffled voices. "Annie, it's Faye." She heard a gush of Annie giggles, then some thumps. The trailer door swung open: Roger stood in front of her, naked.

"It's the producer, all right," he said.

Faye glanced at his nakedness. "I want to talk to you about your wardrobe," she said straight-faced.

From inside, Annie said, "Faye, get out. We're busy."

"Oh, great, you made it after all!" Smokey said.

Faye had the feeling she'd walked into someone else's play. Herb Yount and others were seated at a large table with pads and pencils at each place. A recessed monitor in one wall showed a test pattern. "I came to see Mark," she said.

"Sit down, Faye, what can we get you?" Smokey snapped his fingers at a submissive aide.

"Perrier's fine," she said, bewildered.

"We've just seen the first spot—got two more."

The media consultants' review of Drummond's television spots! She'd forgotten all about it.

"Hello, all," Mark said, coming into the room. "Faye, great of you to be here." He went around the table, shaking hands, thanking them for their "valuable insights." Then he left for a call.

"Have you talked with Tony?" she asked Herb as she sat down next to him at the table.

"Yes," he said tightly. In his public voice, he said, "All set for the big day?"

She smiled at the assorted media people around the table. "We're blowing up Herb's back lot in a couple of days. Anyone who wants to come just let me know."

"I'm Smokey's new media hand," one of the men said, "and these spots are our responses to Sparks's charges that Mark favors people on welfare over 'average working Americans.' We're not happy with these spots and we need your reaction."

"You're making new spots?" Herb asked.

"Probably. But if these work for you, we'll also air these."

A spot came up. Drummond was walking through a wooded area, speaking about "building lives as tall and strong as trees." When it ended, Herb asked, "What age group are these spots aimed at?" Another man talked about "the background being too busy." The consensus: the spot was soft.

The next spot was hard-hitting, hinting that Sparks profited from substandard materials in construction deals, that he was paving California. The visuals were potent—houses as far as the eye could see—no trees, no ocean, no people. A beautiful shot of California came up. The narrator boomed: "Vote for Mark Drummond, the senator who protects California."

This spot was lauded. "Didn't cost us a dime," Smokey said. "The environmentalists put their pennies together."

Mark came back as the meeting broke up; busy executives shook hands and rushed off.

"Mark, could I see you for a minute?" Faye asked.

"This way," he motioned. They went down the hall to his office with the old, brown leather furniture. She remembered him standing by the closet mirror, changing his shirt. It seemed very long ago.

"I was extremely upset to hear about Nadine, Faye. A terrible blow for you and Rob and the families." He shut the door. "I told Rob to take time off, but he won't. I'm worried about him. How are you holding up? You've been through hell. I've missed you." He paused in front of her and kissed her cheek, then led her to a chair. "How's your dad doing?"

"Better, thank God. He's back home."

"Good. Tell me how the campaign's going from your point of view."

"Sparks seems very aggressive. But you've picked up a lot of Latino support," she said. "Were you surprised?"

"No, no, not really. We worked hard to make those ties."

"I remember you seeing Royal Diaz at Della's funeral."

Mark shook his head. He seemed puzzled. "That was an upsetting day—for you most of all."

"Are you really supporting him or is it pro forma?"

"Oh, I don't believe the rumors about him."

"Well, he was a judge in El Salvador. And he did let those death squad people off."

Mark gave her a warm but worried look. "The case against them wasn't proven, Faye. We don't know he wanted to let them off. But you didn't come here to talk about Diaz." His full attention was on her. "What can I help with?"

"Are you coming to the lot for my explosion scene?"

"Well, the schedule's crowded—"

"Going to be a lot of press out there. I'm putting pressure

on Rob to make a hole in your schedule."

"I'll certainly give it my best shot. I'd like to be there."

"I want Diaz there, too."

"Why?"

"Della mentioned him as she was dying."

"An accusation?" he asked, alert.

"No, no. Nothing like that. I just thought he'd be interested in the scene. The character Annie's playing is modeled on Della." She examined his face to see if her story was working. But Mark was glancing at the clock on his desk. "I need Nadine's notes back."

He was behind his desk, his fingertips resting on the glass top. "Hum. That's difficult, Faye. They're part of an investigation, the property, so to speak, of the Senate."

"*Is* there an investigation?"

"There's so much paperwork in these things," he said regretfully, "it's a wonder anything's investigated. I'm still not sure it's the way to go."

"After what's happened to Nadine?"

He inclined his big golden head sadly.

"There really isn't any investigation, is there, Mark?"

"Of course there is."

"So, I can't have Nadine's notes or the disk back?"

"Not at present. Later, of course, I'll see they're returned to you." His eyes settled on her again.

She realized she was standing near the spot where they'd made love. There was no sign of it, of course, and she herself felt little trace of it, either.

He came around the desk to her, reached out and touched her hair. "I shall always remember you and the beauty you brought into my life," he said softly.

"I'm glad of that, Mark, but you know what? It's time for more women in the Senate."

She swung out the door with her lively gait, her red-brown hair rolling on her shoulders. Mark Drummond gazed after her. He could barely remember the feeling of first running for office with her help.

Verdi's *Rigoletto* was soaring through the Ferrays' house when Faye arrived later that evening. "Mom?" she shouted over the music. Cricket sniffed the room and made a beeline for the hallway.

Jerry was dressed, lying on his bed. The shades were up, the sun slanting through the eucalyptus trees, lighting up the shades. "Gee, Pop, you look better."

His eyes opened. He reached over from the bed and turned down the CD. "I always get better as soon as I get out of the hospital. Can't play my *Rigoletto* there."

"You could have had a headset."

"Not the same." He frowned.

She pulled up a chair amid the clutter of magazines, books, stacks of CDs, faded flowers. This room was her parents' bedroom, but now it was Jerry's; Coo had moved into the guest room. "Where's Mom?"

"At a meeting to save the Malibu monarch butterfly."

"Oh, good."

"Yeah, if those people can't save a frigging butterfly, I don't know who can." From another room, the canary's song trilled in the quiet. "Isn't that magical?" he asked.

"I'm glad you're here, Pop, because there's going to be some media noise about Buck and Nadine. That body he identified isn't hers." Her father looked shocked and deeply upset. "I'm sorry to tell you about this."

"What the hell's going on? What's this doing to Robbie?"

She took his bony hand in both of hers, stroking gently. "I think everything will be all right, Pop, and Rob's okay. But the body Buck identified—a suicide—wasn't pregnant. Nadine was."

Jerry let a faint smile slip. "Oh, yeah? Robbie's?"

"Of course! Honestly, Pop. She was ecstatic about being pregnant, but she didn't want to tell Rob over the phone, so she waited. No one knew about that—except me."

Gradually, she realized her father had been drinking. As the suspicion took root and grew, she fought it. "I'm trying to figure out why Buck would do that. Would you ask him when he gets back? The police are bound to, but—"

"Ask him yourself."

"I can't. He hung up on me—he's blaming Rob for everything."

"*Rob?* That's crazy."

"Yes." She couldn't mention Rob's affair with Claire.

"So what am I supposed to think here? That Nadine's okay?"

"I just don't know. The detective thinks she's dead—I can see that in his eyes. All I know for certain is that Nadine's wasn't the body Buck identified. Please, talk to him when he gets back."

Jerry shifted uncomfortably. "His hearings opened today."

"What happened?"

"A lot of old senators jabbering. No sparks."

Faye knew her father wanted her to leave. "What's going on here, Pop? Are you lying here trying to drink yourself to death as quick as you can?" Jerry flinched. "Well, it really pisses me off! How can you do that to us? Why aren't you thinking about how important you are to us? Damn you. *Damn* you! I know you're in pain but why don't you give your body a break, give us all a break!"

Years of refusing to face the terrible duality in him broke over her. She leaped up abruptly, went down the hall, through the kitchen, stopping finally in the dining room. There was an unused feeling in the room—no more family dinners or parties. Cricket trotted in after her, taking up a position below the bird cage. Faye pulled out a chair at the table and sat down.

She heard Jerry coming up behind her.

He took a chair. "I don't want to hurt you, Faye. Don't shame me anymore," he said huskily.

"I didn't mean to."

He sighed. "Okay, okay. I'll stick around as long as possible, in great pain if that'll make you happier." His hand lifted her chin so he could look at her face. "So, what were we talking about?"

She shook her head, feeling short-circuited, scorched.

"You asked me to talk to Buck, right?"

"Yes." She picked up a tail of his shirt and dried her eyes. "When I saw you in the hospital, you said something about Buck and Leo and Sam."

"So? They're old friends."

"Something about campaign high jinks?"

He shrugged. "There was a rumor about Buck's run for lieutenant governor—that the boys fixed his election."

"Fixed it how?"

"Not sure. They had a lot of money, were way ahead of the game on their TV spots. So I don't think they did anything illegal exactly, but there *were* rumors." He let his palm slide down her hair. "Ah, Faye, we're all so fallible."

At six o'clock, she left Jerry's with Cricket. Her bodyguard that night was Dave, a beefy six-footer with pale blue eyes.

"I'm going to make some calls from my car," she told him, "then go on home."

Her last call was to Detective Phelps, but he was out. "I'll have him beeped," his assistant said.

Faye pulled away from her father's house with Dave following her. When Phelps called back, she was on the freeway. He sounded distracted; she heard tense conversation in the background. "I want you to come to the filming and witness the witnesses," Faye said.

"What the hell's that about again?"

"The big explosion scene, Phelps."

"I— Huh, what?" he barked at someone near him. Then to Faye, "I can't come to your—whatever."

"I think it's important."

"Where are you?"

"Hollywood Freeway."

"I'm at Franklin and Highland." He hung up.

"Oh, hell." At least she was on the right freeway.

New buildings were going up in the area, but one vacant lot had been leased to a small traveling carnival: rickety rides, a shooting gallery, refreshment stands. A ring of men in suits and uniforms were staring at a body on the dirt right beside the Flying Tiger ride. Phelps broke away from the men and came toward her.

"What happened?" Faye asked.

He steered her away from the scene. "Someone shot a woman with a rifle."

"God, *this* is what you do all day—bodies?"

"Drugs and bodies go together. I'm off now. Follow me down to Musso's. I gotta eat."

Musso and Franks was an old traditional Hollywood restaurant serving old traditional food. Faded murals were disappearing into the wall, the floor was divided by worn wooden booths. Musso's, a hard room, was always in an uproar.

Phelps ordered liver with bacon and mashed potatoes. "Brain food," he said with a wry smile.

"Bypass rations."

"Have something to eat on the city?"

"No, thanks."

"Look, this scene you're filming? If I'm there, I might tip your hand. Some people in this town recognize me."

"Oh, nuts, Phelps. I need an official witness, just in case. I don't think that's out of line at all."

His sorrowful, penetrating gray eyes regarded her neutrally. "I'll put a man there, but you shouldn't go on with this shoot."

"Too late now for second thoughts. It's the only ammo I have." She fired a wide, mocking smile his way.

"Leave that to people who know what they're doing."

"It's just that I haven't seen a lot of action from your office, starting in March, the day after Della was murdered."

"You think Diaz blew her up? Fine. Get me some proof! A motive, at least. Another thing: your sister-in-law's identified as a suicide and you say the body wasn't hers. Okay, I happen to agree with you. But what possible motive would her father have to pretend she's dead? And if she's not, where the hell *is* she? Be reasonable."

"No." Across the aisle, a pair of hot writers were deep in conversation. "You think she's dead, don't you?"

He sighed. "Yes."

She pulled a glass of water to her. The surface was wet and cold. "The computer disk connects her to Della, you see that now, don't you?"

He cocked his head at her and narrowed his chilly eyes. "Gee, I guess so. Duh, duh."

"Okay, cut it out."

"You think we're stupid?" He hunched his big shoulders over the table. " 'Course the disk linked her to Della, but do you or Nadine know exactly what it meant?"

"No, but Nadine knew some of it, how all the names on the disk were connected through interlocking boards—"

"Yeah, yeah. But what happens to the money when it gets back from the offshore banks? Where does it go? To what end? I got paper chasers, too, but this one takes resources like the Justice Department, and I don't have those. *My* assignment was to find out who blew up Della Izquerra."

"And since you haven't done that, I'm going to go on doing what I can. It's all I have."

He sighed again. His liver arrived. "Look, don't get the wrong idea. I've had six men working with me on this since it landed in my lap. I've had cars watching your house, we've tracked every lead, you've sicced Senator Drummond on us and Judge Stern and Samuel Pike—so don't think there hasn't been a lot of shamans breathing down my neck."

He stabbed his fork into the liver. "My superiors've been on me to clear it up pronto—from the beginning, real pressure. But I fended them off." In a lower voice, he said, "Don't think I don't know what you've been through or how frustrating it is when friends die and no one's punished. I know it's hell."

For an instant, his eyes changed, revealing the sorrow and compassion beneath their cool flinty color. She felt touched. It wasn't in her to criticize him anymore. "Yeah, I guess you do. Thanks for that." She watched him dip his fork into his mashed potatoes. "Why is it that I always seem to end up with you during a meal?"

"We haven't had breakfast yet. Besides, you never eat." He smiled, wrinkling the lines around his eyes. "These are the best mashed potatoes in this town."

"Were you born in L.A.?"

"Right here in Hollywood, Beachwood area. My father was an architect and my mother taught music. I moved back into their house when my mother died last year. The timing coincided with my last divorce. It's a great old place, real Hollywood bungalow on one of those twisty back streets. Great view, too. I got an old avocado tree, a gem of a lemon tree, and a persimmon." His voice warmed up. Tension lines that had seemed innately part of his granite face disappeared.

"I love avocados," she said.

"Want some? I got a ton. This year that sucker went wild—avocados raining down like cannonballs." He spotted her bodyguard at the counter. "Maybe I can get rid of some more on him. I take a lot down to the church—homeless program."

Their three cars pulled up in front of a two-story clapboard house off Beachwood Drive. Phelps opened his front door and turned on some lights. The house was spacious, crammed with delicate antiques sandwiched between neat, serviceable fifties furniture. "Come in," Phelps said.

"What are these?" Faye asked, staring at framed drawings on one living room wall.

Phelps stood beside her. "I collect them—original set sketches from the stage."

"They're nice," she said. "Why'd you start doing that?"

"Long story." She glanced up at him. He was gazing dreamily at the sketch.

They went through the house and out onto a back patio. The garden was small, but fragrant and inviting. On a summer afternoon, it would be cool there under the trees. An array of showy Hollywood lights spread out below a border fence.

Phelps picked up a box of avocados. "Just a few for me," Faye said.

"Dave, you take this box then; I'll get a sack for hers."

They all went back through the house and out the front. Phelps put the sack on her front seat next to Cricket. "Thanks," Faye said. Phelps's arm was on the open window. "Anything else?"

He straightened up, slapped the car roof. "Nothing."

She started her engine. Phelps went back inside the house. She sat in her car, staring at the dark quiet street, slowly aware she was overwhelmed by a sensation rolling inside her, expanding. She could not ignore it. It was gigantic. When had this feeling begun? What act or word had triggered it? Regardless, she did *not* want this emotion.

She revved the engine and shot down the narrow street, ripping around curves until she came to Beachwood, the main thoroughfare.

Dave jerked to a stop behind her. She hopped out of her car and shouted: "We have to go back." Dave didn't look surprised, displeased, or glad. He backed into a driveway while she turned around and headed back up the hill.

"I won't be long," she hollered at him when she got out in front of Phelps's house.

She rang the bell. Phelps opened the door, standing in the center of the frame, looking tense. "Enter," he said. She stepped inside. He shut the door.

"What is happening here?" she demanded.

"I thought you knew. Don't you?"

"I—I'm not sure."

"Yes, you are, Faye," he said gravely.

"I'm not."

"Then why are you here?"

"I came back because I had to know what's . . . with you." She looked into his face but he gave nothing back.

He shifted his weight. "Would you care to discuss it, chew it to death? We could go out back, have a drink."

She was following him through the house again. "I won't stay," she muttered to herself, "I don't know what to do about all . . . this."

"Well, yes, you do," he said without looking back.

"*That's* maddening, Phelps. Are you always like this?"

"No." He opened the back door. She stepped out on the shadowy patio. The night was utterly still.

"Oranges, too, I see," she said, pointing to a far tree.

"Yeah, oranges, too."

She turned. "Well, why aren't you helping? Why are you just standing there not saying anything?"

He raised his hands, palms up, and hiked his strong shoulders. He seemed helpless, almost lost. That look vanished suddenly. "I'm—as stunned as you are," he said finally.

"Since when?" she whispered.

She had a way of moving her head that he found distinctive and familiar now. She tilted it left and hoisted her chin at him.

He glanced off as if to contemplate dates. He knew, but wasn't about to say. The night of the Oscars. He shrugged again. "Since now."

"Well, I don't want this."

"No, I know you don't. You should leave."

She brushed a low-hanging branch of the mighty avocado. He was standing there, arms at his sides like a prisoner awaiting execution. She was no better, she realized. She was standing there, too, her heart banging and banging, dewy sweat on her forehead as if there weren't another soul on the planet, as if Pop were well instead of dying, as if Nadine were with Rob instead of God knew where, as if Gabe weren't waiting for her call, worrying.

In the quaint garden, time and motion halted.

"Yes, I should leave," she said. She glanced up. "Yes, thank you."

She ambled toward the house. He walked slowly behind her. The immense emotion gathered force, whipping through her again. She stopped, head up, hands deep in her pockets, back to him. "You know what I feel? That if I walk out of here, I'm failing, I'm not facing what is. Now that's crazy."

"No, it won't change anything, Faye."

"It'll change me."

"I suspect you can't be changed in that way."

"What do you feel?" She turned and caught her breath. He hadn't expected her to look at him.

His face was raw with an unsuppressed hopeless hunger. He swallowed. "If you leave . . ." His voice was hoarse. "Whatever you do, Faye, will be right. I'm not—this is an accident, a collision. But no one's been hurt."

She nodded, running her hand through a clematis vine trailing down her side of the patio. She went on through the house and out to Dave's car.

Phelps sat down on the back steps, resting his head against the railing. He knew what she was doing. She was letting Dave go back to her house with the dog, saying Phelps would take her home, that she was safe with him. He didn't know if he was safe with her. When he heard her footsteps coming back, he got up and walked out into the garden.

She marched across his yard—erect, determined, a woman girded for battle. She had rearmed herself. She was a wild thing, alluring, but she couldn't back off, even if she had wanted to.

He stepped back. "No," he said, "stop." He raised a hand. She slowed. Her face was in shadow. He moved away from her. "Sometimes I come out here at night and just listen, look at the lights. . . ."

He had to say something to bridge the force of her decision, to make it seem less irrevocable to her. She had to know she could leave again or she wouldn't allow herself to feel anything.

"It takes the curse off the days. Maybe I think about my book, about what the city was like when I was growing up, how much it's changed, about how we're slouching toward Armageddon and we could halt that if we wanted to.

"I used to be a real conservative guy. Not so much anymore. Some of the guys get jagged on the danger—I used to till I saw it was just misery out there. So I come home here, think about my daughter or about what I'm going to plant when I get a day off. I like going down to the garden stores and wandering around till I find something just right for a spot out here. You know, in terms of light, the sunlight. Sometimes the color."

Her touch on his hand was electric, mortal. There would be no reprieve for him. She'd tucked her hand inside his. The breath went out of him. He closed his fingers around her wrist, his hand crept up her arm. She was close, facing him in the shadow of the tree.

"Oh, my darling," he whispered, pressing his hands across her back. She hung on his shoulders, her cheek landed on his. Her hair was brushing against his lips, she smelled of lavender. No pain was sweeter than this pain, this certain agony of the heart.

They made love all night, he, like her, giving himself to intimacy without a shield. There was no distance between them, no hesitations. They could not stop touching each other. Once he said, "I can't believe I'm doing this like it's 1964, and I'm eighteen . . . no commitments."

"You're not eighteen and you know the costs as well as I do. Come here." His body was heavy, his eyes, not leaving her, drank her, sealed her to him. Even when they dozed or lay quietly, one of his hands rested on her somewhere, keeping her.

Later she said, "It's time for me to go. I think it's dawn." But it was only three A.M. and she wasn't leaving, she was reaching for him, crawling over his hard, flat, husky body, sinking her mouth against his mouth.

At six, he followed her home. A new bodyguard was at her door with Cricket beside him wagging her tail. "Has Gabe been here?" she asked. He hadn't.

Phelps waited until she opened her front door. She looked back at him. Smiled. He drove on, feeling the engulfing loneliness as he knew he would.

TWENTY-NINE

THE INTERSECTION SET on the back lot was blocked off while the crew placed cameras and lights, lugged cables. By nine that morning, the extras arrived who'd be the rubberneckers at the accident. The traffic cars driven by teamsters were rolled into place.

Gabe and Lonny sat on the crane, which, like a long-necked bird, lifted and dipped over the intersection. Gabe's calm voice came over the bullhorn: "Car number one, start moving . . . Extras!" Gabe had done the choreography many times, but today, because of the show Faye wanted, the scenes had to be performed like a live act in sequence from start to finish. Sound men were testing mikes for Annie and Roger on their stand-ins, making sure every sigh could be heard. By ten-thirty, they'd solved all the niggling problems, including Roger's desire to wear a hat, which, it was determined, would screw up camera angles. By eleven-fifteen, the set area had a frantic but festive atmosphere. Guests and press were arriving by carts and escorted to the storefront where the huge armored window looked out on the intersection. Inside the "store," a simple buffet table had been set up with sandwiches, wines, and mineral water. Two rows of chairs were behind the window.

Near a video monitor, Faye paced an area behind the crane about half a block from the intersection and across the street from the storefront. By stepping back, she had a clear view of both. Señor Diaz and two of his staff were standing behind the window with Rob and Mark and a campaign aide. Slightly behind them were Sam Pike, Herb Yount, and Tony Valdi. The light inside was sharp enough for Faye to pick out Coo and Norma Goldstein in a corner with some press. She did not see Phelps.

"All the important guests are here," Faye said over her walkie-talkie to Gabe. "Take it away when you're ready."

"Quiet!" Dino was yelling. "Background traffic! Car number one ready . . . Sound!"

"Action," Gabe said serenely.

Car number one, a dark Buick like Della's, was Celia's car. It moved into the shot and pulled to a stop at the curb. Roger got out carrying a briefcase, then leaned toward the open window. Faye held her breath. Roger spoke Congressman Joe's first line. "Honey, get a lawyer." The amplified sound system worked: every syllable was clear and crisp.

Celia, inside the car, said: "Yes, I guess it's time."

"And keep in touch with me?" said Congressman Joe.

"I promise."

The crane moved up, the Buick accelerated from the curb. "Damn you, Celia!" yelled Congressman Joe, leaping back. The car shot into the traffic, skirting a slow-moving Chevy. "Watch out!" The crane stopped as the Buick halted at the intersection waiting to turn left; other cars stopped beside it. Congressman Joe bent down to retrieve the briefcase he'd dropped on the sidewalk.

"Cut!" Gabe yelled on his amplified bullhorn. "Good!"

Roger's minions rushed out of side streets to give him a cigarette, a drink, to powder him down and comb his hair; technicians descended on the Buick. Annie stepped out, a dummy dressed like Celia was put into the car, Billy was having the car armed as quickly as possible, Dino was shouting at extras. Faye was watching the video monitor; it seemed like a real intersection, and she shivered when the men put the yellow-frocked dummy of Celia into the Buick.

Billy signaled Gabe he was ready, Dino was bawling for

background, Roger slouched by the signpost. Gabe said, "Action." Instantly, Roger became an irritated Congressman Joe, staring furiously after the Buick at the intersection as it waited to make a left turn.

The amplified sound of the explosion was everything Billy had promised; even Faye jumped. The Buick's bumpers blew off and four stories of front windows shattered. The car canted to one side as if the two right tires, front and back, had suddenly deflated. Smoke poured from it. At the same time, covered by another camera, Roger's double rocked back against the signpost and flopped heavily to the curb, briefcase flying.

"Cut!" Gabe cried. Some of the watching crew applauded. "C'mon," Gabe yelled, excited now, "move it, move it!"

"This has to be really fast," Faye said into her walkie-talkie. She glanced at the storefront: people inside were talking, but Drummond was getting ready to leave. This was the moment she'd feared, that after the explosion people would drift away, but the explosion was only the prologue to her real script. "Julie! Go over there and remind our guests there's another crucial scene, not to be missed. Keep them there! And see if Phelps is there."

Annie was being helped into the Buick, the crane was moving down for the master shot, extras were milling about, smoke was blowing. "Let's *move!*" Gabe was calling out from the crane. "Let's do it—Roger's big scene now." Roger flipped Gabe the V sign.

There was a mike problem on Annie. Faye groaned, slapped her arms against her side, turned around, turned back, watched the sound man dickering with the wireless mike, watched the guests. Phelps was there, way in the back. A shiver shot through her. Gabe was staring into the sky.

"We're making it," Gabe finally called out. Lonny, directing his cameras, was shouting into his phone.

"Sound! Camera! Background! Action!"

Roger was struggling to his feet. An extra screamed, another bellowed something. "Dazed" extras were getting out of their cars. In the background, cars slowed, drivers gawked. Roger was staggering toward the smoking Buick as the crane drifted down to hover by him as he reached the car.

Faye's video monitor showed a tight shot of Celia inside the car, her head resting on the steering wheel. Someone was calling, "Get an ambulance!" Outside the car, an extra accosted Roger. "Don't touch her, she'll sue!"

Roger yelled, "This is the woman I love—get away from me." He leaned in, trying to hear what Celia was saying.

"Take care of my twins . . ." Celia whispered distinctly. The whole set could hear her.

"Yessss!" Faye hissed, punching her fist out in front of her.

A crowd of extras had circled the car. "Call for help!" Roger reached down and stroked Celia's head. "They're coming, Celia, hang on . . ." He seized the door handle, ripping off his belt at the same time. "She's bleeding to death. Get them to hurry up!" The door would not budge.

"Joe . . ." Celia said, moaning.

"Right here. Hang on. Fight. You're good at that."

"Am I hurt?"

Joe leaned across the open window. "Yes. Bad. You gotta fight hard."

"Bomb?"

"Who would do that?" he said. He yanked at the door again. The car rocked.

Over the mike, Celia was whispering. Joe leaned closer. "Sham . . . selections . . ." said Celia.

Sam Pike, at the window of the storefront, listened and watched intently. What a show, he thought, what a show. Out of the corner of his eye, he spotted Diaz staring at him.

"Tia . . ." said Celia over the sound system.

"What about tia?" asked Joe.

"Bigger . . ." she muttered. "Bigger than I said."

Joe leaned over the car window, trying to hear.

"Celia, I'm going around the other side."

Slowly, the effect of the scene on the street was draining Faye. She hadn't felt as immersed in Della's death since the day it happened, and now it was back with hideous force. Instead of the set and the crew, she saw Della's face, her chin slumped on her chest, her black hair shooting down one side of her face like a curtain, and the blood oozing from beneath the car. Roger was saying his lines to the arriving paramedics.

Faye saw her own paramedic of months ago peer inside the car, look underneath it as her actor was now doing. Faye felt tears on her cheek.

Paramedics were yelling at each other. The crane was moving back. A squad car pulled up. Joe was back at the window. "Celia, who put the bomb in the car?" The paramedics were trying to open the passenger door. On the other side, Joe hung onto the windowsill, his forehead touching it.

Annie's weak but clear voice, speaking the new lines Faye had supplied just for this scene, floated over the set:

"Warn Nadine. Stay clear . . . Bigger than I said . . . CDEE selections . . . Sham . . . Bye . . ."

Faye thought, She isn't saying "bye" right, it's too soft. Bye . . . Della's voice echoed inside her head. "Bye" had sounded sharper, more like "bike."

"No good-byes," Joe said brokenly.

Celia was saying "Diaz . . . Diaz . . ."

A beat. "Cut!" Gabe yelled.

The crane was coming down. Faye yanked herself out of the past and back to the set. The guests in the storefront were smiling, chatting, getting ready to leave. Diaz, talking to a reporter, had a fixed smile on his face, but except for that, he seemed relaxed. Faye felt deflated. He didn't look guilty to her.

"Gabe," Faye said into the walkie-talkie, "don't let those video cameras stop rolling, inside and out." She saw Gabe nod from the crane. In the storefront window, Diaz was talking to Drummond and Rob, who were shaking hands with Herb and Tony in a congratulatory tangle.

Suddenly, Faye felt irrationally elated. It wasn't over yet. She still had the videotapes. She caught up with Roger and Annie. "Just great!" she crooned at them. "Come meet the guests for a sec."

"How'd you like that reading on the paramedic line?" Roger asked. Faye congratulated him again. He was reaching out for Mark's extended hand. Rob was waving at Annie; he tossed Faye a salute. She couldn't see Phelps anywhere. There was an opening around Diaz and his people. "Señor Morales, Señor Diaz," she called out, "I'm glad you could make it!"

Both men shook her hand. Diaz held on a moment too long. "I did not know," he said, "that I would be playing a part in the film." His voice was soft and firm. His large black eyes traveled across her face.

"Is that in the script, Señor Diaz's name?" Morales asked, irritated.

"Oh, no," Faye replied, "it'll all be dubbed over. That was for today, as a bow to our invited guests. I could have used Senator Mark Drummond, but—! Too many syllables!" Morales still seemed uneasy. "I'm glad you could come by. I hope you're not upset."

"No, no," Diaz said. "A gesture, I understand. I hope your movie brings lasting results. I'm afraid I have an appointment. Perhaps we will meet again?" He reached out for her hand, squeezed it, smiled, then turned and took the steps lightly for a man of his size.

She gazed after him. Did you do it, she wondered. He sure didn't act like it. She'd wanted to feel sweet revenge and joy knot together inside her. They hadn't.

Sam Pike was saying to Herb and Tony, "Why do you let these pretty women play with explosives? So dangerous." Sam cackled dryly.

"Did you have a good time?" Faye asked them.

"Yes, indeedy," Sam said, "and you know what I like best about movies? The audience never sees beyond the frame—the frame is God, and mighty selective, too. Why, we could see a film of a home burning down and it's just a wee little model someone put a Zippo to before the camera started turning. But on film it looks like a great big five-bedroom home!" Faye couldn't help liking Sam Pike, his bounce and his canny enthusiasm.

"The magic of movies," Tony purred. "I shudder to think of what all that extra crew and gear cost."

"It was a great show, Faye," Herb said.

"Does Annie's character die?" Sam asked her.

"No. In the story, the bomb was set wrong, a dud."

"Real clever, Faye, I sure take my hat off to you." Sam smiled at Herb and Tony, then at Faye. "But," he said more quietly, "Della died."

"Yes. Why do *you* think she died?"

"Haven't the faintest!" he exclaimed, including Herb and Tony in his gestures. "Someone loses their head, always the way, isn't it?" He put a protective arm around her and turned slightly away from Tony and Herb who were discussing Roger. "Aren't you on thin ice using Diaz's name?"

"That's what Della said."

"She *did*?"

"It took a long time for me to remember it. Can you improve on the story in the scene?"

"Me? No. I don't know what 'sham' or 'selections' mean."

"Maybe 'sham election'?"

" 'Sham affection' is always dynamic in stories. 'Course, we're just talking here for dramatic purposes." He leaned close to her, his pale eyes bright with interest. "Don't be a self-appointed gatekeeper, Faye. Some people are a lot more nervous than others." He patted her shoulder. "Gabe! What a great show!" His hand slid down Faye's arm lightly; when his fingers reached her wrist, he broke away, raising his arm as Gabe strode toward them.

Gabe hugged him. Over Sam's shoulder, he gazed at Faye, reached out and stroked her cheek.

Sam broke the hug. The men turned, as Gabe, six inches taller than Sam, dropped an arm over his mentor's shoulder, bending down to hear whatever Sam was saying, nodding thoughtfully, looking back at Faye, turning back to Sam, shortening his long strides so as not to outdistance the man who meant so much to him.

She turned away and saw Phelps to one side of the crowd. "Thank you," she said, standing close to him, her arm touching his. "Did you see anything useful?"

"No. I think you punted."

"Sorry to have wasted your time."

He gazed at her. "It was not a waste."

Later that afternoon, in a screening room on the lot, after looking at dailies of the last day's shoot, the core group remained: Gabe and Faye; Julie, Dino, and Zack. "Video time," Gabe called out. "The guests." A cassette was inserted. Two large monitors brightened.

"Video of what?" Zack asked.

"The guests," Gabe said.

Faye, sitting at the back with Julie, saw a crack of bright daylight shoot across the aisle. Her bodyguard, Carl, stepped inside, followed by Phelps. Faye moved over a seat so he could sit beside her. "This is Detective Phelps everyone, and Carl," she said.

A wide shot of the storefront came up; in the left-hand corner of the screen numerals counted down minutes, seconds, and tenths of seconds. The camera settled on three people in the front right of the window. Over the shot, the dialogue of the filmed scene could be heard: "Honey, get a lawyer," Roger's Joe was saying.

"Oh, so this is what those extra video operators were for," Zack said. "But why are we looking at the guests?"

"An experiment," Gabe said. "Phelps, this is mainly for you, right? Compliments of the producer." Gabe's voice was tired and sarcastic.

"When do you see the footage you shot today?" Phelps asked.

"Tomorrow," Gabe replied. "That was film—it has to be processed. This is instant gratification tape."

"You can tell from the dialogue where we are," Faye said to Phelps. In the dark, Phelps brushed his hand over hers. Cricket whined; Faye shushed her. Cricket lay on the carpet, but kept a watchful, impatient eye on Faye. "The cameras won't move from the window," she said. "This camera is the long shot, there are others doing close-ups."

Boom! All the guests flinched except Sam. Gabe laughed. "He's so cool." He stretched his long legs into the aisle.

As the dialogue went on, Diaz stiffened. He turned to look at Sam Pike, standing to the right and behind; Sam gave Diaz an incremental nod, but he didn't break his attention from the scene. "So Sam knows Diaz," Faye said.

"He knows everyone," Gabe said.

Annie was saying, "Selections . . . sham . . . bye . . . Diaz."

Diaz sucked his chin back into his neck. His lips formed a word.

"Do you have Spanish lip-readers down at the station?" Faye asked Phelps.

The close-ups from other cameras began. The first shots

included Diaz. "Is that guy upset?" Dino asked.

"Maybe," Phelps said. "If he is, he's handling it well."

"Not what I expected," Faye muttered.

"Just because you heard your friend say his name doesn't mean much."

"You're a real hardass," Faye said. "Do you know what it cost to have these cameras trained on these guys? Diaz looks more disturbed here than he was with me after the shoot."

"Ms. Ferray, he's not unnerved," Phelps said. He brushed his hand against hers again.

"No, he isn't," she admitted.

"Let's all be glad," Gabe said.

The next close-ups were of Rob, Coo, Drummond, and Herb Yount. Rob looked dazed and sad. Herb was pointing at the setups for Mark's benefit, both listened carefully to the dialogue and peered at the action. Then Mark reached behind him, tapped Sam, and said something. Sam shook his head.

Other close-ups followed. Cricket whined again. "I'll take her out," Julie said.

The footage from the camera Faye had inside the storefront began. Phelps was drifting around at the back of the room like Hamlet's ghost, dour, contained. A close-up of Sam showed him fixed on the action. His eyes snapped, he seemed expectant, waiting for the next line, the next surprise. Gabe sat up. Julie, with Cricket, momentarily blocked the monitor; Gabe craned around her. He'd missed something that had struck him as odd. "Wait a minute, roll it back," Gabe said.

On the tape, Mark was turning back to look at Sam, but Sam's expression conferred a brief agreement mixed with a slight irritation as if he didn't want to miss a moment of the unfolding drama. The door to the screening room opened again, sending a shaft of light across the monitors. Gabe turned around, irritated. When he turned back, the scene was over. Now Sam was looking at Diaz, then falling into a lively conversation with Herb and Tony.

"That enough?" Dino said. "You want to see it again?"

"I'll see it later," Gabe said, feeling his fatigue.

The close-ups rolled on, but Gabe still saw Sam smile his impish smile and doing something. What? Where in the dialogue had Gabe's uneasiness begun? He couldn't bring it back.

Faye leaned over to Zack. "Get someone to catalogue this tape for me. Whenever someone—especially Diaz—looks at another person, or says something, I want to know which lines of dialogue it happens around."

The lights came up. "An interesting use of the hidden camera, Ms. Ferray," Phelps said.

"What do you think?"

"Zilch." His thick body unfolded smoothly as he stood.

"Nice try," Gabe said.

"I guess," she said, defeated.

"Give me a dub of that tape and I'll have one of the department's psychologist types go through it. In the meantime," Phelps said, "beef up your security, just in case."

"Carl's here," she said.

Carl was a big man with a slow smile. "You got backup?" Phelps asked him. Carl nodded. "We're dealing with real pros, whoever they are. They're not going to give themselves away."

Gabe got up. Dino handed him the cassettes. "Dino, seven A.M. tomorrow." His voice was tight. "We got to polish off every single lab scene unless our producer gets us more time." They all walked outside.

"Where's Julie and Cricket?" Faye asked. "They've been gone for half an hour."

Gabe touched her back. "We'll find them, we'll find them," he said tensely. "Don't worry."

"I am worried."

Phelps, his back straight, eyes sharp, was looking down the alley.

"Faye!" Julie called from down the block of dark offices. Cricket barked.

"I was worried," Faye cried.

Julie snapped off the leash; Cricket came running up to Faye. She scooped her up.

"Sorry," Julie said. "I walked her to your trailer, got her some dog biscuits."

The group broke up. Julie, Zack, and Dino went off on a cart. "Where are you parked?" Phelps asked Carl.

"Up in the lot," he said.

"Mine's here, I'll drive you," Phelps said. They all fell into step.

"Are you all right, Gabe?" Faye asked. "You seem . . . funny, not yourself."

"I'm fine. Just tired. You want some company tonight?"

"I think I'll take a change of clothes and go see the folks."

He nodded. "Sorry it didn't work the way you wanted."

"Oh, it was a stab in the dark, I knew it." She felt Gabe walking beside her and watched Phelps striding on ahead. Making love to him all last night seemed as far away as another life, and as near to her as the next step. Gabe draped an arm over her shoulder. She looked up at him. "Do you think any of us know what we're doing? Don't you feel we're all hanging out there over the ravine and praying the limb will hold?"

He laughed, warm, magical. "All the time!"

Phelps was not a drinking man, but that night, he went to a hotel bar in Hollywood and ordered a beer. That morning he'd asked that the Della Izquerra case be turned over to his second man on the team. "I got too much on my plate."

"The thing's dead, anyway," his commander had said.

Phelps sipped his beer and felt the chill of the glass and saw Faye's mouth moving, saw her long arms rising. He shut his eyes.

Faye parked her car on the winding, hilly street and got out. Cricket jumped out after her as Carl drove up and stopped. She stared at her house. "I think I'll pick up some clothes and stay with my folks tonight," she said to Carl. "I need to think a couple of things out. Where's Dave?"

"I don't know," he said. "You wait here while I take a look around."

It was a routine now: checking outside and in before Faye entered. Carl went up the narrow passage that led around to the door at the back. She waited by the front door, hunting for her keys. Cricket growled. "Yeah, yeah, I know, dinner." She put her key in the lock, and opened the door. "Carl, c'mon! A hungry dog here."

Cricket, yipping, rushed inside through the narrow opening. "Carl!" Faye called. "Oh, nuts."

Baying, Cricket was heading straight into the living room, her nails sliding on the hardwood floor. "Cricket, stop!" Faye rounded the turn from the dark hall, banged into the corner of a table, and entered the even darker living room, just as Cricket's silhouette leaped at a figure looming against the far window. An arm shot out, backhanding the dog. Cricket yelped and flew across the room, hitting the wall. She fell in a heap. A sound like a faint yip came out of her.

"Buenas noches, Señora Ferray."

Diaz.

She hesitated, torn between rescuing Cricket and running. She lost the chance to escape.

But she made a try. She swung around and ran for the arched entrance to the living room, but he was on her, a thick, powerful man. His hands felt like iron, not flesh. She was flat on her belly, he was on top of her. He grabbed her hair and lifted her with it. She screamed. His iron hand slapped over her mouth.

Oh shit oh shit oh shit. Where's Carl? Faye was trying to breathe and trying not to let her terror ride her.

"Don't scream," he said.

She shook her head.

"I wonder if I trust you."

Keep your head keep your head keep your head, she was repeating over and over inside her panic.

He removed his hand. She gasped for air.

"Sit up." He yanked her hair.

She sat up, her back to him, on her knees.

"That is the right place for you, *coño*, bitch. On your knees."

She could feel the breeze from the front door—it was open. *Can I make it to the door from here?* She didn't think so; it was around the bend and at the end of the hall. To the left of the arch in front of her was the stairwell leading down to her bedroom. She heard Cricket whimper. She raised her head.

"No bodyguards." He chuckled. "They are dead to the world."

Fear froze her. Her mouth was dry. Diaz was moving behind her. He was trying to figure out what to do with her, she could feel it.

"I wanted this satisfaction myself," he said. He kicked her in the back. She screamed. The blow drove her closer to the opening between the living room and the hall. She got up on her hands and moved toward it, moaning. He seized her hair and hit her face. She twisted, fell on her back, closer to the entrance. Her face was on fire; her head felt split.

"Don't hit me," she wailed, inching away from him along the floor. "Tell me what to stop doing and I will." Tears were pouring down her cheek. She couldn't see how far she was from the hall.

He stopped pacing and stood over her in the dark. She inched away, fearing another kick as much as she longed to reach the door.

She made her voice whiny and scared; it wasn't hard. "I shouldn't have used your name in the script . . . but no one else even noticed. It was silly, I wanted to make you mad, and . . ." She tried to swallow. He paced to the window. She slid a few inches toward the entrance. He turned and strode back to her.

She dragged herself to her feet. She tried to collect her thoughts but her mind felt stiff with terror. "It would be hard to explain if I died now," she managed to say. Her tongue stuck to her lips, her head throbbed. "I've told the police I heard your name . . . Della told me your name."

She couldn't see his face, but she could feel him considering that news. She remembered he had been a judge. Her voice was shaking so much she wondered if she could be understood. "Legally, it means nothing, but it will mean more if I turned up dead. You are much safer if I'm alive."

"Della," he said and in that instant, she knew he'd killed her.

The blow when it came snapped her head back and around and knocked her into the wall. The terror fired, her palms slapped the wall. "I am not a victim!" Was she yelling that? "I am not a victim!" She pushed away from the wall, staggering toward the entrance. He seized her again, his hands clamping on her arm, twisting it behind her. She screamed, fought against him, kicking.

He was panting, aroused, it was unmistakable. She was so frightened she could not make any sound at all. He was going to beat her to death. His knee came up into her spine as he pulled her arms back, bending her backward over the blow. He had done this before, he enjoyed it. One hand let go of her arm and slammed into the back of her head.

She was flying and fainting and exploding. She had no idea where she was, everything was brilliantly colored and still dark, without definition. Her head felt twice its size. She felt her ribs crack against something and reached for it. The railing around the stairwell. She was out in the hall. Cricket was yipping somewhere, a high, pained cry.

Faye didn't know where Diaz was. Something was streaming down her face. She turned, trying to stay upright. Diaz was coming through the arch, coming fast, swearing in Spanish, slapping at Cricket whose jaws were buried in his leg. Faye was trapped. If she could find the stairs, she could run. She darted left as she felt his outstretched hand brush against her. He hit the railing hard and she heard it crack. She stumbled on the first stair, twisting her ankle, scraping the wall, losing balance, hearing the strange, strangled sounds from Cricket. Diaz was yelling, wood was breaking.

He crashed onto the landing directly below the railing. The sound was awful, thick and hollow as he hit. Drops of moisture spattered her as her body slapped against the wall beneath the three steps before the turn. Her leg buckled and she felt herself falling.

She landed beside Diaz. Repulsed and terrified, she put out a hand and felt his hair, silky and sticky. She started screaming, but she couldn't get free of him; everywhere she reached, she felt part of him. She clawed her way off him, sliding over his thick legs to the base of the stairs. She got up on her hands and knees. Diaz wasn't moving. *Get out get out get out*. Diaz blocked her way up the steps. She couldn't see; she wiped her eyes. Her fingers and face were sticky with blood. *Oh, God, oh, God, let it be hers, not his*.

She grabbed the lower railing and pulled herself up, stepping between his legs, feeling her own in spasm, trembling so hard she had to hold on to the railing with both hands, stepping up to his waist, putting her foot down beside his head, swaying, balancing, recoiling, stepping over his head and onto the stair. Her knees collapsed. She crawled up the steps, *get out get out get out,* counting, one, two, three, using the wall to get to her feet. She heard herself moaning. She could not run, every motion was heavy, time was danger.

She hit something with her foot. Was she moving? She felt the breeze from the front door ahead of her. She leaned down and touched whatever her foot had struck. It was Cricket, a limp lump. She pulled at it, grabbed it, lifted it, and blinded by the moisture in her eyes, felt her way to the door. She tripped on the stone stair, crashed down on one knee, grabbed at a shrub, steadied herself, still clutching the dog, rose, and stumbled to her car. It was locked. Her car phone was inside. *Get out get out get out.* She turned wildly, wiping her eyes, screaming with pain when she raised her arm. Holding on to the shrubs, holding on to Cricket, she started up the street, willing herself not to faint.

Headlights coming around the bend jabbed the darkness, lighting up the door in front of her. Panicked, she leaned on the bell and banged at the door as she heard the car screech to a stop. The front door flew open.

"What the hell's going on?" It was Boyd, her snotty neighbor. She'd never been happier to see him.

"Faye!" Phelps called from the car in the street. "Faye!"

Two strong hands grabbed her before she went down.

THIRTY

THE FIRST PERSON Faye saw was her mother, nestled in a chair near the bed. Rob and Annie floated in and out, but her mother stayed. Gabe was beside her for a long time, stroking her arm, talking to her. Julie leaned toward her once, her dark face sad and caring, her voice upbeat with effort. Phelps was in the room, moving slowly, circling, speaking to Coo, his manner abrupt and embarrassed, the Phelps of old. She was reaching out to him and a hand met hers. She opened her eyes. No one was there. She felt the bandage on her throbbing head and sat up in bed.

She was back.

The plainness of the room revived her after gaudy dreams. The windows framed an orange dawn. She was alone, and realized with the clarity of recovery that whatever she did now she'd probably do for the rest of her life. It felt good to understand that.

"How goes it?" Gabe was holding a bouquet of yellow tulips.

Faye turned toward him, feeling the pain slice through her back. She felt ugly, her face bruised, her scalp stitched. "I can't remember what people have said," she whispered. It was hard to concentrate. "Where's Diaz?"

"Dead," he said gently. "Broken neck. Phelps went berserk, quite a temper."

"I'll bet."

"You went across the street? To your neighbor. Phelps was just driving up, remember?"

Her head was in Phelps's lap. Everything around them was coming apart. Someone behind them on the street was shouting. Someone was driving, a siren was squealing, the car rocked. Phelps was breathing hard. His hand smoothed her and brushed blood out of her eyes, his other hand kept her head from moving. He kept yelling, "Faster, you son of a bitch."

"Where's Carl?" she asked Gabe.

"He'll pull through. Fractured skull, stab wounds. Diaz popped him at the back door, then walked in. He'd already killed Dave."

She shut her eyes and saw Dave carrying the box of avocados out of Phelps's house.

"You have a fractured rib, a bruised kidney, a concussion, bruises on your face, and a cut on your scalp—that's why you bled so much. Scared the shit out of your neighbor."

"I hate Boyd."

"Boyd drove Phelps's car to the hospital."

"Oh."

Gabe took the top off the water container and stuck the tulips in it.

"And . . . Cricket?"

"You carried her out of the house and wouldn't let go of her even when Phelps put you in the back seat of his car, he told me. Coo called me and when I got to the hospital, there's Cricket on a tray in Emergency. They wouldn't let me in to see you, so I just took her, got Keith on the phone, he got her to his vet. She has a concussion, a broken leg, and a busted rib. She'll be all right."

"She was a tiger. I—I remember Diaz running toward me, trying to get her off his leg, and crashing through that railing—off balance because of Cricket." She sank back on the pillows. "Thank you for giving her to me." She reached out for his hand. "How could I ever think of giving her away?"

"You were different then," he said, squeezing her hand.

"Yes. Where's Phelps?"

"I don't know. Some other guy's heading up Della's investigation, which has expanded because of you."

She lay still, head pounding. "I'd like to see Phelps."

"Sure."

"Nadine?"

"Sorry, Faye. Nothing. But the Senate confirmed Buck. He's on the Court." Gabe rose and started touring the room, stopping at an immense floral arrangement. "All these orchids are straight from the Senate's florists."

"How's our picture? Gee, why aren't you shooting?"

"It's only seven in the morning, Faye. I'm on my way there. We're finishing it as fast as we can, but the rush is really killing us. Tony came by yesterday, smiling, thumbing through the script. I think he's going to pull the plug soon."

"Oh, Lord . . . When can I get out of here?"

"Oh, no, you don't. Here you stay."

"I'm afraid to be here. Who knows who Diaz was really working for?"

That startled him. "There's security outside—"

"No, I want out," she said. But she lay back. The pounding in her head was spreading to her whole body. "Annie didn't say that line right . . . not the way Della said it."

"Which line?"

"The one with 'bye' in it. Did Diaz kill Della?"

"I don't know, sweetheart. Ask Phelps."

She looked away, frowning. "Della's gone forever and Nadine's still dead or missing," she murmured. "What am I going through all this for?"

The door swung open. Julie, Zack, Dino, Annie, and Roger stood in the doorway, carrying a stuffed dog and more flowers. "We heard you were receiving," Julie said. "Tony sent you a computer dictionary." She put it on the table.

"This is from me, until Cricket gets well," Zack said, setting the silly oversized spotted dog on her bed.

Roger took center stage and studied her in an actor's way. "You've got to be tougher, Faye." Inside an ornate box was a certificate: a year of judo lessons. "Herb's more traditional, as we all know." He'd sent a Tiffany pin.

Annie pressed her face close to Faye's; her perfume was sweet and heavy. "Could anyone have a braver sister? I brought you something for the dog," she said, handing over a box, but she couldn't resist announcing the gift before Faye got it open. "It's a tag for her collar: 'Beware. Man-eater.'"

That evening, Faye watched Tot on the network news. "The National Security Council again came under fire today when it was revealed that Congress has raised questions regarding the Council's program expenditures. Sources within the NSC have cited one program, the Office of Public Information, which was developed to educate foreign countries about how democracy works, that may have diverted its funding into American profit-making corporations."

A clip of Leo Townsend: "The charge is ludicrous," he was saying. "All budget expenditures are available for review to the appropriate Congressional committees."

Tot picked it up: "This program was under an in-house investigation by the deputy legal adviser, Nadine Ferray. Earlier this month, Ms. Ferray was accused of leaking unrelated information to the press and dismissed. Ms. Ferray subsequently died by suicide. Her father, Judge Stern, who has just been confirmed as an associate justice of the Supreme Court, has been unavailable for comment. Reports from the White House regarding its own investigation of the NSC are focusing on Jay Harold Harper, special assistant in charge of the OPI program."

In his Los Angeles office after a long day of campaigning, Mark Drummond was also watching Tot's perky face and clipped tone. He opened his desk drawer with a key. Inside were Nadine's notes and the disk. He wondered if he should destroy them. He decided to keep them for insurance—against what, exactly, he didn't know. He shut the drawer and relocked it.

Eighteen miles to the east, in his downtown L.A. office, Cowboy watched Tot's first barrage. His telephone buzzed.

"It's hitting the fan, Cowboy," the man said. "You watching this?"

"Yes, Chief, I am. I did warn about this at our last meeting you'll remember."

"*I* wanted that damned organization out but *you* said we had too much invested—"

"Yes, Chief. Mistakes were made," Cowboy said wearily. "But if we keep our heads, we can clean it up."

"We'll all go to jail! Listen to this reporter! That's national news she's on!"

"Chief, no one's going to jail," Cowboy said. "That's not the question. It's who wins and who loses—*that*'s the question. Always has been." He felt his heart beating fast, pumping a flush into his face. He picked up his gold penknife and toyed with it. "Sit tight. Not one damned thing can be proved." He deliberately changed his tone. "Chief, the hearings went well, didn't you think?"

Judge Buck Stern calmed himself. "Yes, Cowboy, they were quiet and dull. Thank God."

Diaz was always close to her, she could feel his breath, feel the shape of him and the anger of him. To ward him off, she stared at the white blinds, the water cup, the TV set. When she did allow herself to think about him, she wondered if she had been brave. She hoped she was.

Faye was dozing that night when Phelps came into her room. Gently, his hand picked up hers and stroked it.

"Phelps," she said, pleased. "Am I dreaming?"

"No." He'd placed his body between her and the door so no one could see him holding her hand.

"I did dream you were here before, but you weren't when I woke up."

"I was here once. I met your mother. I'm afraid I was upset. I should never have let you out of my sight. He got the jump on me."

"I'm tough."

"Yes. But he died on me. We've pulled in everyone from CDEE. No one's talking, but they will. The prosecutor's finally interested, too."

"Gabe said you weren't in charge of the case now."

He stroked her hand. "Conflict of interest. I intend to retire with an unblemished record. I gotta finish my book. But I have some friends keeping an eye on you here."

"Kiss me, Phelps."

"Oh, darling, darling Faye." He bent down. The smell of the night came with him. He'd just shaved and his cheek was smooth. His lips brushed hers. Then he withdrew.

The next afternoon, Herb Yount was sitting in the armchair by Faye's bed. Herb always went the extra mile when it came to the courtesies of life.

Herb tented his fingers. "I really admire you, Faye. Must've been a terrifying experience. Gabe told me some of what was going on. Did you have that scene of the car blowing up for the movie all along? I mean, is that what happened to you? Was it a re-creation?"

"No, Herb," she lied, "it just occurred to me when we couldn't get the insurance for the Chesapeake Bay scenes."

"The footage is good, not earthshaking, I mean, buildings didn't explode—that's what audiences want, to see half a town taken out. Did you always think that guy Diaz killed your friend?"

"Della. No, I didn't know." Herb nodded. "Thanks for the pin, Herb, a wonderful gift." He nodded again, acknowledging his generosity. "Herb, I need your help."

"Anything, Faye."

"BeverCo's broke. You know that. Gabe's breaking his neck to finish before the ax falls, but the film's suffering. I need you to assume the cost to finish it right."

She stopped talking.

"I'll start the paperwork," he said.

She'd expected a long, tiring argument. "Really?"

He leaned forward confidentially. "Of course. I want to do this for you, Faye. Let's finish the picture! Tell your people to get me figures." Herb smiled, raised a protesting hand. "Now, I don't want you to worry. You should be recovering." The lovefest was over.

Herb *did* want to finish the picture right, and he was moved by her ordeal, but he wasn't finishing it for her. He was doing it because of Roger Reynolds. And that was okay with Faye because right up on the credits audiences were going to read, "In Memory of Della Izquerra."

Dressed in red, Tot swung through the door. Her curly brown hair was bobbed and smartly styled. Sam Pike was behind her in a vanilla-colored suit. Both carried more flowers.

"When did you get out here?" Faye asked her.

"Today. You look fine—except for those bruises."

"Sure—the steel plate in my scalp will never show," Faye said.

"What?" Herb said, alarmed.

"Joke," Faye said.

Herb pulled out an armchair for Tot. "Been seeing you on TV, Tot," he said. "What the hell's going on back there, anyway?" Herb was deeply suspicious of the executive branch.

"Yes, Tot," Sam said, sitting down, "you are certainly on your toes with that story."

"Congress is beginning to make noises about an investigation into possible illegal activities," Tot said.

"Where'd you get your leads?" Sam asked.

"You know better than to ask me about my sources."

"What's this Office of Public Information?" Herb asked.

"Just one of the many programs operated by the executive branch, Herb," Tot said.

"Well, you seem to have shaken Congress out of its lethargy," Sam said.

Tot glanced at Faye; Tot had much more to say, but would not.

"I suppose legitimate programs go astray when the people at the top aren't minding the store," Faye said.

"Like whoever's head of the NSC?" Herb asked Tot.

"Higher."

"I knew it!" He slapped a hand on the table and made the glasses jump. "The Veep strikes again! Who's this Harper?"

"Just a mid-level staffer. He's been reassigned to the Pentagon. The whole press corps has thrown its soldiers into the field looking for the mines and tunnels, so now staff people are leaking. But that works both ways. I mean, Harper stroked columnists to write articles favorable to him and the program and manipulated the news like everyone else."

"So what's the next story, Tot?" Sam asked.

"Unh, unh, unh." Tot shook her finger at him. "No previews."

Sam laughed. "What's the point of knowing you important journalists if you won't ever tell us anything?"

"My theory, along with a lot of other people, is always follow the money," Tot said evenly.

"So, where's it going?" Herb asked.

"If the OPI program is not informing, say, Kenya about the principles of democracy, what *is* it doing with its budget?" Sam and Herb waited expectantly. "One lead relates to Señor Diaz. His outfit is called the CDEE, the Educational Center for International Economics and Ecology. It was a subcontractor to the OPI program."

"Oh, how could that be," Sam said, "if it's some kind of ecology center?"

"Yes, odd, isn't it?" Tot said. "With the money that came out of OPI, CDEE hired a consultant who specialized in educational concepts. The consultant took his percentage and banked the money offshore!"

"Then what?" Herb asked.

"There are several theories," Tot replied, shrugging her little shoulders. "Wait and watch TV."

"She's toying with us," Sam said to Herb.

Herb was rising. "I hope it takes this administration apart. I hope it's another Watergate. Faye, this room is drab. Why don't you go out to my house in Malibu, get a little sun?"

"Herb, thank you, I'd like to be—out of the traffic for a while."

"Good. I'll make the arrangements."

"I have to leave, too, Faye," Sam said, rising. "I'm glad to see you looking so chipper." He bent down to kiss her cheek; the faint rank odor of sour sweat clung to him.

As soon as the men left, Faye said, "I look like hell, don't I?"

"No, not so bad. The worst bruise is that big one on your cheek. Any word about Nadine?"

"Nothing. Tot, what's really going on?"

"Adrian's been helpful, but he's leaving the NSC soon.

Some people have talked. Here's what we think's going on, but there's no proof yet. The consultants bank the money offshore, and *then* the money goes into *domestic* political campaigns through 'independent' television spots."

"What are those?"

"Monies from independent, noncampaign sources that have a point of view favorable to a candidate—like the Willie Horton spots for the Bush campaign."

"Tot, what's this mean?" Faye asked, excited.

"That certain people, inside or outside the NSC, are using that office, and maybe other agency budgets, to siphon federal money to certain U.S. candidates! The OPI program wasn't just running a little foreign war from a desk, it was trying to change the face of our elections. CDEE is part of it, but so are a slew of private subcontractors."

"Who's running it? Who's picking the candidates?"

"Unknown. But after you were attacked, I got a call from someone at CDEE, and he talked a little—"

"Who?" Tot shook her head. "Okay, okay, I won't ask."

"CDEE is part of a program of national campaign bribery."

Tot was caught up in the story of a lifetime, but Faye felt personally affronted. "How dare they?" she said. "How dare they buy our elections!"

"I suppose you think elections are sacred and have never been bought."

"Don't you try that tone on me," Faye said. Her head was pounding. "Of course elections have been bought before—but not like this! They're—whoever 'they' are—taking our tax money and shunting it off into candidates *they* think ought to be in Congress, and I resent it! Damnit, I resent it! It's arrogant! It says no one believes in democracy anymore, that our system doesn't work, but we're exporting it anyway all over the world—"

"You're getting better, I see," Tot drawled.

"Aren't *you* upset?"

"Yes, but lots of people here don't believe in democracy. Never did. The OPI's a big scam, but for a lot of it I don't have second sources, so I can't release it. All I was working with was what Nadine *told* me and your copy of the disk.

But I don't have her notes. Mark has them."

"This is why Della died, isn't it?"

"I think so. She was on to it and someone found out."

"But Diaz wasn't running the overall program. He was only one cog."

"Correct." Tot uncrossed her legs and stood up. "So we've still got a lot of ground to cover."

The first sound Faye heard when she and Gabe arrived at Herb's Malibu house the next day was ocean under the deck.

Malibu homes are dry beach or wet beach. Herb Yount's was wet beach, a low house jutting from the rocky shore, built over the water in defiance of nature. The house was grand and secluded, facing the ocean with a spacious wrap-around deck like a grin. Ten feet below, the jagged beautiful rocks were drenched with surf at low tide, covered by the sea at high. A windbreak made of thick redwood separated the house from the adjoining property; the north side dropped off to rocks and sea. At one end of the deck, screened from the wind by a glass wall, but with a northern view of the rocks, was a hot tub.

On Saturday morning, Faye was sleeping in a bedroom. In an alcove where Herb kept his media center, Gabe was sorting through his production bag when he found the cassette Dino had given him the night they'd seen the videos. He put it in the VCR and fast-forwarded to the close-up shots of the guests. He stopped at a close shot of Sam concentrating on the action.

Gabe turned away looking for his pen when he heard "Ping ping." On the tape, Sam was tapping the elongated nail he cultivated on his little finger against his cup, ping ping.

Gabe frowned. That hadn't bothered him in the screening room—Sam did that a lot. He let the tape roll. Mark was trying to get Sam's attention but Sam seemed irritated, as if he didn't want to miss a moment of the action.

Suddenly, Gabe saw it. Sam's left hand came into the frame, moving toward his face. He scratched his long nail against his cheek.

Gabe pressed rewind. On the sound track, Annie was

saying her line, "Selections . . . Sham . . . Bye . . ." On the
tape, Sam was smiling his impish smile and scratching his
cheek with his nail.

Until that moment, Gabe had been ready to close the chap-
ter. He'd rehearsed what he'd say to Faye, how she'd done
everything she could, used all the advantages and technical
facilities she could command, and, he'd been prepared to say,
now she had to leave it with the police or Phelps, and she,
Faye, had to live with whatever they discovered or failed to
discover.

But everything had changed. He replayed the tape twice.
Then he shut off the VCR.

He went into the white-on-white bedroom. One wall was
mirrored, reflecting the busy sea. Faye was lying on her back,
staring through the ceiling.

"I'm going into town for a couple of hours," he said.

"Bring me my production notes and my laptop from the
house, will you?"

"You ought to rest."

"I'm well enough to make a few calls. Nothing exciting,
I promise."

He went outside, nodded at the security man, and started
the drive into Los Angeles. The image of Sam scratching his
cheek stayed with him. Sam once had a small mole there
until the night Gabe, aged sixteen, had seen him scratch it
so hard he'd made it bleed. The next day, Sam had had the
mole removed. Gabe had known by then that the nail against
his cheek was Sam's only signal of intense inner rage.

During the summer between Gabe's first and second years
of college, he had worked in Sam's office. At that time, the
head of the foundation, a middle-aged man named Fred
Bell, had successfully turned the board and a prominent
review committee against a project Sam had long nurtured
and supported. Outwardly, Sam had taken the defeat well, but
through the summer and into the fall, he'd worked to unseat
Bell with a progressively more powerful siege of innuendo
about his professional ethics and personal lifestyle.

Gabe had not learned much about it from Sam, though he
had heard some comments from friends he'd made at the
foundation. They'd taken sides—Sam's or Fred's. Whenever

Sam spoke about Bell, he'd scratched at his cheek. Later, Gabe had questioned him about what was being whispered. Sam had said of the contest and its sad outcome: "Just business as usual, son." But it hadn't been business as usual and Gabe knew it. At the end of the year when the story came out in the press, Bell's reputation was destroyed. He was forced to resign and Sam took over the foundation.

When he stayed in town, Sam Pike owned a condominium not far from his office. He also had quarters available to him at the Jonathan Club on Figueroa Street, a massive old building where California governors and senators had been anointed and discarded.

Sam was in the club's reading room, sitting in a large leather chair, writing a note, when Gabe found him. He hesitated. He did not want to have this conversation.

"What a surprise," Sam said, folding the paper and slipping it in his pocket. "I was just going to have some lunch. They do a pretty fair leg of lamb here."

"Got time for a walk around the block, Sam?"

"Let's make it, as the kids say. How's Faye doing?" Sam asked. "I have to admit, I'm glad that bastard got his."

They were on Figueroa, a boulevard lined with high-rises and hotels. On weekends, traffic was light; they had the sidewalk to themselves.

"Sam, I wonder if you could tell me why you worked so hard to get *The Jungle Gym* mounted. Was it for Annie?"

Sam Pike looked up at Gabriel. "Guess I can't keep anything secret. You disappointed in me, cuddling that beautiful Annie?"

"No. But was it for Annie?"

"Partly. Also for Faye."

"Why?"

"*Why?* I had hopes you two might get back together, that's why!" They turned the corner, heading east.

"I think we might get back together. But was there any other reason, Sam?"

"Okay, you're going to get it out of me, you always do. Right after Della was killed, Faye was running around town, trying to get her picture mounted and I saw her at that dinner at the Sterns'. She was talking sort of wildly about Della, how she had to find out who'd killed her, and I thought that if I could give her a hand, and Annie, too, it might get Faye's mind off everything. And maybe keep her out of harm's way."

"Keep *Faye* out of harm's way? What do you mean?" Gabe felt his insides clutch tight.

"Well, son," Sam said quickly, "that's kind of overstated. Señor Diaz—no, I shouldn't say anything. I've only heard a couple of rumors."

"What? Did you know he was dangerous?" Gabe was forcing the questions out of his mouth, not wanting to ask them. He just wanted the answers to explain and exonerate.

"No, of course not."

"What did you hear?"

"Nothing you could hang your hat on."

"One of Detective Phelps's men has finally done a real check on him. Diaz was unsavory even in El Salvador."

"Really?" Sam said. He stopped walking. "Now, *that's* something you *can* hang your hat on. But how unfortunate, a man in his position. Bound to affect how people see Latin Americans. There's a lot of people come up here from down there and they're decent, hardworking people," Sam said with energy, "best kind of people, but I guess he wasn't one of them."

"Let's get back to keeping Faye out of harm's way," Gabe said.

"Yes. Faye doesn't know how to tread lightly, you know," he went on, smiling up at Gabe. "The press is beating the drum about Della's murder, and Faye's blurting out to anyone who'd listen that she wasn't going to rest until the killer paid for it—not smart. I mean, who would have thought Faye would be standing beside Della, listening to her last words? And then there was that terrible scare to her on Oscar night. Well! I just thought she'd be better off with a film to keep her busy. Time heals grief, always does." They started walking again. Sam passed a tree and plucked a leaf from it. "If I did wrong to use Annie a little to deflect Faye, get the picture financed, you tell me. But I don't think I did." He squashed the leaf.

"No, but you might have warned me if you thought Faye was in danger."

"Son, if I'd ever thought that, I would have told you."

Gabe stared at Sam, gauging the words against the eyes.

"I didn't think she was in danger, Gabe. Not even the cops thought that."

"What about Nadine, Sam?"

"Nadine?" Sam said, surprised.

"Faye gave her Della's disk. Nadine was libeled and fired because she was investigating some of the stuff Tot's talking about right now. There's a tie."

"Well, you may be right," Sam said. "But one thing I've learned is that what we think is true often turns out not to be."

"But it's awfully convenient, Nadine's disappearance."

"She committed suicide."

Now Gabe stopped walking. "Buck identified the wrong body. It wasn't Nadine. Faye proved it with the detective."

"What?"

"Nadine was pregnant, but the body Buck identified was not."

Sam was frowning. Gabe waited. "Well, I can see how Buck might have done that, having to look at a woman you fear is your daughter, not looking close, tears in his eyes. Buck cared the world for Nadine—"

"That is not true," Gabe said. He felt sick.

"Gabriel, how can you say that?"

"In all the years I knew them, they never showed they cared about her. And then Buck had that body cremated!"

Sam put his hand on Gabe's arm. "Gabriel, don't judge them too quickly until you've been there yourself."

Gabe's heart was thudding against his ribs. "I saw you on tape, while you were watching the explosion scene in the movie. Faye taped all the guests."

Sam gaped at him.

"I saw you scratch at your cheek with your nail. I'm probably the only person who knows what that meant. You were furious watching that scene."

Sam dropped Gabe's arm. For a few seconds, he said nothing. His eyes searched Gabe's face. "I thought it was stupid of Faye to do that scene. Too risky. Maybe I should have warned you Faye was making too much noise about Della, and after that horrible thing after the Oscars, I should have spoken to you about my concerns." He gazed at the massive front door of the club. "Look, this has all been a shock to everyone, but whatever Diaz was involved in, whatever Nadine was investigating—it's better we let the professionals handle it—"

"Tell me the fucking truth!" Gabe shouted, agonized.

Sam stared at him. "Gabe, that is the truth," he whispered, "it's what I know to be true."

Gabe stood on the sidewalk feeling contrite, hating the feeling, distrusting it, hoping he had reason for contrition. But something was very wrong. Sam wasn't leveling with him. Sam was "handling" him.

"C'mon," Sam said gently. "Lunch is on me."

"Can't," he said, "I have to get back to the studio." He wasn't going anywhere near the studio that Saturday afternoon but the excuse had just leaped out of him.

"Then some other time, yes?" Sam said.

"Sure." Gabe turned and strode down the block.

The man who loved him, the man known in one exclusive circle as Cowboy, went into his club and sat down in the reading room. Sam Pike had barely skated through. It'd take a long time to heal the distrust he'd seen in Gabe's eyes. Who would ever have thought that Della Izquerra and Faye Ferray could have produced all this wreckage? He knotted his fist, thinking back to the time around the explosion, the leaks about Diaz's past coming to the surface, how nervous the Friends had been, Della's death.

She'd undoubtedly discovered the subcontracting through CDEE. Sam suspected Diaz had hired the explosion out of fury as well as fear. Her public killing had had two goals— to silence Della and to send a message to the Friends: don't dump me. Sam could still hear the rage in Diaz's voice when he'd learned Della hadn't died instantly, that some friend had been with her.

Sam had wanted to cancel CDEE's participation in the plan, but he was wary. Diaz might talk about the source of the money flowing in such a tidal wave through CDEE, so

Sam had calmed down Diaz and the Friends. Then, Faye had shown up in person at CDEE and her visit had set Diaz off.

Cowboy went into the bar. "Phil, give me a tomato juice," he said to the bartender.

"Hard day, huh, Mr. Pike?" he cracked.

"Some days the only thing you can do is keep going like a dray horse." He was glad Diaz was dead. CDEE was lost, but the Friends had other connections, and even though OPI was exposed, they were already moving their operation. Millions of dollars were already in the chute, so the core operation would go on. But how much did Faye know? Did she have any proof? Faye's tenacity had cost him. Despite everything, she hadn't quit. She'd smoked out Diaz and now her stubbornness threatened his relationship with Gabe. Cowboy had let Diaz finally take action against her and Diaz had failed!

Sam was scratching the phantom mole on his cheek. With a studied gesture, he pulled back his finger, let his hand drop.

Gabe was driving aimlessly, feeling low and uneasy. He took a ramp onto the Santa Monica Freeway, streaming with cars rushing east and west. He punched in Keith's number on his car phone. "I need to talk," Gabe said, when Keith answered. "I won't stay long."

"Come ahead."

When he reached Keith's, Gabe took a seat in the kitchen. "I have a question for you," he said. "What would you do if your father turned out to be a dishonest son of a bitch?"

"I loved my father and he *was* a dishonest son of a bitch," Keith said, popping open the beers.

"What if he had the ethics of a snake?"

"He did!"

"What if he'd been dangerous?"

"Dangerous? *Dad?*" Keith squawked.

"Hypothetically dangerous."

"Well, there's dangerous and then there's *dangerous*. What do you mean? Homicidal?"

"No. No." Gabe curled his palm around the cold beer. "I'm thinking through a character."

"The hell you are."

"I'm getting ready to be disillusioned."

"Want to see a surprise?" Keith asked.

"No."

Keith pulled Gabe's arm. In the bedroom, Cricket was lying in a dog bed, her leg in a cast, half her head shaved.

"I'll be damned. How you doin', Crickie?" Gabe said, kneeling.

She tried to get up. "No, no," Keith said, "stay." Cricket struggled back down, beating her tail against the side of the bed. Bob, sitting nearby, barked. It sounded like a cannon.

Faye was talking to her father and listening to the surf roaring in the background. "I wanted to let you know where I am and that I'm not picking up Herb's phone, but you can reach me on my portable. And take down this Detective Phelps's number—he'll always know where I am."

"Don't talk so fast, I can't get all this down." Papers rustled. "I'm going up to see Buck tomorrow and I'll call you when I get back."

"Are you well enough to do that?"

"Are *you* well enough to hold a phone? I'll rent a car and driver! When can you come see me?" Hearing her father's voice made her feel normal again.

"I'm ambulatory now, Pop. My muscles feel weird, sore; my head aches. How about tomorrow or the next day?"

When they hung up, Faye felt the tension return. She swung between a feeling of safety and one of extreme danger.

Faye made a call on Herb's bedside phone.

"How are you?" Phelps asked.

"Fine."

"I don't like you being out there. Too far. Not good security."

"I have security—Carl's brothers-in-arms from the agency. And this place has only one door—the other sides are all rocks and sea. I'd like to talk to you when I'm better."

"We don't need to talk, Faye. I have no expectations. What is, is. I will always . . . you'll . . . it won't change, whether I'm with you or not."

"I'd like to call you later. Gabe's—"

"And that's another thing. If you're going to stay with Gabe when you're all recovered, fine. But you can't see me. No double games."

She watched the sea washing the rocks. "I wouldn't expect them of you."

"I want to come out later today, see the setup, the house. Do you feel safer out there? What's your gut tell you?"

"Safer."

"Okay. I'm dropping by your house in town, just to take a look around again."

"I thought you weren't on this case."

"A look around isn't on a case, believe me."

"Phelps?"

"Yes?"

What she wanted to say couldn't be said in words. "I'll see you later today, then."

"Right. Bye, Faye."

THIRTY-ONE

THE LIGHT WAS strange. The clouds over the sea seemed to glow from the inside.

Faye, immersed in the hot tub, put her head back and shut her eyes. The warm water was balm. Inside, Herb's phone rang but not for her; no one knew she was there. Knowing that was relaxing in itself. She'd stepped outside her life into serenity. She drifted, listening to the orchestration of the waves. She imagined the nautilus gliding beneath the deck, but now its milky-white tentacles and arching shell seemed beautiful, benevolent. For the first time, she remembered Della without despair, thinking of all the good times with her, of their last day, of Annie saying her words, "selections . . . sham . . . bye . . ." It didn't matter now, but Annie hadn't said "bye" right—it was more like "bike." Faye let herself slide lower into the toasty water. Elections. Sham. Bike. She opened her eyes. Sham Bike? She sat up. Had Della been saying "Sam Pike"?

The water was almost scalding. The sky was growing clouds with pink rims, the sea turning gray. The rocks seemed sharp as knives. Della could *not* have been saying "Sam Pike."

Pop! A cork?

"Gabe?" she called. She heard steps coming out on the deck. Behind the screen, Faye was half in and half out of the tub. "Gabe?"

A hand came around the screen holding a glass of red wine. "Have some of the best wine in the country!"

Sam Pike.

"Go ahead," his voice said cheerfully, "take it."

She stared at the glass and the hand attached to it. Her heart was pounding. She took the glass.

"Are you decent?"

"No," she said hoarsely. She wrapped herself in a robe, holding it against her tightly. Her damp hair felt cold on the back of her neck, her body still ached. She didn't want to go out there. She touched the bruise on her forehead, arranged her expression.

She swung out from behind the screen with more energy than Sam expected. "You're getting well," he said, "that's good! Did you try this wine? Isn't it good? I was just down at Roger's and remembered Herb had loaned you his place. Gabe around?" He walked to the railing. "Great deck." He looked down.

"And you're so close to the water you could practically dive in. Guess it's about fifteen feet, right? It's high tide, isn't it? The rocks down there are covered with surf." On the north side of the deck a stairway led down literally into the water. "I suppose at low tide you can get under the deck," he said.

Sam was wearing Malibu calling clothes, slacks, open-necked white shirt, loafers. "How'd you get in?" she asked.

"Oh, those security men know me," he replied, gesturing toward the front of the house. "I recommended them to Gabe. I was just going to leave the bottle, but they said you were awake, telephoning, whatever."

She let herself down on a lounge chair. "Gabe will be back soon," she said.

He pulled a deck chair around, sat down near her and peered at her happily. "Are you and Gabe getting back together?"

"You'll be the first to know."

Sam chuckled and sipped his wine. "Well! I hope everything's over, Faye, so we can all get back to normal. Though

I don't suppose anyone knows the why of it all."

"You mean why Della was killed, why Nadine disappeared, why I was attacked? Not to mention Nadine's friend in Washington, Pamela—"

"Wait a minute. You don't believe Nadine killed herself?" He tilted his head, looking at her with admiration, wondering what Gabe had told her.

"No. Do you?" Faye asked.

"Well, yes. Why don't you?"

"Because she was pregnant."

"Ah." Sam gazed at the clouds spawning in the sky. "Did you tell Buck?"

"Yes. He hung up on me."

"Distraught, I suppose. No grandchildren. Hard to face at our age." He looked off, as if contemplating that disappointment. He pointed at the deck. "How deep is the water under there?"

"I have no idea—ten feet?" She sipped the wine and glanced at the swelling sea. But her heart was thudding. She was afraid.

Forty miles inland, Gabe gave Detective Phelps a wave as he parked in front of Faye's house. "What are you doing here?" Gabe asked.

Phelps was standing by the open front door. "I've taken some time off. I'm just nosing around," he said. "That neighbor across the street, Boyd Matson?" Gabe nodded. "He's still insisting he saw two men around Faye's house the night of the attack, Diaz and someone else. That bugs me."

"How about other neighbors?"

"The guys interviewed them again. Nothing."

Gabe walked inside. "I'm here to pick up some notes for Faye." He was impatient; he wanted to get back to Malibu.

"That Boyd Matson," Phelps mumbled, "I just can't . . ."

"Burr under your saddle," Gabe supplied.

"Yeah."

Gabe started for Faye's study. Phelps took in the unfinished walls, the light larky furniture. He examined a painting. When Gabe returned, he was carrying two loose-leaf notebooks and Faye's laptop.

"They just want to shut this case down, you see," Phelps said. "By the way, I want to check the layout of that Malibu house."

"I thought you were on vacation."

"I'll send one of the guys."

"Sure, but we got security."

"I saw them at the hospital. They're not from the group I suggested back then."

"No, I got them through my friend, Sam Pike."

Phelps nodded. "How's she doing?"

"Better."

Phelps nodded again. Gabe was likable. He had good instincts, too—he was looking at Phelps and something was bothering him. "What?" Phelps said.

"Nothing," Gabe said, after a moment.

Phelps began picking through a box of small tagged items, each in a plastic bag. "My men found these on the floor, under chairs, that sort of thing," he said.

A matchbook, a comb, three different earrings, coins, a gold penknife. Gabe picked up the penknife. "Where was this found?"

Phelps turned over the tag. "Under the telephone in the front hall. Probably slid under it by accident."

Two hands clasped in friendship were engraved on Sam Pike's penknife.

"Beautiful place to get well," Sam was saying to Faye. He walked to the end of the deck, then back again to his chair. "You know what Gabe told me once? That he ought to apologize to Tot because he'd unwittingly used her to get a rest from you. Of course, Gabe expressed it with a good deal more charm, but that was the essence."

Tot and Gabe and their connection seemed as distant as a college romance to Faye.

"Would you mind a little advice from a friend of the family?" He peered at her. "Don't let him go. You two have had your problems, but you're awfully good together."

Faye smiled. The hot tub had dulled her. Or maybe the wine. Sam was pouring more into her glass. "No more for me, Sam."

"That Tot," Sam said, "she's a whiz at what she does, but there's something cold inside her that puts me off." He raised a hand as if she'd made an objection. "I know, I know, she's alluring—she tempted Gabe—but she's got a mission in life, and people with missions are chilly. Or am I crazy?"

She could feel her muscles relaxing. She tightened her legs. "Tot always said follow the money," Faye heard herself saying. "I always followed the people."

"Quite right, too. People always teach us something."

She picked up her glass. "Annie finally told me you were the one who suggested BeverCo for the picture," she said.

He held up both hands. "I give! I already confessed to Gabe about that! I shouldn't have interfered. But I meant it for the best."

Faye felt blank. "I wasn't going to accuse you of anything. But I didn't like having Annie forced on me. Or Gabe, either."

"I had nothing to do with Gabe—that was all Herb, and Roger, of course. But about Annie, I'm afraid I got carried away. An old man's fling."

"You don't look a day over fifty."

"I try to keep fit. I work out."

Her body was turning to water. She almost dropped her glass.

"The sea air," he proclaimed. "Nature's relaxant." Faye was frowning. "What bothers you?" he asked, leaning forward.

"Annie told you Nadine was with me, in my production."

"Annie? I don't recall that," Sam said, looking sideways at her with delight. He scraped his nail along his cheek.

Faye suddenly felt wonderful. "Oh, yes, she did."

"Well, if so, I forgot. It wouldn't have meant anything to me where she was."

"No, but at the time . . ." She'd lost her thought.

Sam was staring at her hard. "At the time what?"

"I mean, later, when I knew Buck had misidentified Nadine, it made me start thinking about you and Leo."

"Why Leo?"

"Because he was the only person who wanted Nadine out of his picture."

"I see." Sam felt morose. She was doing it again. He had hoped it could all be quietly put to rest. "Why me?"

She hesitated. Don't answer, she thought. But she had to know. "The night of Buck's party Nadine and I overheard the three of you in the study. You were talking about elections."

Sam trained his eyes skyward. "Really?"

"And how power comes rolling out of California *to* the Capitol now, not the other way around." She was amazed her laugh sounded natural.

"Well, so it does, my dear. *Now,* it does."

"I think Pop mentioned once that you and Buck were old friends. So, when I knew the woman Buck had identified as Nadine *wasn't* pregnant, I started to doubt Buck—"

"And then you thought of *me*? But why?"

"I don't know." She couldn't think at all. She forced herself to get to her feet and walk. "Nadine was making real problems for someone and it went through Annie to you to Buck—that was the only way Buck could find Nadine." She wound her fingers around the cool railing.

"Leo and I didn't care where she was."

"No, not Leo—he wanted her out. But Buck cared. They had a terrible argument on the phone." She turned around. "You're the only way he could have learned where she was."

Sam seemed puzzled. "I honestly don't think Annie ever mentioned Nadine to me, Faye."

She said nothing. She knew she wasn't safe; a familiar sensation and she didn't question it. The windbreak was a high solid wall. No one could see them through its one-way glass. She looked at the indifferent sea and the distant lowering clouds. She thought of yelling for the security man, but she didn't trust him now. What had Tot said? Who inside or outside the government was running the program? Who was picking the candidates?

Sam felt her looking at him with new eyes. He jogged his glass at her in a salute. "Faye, you know me. I'm an arts man. That's all I care about. Sure, I'm interested in politics, I've worked for candidates I've believed in, I make connections for people when I can."

The surf sounded louder. She went back to her chair.

"What did you say?" she asked.

"Oh, I was talking about what I like doing. What did you think of all Tot's theories? Sounded like she's on to a big story."

Faye felt panicky. There was something wrong with her body. *The wine!* Was it drugged? When would Gabe get back? When was Phelps coming?

"On to . . . ?"

"The scam!" he said happily. "It sounded big."

"Is it?"

"Why, yes, it is."

She glanced away again. "I don't care."

"You always care!" He cackled.

"No, I don't," she lied. "Everything will come out. It always does."

"What will come out, Faye?"

Talking took great effort. "Weren't you talking about Tot?"

"Yes, about all that money buying elections," he said. "The scam through Harper's program, going into the organizations and back into our elections. But the beauty of it is that the money never touches the campaigns—it's legal money for communications." Sam seemed smug. He was going to make one last try to save her. "You know, even if Tot has all that, life will go on—business as usual. I guarantee it."

She realized Sam had planted his chair between her and the sliding doors into the house.

"It matters what happened," she whispered.

"Yes, but it doesn't matter *that* much. Don't be naïve," he said, sucking deeply on the salt air. "These things . . . Well, have you ever been scuba diving? Floor of the sea's just littered with beautiful shells and not one of them shows, they're all covered up by the sand. Maybe Tot can keep the story going, but eventually the media will lose interest, always another story out there like sand over shells . . . then the public loses interest. No one will even remember where those shells are."

She opened her eyes. "What?"

He had shoved his face close to hers. "Faye. Best thing is to go on, isn't it? Leo's moving on soon, and Buck's on the Court." He patted her knee. With effort, she got up and moved toward the rail near the stairs. "Just what is it that you think I did, Faye?"

Thinking had become a kind of frightening trigonometry.

"Why, nothing, Sam," she said, conscious that she had never lied very well. She leaned against the rail, her hands propped behind her.

"Don't kid me, Faye."

She couldn't look at him. "*Did* you do all this, Sam? Is what Nadine was uncovering, is everything yours? Are you running it?" The beads of sweat on her face turned icy.

He walked over to her. She was looking out at the sea. The breeze blew her hair across her profile like a veil. "I'm a small fish," he said. "I report to bigger fish—sort of a consortium. That's my dilemma with you."

"What do you mean?" Her heart was pumping so fast she could scarcely breathe.

He glanced at her face sharply. "Faye, just go along, the program's already been moved. It'll continue, it even provides a service—no one's being hurt—"

"No one's hurt?" She swung around and almost lost her balance. "Who do you call no one? Della? Nadine? Me?"

He snapped. "You kept pushing and pushing!" he shouted.

He terrified her more than Diaz, but instinct told her that if she showed any fear, everything would end fast. She had to hold out. So she looked away.

"I can't believe you'd be involved in anything as tawdry as this." Twenty feet below, the surf gnawed at the rocks.

"Tawdry?" He laughed. "Do you think things like this happen without Cabinet involvement? Nosiree, we got a lot of support, inside and outside. Elections can't be left to chance! They're too important!"

"Yes, they are. And who elected you?"

He sighed. "There's a great Latin American poet who wrote about the little people beneath the ocean who cause the waves to break upon the shore. But we know these little people can cause revolutions, too. The pressure, the constant pressure. You're like that. What was so important to you about Della? She was only a friend," he said, "you could have let it go."

"What kind of person would abandon her friend?"

He leaned very close. "It is your own character that's led you here to this moment. *You* are to blame."

She turned and nearly screamed. The Sam she'd known for years had vanished. The face she saw without its affable mask was venomous. Only his teeth were smiling at her.

"Little Faye, what a thorn you are," he sniped nastily.

"Sam! You know me!" She couldn't prevent herself from stepping back.

He inched toward her. "Yes. Why can't you ever leave anything alone? I tried to warn you, but you were so stubborn." An eerie note of patience slid into his tone, spurious, menacing. "You haven't learned your lesson. You always want things your own way—but no more. It makes me sad because I like you and I tried to protect you. I gave you your movie, I tried to distract you from Della's death, and I had nothing to do with that—it was stupid, tragic—I took your side with Gabe, I tried to get you two together because he'd distract you, too. But you just would not quit! That's what drove Gabe away the first time."

"Sam! Don't do this! Think what it would do to Gabe!"

He looked at the ocean. "It'll be painful for him," he said coldly. "But I can't allow you to go on wrecking everything." His teeth were bared in the face that was no longer his. "You can hardly keep your eyes open, Faye, and in a while you will go to sleep. When I put you in the water, you will welcome it."

The urge to sleep was like a weight, she could feel herself drifting into it as into some other space. She refused to give in. The windbreak—too far. Beside her, around the railing, the steps went down into the thrashing surf. Would he follow her there? She had to get past him to get inside the house— that was the only way out. She couldn't reason with him. Would begging help?

Fuck him, she thought. She stepped away from the railing. "I need some water." She headed across the deck for the living room, walking steadily with enormous effort. Suddenly, he was in front of her, his arm out, stopping her with his palms.

"Cut it out, Sam."

He shoved her back. Her muscles weren't doing what she told them. She was stumbling. When she hit him with her fist as hard as she could on the side of his head, it surprised and infuriated him. He grabbed her shoulder.

She knew he expected her to make a dive for the doors, so she ducked backward and made for the steps, pushing open the gate at the top and plunging down. At the bottom, she threw herself into the surf.

The Pacific chill shot through her, waking her some, but her body felt like lead. She was dragging it behind her as she swam away from the steps toward an outside piling of the deck. She was afraid to swim beneath it: how strong were the currents, how high would the tide rise? She felt submerged boulders touch her feet. The incoming tide thrust her toward the steps; she fought her way to the piling. The surf broke over her, pushing her under the deck. When the ebb sucked her toward the support, she grabbed it. A wave crashed over her.

When she came up for air, she could hear Sam laughing. "I'm staying right here, Faye! Before long you won't be able to hang on to anything down there. You'll just slip away."

He was right about that. She'd boxed herself in. To her left, beyond the deck, was the vertical cliff beside the house, a seething foam sea that only a few hours ago was a placid stretch of elephantine rocks she'd seen from the hot tub. To her right, much farther away, the surf pounded below the house next door, positioned higher on the cliff than Herb's. Behind her, farther under the deck, the swells pounded against the cliff to which Herb's house was attached. Spume sprayed back into her face off the cliff. There was no place to rest out of the water except the steps. She hung on tight, but her muscles didn't belong to her. She looped her arms around the piling and clasped her hands together as the sea surged up and down under the deck.

Above, Sam leaned out over the railing trying to spot her, but the deck supports angled back under it. He couldn't find her. Slowly, he straightened, glanced at his watch, and studied the sea, thinking it through. He took off his loafers.

Faye felt herself losing consciousness. Oh, Phelps . . . She slapped her cheek with one hand, put her face in the water. She hung on, grimly. She had to try to reach the steps. When she let go of the piling, an incoming swell pitched her against the rocks under the deck. She clung to the tip of one, timing the waves.

At the ebb, she let herself be carried away from the back of the deck and the rocks; she windmilled her arms through the water, making for the steps, fighting the pull out to sea. The strong current whisked her straight out beyond the deck. Before the next wave, as she floated in the foam, she felt the nautilus below her, waiting, its ivory tentacles drifting through the dark water.

A swell swept her back in and once more she tried to claw her way, swim her way north, to get to the steps. A giant gray wave broke just beyond the deck and the swell lifted her straight up. Her face slammed the underside of the deck. *I will drown here.* Terror galvanized her. She shook herself out of the heavy bathrobe and fought, rock by rock, wave by wave, toward the steps.

She grabbed the railing and hung on, her naked body half in, half out of the shadow of the deck. She pulled herself up a step, looking for a foothold. She did not see Sam poised like a marksman on the top step, studying her.

A hand, palm open, pressed on the crown of her head. She jerked, crying out. The hand was pushing her under the surface. She struggled, gripping the rail, but the only way to get away was to let go, let the sea carry her away. Straining, she twisted her head. Sam grimaced at her. The pressure on her head was relentless.

She went under. A wave broke and ebbed. When she let her hand slide down the railing, he seized her hair to hold her. She fought, afraid to let go of the rail, afraid of the sea, afraid of him.

His hand found her face and forced it back into the water. Her lungs were going to blow her up. She let go. An incoming wave flung her against him, knocking him back against the steps. She clawed at him, climbing him, desperate, gaining, grinding her fingernails in his face, grabbing the rail, heading up.

"Let me save you!" he howled, a monstrous sound. He grabbed her ankle. She lunged upward but he held on, then yanked her downward. A wave hit them. She seized the back of a step with both hands, felt her shoulder giving, felt her nails clawing over the iron and wood as he drew her down.

The stairs were shaking. A hand reached down and grabbed her under her arm. Gabe, above, was yelling at Sam. Sam let go of her ankle.

She started crawling up the stairs, then Gabe was lifting her. Her toes touched the steps then another arm swung her up. She was on the deck in front of Phelps. He ripped a blanket off a chair, threw it over her shoulders, and hugged her tight.

"Gabe!" Sam was shouting from below. He was hanging on to the lower railing.

Phelps, his arm sealed around her, started to turn her toward the house. "No!" she said. "I want to see him!"

Gabe was going down the steps, the spray from the waves hitting him. Sam, holding on with one hand, raised the other for Gabe to pull him out. But Gabe stopped on a middle step. "Gabriel!" Sam screamed.

Gabe knotted his fist into Sam's collar, dragged him out of the sea, flung him onto the stairs, leaped over him, reached down and yanked him up again, pushing and dragging, all the way to the deck.

Sam flopped onto it. "It's a miracle I came out here," Sam gasped.

Faye started; the blanket fell open. "It's a miracle I'm *alive!* You tried to drown me!" Phelps drew the blanket around her again with one hand. He had a gun in the other. He watched Gabe warily.

"Get up," Gabe said to Sam.

Sam started to rise, but not fast enough. Gabe jerked him to his feet. Off balance, Sam reached out for a chair to right himself. "She's out of her head," Sam panted.

With an agonized cry, Gabe smashed Sam backward against the railing.

"I was trying to save her!" Sam shrieked, both hands covering his face. "She kept fighting me! She panicked!" He pulled himself along the railing until he reached a bench and collapsed on it. He seemed old. He grabbed Gabe's sleeve. "I was trying to help her—"

Gabe shook him off.

"He had my head underwater!" Faye yelled furiously.

"I didn't, oh, Lord, Gabe," Sam cried, "I wouldn't hurt her. But don't blame her, she was almost unconscious. I was trying to get her *out* of the water. I swear it. She was passing out, I had to keep hold of her, but I didn't have the strength to pull her out so I tried to keep her head above the water, but she kept slipping back in." Sam's agitation shook his body. "Gabe, believe me, I'd never hurt anyone." He looked up at Gabe, desperate and wary.

"He tried to kill me, Gabe," Faye said.

"I was only trying to help," Sam whispered. "Faye, I didn't mean to frighten you. I'm so sorry." His eyebrows jumped up, wrinkling his forehead.

Phelps had had enough. He put his gun in his holster and walked over to Sam. "Get up, please." Sam rose shakily. Phelps snapped a pair of handcuffs on him.

"What's going on?" Sam asked, alarmed and shocked.

"I am arresting you for the attempted murder of Faye Ferray." He read Sam his rights, then left the deck to use the telephone.

Sam was moaning. "My God, *Gabriel*! This is a nightmare. None of it's *true*!"

Gabe stared at him with disgust mixed with sorrow.

Sam straightened his back and moved away. He didn't look as old as he had only a moment before. "I'll have bail posted in an hour," he said icily. "And it'll be my word against yours, Little Faye. Something to think about."

Phelps came out on deck, took Pike under one arm. "You'll have to follow me," he said to Gabe.

Gabe nodded, watching Sam. Then he turned away.

Sam called out, "Love you, Gabe."

When they'd left the deck, Gabe sat on the bench, his head in his hands, his shoulders shaking, sobbing. Faye sat beside him and put her arms around him.

THIRTY-TWO

JERRY HAD BEEN unable to reach Buck, even though he knew they were back from Washington. Buck's curious distress that day at the house, talking about the children, had stayed with him, but Faye's appeal that he ask Buck about Nadine had made Jerry hire the car and head north.

El Contento glowed in the summer sun. Bright pouches of flowers bloomed around the oak tree Helena had long since dubbed "Mr. Sentinel." It stood proudly in the front, motionless and noble in the morning heat. Salt spray perfumed the air. Jerry drew a deep breath; the drive had not depleted his energy as much as he feared.

"Jerry!" Buck's tone was a mix of pleasure and caution. He was standing in the red-tiled entrance hall as Edward opened the front door.

"Congratulations! Do we call you Justice Buck now?"

Buck laughed, proud and satisfied. "You come all the way up here for that?"

"No. Got to talk, Buck."

"Sure, sure." The Judge, now the Justice, wearing slacks and a sports shirt, looked ruddy with good health. He steered Jerry into a sunny plain of white sofas and ruby-red rugs. "How're you feeling?"

"Great," Jerry said. "Remission, docs say." He sat down gratefully. "Buck, I'll get right to the point. You came to see me a while ago real upset. Now something's going on I don't understand, and my daughter's almost killed by a man the police believe was responsible for Della's death—"

"Hey, hold on, Jerry. I've been in Washington—I don't know what the cops are doing out here." He pulled in his chin, his face a picture of avuncular concern. "I did hear about Faye and her trouble and I'm very sorry. I trust she's improving."

"Why, Jerry!" Helena said. "Such a surprise to see you here!" She stopped just inside the doorway.

"Jerry and I are going out to the terrace, my dear. Perhaps you'd have Cindy bring us something."

"Of course, good to see you again, Jerry," she said without interest.

Buck opened the double glass doors to the terrace and waved at a table and chairs outside. "I don't know anything about this Diaz character, Jerry."

"Let me finish," Jerry said, sitting down. "Faye and Nadine were looking into Della's death."

"I don't want to talk about Nadine."

Helena's voice rose from the interior. "Dear, could I see you a moment?"

"Excuse me, Jer," Buck said, relieved.

Jerry rested, gazing at the beautiful, gaudy garden tended by a battalion of attendants.

"Where were we? Oh, yes, Faye," Buck said, sitting down again.

"No, not Faye exactly, but what happened to her is connected to Nadine because my Faye asked Nadine to check into something Della left, and your girl did."

"Oh, how do I know what they were up to?" Impatiently, Buck drew his palm across the glass tabletop.

"Who's this Diaz prick who almost killed Faye?" Jerry said angrily.

"Keep your voice down," Buck said. "This place is a hive. I didn't know him!"

"Buck, never in a million years would you not know Nadine if she were lying on a slab in the morgue. Now

you tell me what's going on, I want to hear it from you
because my daughter's lucky to be alive!" he roared and felt
half his energy drain from his body.

"Goddamn you," Buck said, low and angry, going on the
offensive. "You don't walk in here making demands—"

"Yes I do!" Jerry snapped. Buck was hiding behind anger.
"You know the only great thing about being terminally ill?
I can do or say anything. I have nothing left to lose."

"Nadine got into some trouble back East," Buck said reluctantly. "I don't know what it was about, but she couldn't handle it. So back off."

"What's Sam Pike got to do with all of this?"

"Sam?" he said, incredulous. "You know Sam!"

"Yeah, but who is he, really?"

"I don't know him that well. He runs a big foundation,
well connected."

"In government or the private sector?"

"Both. I don't know, for chrissakes, Jer." The Friends were
in deep shit if people were catching on to Cowboy's shadows.
"The only thing I know about Sam is that he'd like to think
he knows how to run the country the way it ought to be
run. And I know fifty more who think the same way—and
so do you!"

"Tell me about Nadine, Buck," Jerry said, "or I swear
to God I'll make more trouble for you and Helena than
you ever believed possible. I mean it. I don't care anymore."

Buck jumped out of the chair. "Don't you threaten me!"

"I'll do more than that. You've never talked to a dying
man! I tell you, Buck, I have four aces here!"

Justice Stern's fury was evaporating into second thoughts.
The lines and folds in his face loosened, his shoulders
slumped, his fists relaxed.

"I thought that woman in the morgue really was Nadine,
Jer. She had blond hair, same build, but she was beaten,
pretty badly decomposed, wrists slashed. I didn't look too
closely. I didn't take Helena, couldn't put her through it. It
was horrible, fearing all sorts of things about your daughter,
then learning the worst." He put his hands to his face. "Then
Faye called, said Nadine was pregnant. I'd read the autopsy

report, I knew that woman wasn't pregnant."

Jerry turned away. What father could read his daughter's autopsy report? Not even Buck could have done that.

"Bucky, spare me the public version," he said briskly. "I want to know what really happened."

Buck removed his hands from his face and glanced up. It wasn't washing. He surveyed the garden. "She's safe."

"Thank God for that, but it really pisses me off! How *could* you put my son and daughter through this hell?"

"Misidentifying her was the only way I could save her!" His big face twisted. Jerry believed him.

"How come?"

"She'd had a fight with Rob and I knew she was in hot water at her work, too. Then she vanished. I learned she was with Faye and the production. I had her followed and knew when she'd taken a train coming out here. She checked into a hotel. I went to see her, we had a good talk and she—went to the clinic."

"A clinic? Why?"

"She was in danger, Jerry. I had good advice that she was in danger. She was on to some operation inside the NSC. And she was being impossible about it. I was afraid for her!"

That struck home to Jerry. Still, he was uneasy. "But why put her in a clinic?"

"Where else can you disappear for a while? Hawaii? No. It's a very fine clinic up north, Jer. I put her in there because when I saw her in this hotel in L.A., she refused to knuckle under!"

"Knuckle under? Jesus, Buck—"

"You know what I mean. She was disoriented, she didn't know what she was up against! She had to keep her head down, but she—" Nadine's pale angry face in the hotel room haunted him. "You wouldn't have believed some of the things she told me. She actually thought Senator Drummond was mounting an investigation on her notes."

"Was he?"

"Of course not."

"Tot's got some mighty interesting stories out now. It doesn't sound as if Nadine or Faye were so disoriented."

"Maybe not, but other people were. Della was killed for knowing less than Nadine. We know a lot more now than we did even two weeks ago. And I thought I could handle it, you know, we always think we can handle it."

"But what were you thinking of? How long were you going to keep her there? How are you going to explain her sudden reappearance?"

Buck was at ease again. "Oh, you know, the press can always be dealt with. I'd've said something to them like, 'It's terrible believing your only daughter's dead. But we've been reprieved. Let's not wreck this wonderful joy. She checked herself in to a clinic, she's received the treatment she needed, all is forgiven, she's home again . . . ' "

"I wasn't asking about the damned press. What about Nadine, how long were you going to keep her locked up? She didn't check herself in, so she can't get out herself, right?"

Buck gazed at a patch of thick Shasta daisies. "Now that we know what's going on, that rogue Diaz and everything, she's not in danger anymore."

Jerry was disgusted. "Diaz? He was after Faye, not Nadine."

"He probably thought Faye had communicated with Nadine."

"Can it, Buck. You couldn't have thought that—"

Buck grabbed Jerry's arm, his voice intense. "I wasn't thinking clearly. She's my only child, Jer. What if you only had Faye? You'd move heaven and earth to keep her safe. And you have to remember the time frame here. We didn't know about Diaz. All I knew was something funny was going on at the NSC and she was in the way, or appeared to be."

The time frame. Yes, Jerry thought, things were different a few weeks ago. He cast back and it chilled him. "You were going into Senate hearings. You put her away because *she* was dangerous to *you*!" He made himself shut up and breathe slowly. "You're connected somehow to what she was investigating," he whispered, horrified.

"No," Buck roared. "You asshole, no! It wasn't that way! I didn't want her of all people to know I made a mistake, I miscalculated. I was ashamed—"

The full blast buffeted Jerry. He felt desperately ill. "You rotten son of a bitch. I'm too old to buy your lies. You didn't do any of this for her or because you were ashamed of whatever misdeed you were involved in. You did it for yourself. You were being confirmed! No one, not even your daughter, could be allowed to interfere with that!"

The nausea wave smashed into him. He hung on to the back of a chair and vomited. He shook his head when the spasm ended and wiped his mouth on his handkerchief. Buck hadn't moved. His face was pale; one leg was crossed over the other, his hands folded in his lap. Jerry spat at him.

When the car dropped Jerry at his home hours later, Coo had to help him up the steps and into bed. Every cell in his body ached. "I have to call Faye," he said.

"Later."

"Now."

"If you don't stop socializing, you'll be back in the hospital. Do you want that?"

"No. You call her, tell her to come over here. And put on some healing Verdi, Coo. I have to wash Buck Stern out of my system."

After Sam's arrest, Faye spent the night at Herb's dreaming of Sam holding her face in the water, waking up, dozing. Phelps had three men on the door, but the last time she'd awakened just before dawn she sensed they weren't needed. It was over.

Gabe left early the next morning for the studio, but when she got Coo's call, she was surprised to discover Gabe in the living room, lying on a couch, staring at the gray-blue Pacific.

"Keith's coming over in a while, bringing Cricket," she said, sitting beside him. "How are you?"

"Not good, honey, not good. I'll get better." He stroked her cheek. "I'm so sorry, Faye, I feel responsible for what Sam put you through. I was thinking back and there were times I should have seen what he was really like."

"You're not responsible. We both loved Sam."

"He's crazy—that's the best we can say about him."

"But he loved you, in his way. None of the good things are erased."

He didn't smile, nod, agree, disagree. He turned his face away, grieving. "I want us to go away when we finish shooting?"

She smoothed his hair back from his forehead and ran a finger down the deep line in his cheek. "All I can manage is one day at a time. Let's talk about that later. In three days, we start shooting again, but right now, I'm going to see Pop."

"Are you up to that?"

"All my muscles ache, my cuts ache, but I feel okay."

"You shouldn't drive." He was lifting himself off the couch. She put her hand on his chest, pressing him back.

"One of the cops outside will drive me."

The canary serenaded the hot still air. Jerry was on his deck in a chaise. "Look what your mom brought me," he said, waving at the trilling bird in a big wicker cage. "Canary condo." He held out a piece of paper.

Four lines were written on the paper. "What does this mean?"

"Nadine's there in a clinic."

"A clinic?"

"Sit down, Faye." He pulled at her hand. "Buck put her there. He was protecting himself."

"This is how he's protecting himself? Locking her away? Did he think no one would notice or care?"

"Old-fashioned powerful fathers think they have the right."

"Pop, that's crap. What did he say?"

Jerry's face was thin and pale, his prominent nose more beaklike, his eyes flinty. "He said he was protecting Nadine."

"If he wanted to protect her," she said, amazed, "he must have *believed* her, he must have felt she *needed* protection." But Jerry was watching the canary. "We didn't think anyone would believe us."

Jerry's eyes narrowed, the lines between them deepened. "He wasn't protecting her, honey lamb, he was protecting himself. His daughter was going off the deep end, running away from her husband, making out-of-channel accusations about improper programs at the NSC, and he was going into the Senate for confirmation. Such a sweet guy."

She pressed her fingertips against her throbbing head. "This is terrible, terrible. And what's she supposed to do now—just reappear? Take her place in society?"

"Ummm, well, the family might say she'd had a little breakdown—no one wants to inquire too deeply into those. If they started looking into the misidentifying of the girl in the morgue, Buck would talk about being so grief-stricken he couldn't bear looking too closely."

"Oh, don't be ridiculous, Pop!"

"I didn't buy it, either. Anyway, obviously, Nadine would come 'back from the dead.' But whatever he'd say, I have a feeling Nadine would back him up, it would all be smoothed over, and maybe Nadine'd go on a long trip. With that kind of money, backed by a complete absence of morals, anything is possible."

"Aren't you forgetting about Nadine here? She'd never go along."

"We'll see. Family ties are strong—even against our will sometimes. Whatever she says or does, Buck's on the Court and, short of murder or rape, he'll stay there. A great dream has been realized," he added sarcastically. "Ain't life a wonder?"

"Yeah. And Nadine's paying for it." Faye was pacing up and down in front of the potted plants by the railing.

"Faye, she's alive!"

"Yes, but how is she? Has she been drugged, shocked— is the baby okay? My God, I can't believe this." Her hands fluttered toward her face. "How can he do this to her, Pop?" She waved the paper. "Where *is* this place?"

"Outside Sacramento, in the foothills. Faye, let your brother go and get her."

"Pop—!"

"Just think about it. Sit down and think about it."

Faye sat. There was a bottle of apple juice peeking out of a bucket beneath the table, and a stack of little paper cups. Her head ached dully. She felt her mind wander, taking a turn, fading out. She saw the ocean slapping against the rocks. Only yesterday. She saw Sam's evil face. He'd probably be out on bail by tonight. She pulled herself back.

She touched the lid of the apple juice. "I'll tell Robbie, Pop. You're right."

From her parents' house, she telephoned first Rob, then Phelps about Nadine. An hour later, she was back in Malibu.

"Oh, there you are," Faye cooed as Keith put Cricket down in Herb's living room.

Cricket teetered toward Faye like a damaged toy, her rear left leg stiffened in a cast, her front legs trying to compensate, eyes hopeful, tail wagging. She dipped her head. Faye sat down on the floor and petted her.

"Now she'll cry," Gabe said, arms folded across his chest, eyes happy.

"Nah," Keith said, "dogs don't cry."

Faye put her arm around Cricket and pressed her face against her neck. "I can't thank you enough, Keith," she said, crying. Cricket was humping toward Gabe.

"I'm glad she turned out to be fierce!" Keith said, laughing. "Twenty pounds of attack dog!"

"With a heavy-metal attitude," Gabe said.

"So, what's the program?" Keith asked.

"We're waiting for Rob, then he's taking off to see Nadine," Faye said.

Rob was late. His once wholesome, open face was tired and closed, his dark hair slicked back, cut short.

"Gabe," Rob said nervously, offering his hand.

"Rob." They shook hands firmly.

"I've been a bastard to you, Gabe. I'm sorry."

"Forget it."

"No, I mean it, I was a rat."

"Okay, you stand here and beat on yourself while I go get the beer," Gabe said. He put a hand on Rob's arm.

Rob hugged Faye. "You never believed she was dead, did you?" She shook her head. "So how'd Pop find out she was at this clinic?"

"I asked him to talk to Buck," Faye said. "Pop won't tell me much, Robbie. He just gave me this address and said she was there."

"But why?"

"All he said was Buck wanted to protect her. You'll have to get the rest from Nadine."

Rob bent down and petted Cricket to give himself time to control the feelings boiling inside. But he couldn't stem the rush. He sat down heavily. "I did believe she was dead," he said, brushing tears from his cheek. "Another thing I can't forgive myself for. I was angry at her at first, going off, then I was worried, I mean, heartsick worried . . . it really surprised me, how deeply I felt that. Then I stopped hoping. Now I'd do anything if we could just have another chance."

"There's always a second chance," Gabe said.

Rob nodded. "Does she know we're coming?"

"I don't know," Faye said. "I thought you'd like to make the call to this clinic."

"Why hasn't anyone heard from her?"

"You know Nadine," Faye said. "If she could have called, she would have."

"She won't want to see me. You go, Faye."

"No."

Rob threw his head back. "I can't do this alone! If you're up to it, please come with me. We can be back in a few hours. I need your support, Faye."

The clinic was a massive Italianate Victorian building in the Sierra foothills. It looked grand and silly dumped there beside the forests and farms, an improbable mass of bay windows and fanciful pediments. The perimeter wrought-iron fence crowned by coiled lengths of razor wire was the only serious thing about it.

Gabe caught her arm. "Beautiful," he said, "but sinister." Faye looked up at the small ancient windows. They were barred. "Poor Nadine. Like she'd been shelved. Not useful anymore." The lawn smelled newly cut, the grounds perfect and apparently unused. No sign of life came from inside the building.

Inside, the place was clean and stern. An officious woman in gray—to differentiate her from the nursing staff—directed them to Nadine's room on the top floor. The heavy door shut silently behind them.

The room astonished Faye: it was luxuriously furnished in rich fabrics and soft furniture. But Nadine, sitting on the foot of the bed, wore an institutional dress that contrasted starkly with the plush room. Her blond hair was emerging again. Her pregnancy was just beginning to show.

"What took you so long?" she cried, raising both arms like a child. Faye waited for Rob, but he held back, staring at Nadine. Then Faye laughed and hugged her. Gabe kissed her cheek. "Faye brought you some new clothes," he said, putting a suitcase down on the bed.

Rob moved toward his wife, solemn, sad, then swept her into his arms. "Oh, honey . . ." She tolerated his embrace.

"What is this place?" Faye asked.

"It hides troublesome rich girls, and believe me, we don't have any freedom of movement." She leveled a look at Faye. "Tell me the truth."

"Of course. Always."

"I haven't heard it in a long time," Nadine mumbled. "Can I get out of here?"

"As far as we know," Gabe said.

An air of discomfort drifted into the room.

"How's the film?" Nadine asked, filling the silence. "And Dino, the extras' slave driver, how's he? How's Annie?"

"They all ask after you," Faye said.

"Annie causing problems?" Nadine asked.

"No, she's going to be really good in the film," Gabe said.

"She's having a hot affair with Roger," Faye said, telling her about Roger opening Annie's trailer door stark naked. The laughter that followed was too loud.

"I wanted to get word to you," Nadine said, pulling at the neck of her sack dress. "But there was no way. No letters in or out, no phone calls, I had nothing to bribe them with, my clothes were taken away."

"How have they treated you?" Rob asked.

"All right, for a prison. That's essentially what it is. I obeyed, for the baby's sake."

"Buck told us you were dead," Faye said.

Nadine's eyes opened, her mouth drew back in that peculiar and moving way of hers, the shock inside making the skin outside retreat.

"Dead?"

"Pop said that now Buck may tell the world that you had a little breakdown," Faye said, wanting it all out, "that you'd back him up, maybe go on a long trip . . ."

"A long trip? A breakdown? Has everyone lost their minds?" She seemed both outraged and scared. "He put me in here to save himself! Would any of you have believed that sticking a daughter away in a clinic against her will could be done today? Well, he did it."

Her voice was rising. "I was drugged by my own father and I woke up here. Even Dad," she said to Faye, squinting against her tears, "even Dad . . . how could he do that to *me*?" She was wailing. Rob, horrified, didn't move. It was Gabe who went to her, put an arm around her. "I'm not going on any long trip, and I'm not telling the press or whoever that I had a little breakdown. All I want to do is get out of here!" She was calmer, but it was as if a lid had been clamped tight on her feelings.

"You'll leave here today," Faye said. "I promise you."

Nadine snapped open the suitcase with tight movements. "Just give me a minute to change."

"Gabe and I will wait downstairs," Faye said. "And then, we'll really start catching you up, Nadine, because Tot's been breaking the OPI story."

Nadine put a hand on her throat. "That seems very far away."

"Do you want me to stay, Nadine?" Rob asked.

"Yes," she replied coldly.

Gabe and Faye sat on a bench outside under a dark, old oak. "Something's wrong with Nadine," he said.

"I know. But she's been shut up."

"It hasn't been that long, Faye."

"I think she's been heavily sedated. I hope the baby's all right."

Gabe sighed, watching a squirrel charge across the perfect lawn. He took a packet out of his jacket pocket. "I found this in Malibu." It was half a nautilus shell, shaped like a big comma, curling back, each segment of shell dwindling in size into the conical tail.

She turned it around in her hands. "I was dreaming of the nautilus last night, first time in a long time. I was inside it, going from section to section," she said, tracing the segments of the shell with her finger. "There was a moment on the deck with Sam when I thought the nautilus was beneath me in the sea, waiting. Those dreams, they goaded me, forced me to work out the problem, to remember . . ."

"See, what I like about this creature," he said, "is that it packs where it's been on its back, a record of growth."

"Yeah," she said, "but sometimes it isn't growth, just painful old stupid experience." She felt his arm touch hers. "Gabe, tell me about finding Sam's penknife at my house."

"It was . . . horrifying," he murmured. "Sam had had that knife for years. I knew you hadn't had him over. Phelps and I were in the hall and he'd just been telling me the neighbors had seen a second man with Diaz, a man who left before you arrived. I don't know why Sam was there with Diaz. I'd like to think he was there to stop him, but maybe he was there to tell your bodyguard to let him in—they were his men, as we know . . . I trusted Sam so much."

She put a hand on his knee. "You were right to trust. It's just harder to trust again when it's broken." She gazed at the shell. "I love you, Gabe, and I love our work. But maybe our work took over and we substituted it for what we first had together. You remember when Pop had his heart attack and we were sitting in the restaurant down the street? You said things hadn't been good between us for a long time, that we'd been the town's hot team, always talking film day and night, that what we'd really had after a while was a limited partnership. I refused to believe it and I got upset. But you were right, Gabe. And now I feel as if I'm coming out of the past, really coming out of it, and you can, too, if you give yourself a chance. Last night, I had one of those telephone dreams from Della. She said, 'Look in on my twins, will you, *querida*?' She didn't say 'Look out for them,' or 'Watch out for them.' There wasn't any alarm." Another squirrel bounded across the grass and dashed up a tree. "When we finish the film, I want to go away for a while."

"Yes, we'll go away."

"No. Not together. Maybe that later." She was at a crossroad, but she wasn't ready to step into it yet. "When we're finished with the film I'm taking some time off."

"What's happened?"

"I'm not sure."

"You're upset—Diaz, Sam, now Nadine. You can't expect to feel . . ."

"Feel what?"

"Like yourself, honey."

"You remember when you used to say to me, 'I have to think my thoughts'? That's what I have to do. When we get back tonight, I'm not staying in Malibu. I think I'll go with Rob and Nadine to the folks' for a couple of days."

"Oh, Faye," he said gravely, taking her hand.

"Life is short, Gabe. I have to find my way."

They weren't going to let Nadine out. Faye, Gabe, Nadine, and Rob were standing at a counter in the front hallway as a nurse and an administrator were opening and closing files, punching things up on a computer. The administrator, a woman about fifty with a streak of gray in her hair, kept saying, "You understand paperwork, it must be done properly. It won't take long, but if you'll just have a seat . . ." Behind a partition, a secretary was frantically phoning.

The administrator snapped to the nurse, "This isn't the right charge sheet!" Two large men in white moved toward the front door. Down the long hall, patients were peeking out, staring. Chimes sounded from somewhere.

"Let's get a move on," Rob said to the administrator.

"We'll have all the papers ready soon," she replied with a condescending smile. "If you'll just be patient." She went behind the partition. "Is he there?" she hissed. After a short, staccato conversation on the telephone, she came out.

The secretary handed her a fat file. She started going through it, nodding and making check marks.

"Now, we'll have to have some signatures," the administrator said brightly, as if to children. Behind her, a printer was discharging continuous sheets. "Please sit down, you'll be more comfortable." She turned to the secretary and said quietly, "Find that release." She pivoted back, new sheets of paper in her hands. "Mrs. Ferray, I need your signature on this paper."

"Wait," Faye said, "let's take a good look at that." Faye read it carefully. "It says you voluntarily checked yourself into this gothic horror, that nothing bad happened to you here, you received treatment and you are now checking yourself out."

The administrator smiled at Faye. "Doesn't she look wonderful?"

"Nadine looks like hell and you know it."

The administrator sucked in her breath and squared her jaw. She pushed the papers toward Nadine. "If you'd sign here," she said coldly.

"Hey," Faye said, "what *is* this?"

Gabe took her arm, his slow smile widening.

Nadine swung around from the counter. "Right, what are we doing here?"

Faye and Gabe were at the door. The two guards shifted their weight uneasily. The administrator shouted, "You can't leave! We haven't finished!"

"*I'm* finished!" Nadine brushed past the men and pushed open the door.

"Now just a minute!" the administrator cried out. "There are rules, we have regulations here! You can't do this!"

Faye called out, "Oh, yes we can!"

Nadine was laughing. She broke into a run, bobbing down the steps and out onto the green lawn. "Where's the car?"

Rob pointed at the parking lot. Gabe took Faye's hand and they all made for it.

Faye looked back. No one was following them.

By ten o'clock that night, Nadine, Rob, Coo, and Jerry were in the living room rehashing the entire experience. The costs were yet to be added up.

Outside the house, Faye had hugged Gabe hard. "I'll see you in two days," she'd said. Now, she was sitting in the kitchen, staring at the telephone. She hadn't used one for a private and unguarded conversation in months. The only person she wanted to talk with was a forty-six-year-old police detective who was writing a novel like everyone else in the country, whose job made his eyes on a good day resemble permafrost.

She picked up the phone and called him.

"He's been looking for you," a clipped, distracted voice said. "I can't reach him right now. He's on a call."

Some note in the woman's voice alerted Faye. "Is he all right?"

"I cannot give you—will you hold on, please?"

Faye hung on in a vacuum, waiting for disaster, waiting for joy, waiting. What had he said that night she'd been with him in his garden? That this was an accident and no one had been hurt? Yes and no. A collision had occurred and the aftershocks were still rumbling. She stared at the receiver, commanding it to speak to her. She was in a void. She hadn't known him long enough to feel so profoundly anxious. But in another way, on another level, she felt known, deeply known by him. That was asinine. She hung on in the telephone limbo. Had he been shot? No, he was a desk man. He couldn't have been shot. Could he? The phone clicked. Nothing. This was insane, this jumbled spastic emotional tide. A measure of her innate insecurities, her unstable nature. She hung on. She heard Coo's faint bubbling laugh from the dining room. She heard Nadine say something sharp and impatient to Rob.

Phelps was on the line, strong and tense. "Where are you?"

Faye's body sank back in her chair. She dropped the phone on the table. "Faye!"

"I'm here. I'm at my parents' house."

"Good, good. I was concerned. Hold on." He was gone for a few seconds, then he was back.

"And your sister-in-law?"

"Out of the slammer."

"That's good. So, what are your plans?"

"I'm not going to Malibu."

She heard him suck in his breath. "Stay where you are. Someone will pick you up."

The driver was a woman in her twenties who handled the car expertly and drove fast. Faye thought of asking her where they were going, but decided against knowing. There was something reviving about not knowing the destination. Then the driver turned onto Beachwood Drive.

Phelps was standing in the open door.

"I thought you were out on some big emergency," she said. His shirt sleeves were rolled up, he wasn't wearing a tie, his trousers were wrinkled by hours of work. His face was taut. She couldn't see his eyes.

"That was done with an hour ago."

"Was it bad?"

"It's always bad. Everything's breaking down."

"They sounded like you were—"

"Will you step inside?"

She went in. He closed the door and immediately began walking into the living room. "Phelps."

"What?" He was still walking, turning into the dining room.

"I was worried about you."

"No need."

They reached the patio. He was going down the steps. "Phelps! What are you doing? What's going on?"

At the bottom, in the light, he turned. "Take a good look at me, Ms. Ferray. You are not looking at a hotshot anybody."

She sat down on the top steps. "Maybe not, but a pretty fair human being. I'm looking at that."

He was impatient. His shell was crumbling. She could see it in his eyes. "Yup, I'm a real decent guy, living in his parents' old home, waiting for retirement, with a grown daughter in college."

"You got debts? You own a car? How about a savings account—you got one of those? A pension?" She shot to her feet. "Do you really want to talk about this crap?"

He turned and walked away from her. "No." He stopped, resting his back against the trunk of the old avocado tree.

She went up to him but did not touch him. "I'm scared, too. But it's good scared, not bad. We both know the difference."

His expression changed, reservations slid away. She touched his cheek. His skin shivered.

"I didn't expect you," he said.

"Makes two of us."

Mollie Gregory

__PRIVILEGED LIES
0-515-11266-6/$4.99

When power is the ruling passion, telling the truth can be deadly. Los Angeles film maker Faye Ferray knows her friend Della's death is no accident and that it must be related to Della's work as a lawyer. Faye and her friends from law school–a top Washington attorney and a television reporter–put old rivalries aside as they dig through influential Washington and Los Angeles circles for the key to Della's murder.

__BIRTHSTONE
0-515-10704-2/$4.99

"Finely-etched characters, intricate plotting, and raw human emotion..."-Carolyn See, author of <u>Golden Days</u>
Nearly destroyed by a shocking crime of passion, the Wyman family has triumphed over their tragedy: award-winning director Sara, noted movie critic Vail, and their steel-willed mother Diana are in the spotlight of fame and success. Then, Sara's daughter Lindy returns, forcing secrets out of the shadows...

__TRIPLETS
0-515-10761-1/$5.50

"Sexy, slick, searing and shocking!"-<u>Los Angeles Times</u>
The Wyman triplets had everything money could buy, and more-beauty, intelligence and talent. Sara, Sky, and Vail shared a special closeness...until the day their crystal dreams were shattered, turning their trust and loyalty to deception and dishonor.

Payable in U.S. funds. No cash orders accepted. Postage & handling: $1.75 for one book, 75¢ for each additional. Maximum postage $5.50. Prices, postage and handling charges may change without notice. Visa, Amex, MasterCard call 1-800-788-6262, ext. 1, refer to ad # 377b

Or, check above books and send this order form to:	Bill my: ☐ Visa ☐ MasterCard ☐ Amex	
The Berkley Publishing Group	Card#_____	(expires)
390 Murray Hill Pkwy., Dept. B		($15 minimum)
East Rutherford, NJ 07073	Signature_____	
Please allow 6 weeks for delivery.	Or enclosed is my: ☐ check ☐ money order	

Name_____	Book Total $_____
Address_____	Postage & Handling $_____
City_____	Applicable Sales Tax $_____ (NY, NJ, CA, GST Can.)
State/ZIP_____	Total Amount Due $_____